PRAISE FOR
ISLANDS IN THE NET

"Sterling's genius lies in the elaboration of significant details . . . *Islands in the Net* reconstructs a world so the imagined future reveals the equally elaborate strangeness of our own time."

—*Locus*

"Sterling has expanded my mind . . . he's better than drugs—there's none of the nasty side effects."
—John Shirley, *Science Fiction Review*

"*Islands in the Net* is the kind of writing Bruce Sterling does better than anyone else . . . every event, every character, every detail of background seems inevitable . . . This is the high-tech future as it might actually look, explored through a story in which the tension never stops."

—Nancy Kress, author of *An Alien Light*

"Sterling's picture of ordinary life . . . in the midst of cyberpunk's high-tech underworld is refreshing!"
—*Publishers Weekly*

BRUCE STERLING

ISLANDS IN THE NET

ACE BOOKS, NEW YORK

This Ace book contains the complete
text of the original hardcover edition.
It has been completely reset in a typeface
designed for easy reading and was printed
from new film.

ISLANDS IN THE NET

An Ace Book/published by arrangement with
Arbor House

PRINTING HISTORY
Arbor House edition published 1988
Ace edition/March 1989

ISBN: 0-441-37423-9

Ace Books are published by The Berkley Publishing Group,
200 Madison Avenue, New York, New York 10016.
The name ''ACE'' and the ''A'' logo are
trademarks belonging to Charter Communications, Inc.

PRINTED IN THE UNITED STATES OF AMERICA

10 9 8 7 6 5 4 3 2 1

1

THE sea lay in simmering quiet, a slate-green gumbo seasoned with warm mud. Shrimp boats trawled the horizon.

Pilings rose in clusters, like blackened fingers, yards out in the gentle surf. Once, Galveston beach homes had crouched on those tar-stained stilts. Now barnacles clustered there, gulls wheeled and screeched. It was a great breeder of hurricanes, this quiet Gulf of Mexico.

Laura read her time and distance with a quick downward glance. Green indicators blinked on the toes of her shoes, flickering with each stride, counting mileage. Laura picked up the pace. Morning shadows strobed across her as she ran.

She passed the last of the pilings and spotted her home, far down the beach. She grinned as fatigue evaporated in a flare of energy.

Everything seemed worth it. When the second wind took her, she felt that she could run forever, a promise of indestructible confidence bubbling up from the marrow. She ran in pure animal ease, like an antelope.

The beach leapt up and slammed against her.

Laura lay stunned for a moment. She lifted her head, then caught her breath and groaned. Her cheek was caked with sand, both elbows numbed with the impact of the fall. Her arms trembled as she pushed herself up onto her knees. She looked behind her.

Something had snagged her foot. It was a black, peeling length of electrical cable. Junked flotsam from the hurricane, buried in the sand. The wire had whiplashed around her left ankle and brought her down as neatly as a lariat.

She rolled over and sat, breathing hard, and kicked the

loosened wire off her shoe. The broken skin above her sock had just begun to bleed, and the first cold shock gave way to hot smarting pain.

She stood up and threw off the shakiness, brushing sand from her cheek and arms. Sand had scratched the plastic screen of her watchphone. Its wrist strap was caked with grit.

"Great," Laura said. A belated rush of anger brought her strength back. She bent and pulled at the cable, hard. Four feet of wet sand furrowed up.

She looked around for a stick or a chunk of driftwood to dig with. The beach, as usual, was conspicuously clean. But Laura refused to leave this filthy snag to trip some tourist. That wouldn't do at all—not on her beach. Stubbornly, she knelt down and dug with her hands.

She followed the frayed cord half a foot down, to the peeling, chromed edge of a home appliance. Its simulated plastic wood grain crumbled under Laura's fingers like old linoleum tile. She kicked the dead machine several times to loosen it. Then, grunting and heaving, she wrenched it up from its wet cavity in the sand. It came up sullenly, like a rotten tooth.

It was a video cassette recorder. Twenty years of grit and brine had made it a solid mass of corrosion. A thin gruel of sand and broken shell dripped from its empty cassette slot.

It was an old-fashioned unit. Heavy and clumsy. Limping, Laura dragged it behind her by its cord. She looked up the beach for the local trash can.

She spotted it loitering near a pair of fishermen, who stood in hip boots in the gentle surf. She called out. "Trash can!"

The can pivoted on broad rubber treads and rolled toward her voice. It snuffled across the beach, mapping its way with bursts of infrasound. It spotted Laura and creaked to a stop beside her.

Laura hefted the dead recorder and dropped it into the open barrel with a loud, bonging thump. "Thank you for keeping our beaches clean," the can intoned. "Galveston appreciates good citizenship. Would you like to register for a valuable cash prize?"

"Save it for the tourists," Laura said. She jogged on toward home, favoring her ankle.

Home loomed above the high-tide line on twenty sand-colored buttresses.

The Lodge was a smooth half cylinder of dense concretized sand, more or less the color and shape of a burnt bread loaf. A round two-story tower rose from the center. Massive concrete arches held it a dozen feet above the beach.

A broad canopy in candy-stripe red and white shaded the Lodge's walls. Under the canopy, a sun-bleached wooden walkway girdled the building. Behind the walkway's railings, morning sunlight gleamed from the glass doors of half a dozen guest rooms, which faced east to the sea.

A trio of guest kids were already out on the beach. Their parents were from a Rizome Canadian firm, and they were all vacationing at company expense. The kids wore navy blue sailor suits and nineteenth-century Fauntleroy hats with trailing ribbons. The clothes were souvenirs from Galveston's historical district.

The biggest kid, a ten-year-old, ran headlong toward Laura, holding a long wooden baton over his head. Behind him, a modern window-sculpture kite leapt from the others' arms, wing after tethered wing peeling loose in blue and green pastels. Yanked free, each fabric aerofoil flapped into shape, caught the wind, and flung itself into flight. The ten-year-old slowed and turned, fighting its pull. The long kite bucked like a serpent, its movements eerily sinuous. The children screamed with glee.

Laura looked up at the Lodge's tower roof. The flags of Texas and Rizome Industries Group slid up the tower's flagpole. Old Mr. Rodriguez waved at her briefly, then disappeared behind the satellite dish. The old man was doing the honors as usual, starting another day.

Laura limped up the wooden stairs to the walkway. She pushed through the heavy doors of the front lobby. Inside, the Lodge's massive walls still held the coolness of night. And the cheerful reek of Tex-Mex cooking—peppers, cornmeal, and cheese.

Mrs. Rodriguez was not at the front desk yet—she was a late riser, not as spry as her husband. Laura walked through the empty dining room and up the tower stairs.

The tower's trapdoor slid open at her approach. She emerged

through the tower's lower floor, into a round conference room lined with modern office equipment and padded swivel chairs. Behind her, the trapdoor accordioned shut.

David, her husband, was stretched out on a wicker couch, with the baby on his chest. They were both fast asleep. One of David's hands spread cozily across little Loretta's pajama'd back.

Morning light poured through the tower's thick, round windows, slanting high across the room. It lent a strange Renaissance glow to their faces. David's head was propped against a pillow, and his profile, always striking, looked like a Medici coin. The baby's relaxed and peaceful face, her skin like damask, was hauntingly fresh and new. As if she'd popped into the world out of cellophane.

David had kicked a woolen comforter into a wad at the foot of the couch. Laura spread it carefully over his legs and the baby's back.

She pulled up a chair and sat by them, stretching out her legs. A wash of pleasant fatigue came over her. She savored it a while, then gave David's bare shoulder a nudge. "Morning."

He stirred. He sat up, cradling Loretta, who slept on in babylike omnipotence. "Now she sleeps," he said. "But not at three A.M. The midnight of the human soul."

"I'll get up next time," Laura said. "Really."

"Hell, we ought to put her in the room with your mother." David brushed long black hair from his eyes, then yawned into his knuckles. "I dreamed I saw my Optimal Persona last night."

"Oh?" Laura said, surprised. "What was it like?"

"I dunno. About what I expected, from the stuff I read about it. Soaring and foggy and cosmic. I was standing on the beach. Naked, I think. The sun was coming up. It was hypnotic. I felt this huge sense of total elation. Like I'd discovered some pure element of soul."

Laura frowned. "You don't really believe in that crap."

He shrugged. "No. Seeing your O.P.—it's a fad. Like folks used to see UFO's, you know? Some weirdo in Oregon says he had an encounter with his personal archetype. Pretty soon, everybody and his brother's having visions. Mass hysteria, collective unconscious or some such. Stupid. But modern at least. It's very new-millennium.'' He seemed obscurely pleased.

"It's mystic bullshit," Laura told him. "If it was really your Optimal Self, you should have been building something, right? Not beachcombing for Nirvana."

David looked sheepish. "It was just a dream. Remember that documentary last Friday? The guy who saw his O.P. walking down the street, wearing his clothes, using his charge card? I got a long way to go just yet." He looked down at her ankle and started. "What'd you do to your leg?"

She looked at it. "I tripped over a piece of hurricane junk. Buried in the sand. A VCR, actually." Loretta woke up, her tiny face stretching in a mighty toothless yawn.

"Really? Must have been there since the big one of '02. Twenty years! Christ, you could get tetanus." He handed her the baby and fetched a first-aid kit from the bathroom. On the way back he touched a console button. One of the flat display screens on the wall flared into life.

David sat on the floor with limber grace and put Laura's foot in his lap. He unlaced her shoe and glanced at its readout. "That's pretty rotten time. You must have been limping, babe."

He peeled off her sock. Laura held the wriggling baby to her shoulder and stared at the screen, distracting herself as David dabbed at her raw skin.

The screen was running David's Worldrun game—a global simulation. Worldrun had been invented as a forecasting tool for development agencies, but a glamorized version had found its way onto the street. David, who was prone to sudden enthusiasms, had been playing it for days.

Long strips of the Earth's surface peeled by in a simulated satellite view. Cities glowed green with health or red with social disruption. Cryptic readouts raced across the bottom of the screen. Africa was a mess. "It's always Africa, isn't it?" she said.

"Yeah." He resealed a tube of antiseptic gel. "Looks like a rope burn. It didn't bleed much. It'll scab."

"I'll be okay." She stood up, lifting Loretta, and disguising the pain for his sake. The rawness faded as the gel soaked in. She smiled. "I need a shower."

David's watchphone beeped. It was Laura's mother, calling from her guest room in the Lodge, downstairs. *"Ohayo,* y'all! How about helping Granny surround some breakfast?"

David was amused. "I'll be down in a minute, Margaret. Don't eat anything with the hide still on it." They went upstairs to their bedroom.

Laura gave him the baby and stepped into the bathroom, which shut behind her.

Laura could not understand why David actively liked her mother. He'd insisted on her right to see her grandchild, though Laura hadn't met her mother face to face in years. David was taking naive pleasure in his mother-in-law's stay, as if a week-long visit could smooth over years of unspoken resentment.

To David, family ties seemed natural and solid, the way things should be. His own parents doted on the baby. But Laura's parents had split when she was nine, and she'd been raised by her grandmother. Laura knew that family was a luxury, a hothouse plant.

Laura stepped into the tub and the curtain shunted shut. The sun-warmed water washed the tension from her; she put family troubles out of mind. She stepped out and blew her hair dry. It fell into place—she wore a simple cut, short, with light feathery bangs. Then she confronted herself in the mirror.

After three months, most of her postnatal flab had succumbed to her running campaign. The endless days of her pregnancy were a fading memory, though her swollen body image still lurched up sometimes in her dreams. She'd been happy, mostly—huge and achy, but cruising on motherhood's hormones. She'd given David some rough times. "Mood swings," he'd said, smiling with fatuous male tolerance.

In the last weeks they'd both been spooked and twitchy, like barnyard animals before an earthquake. Trying to cope, they talked in platitudes. Pregnancy was one of those archetypal situations that seemed to breed clichés.

But it was the right decision. It had been the right time. Now they had the home they'd built and the child they'd wanted. Special things, rare things, treasures.

It had brought her mother back into her life, but that would pass. Basically, things were sound, they were happy. Nothing wildly estatic, Laura thought, but a solid happiness, the kind she believed they had earned.

Laura picked at the part in her hair, watching the mirror. That light threading of gray—there hadn't been so much before the baby. She was thirty-two now, married eight years. She touched the faint creases at the corners of her eyes, thinking of her mother's face. They had the same eyes—set wide, blue with a glimmer of yellow-green. "Coyote eyes," her grandmother had called them. Laura had her dead father's long, straight nose and wide mouth, with an upper lip that fell a little short. Her front teeth were too big and square.

Genetics, Laura thought. You pass them on to the next generation. Then they relax and start to crumble on you. They do it anyway. You just have to pay a little extra for using the copyright.

She lined her eyes, touched on lipstick and video rouge. She put on hose, knee-length skirt, long-sleeve blouse in patterned Chinese silk, and a dark blue business vest. She stuck a Rizome logo pin through the vest's lapel.

She joined David and her mother in the Lodge's dining room. The Canadians, here for the last day, were playing with the baby. Laura's mother was eating the Nipponese breakfast, little cakes of pressed rice and tiny popeyed fish that smelled like kerosene. David, on the other hand, had fixed the usual: cunningly disguised food-oid stuff. Fluffy mock scrambled eggs, soybean bacon, pancakes from batter made of thick, yellow scop.

David was a health-food nut, a great devotee of unnatural foods. After eight years of marriage, Laura was used to it. At least the tech was improving. Even the scop, single-cell protein, was better these days. It tasted all right, if you could forget the image of protein vats crammed with swarming bacteria.

David wore his overalls. He was going out house wrecking today. He had his heavy toolbox and his grandfather's old oil-company hard hat. The prospect of bashing up houses—filthy, crowbar-swinging muscle work—always filled David with childlike glee. He drawled more than usual and put hot sauce on his eggs, infallible signs of his good mood.

Laura's mother, Margaret Alice Day Garfield Nakamura Simpson, wore a Tokyo original in blue crepe de chine, with a trailing waist sash. Her woven-straw sun hat, the size of a bicycle wheel, was tied across her back. She called herself Margaret Day, since she had recently divorced Simpson, a man Laura scarcely knew.

"It's not the Galveston I remember anymore," Laura's mother said.

David nodded. "You know what I miss? I miss the wreckage. I mean, I was ten when the big disaster hit. I grew up in the wreckage down the island. All those beach homes, snapped off, washed up, tossed around like dice. . . . It seemed infinite, full of surprises."

Laura's mother smiled. "That's why you stayed here?"

David sipped his breakfast juice, which came from a powdered mix and was of a color not found in nature. "Well, after '02, everyone with sense pulled out. It left all the more room for us diehards. We BOI's, Born on the Island folks, we're a weird breed." David smiled self-consciously. "To live here, you have to have a kind of dumb love for bad luck. Isla Malhaldo, that was Galveston's first name, you know. Isle of Bad Luck."

"Why?" Laura's mother said obligingly. She was humoring him.

"Cabeza de Vaca called it that. His galleon was shipwrecked here in 1528. He was almost eaten by cannibals. Karankawa Indians."

"Oh? Well, the Indians must have had some name for the place."

"Nobody knows it," David said. "They were all wiped out by smallpox. True Galvestonians, I guess—bad luck." He thought it over. "A very weird tribe, the Karankawas. They used to smear themselves with rancid alligator grease— they were famous for the stench."

"I've never heard of them," Margaret Day said.

"They were very primitive," David said, forking up another scop pancake. "They used to eat dirt! They'd bury a fresh deer kill for three or four days, until it softened up, and—"

"David!" Laura said.

"Oh," David said. "Sorry." He changed the subject. "You ought to come out with us today, Margaret. Rizome has a good little side biz with the city government. They condemn it, we scrap it, and it's a lot of fun all around. I mean, it's not serious money, not by *zaibatsu* standards, but there's more to life than the bottom line."

" 'Fun City,' " her mother said.

"I see you've been listening to our new mayor," Laura said.

"Do you ever worry about the people drifting into Galveston these days?" her mother said suddenly.

"What do you mean?" Laura said.

"I've been reading about this mayor of yours. He's quite a strange character, isn't he? An ex-bartender with a big white beard who wears Hawaiian shirts to the office. He seems to be going out of his way to attract—what's the word?—fringe elements."

"Well, it's not a real city anymore, is it?" David said. "No more industry. Cotton's gone, shipping's gone, oil went a long time ago. About all that's left is to sell glass beads to tourists. Right? And a little, uh, social exotica is good for tourism. You expect a tourist burg to run a little fast and loose."

"So you like the mayor? I understand Rizome backed his campaign. Does that mean your company supports his policies?"

"Who's asking?" Laura said, nettled. "Mother, you're on vacation. Let Marubeni Company find their own answers."

The two of them locked eyes for a moment. *"Aisumimasen."* her mother said at last. "I'm very sorry if I seemed to pry. I spent too much time in the State Department. I still have the reflexes. Now that I'm in what they laughingly call private enterprise." She set her chopsticks across her plate and reached for her hat. "I've decided to rent a sailboat today. They say there's an offshore station—an OPEC, or something like that."

"OTEC," David corrected absently. "The power station. Yeah, it's nice out there."

"I'll see you at supper then. Be good, you two."

Four more Canadians came in for breakfast, yawning. Margaret Day filtered past them and left the dining room.

"You had to step on her toes," David said quietly. "What's wrong with Marubeni? Some creaky old Nipponese trading company. You think they sent Loretta's grandma here to swipe our microchips or something?"

"She's a guest of Rizome," Laura said. "I don't like her criticizing our people."

"She's leaving tomorrow," David said. "You could go a little easier on her." He stood up, hefting his tool chest.

"All right, I'm sorry," Laura told him. There wasn't time to get into it now. This was business.

She greeted the Canadians and took the baby back. They were part of a production wing from a Rizome subsidiary in Toronto, on vacation as a reward for increased production. They were sunburned but cheerful.

Another pair of guests came in: Señor and Señora Kurosawa, from Brazil. They were fourth-generation Brazilians, with Rizome-Unitika, a textile branch of the firm. They had no English, and their Japanese was amazingly bad, laden with Portuguese loan words and much Latin arm waving. They complimented Laura on the food. It was their last day, too.

Then, trouble arrived. The Europeans were up. There were three of them and they were not Rizome people, but bankers from Luxembourg. There was a banker's conference in the works tomorrow, a major do by all accounts. The Europeans had come a day early. Laura was sorry for it.

The Luxembourgers sat morosely for breakfast. Their leader and chief negotiator was a Monsieur Karageorgiu, a tawny-skinned man in his fifties, with greenish eyes and carefully waved hair. The name marked him as a Europeanized Turk; his grandparents had probably been "guest workers" in Germany or Benelux. Karageorgiu wore an exquisitely tailored suit of cream-colored Italian linen.

His crisp, precise, and perfect shoes were like objets d'art, Laura thought. Shoes engineered to high precision, like the power plant of a Mercedes. It almost hurt to see him walk in them. No one at Rizome would have dared to wear them; the righteous mockery would have been merciless. He reminded

Laura of the diplomats she'd seen as a kid, of a lost standard in studied elegance.

He had a pair of unsmiling companions in black suits: junior executives, or so he claimed. It was hard to tell their origins; Europeans looked more and more alike these days. One had a vaguely Côte d'Azur look, maybe French or Corsican; the other was blond. They looked alarmingly fit and hefty. Elaborate Swiss watchphones peeked from their sleeves.

They began complaining. They didn't like the heat. Their rooms smelled and the water tasted salty. They found the toilets peculiar. Laura promised to turn up the heat pump and order more Perrier.

It didn't do much good. They were down on hicks. Especially doctrinaire Yankees who lived in peculiar sand castles and practiced economic democracy. She could tell already that tomorrow was going to be rocky.

In fact the whole setup was fishy. She didn't know enough about these people—she didn't have proper guest files on them. Rizome-Atlanta was being cagey about this bankers' meeting, which was most unusual for headquarters.

Laura took their breakfast orders and left the three bankers trading sullen glares with the Rizome guests. She took the baby with her to the kitchen. The kitchen staff was up and banging pans. The kitchen staff was seventy-year-old Mrs. Delrosario and her two granddaughters.

Mrs. Delrosario was a treasure, though she had a mean streak that bubbled up whenever her advice was taken with anything less than total attention and seriousness. Her granddaughters mooched about the kitchen with a doomed, submissive look. Laura felt sorry for them and tried to give them a break when she could. Life wasn't easy as a teenager these days.

Laura fed the baby her formula. Loretta gulped it with enthusiasm. She was like her father in that—really doted on goop no sane person should eat.

Then Laura's watchphone beeped. It was the front desk. Laura left the baby with Mrs. Delrosario and took the back way to the lobby, through the staff rooms and the first-floor office. She emerged behind the desk. Mrs. Rodriguez looked up in relief, peering over her bifocals.

She had been talking to a stranger—a fiftyish Anglo woman in a black silk dress and a beaded choker. The woman had a vast mane of crisp black hair and her eyes were lined dramatically. Laura wondered what to make of her. She looked like a pharaoh's widow. "This is her," Mrs. Rodriguez told the stranger. "Laura, our manager."

"Coordinator," Laura said. "I'm Laura Webster."

"I'm the Reverend Morgan. I called earlier."

"Yes. About the City Council race?" Laura touched her watch, checking her schedule. The woman was half an hour early. "Well," she said. "Won't you come around the desk? We can talk in my office."

Laura took the woman into the cramped and windowless little suboffice. It was essentially a coffee room for the staff, with a data-link to the mainframe upstairs. This was where Laura took people from whom she expected the squeeze. The place looked suitably modest and penurious. David had decorated it from his wrecking expeditions: antique vinyl car seats and a modular desk in aged beige plastic. The ceiling light shone through a perforated hubcap.

"Coffee?" Laura said.

"No, thank you. I never take caffeine."

"I see." Laura put the pot aside. "What can we do for you, Reverend?"

"You and I have much in common," Reverend Morgan said. "We share a confidence in Galveston's future. And we both have a stake in the tourist industry." She paused. "I understand your husband designed this building."

"Yes, he did."

"It's 'Organic Baroque,' isn't it? A style that respects Mother Earth. That shows a broad-minded approach on your part. Forward-looking and progressive."

"Thank you very much." Here it comes, Laura thought.

"Our Church would like to help you expand services to your corporate guests. Do you know the Church of Ishtar?"

"I'm not sure I follow you," Laura said carefully. "We at Rizome consider religion a private matter."

"We Temple women believe in the divinity of the sexual act." Reverend Morgan leaned back in her bucket seat, stroking her hair with both hands. "The erotic power of the Goddess can destroy evil."

The slogan found a niche in Laura's memory. "I see," Laura said politely. "The Church of Ishtar. I know your movement, but I hadn't recognized the name."

"It's a new name—old principles. You're too young to remember the Cold War." Like many of her generation, the reverend seemed to have a positive nostalgia for it—the good old bilateral days. When things were simpler and every morning might be your last. "Because we put an end to it. We invoked the Goddess to take the war out of men. We melted the cold war with divine body heat." The reverend sniffed. "Male power mongers claimed the credit, of course. But the triumph belonged to our Goddess. She saved Mother Earth from the nuclear madness. And She continues to heal society today."

Laura nodded helpfully.

"Galveston lives by tourism, Mrs. Webster. And tourists expect certain amenities. Our Church has come to an arrangement with the city and the police. We'd like an understanding with your group as well."

Laura rubbed her chin. "I think I can follow your reasoning, Reverend."

"No civilization has ever existed without us," the reverend said coolly. "The Holy Prostitute is an ancient, universal figure. The Patriarchy degraded and oppressed her. But we restore her ancient role as comforter and healer."

"I was about to mention the medical angle," Laura said.

"Oh, yes," said the reverend. "We take the full range of precautions. Clients are tested for syphilis, gonorrhea, chlamydia, and herpes, as well as the retroviruses. All our temples have fully equipped clinics. Sexual disease rates drop dramatically wherever we practice our art—I can show you statistics. We also offer health insurance. And we guarantee confidentiality, of course."

"It's a very interesting proposal," Laura said, tapping her desk with a pencil. "But it's not a decision I can make on my own. I'll be happy to take your ideas to our Central Committee." She took a breath. The air in the tiny room held the smoky reek of the reverend's patchouli. The smell of madness, Laura thought suddenly. "You have to understand that Rizome may have some difficulties with this. Rizome favors strong social ties in its associates. It's part of our corporate philosophy. Some of us might consider prostitution a sign of social breakdown."

The reverend spread her hands and smiled. "I've heard about Rizome's policies. You're economic democrats—I admire that. As a church, a business, and a political movement, we're a new-millennium group ourselves. But Rizome can't change the nature of the male animal. We've already serviced several of your male associates. Does that surprise you?" She shrugged. "Why risk their health with amateur or criminal groups? We Temple women are safe, dependable, and economically sensible. The Church stands ready to do business."

Laura dug into her desk. "Let me give you one of our brochures."

The reverend opened her purse. "Have a few of ours. I have some campaign pamphlets—I'm running for City Council."

Laura looked the pamphlets over. They were slickly printed. The margins were dotted with ankh symbols, yin-yangs, and chalices. Laura scanned the dense text, spotted with italics and words in red. "I see you favor a liberal drug policy."

"Victimless crimes are tools of Patriarchal oppression." The reverend dug in her purse and produced an enameled pillbox. "A few of these will argue the case better than I can." She dropped three red capsules on the desktop. "Try them, Mrs. Webster. As a gift from the Church. Astonish your husband."

"I beg your pardon?" Laura said.

"Remember the giddiness of first love? The sense that the whole world had new meaning, because of him? Wouldn't you like to recapture that? Most women would. It's an intoxicating feeling, isn't it? And these are the intoxicants."

Laura stared at the pills. "Are you telling me these are love potions?"

The reverend shifted uncomfortably, with a whisper of black silk against vinyl. "Mrs. Webster, please don't mistake me for a witch. The Church of Wicca are reactionaries. And no, these aren't love potions, not in the folklore sense. They only stir that rush of emotion—they can't direct it at anyone. You do that for yourself.''

"It sounds hazardous," Laura said.

"Then it's the sort of danger women were born for!'' the reverend said. "Do you ever read romance novels? Millions do, for this same thrill. Or eat chocolate? Chocolate is a lover's gift, and there's reason behind the tradition. Ask a chemist about chocolate and serotonin precursors sometime.'' The reverend touched her forehead. "It all comes to the same, up here. Neurochemistry.'' She pointed to the table. "Chemistry in those pills. They're natural substances, creations of the Goddess. Part of the feminine soul.''

Somewhere along the line, Laura thought, the conversation had gently peeled loose from sanity. It was like falling asleep on an air raft and waking up far out to sea. The important thing was not to panic. "Are they legal?'' Laura said.

Reverend Morgan picked up a pill with her lacquered nails and ate it. "No blood test would show a thing. You can't be prosecuted for the natural contents of your own brain. And no, they're not illegal. Yet. Praise the Goddess, the Patriarchy's laws still lag behind advances in chemistry.''

"I can't accept these,'' Laura said. "They must be valuable. It's conflict of interest.'' Laura picked them up and stood, reaching over the desk.

"This is the modern age, Mrs. Webster. Gene-spliced bacteria can make drugs by the ton. Friends of ours can make them for thirty cents each.'' Reverend Morgan rose to her feet. "You're sure?'' She slipped the pills back in her purse. "Come and see us if you change your mind. Life with one man can go stale very easily. Believe me, we know. And if that happens, we can help you.'' She paused meditatively. "In any of several different ways.''

Laura smiled tightly. "Good luck with your campaign, Reverend.''

"Thank you. I appreciate your good wishes. As our mayor always says, Galveston is Fun City. It's up to all of us to see that it stays that way.''

Laura ushered her outside. She watched from the walkway as the reverend slipped into a self-driven van. The van whirred off. A flock of brown pelicans crossed the island, headed for

Karankawa Bay. The autumn sun shone brightly. It was still the same sun and the same clouds. The sun didn't care about the landscape inside people's heads.

She went back in. Mrs. Rodriguez looked up from behind the front desk, blinking. "I'm glad my old man is no younger," she said. *"La puta,* eh? A whore. She's no friend to us married women, Laurita."

"I guess not," Laura said, leaning against the desk. She felt tired already, and it was only ten o'clock.

"I'm going to church this Sunday," Mrs. Rodriguez decided. *"Qué brujeria,* eh? A witch! Did you see those eyes? Like a snake." She crossed herself. "Don't laugh, Laura."

"Laugh? Hell, I'm ready to hang garlic." The baby wailed from the kitchen. A sudden Japanese phrase leapt into Laura's head. *"Nakitsura ni hachi,"* she blurted. "It never rains but it pours. Only it's better in the original. 'A bee for a crying face.' Why can't I ever remember that crap when I need it?"

Laura took the baby upstairs to the tower office to deal with the day's mail.

Laura's corporate specialty was public relations. When David had designed the Lodge, Laura had prepared this room for business. It was equipped for major conferences; it was a full-scale node in the global Net.

The Lodge did most of its business as telex, straight print sent by wire, such as guest dossiers and arrival schedules. Most of the world, even Africa, was wired for telex these days. It was cheapest and simplest, and Rizome favored it.

"Fax" was more elaborate: entire facsimiles of documents, photographed and passed down the phone lines as streams of numbers. Fax was good for graphics and still photos; the fax machine was essentially a Xerox with a phone. It was great fun to play with.

The Lodge also took plenty of traditional phone traffic: voice without image, both live and recorded. Also voice with image: videophone. Rizome favored one-way prerecorded calls because they were more efficient. There was less chance of an expensive screwup in a one-way recorded call. And recorded video could be subtitled for all of Rizome's language groups, a major advantage for a multinational.

The Lodge could also handle teleconferencing: multiple phone calls woven together. Teleconferencing was the expensive borderland where phones blurred into television. Running a teleconference was an art worth knowing, especially in public relations. It was a cross between chairing a meeting and running a TV news show, and Laura had done it many times.

Every year of her life, Laura thought, the Net had been growing more expansive and seamless. Computers did it. Computers melted other machines, fusing them together. Television-telephone-telex. Tape recorder—VCR—laser disk. Broadcast tower linked to microwave dish linked to satellite. Phone line, cable TV, fiber-optic cords hissing out words and pictures in torrents of pure light. All netted together in a web over the world, a global nervous system, an octopus of data. There'd been plenty of hype about it. It was easy to make it sound transcendently incredible.

She'd been more into it when she'd been setting it up. Right now it seemed vastly more remarkable that Loretta was sitting up much straighter in her lap. "Looook at you, Loretta! Look how straight you can hold your head! Look at you, sweetie-face. . . . Wooga woog-woog-woog . . ."

The Net was a lot like television, another former wonder of the age. The Net was a vast glass mirror. It reflected what it was shown. Mostly human banality.

Laura zoomed one-handed through her electronic junk mail. Shop-by-wire catalogs. City Council campaigns. Charities. Health insurance.

Laura erased the garbage and got down to business. A message was waiting from Emily Donato.

Emily was Laura's prime news source for the backstage action in Rizome's Central Committee. Emily Donato was a first-term committee member.

Laura's alliance with Emily was twelve years old. They'd met in college at an international business class. Their shared backgrounds made friendship easy. Laura, a "diplobrat," had lived in Japan as an embassy kid. For Emily, childhood meant the massive industrial projects of Kuwait and Abu Dhabi. The two of them had shared a room in college.

After graduation, they'd examined their recruiting offers

and decided together on Rizome Industries Group. Rizome looked modern, it looked open, it had ideas. It was big enough for muscle and loose enough for speed.

The two of them had been double-teaming the company ever since.

Laura punched up the message and Emily's image flashed onto the screen. Emily sat behind her antique desk at home in Atlanta, Rizome's headquarters. Home for Emily was a high-rise apartment downtown, a cell in a massive modern beehive of ceramic and composite plastic.

Filtered air, filtered water, halls like streets, elevators like vertical subways. A city set on end, for a crowded world.

Naturally everything about Emily's apartment struggled to obscure the facts. The place abounded in homey quirks and little touches of Victorian solidity: cornices, baroque door frames, rich mellow lighting. The wall behind Emily was papered in paisley arabesques, gold on maroon. Her polished wooden desktop was set as carefully as a stage: low keyboard at her right hand, pen and pencil holders with a slanting peacock plume, a gleaming paperweight of gypsum crystal.

The Chinese synthetic of Emily's frilled gray blouse had the faint shimmer of mother-of-pearl. Emily's chestnut-brown hair had been done by machine, with elaborate braids and little Dickensian curls at the temple. She wore long malachite earrings and a round cameo hologram at her neck. Emily's video image was very twenties, a modern reaction against the stark, dress-for-success look of generations of businesswomen. To Laura's eye, the fashion suggested an antebellum southern belle filled to gushing with feminine graciousness.

"I've got the *Report*'s rough draft," Emily announced. "It's pretty much what we expected."

Emily pulled her copy of the *Quarterly Report* from a drawer.

She flipped pages. "Let's get to the major stuff. The Committee election. We've got twelve candidates, which is a joke, but three frontrunners. Pereira's an honest guy, you could play poker with him by telex, but he can't live down that Brasilia debacle. Tanaka pulled a real coup with that Osaka lumber deal. He's pretty flexible for an oldline salary man, but I met him in Osaka last year. He drank a lot and wanted to pinch me. Besides, he's into countertrade, and that's my turf.

"So we'll have to back Suvendra. She came up through the Djakarta office, so the East Asian contingent's behind her. She's old, though." Emily frowned. "And she smokes. An ugly habit and it tends to rub people the wrong way. Those clove-scented Indonesian cancer sticks—one whiff and you're ready for a biopsy." She shuddered.

"Still, Suvendra's our best bet. At least, she'll appreciate our support. Unfortunately that moron Jensen is running again on a youth platform, and that'll cut into the votes we can swing. But to hell with it." She pulled at a coil of hair. "I'm tired of playing the young ingenue anyway. When I run again in '25 I think we should aim for the Anglo and feminist vote."

She flipped pages, frowning. "Okay, a quick review of the party line. Let me know if you need more data on the arguments. Philippines farm project: no way. Farming's a black hole and Manila's price supports are bound to collapse. Kymera joint project: yes. Russian software deal: yes. The Sovs still have hard-currency problems, but we can cut a good countertrade in natural gas. Kuwaiti housing project: no. Islamic Republic: the terms are good but it stinks politically. No."

She paused. "Now here's one you didn't know about. Grenada United Bank. The Committee's slipping this one in." For the first time, Emily looked uneasy. "They're an offshore bank. Not too savory. But the Committee figures it's time for a gesture of friendship. It won't do our reputation much good if the whole thing is hashed out in public. But it's harmless enough—we can let it go."

Emily yanked open a wooden drawer with a squeak and put the *Report* away. "So much for this quarter. Things look good, generally." She smiled. "Hello, David, if you're watching. If you don't mind, I'd like a private word with Laura now."

The screen went blank for a long moment. But the time elapsing didn't cost much. Prerecorded one-way calls were cheap. Emily's call had been compressed into a high-speed burst and sent from machine to machine overnight, at midnight rates.

Emily reappeared on the screen, this time in her bedroom. She now wore a pink-and-white satin night-robe and her hair had been brushed out. She sat cross-legged in her wooden four-poster bed, a Victorian antique. Emily had refinished her ancient, creaking bed with modern hard-setting shellac. This transparent film was so mercilessly tough and rigid that it clamped the whole structure together like cast iron.

She had attached the phone camera to one of the bedposts. Business was over now. This was personal. The video etiquette had changed along with Emily's expression. She had a hangdog look. A new camera angle, looking down into the bed from a somewhat superior angle, helped convey the mood. She looked pitiful.

Laura sighed, pausing the playback. She shifted Loretta in her lap and nuzzled her absently. She was used to hearing Emily's problems, but it was hard to take before lunch. Especially today. Weirdness beginning to mount. She lifted her finger again.

"Well, I'm back," Emily intoned. "I suppose you can guess what it is. It's Arthur again. We had another fight. A brutal one. It started as one of those trivial things, about nothing really. Oh, about sex I guess, or at least that's what he said, but it came out of the blue for me. I thought he was being a bastard for no reason. He started sniping at me, using That Tone of Voice, you know. And once he gets that way he's impossible.

"He started shouting, I started yelling, and things just went straight to hell. He almost hit me. He clenched his fist and everything." Emily paused dramatically. "I ran back in here and locked the door in his face. And he didn't say a damned thing. He just left me in here. When I came out he was gone. And he took . . ." Her voice shook for a moment and she waited it out, pulling at a long strand of hair. "He took that photo he made of me, the black-and-white one in period dress, that I really liked. And that was two days ago and he doesn't answer his goddamn phone."

She looked close to tears. "I don't know, Laura. I've tried everything. I've tried men in the company, men outside, and it's just no luck at all. I mean, either they want to own you and be the center of the universe, or they want to treat you like some bed-and-breakfast service and expose you to Christ knows what kind of disease. And it's been worse since I've been on the Committee. Rizome men are a lost cause now. They tiptoe around me like I was a goddamn land mine."

She looked off-camera. "C'mon, kitty." A Persian cat jumped onto the bed. "Maybe it's me, Laura. Other women come to decent terms with men. You certainly did. Maybe I need outside help." She hesitated. "Someone put an anonymous post on the trade division board. About a psychiatric drug. Marriage counselors are using it. Romance, they call it. You ever hear of it? I think it's illegal or something." She stroked her cat absently.

She sighed. "Well, this is nothing new. Emily's sob story, year thirty-two. I think it's through between me and Arthur now. He's an artistic type. A photographer. Not in business at all. I thought it might work out. But I was wrong as usual." She shrugged. "I should look at the bright side, right? He didn't ask me for money and he didn't give me a retrovirus. And he wasn't married. A real prince."

She leaned back against the mahogany headboard, looking tired and defenseless. "I shouldn't tell you this, Laura, so be sure to erase it first thing. This Grenada Bank deal—that meeting you're about to hold is part of it. Rizome's sponsoring a meeting on data banking and data piracy. That doesn't sound like anything new, but listen: it's with actual live pirates. Sleazy offshore types from the data havens. Remember the fight we put through to get your Lodge equipped for major meetings?"

Emily grimaced and spread her hands. "Well, the Europeans should be there already. They're the tamest of the bunch— the closest to legit. But you can expect some Grenadians in tomorrow, with one of our security people. The Committee's sent you the schedule already, but not the full details. As far as you know, they're all legitimate bankers. Be nice to them, all right? They may be crooks to us, but what they do is completely legal in their little enclaves."

She frowned. The cat dropped to the floor with a thump off-camera. "They've been taking bites out of us for years, and we've got to talk some sense into them. It looks bad for Rizome to cozy up to pirates, so keep it quiet, all right? I'm being stupid here, because I wanted to give you a break. If it comes out that I leaked this, the Committee will slap me down hard. So you'd better be a lot more discreet than I am. Okay, end of message. Send me a tape of the baby, all right? Say hi to David." The screen went blank.

Well, now she had it all. She erased the tape. Thanks, Em. Pirate data bankers, no less. Creepy little hustlers from some offshore data haven—the kind of guys who chewed matchsticks and wore sharkskin suits. That explained the Europeans. Bankers my eye. They were all rip-off artists. Crooks.

They were nervous, that was it. Jumpy. And no wonder. The general potential for embarrassment in this situation was vast. One phone call to the Galveston police and they could all be in muchissimo hot water.

She was a little mad at the Committee for being cagy about it. But she could see their reasons. And the more she thought about it, the more she recognized it as a gesture of trust. Her Lodge was going to be right in the middle of some very delicate action. They could easily have taken it to another Lodge—like the Warburtons in the Ozarks. This way they were going to have to level with her. And she was going to see it all.

After a late lunch, she took the Canadians into the conference room in the tower. They logged in to Atlanta and picked up their last messages. They killed a couple of hours before departure, grinning into videophones and gossiping. One of the women had run out of video rouge and had to borrow Laura's.

At four, the fall *Quarterly Report* came on line, a little early. The printers chattered hard copy. The Kurosawas picked up their Portuguese translation and left.

David showed up at five o'clock, and he'd brought his wrecking crew. They stomped into the bar, raided the beer, and rushed upstairs to see the baby. Laura's mother arrived, sunburned from her boat trip to the OTEC. Galveston's Ocean Thermal Energy Converter was a civic pride and joy, and one of David's crew had been on the project. Everyone seemed delighted to trade notes.

David was peppered head to foot with grime and sawdust. So were his four wrecking buddies. In their work shirts, denim overalls, and heavy boots, they looked like Depression hoboes. Actually David's friends were a dentist, two marine engineers, and a biology professor, but appearances counted. She tugged his shoulder strap. "Did the European bankers see you, coming in?"

David beamed paternally as his friends admired Loretta's amazing new skill at clenching her sweaty little fists. "Yeah, so?"

"David, you reek."

"A little honest sweat!" David said. "What are we, Marxists? Hell, they envy us! Those Luxembourg paper shufflers are dying for a day's honest work."

Supper with David's friends was a great success. David broke his principles and ate the shrimp, but refused to touch the vegetables. "Vegetables are full of poisons!" he insisted loudly. "They're crammed with natural insecticides! Plants use chemical warfare. Ask any botanist!"

Luckily no one pursued the subject. The wrecking crew called vans and left for home. Laura locked up for the night while the staff loaded the dishes. David took a shower.

Laura limped up to the top floor to join him. It was sunset. Mr. Rodriguez lowered the flags on the roof and tottered back down three flights of stairs to staff quarters. He was a stoic old man, but Laura thought he looked tired. He'd had lifeguard duty. The Canadians' manic brood had run him ragged.

Laura kicked off her sandals and hung her vest and skirt in the bedroom closet. She shrugged out of her blouse, then sat on the bed and peeled off her hose. Her injured ankle had swollen and was now an impressive blue. She kicked her legs out straight and leaned back against the headboard. A ceiling vent came on and cool air poured over the bed. Laura sat in her underwear, feeling tired and vaguely squalid.

David stalked naked out of the bathroom and disappeared into the baby's room. She heard him making soothing goo-goo noises. Laura checked tomorrow's schedule on her watchphone. Her mother was leaving tomorrow. Her departure flight to Dallas was scheduled just before the Grenadians arrived. Laura grimaced. Always more trouble.

David emerged from the baby's room. His long hair was parted in the middle and wet-combed down, flatly, over his ears and neck. He looked like a demented Russian priest.

He flopped down onto the bed and gave her a big, knowing grin. Make that a demented Russian priest with a yen for women, Laura thought with a sinking feeling.

"Great day, huh?" He stretched. "Man, I worked my ass off. I'll be sore tomorrow. Feel great now, though. Lively." He watched her with narrowed eyes.

Laura was not in the mood. A sense of ritual settled over both of them, a kind of unspoken bargaining. The object was to make your mood set the tone of the evening. Souring it was a foul.

There were multiple levels of play. Both sides won big if you both reached the same mood quickly, through sheer infectious charisma. You won second-class if you got your own way without feeling guilty about it. Pyrrhic victory was when you got your own way but felt rotten. Then there were the various levels of giving in: Gracious, Resigned, and Martyr to the Cause.

Fouls were easiest, and then you both lost. The longer the ritual lasted, the more chances there were to screw up. It was a hard game to play, even with eight years' practice.

Laura wondered if she should tell him about the Church of Ishtar. Thinking about the interview revived her sense of sexual repulsion, like the soiled feeling she got from seeing pornography. She decided not to mention it tonight. He was sure to take it all wrong if he thought his overtures made her feel like a hooker.

She buried the idea and cast about for another one. The first twinge of guilt nibbled her resolve. Maybe she should give in. She looked down at her feet. "My leg hurts," she said.

"Poor babe." He leaned over and had a closer look. His eyes widened. "Jesus." Suddenly she had become an invalid. The mood shifted all at once, and the game was over. He kissed his fingertip and tapped it lightly on the bruise.

"Feels better," she said, smiling. He leaned back in bed and got under the sheet, looking resigned and peaceable. That was easy. Victory class one for the Poor Little Lame Girl.

Now it was overkill, but she decided to mention her mother anyway. "I'll be fine when things get back to normal. Mother leaves tomorrow."

"Back to Dallas, huh? Too bad, I was just getting used to the old gal."

Laura kicked her way under the sheet. "Well, at least she didn't bring some obnoxious boyfriend."

David sighed. "You're so hard on her, Laura. She's a career woman of the old school, that's all. There were millions like her—men, too. Her generation likes to get around. They live alone, they cut their ties, they stay fast and loose. Wherever they walk families crumble." He shrugged. "So she had three husbands. With her looks she could have had twenty."

"You always take her side. Just because she likes you." Because you're like Dad, she thought, and blocked the thought away.

"Because she has your eyes," he said, and gave her a quick, snaky pinch.

She jumped, shocked. "You rat!"

"You big rat," he corrected, yawning.

"Big rat," she agreed. He'd broken her out of her mood. She felt better.

"Big rat that I can't live without."

"You said it," she said.

"Turn out the light." He turned onto his side, away from her.

She reached out to give his hair a final ruffle. She killed the lights, touching her wrist. She put her arm over his sleeping body and slid up against him in darkness. It was good.

2

AFTER breakfast, Laura helped her mother pack. It surprised her to see the sheer bulk of bric-a-brac her mother hauled around: hatboxes, bottles of hairspray and vitamins and contact-lens fluid, a video camera, a clothes steamer, a portable iron, hair curlers, a sleeping mask, six pairs of shoes with special wooden lasts to keep them from mashing down in her luggage. She even had a special intaglio box just for earrings.

Laura held up a red leather-bound travel diary. "Mother, why do you need this? Can't you just call up the Net?"

"I don't know, dear. I spend so much time on the road—it's like home for me, all of these things." She packed dresses with a swish of fabric. "Besides, I don't like the Net. I never even liked cable television." She hesitated. "Your father and I used to fight about that. He'd be a real Net-head now, if he was still alive."

The idea sounded silly to Laura. "Oh, Mother, come on."

"He hated clutter, your father. He didn't care for nice things—lamps, carpets, dinner china. He was a dreamer, he liked abstractions. He called me a materialist." She shrugged. "My generation always got bad press for that."

Laura waved her arm about the room. "But, Mother, look at these things."

"Laura, I like my possessions and I've paid for all of them. Maybe people don't prize possessions now like we did in the premillennium. How could they? All their money goes into the Net. For games, or business, or television—things that come over the wires." She zipped her bag shut. "Young people these days, maybe they don't hanker after a Mercedes or a Jacuzzi. But they'll brag like sixty about their data access."

Laura felt impatient. "That's silly, Mother. There's nothing wrong with being proud of what you know. A Mercedes is just a machine. It doesn't prove anything about you as a person." Her watchphone beeped; the van had arrived downstairs.

She helped her mother take her luggage down. It took three trips. Laura knew she'd have a wait in the airport, so she took the baby along, in a canvas travel sling.

"Let me get this trip," her mother said. She slipped her card into the van's charge slot. The door clicked open and they loaded the bags and stepped in.

"Howdy," the van said. "Please announce your destination clearly into the speaker. *Anunce usted su destinacion claramente en el microfono por favor.*"

"Airport," Laura said, bored.

". . . sss . . . ank you! Estimated travel time is twelve minutes. Thank you for using the Galveston Transit System. Alfred A. Magruder, Mayor." The van accelerated sluggishly, its modest engine whining. Laura lifted her brows. The van's spiel had been changed. "Alfred A. Magruder, Mayor?" she murmured.

"Galveston is Fun City!" the van responded. Laura and her mother traded glances. Laura shrugged.

Highway 3005 was the main artery down-the-island. The road's glory days were long gone; it was haunted by the memories of cheap oil and private cars doing sixty miles per. Long sections of tarmac had been potholed into ruin and replaced with plastic mesh. The mesh crackled loudly beneath the tires.

On their left, to the west, bare cracked slabs of concrete fringed the road like fallen dominoes. Building foundations had no scrap value. They were always the last to go. Beach scrub flourished everywhere: salt grass, spreading mats of crisp glasswort, leathery clumps of reed. To their right, along the shore, surf washed the stilts from vanished beach homes. The stilts leaned at strange angles, like the legs of wading flamingos.

Her mother touched Loretta's thin curls, and the baby gurgled. "Does it ever bother you, this place, Laura? All this ruin . . ."

"David loves it here," Laura said.

Her mother spoke with an effort. "Does he treat you all right, dear? You seem happy with him. I hope that's true."

"David's fine, mother." Laura had dreaded this talk. "You've seen how we live, now. We have nothing to hide."

"Last time we met, Laura, you were working in Atlanta. Rizome's headquarters. Now you're an innkeeper." She hesitated. "Not that it's not a nice place, but . . ."

"You think it's a setback to my career." Laura shook her head. "Mother, Rizome's a democracy. If you want power, you have to be voted in. That means you have to know people. Personal contact means everything with us. And innkeeping, as you put it, is great exposure. The best people in our company stay in the Lodges as guests. And that's where they see us."

"That's not how I remember it," her mother said. "Power is where the action is."

"Mother, the action's everywhere now. That's why we have the Net." Laura struggled for politeness. "This isn't something David and I just stumbled into. It's a showcase for us. We knew we'd need a place while the baby was small, so we drew up the plans, we carried it through the company, we showed initiative, flexibility. . . . It was our first big project as a team. People know us now."

"So," her mother said slowly. "You worked it all out very neatly. You have ambition and the baby. Career and the family. A husband and a job. It's all too pat, Laura. I can't believe it's that simple."

Laura was icy. "Of course you'd say that, wouldn't you?"

Silence fell heavily. Her mother picked at the hem of her skirt. "Laura, I know my visit hasn't been easy for you. It's been a long time since we went our separate ways, you and I. I hope we can change that now."

Laura said nothing. Her mother went on stubbornly. "Things have changed since your grandmother died. It's been two years, and she's not there for either of us now. Laura, I want to help you, if I can. If there's anything you need. Anything. If you have to travel—it would be fine if you left Loretta with me. Or if you just need someone to talk to."

She hesitated, reaching out to touch the baby, a gesture of

open need. For the first time, Laura truly saw her mother's hands. The wrinkled hands of an old woman. "I know you miss your grandmother. You named the baby after her. Loretta." She stroked the baby's cheek. "I can't take her place. But I want to do something, Laura. For my grandchild's sake."

It seemed like a decent, old-fashioned family gesture, Laura thought. But it was an unwelcome favor. She knew she'd have to pay for her mother's help—with obligations and intimacy. Laura hadn't asked for that and didn't want it. And didn't even need it—she and David had the company behind them, after all, good solid Rizome *gemeineschaft*. "That's very nice, mother," she said. "Thank you for the offer. David and I appreciate it." She turned her face away, to the window.

The road improved as the van reached a section zoned for redevelopment. They passed a long marina clustered with autopilot sailboats for hire. Then a fortresslike mall, built, like the Lodge, from concretized beach sand. Vans crowded its parking lot. The mall flashed past in bright commercial garishness: T-SHIRTS BEER WINE VIDEO Come On In, It's Cool Inside!

"Business is good, for a weekday," Laura said. The crowd was mostly middle-aged Houstonians, freed for the day from their high-rise warrens. Scores of them wandered the beach, aimlessly, staring out to sea, glad of an unobstructed horizon.

Her mother continued to press. "Laura, I worry about you. I don't want to run your life for you, if that's what you're thinking. You've done very well for yourself, and I'm glad for it, truly. But things can happen, through no fault of your own." She hesitated. "I want you to learn from our experience—mine, my mother's. Neither of us had good luck—with our men, with our children. And it wasn't that we didn't try."

Laura's patience was eroding. Her mother's experience—it was something that had haunted Laura every day of her life. For her mother to mention it now—as if it were something that might have slipped her daughter's mind—struck Laura as grossly thoughtless and crass. "It's not enough to try, Mother. You have to plan ahead. That was something your generation was never any good at.'' She gestured at the window. ''Don't you see that out there?''

The van had reached the southern end of the Galveston Seawall. They were passing a suburb, once a commuter's haven with fresh green lawns and a golf course. Now it was a barrio, with sprawling houses subdivided, converted into bars and Latin groceries.

''The people who built this suburb knew they were running out of oil,'' Laura said. ''But they wouldn't plan for it. They built everything around their precious cars, even though they knew they were turning the downtowns into ghettos. Now the cars are gone, and everyone with money has rushed back downtown. So the poor are shoved out here instead. Only they can't afford the water bills, so the lawns are full of scrub. And they can't afford air conditioning, so they swelter in the heat. No one even had the sense to build porches. Even though every house built in Texas had porches, for two hundred years!''

Her mother stared obediently out the window. It was noon, and windows were flung open from the heat. Inside them, the unemployed sweated before their subsidized televisions. The poor lived cheap these days. Low-grade scop, fresh from the vats and dried like cornmeal, cost only a few cents a pound. Everyone in the ghetto suburbs ate scop, single-cell protein. The national food of the Third World.

''But that's what I'm trying to tell you, dear,'' her mother said. ''Things change. You can't control that. And bad luck happens.''

Laura spoke tightly. ''Mother, people built these crappy tract homes, they didn't grow there. They were built for rip-off quick profit, with no sense of the long term. I know those places, I've helped David smash them up. Look at them!''

Her mother looked pained. ''I don't understand. They're cheap houses where poor people live. At least they have shelter, don't they?''

''Mother, they're energy sieves! They're lathwork and sheetrock and cheap tinsel crap!''

Her mother shook her head. ''I'm not an architect's wife, dear. I can see you're upset by these places, but you talk as if it were my fault.''

The van turned west up 83rd Street, heading for the airfield. The baby was asleep against her chest; Laura hugged her tighter, feeling depressed and angry. She didn't know how she could make it any clearer to her mother without being bluntly rude. If she could say: Mother, your marriage was like one of these cheap houses; you used it up and moved on. . . . You threw my father out of your life like last year's car, and you gave me to Grandmother to raise, like a house plant that no longer fit your decor. . . . But she couldn't say that. She couldn't force the words out.

A shadow passed low overhead, silently. A Boeing passenger plane, an intercontinental, its tail marked with the red and blue of Aero Cubana. It reminded Laura of an albatross, with vast, canted, razorlike wings on a long, narrow body. Its engines hummed.

The sight of planes always gave Laura a nostalgic lift. She had spent a lot of time in airports as a child, in the happy times before her life as a diplomat's kid fell apart. The plane dropped gently, with computer-guided precision, its wings extruding yellow braking films. Modern design, Laura thought proudly, watching it. The Boeing's thin ceramic wings looked frail. But they could have cut through a lousy tract house like a razor through cheese.

They entered the airport through gates in a chain-link fence of red plastic mesh. Outside the terminal, vans queued up in the taxi lane.

Laura helped her mother unload her bags onto a waiting luggage trolley. The terminal was built in early Organic Baroque, with insulated, fortresslike walls and double sliding doors. It was blessedly cool inside, with a sharp reek of floor cleaner. Flat display screens hung from the ceiling, shuffling arrivals and departures. Their luggage trolley tagged along at their heels.

The crowd was light. Scholes Field was not a major airport, no matter what the city claimed. The City Council had expanded it after the last hurricane, in a last-ditch attempt to boost Galveston's civic morale. A lot of taxpayers had quickly used it to leave Galveston for good.

They checked her mother's luggage. Laura watched her mother chat with the ticket clerk. Once again she was the woman Laura remembered: trim and cool and immaculate, self-contained in a diplomat's Teflon shell. Margaret Day: still an attractive woman at sixty-two. People lasted forever, these days. With any luck, her mother could live another forty years.

They walked together toward the departure lounge. "Let me hold her just once more," her mother said. Laura passed her the baby. Her mother carried Loretta like a sack of emeralds. "If I've said anything to upset you, you'll forgive me, won't you? I'm not as young as I was and there are things I don't understand."

Her voice was calm, but her face trembled for a moment, with a strange naked look of appeal. For the first time Laura realized how much it had cost her mother to go through this—how ruthlessly she had humbled herself. Laura felt a sudden empathetic shock—as if she'd met some injured stranger on her doorstep. "No, no," she mumbled, walking. "Everything was fine."

"You're modern people, you and David," her mother said. "In a way you seem very innocent to us, oh, premillennium decadents." She smiled wryly. "So free of doubts."

Laura thought it over as they walked into the departure lounge. For the first time, she felt a muddy intuition of her mother's point of view. She stood by her mother's chair, out of earshot from the sprinkling of other passengers for Dallas. "We seem dogmatic. Smug. Is that it?"

"Oh, no," her mother said hastily. "That's not what I meant at all."

Laura took a deep breath. "We don't live under terror, Mother. That's the real difference. No one's pointing missiles at my generation. That's why we think about the future, the long term. Because we know we'll have one." Laura spread her hands. "And we didn't earn that luxury. The luxury to look smug. You gave it to us." Laura relaxed a little, feeling virtuous.

"Well . . ." Her mother struggled for words. "It's something like that but. . . . The world you grew up in—every year it's more smooth and controlled. Like you've thrown a net over the Fates. But Laura, you haven't, not really. And I worry for you."

Laura was surprised. She'd never known her mother was such a morbid fatalist. It seemed a weirdly old-fashioned attitude. And she was in earnest, too—as if she were ready to nail up horseshoes or count rosary beads. And things had been going rather oddly lately. . . . Despite herself, Laura felt a light passing tingle of superstitious fear.

She shook her head. "All right, Mother. David and I—we know we can count on you."

"That's all I asked." Her mother smiled. "David was wonderful—give him my love." The other passengers rose, shuffling briefcases and garment bags. Her mother kissed the baby, then stood and handed her back. Loretta's face clouded and she began snuffling up to a wail.

"Uh-oh," Laura said lightly. She accepted a quick, awkward hug from her mother. "Bye."

"Call me."

"All right." Bouncing Loretta to shush her, Laura watched her mother leave, blending in with the crowd at the exit ramp. One stranger among others. Ironic, Laura thought. She'd been waiting for this moment for seven days, and now that it was here, it hurt. Sort of. In a way.

Laura glanced at her watchphone. She had to kill an hour before the Grenadians arrived. She went to the coffee shop. People stared at her and the baby. In a world so crammed with old people, babies had novelty value. Even total strangers turned mushy, making faces and doing little four-finger waves.

Laura sat, sipping the airport's lousy coffee, letting the tension wash out of her. She was glad that her mother was gone. She could feel repressed bits of her personality rising slowly back into place. Like continental shelves lifting after an ice age.

A young woman two booths away was interested in the baby. Her eyes were alight and she kept mugging at Loretta, big open-mouthed grins. Laura watched her, bemused. Something about the woman's broad-cheeked, freckled face struck Laura as quintessentially Texan. A kind of rugged, cracker look, Laura thought—a genetic legacy from some hard-eyed woman in calico, the sort who rode shotgun through Comanche country and had six kids without anesthetic. It showed even through the woman's garish makeup—blood-red waxy lipstick, dramatically lined eyes, hair teased into a mane. . . . Laura realized with a start that the woman was a hooker from the Church of Ishtar.

The Grenadians' flight was announced, a connection from Miami. The Church hooker leapt up at once, a flush of excitement on her face. Laura trailed her. She rushed at once to the embarkation lounge.

Laura joined her as the plane emptied. She cataloged passengers at a glance, watching for her guests. A family of Vietnamese shrimpers. A dozen shabby but optimistic Cubans with shopping bags. A group of serious, neatly dressed black collegians in fraternity sweaters. Three offshore oil-rig roughnecks, wrinkled old men wearing cowboy hats and engineering boots.

Suddenly the Ishtar woman drew near and spoke to her. "You're with Rizome, aren't you?"

"Rye-zoam," Laura said.

"Well, then, you'd be waiting for Sticky and the old man?" Her eyes sparkled. It gave her bony face a strange vivacity. "Did the Rev'rend Morgan talk to you?"

"I've met the reverend," Laura said carefully. She knew nothing about anyone named Sticky.

The woman smiled. "Y'all's baby is cute. . . . Oh, look, there they are!" She raised her arm over her head and waved excitedly, the deep-cut neckline of her blouse showing fringes of red brassiere. "Yoo-hoo! Sticky!"

An old-fashioned Rastaman in dreadlocks cut his way out of the crowd. The old man wore a long-sleeved dashiki of cheap synthetic, over baggy drawstring pants, and sandals.

The Rastaman's young companion wore a nylon windbreaker, sunglasses, and jeans. The woman rushed forward and embraced him. "Sticky!" The younger man, with sudden wiry strength, lifted the Church woman off her feet and spun her half around. His dark, even face was expressionless behind the glasses.

"Laura?" A woman had appeared at Laura's elbow, silently. It was one of Rizome's security coordinators, Debra Emerson. Emerson was a sad-looking Anglo woman in her sixties with etched, delicate features and thinning hair. Laura had often spoken to her over the Net and had met her once in Atlanta.

They exchanged brief formal hugs and cheek kisses in the usual Rizome style. "Where are the bankers?" Laura said.

Emerson nodded at the Rastaman and his companion. Laura's heart sank. "That's them?"

"These offshore bankers don't follow our standards," Emerson said, watching them.

Laura said, "Do you realize who that woman is? The group she's with?"

"Church of Ishtar," Emerson said. She didn't look happy about it. She glanced up into Laura's face. "We haven't told you all we should yet, for reasons of discretion. But I know you're not naive. You have good Net connections, Laura. You must know how things stand in Grenada."

"I know Grenada's a data haven," Laura said cautiously. She wasn't sure how far to go.

Debra Emerson had once been a high muckety-muck at the CIA, back when there had been a CIA and its muckety-mucks were still in vogue. Security work had no such glamor nowadays. Emerson had the look of someone who had suffered in silence, a sort of translucency around the eyes. She favored gray corduroy skirts and longsleeve blouses in meek beiges and duns.

The old Rastaman shambled over, smiling. "Winston Stubbs," he said. He had the lilt of the Caribbean, softened vowels broken by crisp British consonants. He shook Laura's hand. "And Sticky Thompson, Michael Thompson that is." He turned. "Sticky!"

Sticky came up, his arm around the Church girl's waist. "I'm Laura Webster," Laura said.

"We know," Sticky said. "This is Carlotta."

"I'm their liaison," Carlotta drawled brightly. She pushed her hair back with both hands and Laura glimpsed an ankh tattooed on her right wrist. "Y'all bring much luggage? I got a van waiting."

"I-and-I have business up-the-island," Stubbs explained. "We be in to your Lodge later this night, call you on the Net, seen?"

Emerson broke in. "If that's the way you want it, Mr. Stubbs."

Stubbs nodded. "Later." The three of them left, calling a luggage trolley.

Laura watched them go, nonplussed. "Are they supposed to be running around loose?"

Emerson sighed. "It's a touchy situation. I'm sorry you were brought here for nothing, but it's just one of their little gestures." She tugged the strap of her heavy shoulder bag. "Let's call a cab."

After their arrival, Emerson vanished upstairs into the Lodge's conference room. Usually, Laura and David ate in the dining room, where they could socialize with the guests. That night, however, they joined Emerson and ate in the tower, feeling uneasily conspiratorial.

David set the table. Laura opened a covered tray of chile rellenos and Spanish rice. David had health food.

"I want to be as open and straightforward with you as I possibly can," Emerson murmured. "By now, you must have realized the nature of your new guests."

"Yes," David said. He was far from happy about it.

"Then you can understand the need for security. Naturally we trust the discretion of you and your staff."

David smiled a little. "That's nice to know."

Emerson looked troubled. "The Committee has been planning this meeting for some time. These Europeans you've been sheltering are no ordinary bankers. They're from the EFT Commerzbank of Luxembourg. And tomorrow night a third group arrives. The Yung Soo Chim Islamic Bank of Singapore."

David paused with a fork halfway to his mouth. "And they're also—?"

"Data pirates, yes."

"I see," Laura said. She felt a sudden surge of chilly excitement. "This is big."

"Very," Emerson said. She let that sink in for a while. "We offered them any of six possible locations for the meeting. It could just as easily have been the Valenzuelas in Puerto Vallarta. Or the Warburtons in Arkansas."

"How long do you expect this to last?" David said.

"Five days. Maybe a week at the outside." She sipped her iced tea. "It's up to us to supply airtight security once the meeting is under way. You understand? Locked doors, drawn curtains. No running in and out.''

David frowned. ''We'll need supplies. I'll tell Mrs. Delrosario.''

''I can take care of supplies.''

''Mrs. Delrosario's very particular about where she shops,'' David said.

''Oh, dear,'' said Ms. Emerson sincerely. ''Well, groceries are not a major problem.'' She picked carefully at the skin of her stuffed pepper. ''Some of the attendees may bring their own food.''

David was stunned. ''You mean they're afraid to eat our food? They think we'll poison them, is that it?''

''David, it's a sign of their great trust in Rizome that the three banks have agreed to meet here in the first place. It's not us that they distrust. It's one another.''

David was alarmed. ''What exactly are we getting into? We have a small child here! Not to mention our staff.''

Emerson looked hurt. ''Would you feel better if this Lodge was full of armed guards from Rizome? Or if Rizome even had armed guards? We can't confront these people by force, and we shouldn't try to. That's our strength.''

Laura spoke up. ''You're saying that because we're harmless, we won't be hurt.''

''We want to reduce tension. We don t mean to arrest these pirates, prosecute them, crush them. We've decided to negotiate. That's a modern solution. It worked for the arms race, after all. It has been working for the Third World.''

''Except for Africa,'' David said.

Emerson shrugged. ''It's a long-term effort. The old East-West Cold War, the North-South struggle . . . those were both old fights. Struggles we inherited. But now we face a truly modern challenge. This meeting is part of it.''

David looked surprised. ''Come on. These aren't nuclear arms talks. I've read about these havens. They're fleabag pirates. Sleazy rip-off artists who won't pull their own weight in the world. So they call themselves bankers, so they wear three-piece suits. Hell, they can fly private jets and shoot boars in the forests of Tuscany. They're still cheap rip-off bastards.''

"That's a very correct attitude," Emerson said. "But don't underestimate the havens. So far, as you say, they're only parasites. They steal software, they bootleg records and videos, they invade people's privacy. Those are annoyances, but it's not yet more than the system can bear. But what about the potential? There are potential black markets for genetic engineering, organ transplants, neurochemicals . . . a whole galaxy of modern high-tech products. Hackers loose in the Net are trouble enough. What happens when a genetic engineer cuts one corner too many?"

David shuddered. "Well, that can't be allowed."

"But these are sovereign national governments," said Emerson. "A small Third World nation like Grenada can profit by playing fast and loose with new technologies. They may well hope to become a center of innovation, just as the Cayman Islands and Panama became financial centers. Regulation is a burden, and multinationals are always tempted to move out from under it. What happens to Rizome if our competitors evade the rules, offshore?"

She let them mull over that for a while. "And there are deeper questions that affect the whole structure of the modern world. What happens when tomorrow's industries are pioneered by criminals? We live on a crowded planet, and we need controls, but they have to be tight. Otherwise corruption seeps in like black water."

"It's a tough agenda," David said, thinking it over. "In fact, it sounds hopeless."

"So did the Abolition," said Emerson. "But the arsenals are gone." She smiled. The same old line, Laura thought. The old baby-boom generation had been using it for years. Maybe they thought it would help explain why they were still running everything. "But history never stops. Modern society faces a new central crisis. Are we going to control the path of development for sane, human ends? Or is it going to be laissez-faire anarchy?"

Emerson polished off the last of her chile relleno. "These are real issues. If we want to live in a world we can recognize, we'll have to fight for the privilege. We at Rizome have to do our part. We are doing it. Here and now."

"You make a pretty good case," David said. "But I imagine the pirates see things differently."

"Oh, we'll be hearing their side soon enough." She smiled. "But we may have some surprises for them. The havens are used to multinational corporations in the old style. But an economic democracy is a different animal. We must let them see that for themselves. Even if it means some risk to us."

David frowned. "You don't seriously think they'll try anything?"

"No, I don't. If they do, we'll simply call the local police. It would be scandalous for us—this is, after all, a very confidential meeting—but worse scandal, I think, for them." She placed fork and knife neatly across her plate. "We know there's some small risk. But Rizome has no private army. No fellows in dark glasses with briefcases full of cash and handguns. That's out of style." Her eyes flashed briefly. "We have to pay for that luxury of innocence, though. Because we have no one to take our risks for us. We have to spread the danger out, among Rizome associates. Now it's your turn. You understand. Don't you?"

Laura thought it over, quietly. "Our number came up," she said at last.

"Exactly."

"Just one of those things," David said. And it was.

The negotiators should have arrived at the Lodge all at the same time, on equal terms. But they didn't have that much sense. Instead they'd chosen to screw around and attempt to one-up each other.

The Europeans had arrived early—it was their attempt to show the others that they were close to the Rizome referees and dealing from a position of strength. But they soon grew bored and were full of peevish suspicion.

Emerson was still mollifying them when the Singapore contingent arrived. There were three of them as well: an ancient Chinese named Mr. Shaw and his two Malay compatriots. Mr. Shaw was a bespectacled, balding man in an oversized suit, who spoke very little. The two Malays wore black songkak hats, peaked fore and aft, with sewn-on emblems of their group, the Yung Soo Chim Islamic Bank. The

Malays were middle-aged men, very sober, very dignified. Not like bankers, however. Like soldiers. They walked erect, with their shoulders squared, and their eyes never stopped moving.

They brought mounds of luggage, including their own telephones and a refrigerated chest, packed with foil-sealed trays of food.

Emerson made introductions. Karageorgiu glared aggressively, Shaw was woodenly aloof. The escorts looked ready to arm-wrestle. Emerson took the Singaporeans upstairs to the conference room, where they could phone in and assure their home group that they had arrived in one piece.

No one had seen the Grenadians since the day before, at the airport. They hadn't called in, either, despite their vague promises. Time passed. The others saw this as a studied insult and fretted over their drinks. They broke at last for dinner. The Singaporeans ate their own food, in their rooms. The Europeans complained vigorously about the barbarous Tex-Mex cuisine. Mrs. Delrosario, who had outdone herself, was almost reduced to tears.

The Grenadians finally showed up after dusk. Like Ms. Emerson, Laura had become seriously worried. She greeted them in the front lobby. "So glad to see you. Was there any trouble?"

"Nuh," said Winston Stubbs, exposing his dentures in a sunny smile. "I-and-I were downtown, seen. Up-the-island." The ancient Rastaman had perched a souvenir cowboy hat on his gray shoulder-length dreadlocks. He wore sandals and an explosive Hawaiian shirt.

His companion, Sticky Thompson, had a new haircut. He'd chosen to dress in slacks, long-sleeved shirt, and business vest, like a Rizome associate. It didn't quite work on him though; Sticky looked almost aggressively conventional. Carlotta, the Church girl, wore a sleeveless scarlet beach top, a short skirt, and heavy makeup. A brimming chalice was tattooed on her bare, freckled shoulder.

Laura introduced her husband and the Lodge staff to the Grenadians. David gave the old pirate his best hostly grin: friendly and tolerant, we're all just-folks here at Rizome. Overdoing it a bit maybe, because Winston Stubbs had the standard pirate image. Raffish. "Howdy," David said. "Hope y'all enjoy your stay with us."

The old man looked skeptical. David abandoned his drawl. "Cool runnings," he said tentatively.

"Cool runnings," Winston Stubbs mused. "Have nah hear that in forty year. You like those old reggae albums, Mr. Webster?"

David smiled. "My folks used to play them when I was a kid."

"Oh, seen. That would be Dr. Martin Webster and Grace Webster of Galveston."

"That's right," David said. His smile vanished.

"You designed this Lodge," Stubbs said. "Concretized sand, built from the beach, eh?" He looked David up and down. "Mash-it-up appropriate technology. We could use you in the islands, mon."

"Thanks," David said, fidgeting. "That's very flattering."

"We could use a public relations, too," Stubbs said, grinning crookedly at Laura. His eye whites were veined with red, like cracked marbles. "I-and-I's reputation could use an upgrade. Pressure come down on I-and-I. From Babylon Luddites."

"Let's all gather in the conference room," Emerson said. "It's early yet. Still time for us to talk."

They argued for two solid days. Laura sat in on the meetings as Debra Emerson's second, and she realized quickly that Rizome was a barely tolerated middleman. The data pirates had no interest whatsoever in taking up new careers as right-thinking postindustrialists. They had met to confront a threat.

All three pirate groups were being blackmailed.

The blackmailers, whoever they were, showed a firm grasp of data-haven dynamics. They had played cleverly on the divisions and rivalries among the havens; threatening one bank, then depositing the shakedown money in another. The havens, who naturally loathed publicity, had covered up the attacks. They were deliberately vague about the nature of the depredations. They feared publicizing their weaknesses. It was clear, too, that they suspected one another.

Laura had never known the true nature and extent of haven operations, but she sat quietly, listened and watched, and learned in a hurry.

The pirates dubbed commercial videotapes by the hundreds of thousands, selling them in poorly policed Third World markets. And their teams of software cracksters found a ready market for programs stripped of their copy protection. This brand of piracy was nothing new; it dated back to the early days of the information industry.

But Laura had never realized the profit to be gained by evading the developed world's privacy laws. Thousands of legitimate companies maintained dossiers on individuals: employee records, medical histories, credit transactions. In the Net economy, business was impossible without such information. In the legitimate world, companies purged this data periodically, as required by law.

But not all of it was purged. Reams of it ended up in the data havens, passed on through bribery of clerks, through taps of datalines, and by outright commercial espionage. Straight companies operated with specialized slivers of knowledge. But the havens made a business of collecting it, offshore. Memory was cheap, and their databanks were huge, and growing.

And they had no shortage of clients. Credit companies, for instance, needed to avoid bad risks and pursue their debtors. Insurers had similar problems. Market researchers hungered after precise data on individuals. So did fund raisers. Specialized address lists found a thriving market. Journalists would pay for subscription lists, and a quick sneak call to a databank could dredge up painful rumors that governments and companies suppressed.

Private security agencies were at home in the data demimonde. Since the collapse of the Cold War intelligence apparats, there were legions of aging, demobilized spooks scrabbling out a living in the private sector. A shielded phone line to the havens was a boon for a private investigator.

Even computer-dating services kicked in their bit.

The havens were bootstrapping their way up to Big Brother status, trading for scattered bits of information, then collating it and selling it back—as a new and sinister whole.

They made a business of abstracting, condensing, index-ing, and verifying—like any other modern commercial database. Except, of course, that the pirates were carnivorous. They ate other databases when they could, blithely ignoring copyrights and simply storing everything they could filch. This didn't require state-of-the-art computer expertise. Just memory by the ton, and plenty of cast-iron gall.

Unlike old-fashioned smugglers, the haven pirates never had to physically touch their booty. Data had no substance. EFT Commerzbank, for instance, was a legitimate corpora-tion in Luxembourg. Its illegal nerve centers were safely stowed away in Turkish Cyprus. The same went for the Singaporeans; they had the dignified cover of an address in Bencoolen Street, while the machinery hummed merrily in Nauru, a sovereign Pacific Island nation with a population of 12,000. For their part, the Grenadians simply brazened it out.

All three groups were monetary banks as well. This was handy for laundering client funds, and a ready source of necessary bribes. Since the invention of electronic funds trans-fer, money itself had become just another form of data. Their host governments were not inclined to quibble.

So, Laura thought, the basic principles of operation were clear enough. But they created, not solidarity, but bitter rivalry.

Names were freely exchanged during the more heated mo-ments. The ancestral lineage of the havens saddled them with an unhelpful and sometimes embarrassing heritage. During occasional bursts of frankness, whole whale-pods of these large and awkward facts surfaced and blew steam, while Laura marveled.

The EFT Commerzbank, she learned, drew its roots mainly from the old heroin networks of the south of France, and from the Corsican Black Hand. After the Abolition, these clunky gutter operations had been modernized by former French spooks from "La Piscine," the legendary Corsican school for paramilitary saboteurs. These right-wing commandos, tradi-tionally the rogue elephants of European espionage, drifted quite naturally into a life of crime once the French govern-ment had cut off their paychecks.

Additional muscle came from a minor galaxy of French

right-wing action groups, who abandoned their old careers of bombing trains and burning synagogues, to join the data game. Further allies came from the criminal families of the European Turkish minority, accomplished heroin smugglers who maintained an unholy linkage with the Turkish fascist underground.

All this had been poured into Luxembourg and allowed to set for twenty years, like some kind of horrible aspic. By now a kind of crust of respectability had formed, and the EFT Commerzbank was making some attempt to disown its past.

The others refused to make it easy for them. Egged on by Winston Stubbs, who remembered the event, Monsieur Karageorgiu was forced to admit that a member of the Turkish "Gray Wolves" had once shot a pope.

Karageorgiu defended the Wolves by insisting that the action was "business." He claimed it was a revenge operation, recompense for a sting by the Vatican's corrupt Banco Ambrosiano. The Ambrosiano, he explained, had been one of Europe's first truly "underground" banks, before the present system had settled. Standards had been different then—back in the rough-and-tumble glory days of Italian terrorism.

Besides, Karageorgiu pointed out smoothly, the Turkish gunman had only wounded Pope John Paul II. No worse than a kneecapping, really. Unlike the Sicilian Mafia—who were so annoyed at the Banco's misdeeds that they had poisoned Pope John Paul I stone dead.

Laura believed very little of this—she noticed Ms. Emerson smiling quietly to herself—but it was clear that the other pirates had few doubts. The story fit precisely into the folk mythos of their enterprise. They shook their heads over it with a kind of rueful nostalgia. Even Mr. Shaw looked vaguely impressed.

The Islamic Bank's antecedents were similarly mixed. Triad syndicates were a major factor. Besides being criminal brotherhoods, the Triads had always had a political side, ever since their ancient origins as anti-Manchu rebels in seventeenth-century China.

The Triads had whiled away the centuries in prostitution, gambling, and drugs, with occasional breaks for revolution, such as the Chinese Republic of 1912. But their ranks had swollen drastically after the People's Republic had absorbed Hong Kong and Taiwan. Many diehard capitalists had fled to Malaysia, Saudi Arabia, and Iran, where the oil money still ran fast and deep. There they prospered, selling rifles and shoulder-launched rockets to Kurdish separatists and Afghani mujahideen, whose bloody acres abounded in poppies and cannabis. And the Triads waited, with ghastly patience, for the new Red dynasty to crack.

According to Karageorgiu, the Triad secret societies had never forgotten the Opium Wars of the 1840s, in which the British had deliberately and cynically hooked the Chinese populace on black opium. The Triads, he alleged, had deliberately promoted heroin use in the West in an attempt to rot Western morale.

Mr. Shaw acknowledged that such an action would only have been simple justice, but he denied the allegation. Besides, he pointed out, heroin was now out of favor in the West. The drug-using populace had dwindled with the aging of the population, and modern users were more sophisticated. They preferred untraceable neurochemicals to crude vegetable extracts. These very neurochemicals now boiled out of the high-tech drug vats of the Caribbean.

This accusation wounded Winston Stubbs. The Rastafarian underground had never favored "steel drugs." The substances they made were sacramental, like communion wine, meant to assist in "i-tal meditation."

Karageorgiu scoffed at this. He knew the real sources of the Grenadian syndicate and recited them with relish. Cocaine-crazed Colombians cruising the streets of Miami in armored vans crammed with Kalashnikovs. Degraded Cuban boat-lifters, speckled with prison tattoos, who would kill for a cigarette. Redneck American swindlers like "Big Bobby" Vesco, who had specialized in the sucker's shell game with a series of offshore fronts.

Winston Stubbs heard the man out peaceably, trying to defuse Laura's horror with skeptical brow wrinkling and little pitying shakes of his head. But he bristled at this last remark. Mr. Robert Vesco, he said indignantly, had at one point owned the government of Costa Rica. And in the legendary IOS scam, Vesco had liberated $60 million of illegally invested CIA retirement funds. This action showed that Vesco's heart was righteous. There was no shame in having him as forefather. The man was a duppy conqueror.

After the second day's negotiations broke up, Laura shakily joined Debra Emerson out on the seaside verandah for a private conference. "Well," said Emerson cheerfully. "This has certainly cleared the air."

"Like lifting the lid of a cesspool," Laura said. A salt breeze blew in from offshore, and she shuddered. "We're getting nowhere with these negotiations. It's obvious they have no intention of reforming. They barely tolerate us. They think we're saps."

"Oh, I think we're progressing nicely," Emerson said. Since the talks had started, she had relaxed into a glazed professional ease. Both she and Laura had made an effort to break past their formal roles and to establish the kind of gut-level personal trust that held Rizome together as a postindustrial company. Laura was reassured that Emerson took the company's principles so seriously.

It was good, too, that the Committee had fully acknowledged Laura's need to know. For a while she had been afraid that they would try some security bullshit, and that she would have to go on the company Net and make a stink about it. Instead they had taken her into the core of negotiations. Not at all a bad thing, career-wise, for a woman still officially on infancy furlough. Laura now felt vaguely guilty about her earlier suspicions. She even wished that Emily Donato hadn't told her anything.

Emerson nibbled a praline and gazed out to sea. "It's all been skirmishing so far, just macho one-upmanship. But soon they'll be getting down to business. The critical point is their blackmailers. With our help, with a little guidance, they'll join forces in self-defense."

A seagull noticed Emerson eating. It swooped up and hovered hopefully above the walkway's railing, its flat yellow eyes gleaming. "Join forces?" Laura said.

"It's not as bad as it sounds, Laura. It's their small scale and fast reflexes that make the data havens dangerous. A large, centralized group will become bureaucratic."

"You think so?"

"They have weaknesses we don't," Emerson said, settling deeper into her reclining chair. She cracked off a chip of her praline and studied the floating bird. "The major weakness of criminal groups is their innate lack of trust. That's why so many of them rely on family blood ties. Especially families from oppressed minorities—a double reason for group loyalty against the outside world. But an organization that can't rely on the free loyalty of its members is forced to rely on *gesellschaft*. On industrial methods."

She smiled, lifting her hand. "And that means rule books, laws, stiff formal hierarchies. Violence is not Rizome's strong suit, Laura, but we do understand management structures. Centralized bureaucracies always protect the status quo. They don't innovate. And it's innovation that's the real threat. It's not so bad that they rip us off." She tossed her chip of candy and the gull caught it instantly. "The problem comes when they outthink us."

"The bigger, the stupider, is that the strategy?" Laura said. "What happened to good old divide and conquer?"

"This isn't politics. This is technology. It's not their power that threatens us, it's their imagination. Creativity comes from small groups. Small groups gave us the electric light, the automobile, the personal computer. Bureaucracies gave us the nuclear power plant, traffic jams, and network television. The first three changed everything. The last three are memories now."

Three more freeloading gulls swooped up from nowhere. They jostled gracefully for space, with creaking screams of greed. Laura said, "Don't you think we ought to try something a little more vigorous? Like, say, arresting them?"

"I don't blame you for thinking that," Emerson said. "But you don't know what these people have survived. They thrive on persecution, it unites them. It builds a class chasm between them and society, it lets them prey on the rest of us without a twinge of conscience. No, we have to let them grow, Laura, we have to give them a stake in our status quo. It's a long-term struggle. Decades long. Lifetimes. Just like the Abolition."

"Mmmm," Laura said, not liking this much. The older generation was always going on about the Abolition. As if abolishing bombs intended to destroy the planet had required transcendent genius. "Well, not everyone shares that philosophy. Or else these data sharks wouldn't be here now, trying to roll with the punches." She lowered her voice. "Who do you think is blackmailing them? One of them, maybe? Those Singaporeans . . . they're so aloof and contemptuous. They look pretty suspicious."

"Could be," Emerson said placidly. "Whoever it is, they're professionals." She threw the last of her candy to the gulls and stood up, shivering. "It's getting chilly."

They went in. Inside the Lodge, a routine had emerged. The Singaporeans always retired to their rooms after negotiations. The Europeans amused themselves in the conference room, running up the Lodge's telecom bills.

The Grenadians, on the other hand, seemed deeply interested in the Lodge itself. They had inspected it from tower to foundation, asking flattering questions about computer design and concretized sand. Since then the Grenadians seemed to have taken an active liking to David. They had gathered with him in the downstairs lounge for the third night running.

Laura went to help with the washing. The staff was bearing up well, despite the security requirements. They found it exciting to have actual live criminals in the place. Mrs. Rodriguez had stuck appropriate nicknames on the guests: Los Opios, Los Morfinos, and, of course, Los Marijuanos. Winston Stubbs, El Jefe de los Marijuanos, was a staff favorite. Not only did he look most like a proper pirate, but he had tried to tip them several times. The Morfino Europeans, however, were on everyone's shit list.

Debra Emerson had not escaped—no one called her anything but "La Espia." Everyone agreed that she was weird. *Poca loca.* But she was Rizome, so it was okay.

Laura had not gone running in three days. Her ankle was better now but the forced confinement was making her antsy. She needed a drink. She joined David and the Grenadians in the bar.

David was showing off his music collection. He collected old Texas pop music—western swing, blues, polkas, *conjunto* border ballads. A sixty-year-old *conjunto* tape played over the lounge's speakers, rapid accordion riffs punctuated with high-pitched wails. Laura, who had grown up with synthesizers and Russian pop music, still found the stuff eerie as hell.

She poured herself a glass of the house red and joined them around a low table. The old man sat slumped in a chair, looking drowsy. Sticky Thompson and the Church woman sat together on a couch.

During the debates, Sticky had been very animated, almost hyper at times. Among his luggage, Sticky had brought a thermos of what he claimed was acidophilus milk. He was drinking it now. Laura wondered what was in it. Sticky couldn't be older than twenty-two or three, she thought. He was a little young to have ulcers.

Carlotta had a glass of orange juice. She had made it clear that she never touched coffee or alcohol. She sat intimately close to Sticky, pressing her black-stockinged thigh against his leg, tugging lightly at the curls at the back of his neck. Carlotta had never taken part in the debates, but she shared Sticky's room. She watched him with animal raptness—like the gulls outside.

The sight of Carlotta and Sticky—young love played at 78 rpm—gave Laura a sense of unease. There was something horribly bogus about their ambience, as if they were deliberately mimicking a romance. She pulled a chair close to David's.

"So what do y'all think?" David said.

"It's better than those yodeling cowboys," Sticky said, his amber eyes gleaming. "But you can't say this is your roots, mon. This is Third World music."

"The hell you say," David said mildly. "It's Texas music, I'm a Texan."

"That's Spanish they're singing, mon."

"Well, I speak Spanish," David said. "Maybe you didn't notice our staff are Texan Hispanics."

"Oh, seen, I notice them," Sticky said. This was the first time Sticky had used such a thick patois. "I noticed you sleep up in the castle tower." Sticky pointed upstairs. "While they sleep down here by the kitchen."

"Oh, you reckon so?" David drawled, stung. "You want those old folks to walk up two flights of stairs, I guess. While we keep the baby down here to wake our guests."

"I see what I see," Sticky said. "You say, no more wage slaves, equal rights in the big mother Rizome. Everybody votes. No bosses—coordinators. No board—a Central Committee. But your wife still give orders and they still cook and clean."

"Sure," Laura broke in. "But not for us, Sticky. For you."

"That's a good one," Sticky said, riveting his hot eyes on Laura. "You talk a good line after those P.R. courses at the university. Diplomatic, like your mother."

There was a sudden silence. "Chill out, Sticky," the old man murmured. "You gettin' red, boy."

"Yeah," David said, still smarting. "Maybe you better take it a little easy on that milk."

"There's nothing in this milk," Sticky said. He shoved the thermos at Laura, who was closest. "You try it."

"All right," Laura said abruptly. She had a sip. It was cloyingly sweet. She handed it back. "That reminds me. David, did you feed the baby?"

David grinned, admiring her bravado. "Yeah."

There was nothing in the milk, she decided. Nothing was going to happen to her. She sipped her wine to wash the taste away.

Carlotta laughed suddenly, breaking the tension. "You're a caution, Sticky." She started rubbing his shoulders. "It's no use you bein' down on Mr. and Mrs. Married Life. They're straights, that's all. Not like us."

"You don't see it yet, girl. You haven't heard 'em talk upstairs." Sticky had lost his temper, and his accent. He was starting to sound more and more like a cable news announcer, Laura thought. That flat Mid-Atlantic television English. Global Net talk. Sticky pulled Carlotta's hand away and held it. "Straights aren't what they used to be. They want it all now—the whole world. One world. Their world." He stood up, pulling her to her feet. "Come on, girl. The bed needs shaking."

"Buenas noches," David called out as they left. *"Suenos dulces, cuidado con las chinches!"* Sticky ignored him.

Laura poured herself another glass and knocked back half of it. The old man opened his eyes. "He's young," he said.

"I was rude," David said contritely. "But I dunno, that old Imperialist America line—it gets me where I live. Sorry."

"Not America, no," the old man said. "You Yankees aren't Babylon. You only part of her, now. Babylon-she-multinational, Babylon-she-multilateral." He chanted the words. "Babylon she come to get us where we live." He sighed. "You like it here, I know. I ask the old women, they say they like it too. They say you nice, you baby's cute. But where she growing up, that baby, in your nice one world with its nice one set of rules? She have no place to run. You think that over, seen? Before you come down on us." He stood up, yawning. "Tomorrow, eh? Tomorrow." He left.

Silence fell. "Let's go to bed," Laura said at last. They went upstairs.

The baby was sleeping peacefully. Laura had been checking her crib monitor with the watchphone. They pulled their clothes off and slid into bed together. "What a weird old duck that Stubbs is," David said. "Full of stories. He said . . . he said he was in Grenada in '83 when the U.S. Marines invaded. The sky was full of choppers shooting Cubans. They took over the radio station and played Yankee pop music. The Beach Boys, he said. I thought he meant the Marines at first. Beach boys."

Laura frowned. "You're letting him get to you, David. That nice old codger and his poor little island. His poor little island is taking a big bite out of our ass. That snotty remark about Mother—they must have dossiers on both of us, the size of phone books. And what about that Church girl, huh? I don't like that business one bit."

"We've got a lot in common with Grenada," David said. "Galveston was a pirate haven, once upon a time. Good old Jean Lafitte, remember? Back in 1817. Hijacking shipping, yo-ho-ho, bottle of rum, the whole routine." David grinned. "Maybe you and I could start a haven, okay? Just a snug little one that we could run from the conference room. We'd find out how many teeth old Sticky's grandmother has."

"Don't even think it," Laura said. She paused. "That girl. Carlotta. You think she's attractive?"

He sank down into his pillow. "A little," he said. "Sure."

"You kept looking at her."

"I think she was high on those Church pills," he said. "Romance. It does something for a woman, to have that glow. Even if it's fake."

"I could take one of those pills," Laura said carefully. "I've been totally nuts about you before. It didn't do any permanent damage."

David laughed. "What's gotten into you tonight? I couldn't believe you drank that milk. You're lucky you're not seeing little blue dogs leaping out of the wall." He sat up in bed, waving his hand. "How many fingers?"

"Forty," she said, smiling.

"Laura, you're drunk." He pinned her down and kissed her. It felt good. It was good to be crushed under his weight. A warm, solid, comfortable crush. "Good," she said. "Give me ten more." His face was an inch away and she smelled wine on her own breath.

He kissed her twice, then reached down and gave her a deep, intimate caress. She threw her arms around him and closed her eyes, enjoying it. Good strong warm hand. She relaxed, sinking into the mood. A nice little trough of chemistry there, as scratchy pleasure melted into lust. The wariness that took her through the day evaporated as she relaxed into arousal. Good-bye, calculating Laura; hello, connubial Laura, long time no see. She started kissing him seriously, the kind she knew he liked. It was great to do it, and know he liked it.

Here we go, she thought. A nice solid slide inside her. Surely nothing was ever better than this. She smiled up into David's face.

That look in his eyes. It had scared her sometimes, the first times, and excited her. That look of sweet David gone and something else in his place. Some other part of him, primal. Something that she couldn't control, that could take her own control away. Sex had been like that in the first days of their affair, something wild and strong and romantic, and not entirely pleasurable. Too close to fainting, too close to pain. Too strange . . .

But not tonight. They slipped into a good thumping rhythm. A good mauling hug and a good solid pounding. Fine solid, dependable sex. Building up to orgasm like laying bricks. Angel architects laid bricks like this in the walls of heaven.

Level one, level two, taking their time, level three, almost done now, and there it was. Climax washed through her, and she moaned happily. He was still at it. It was no use aiming for another one, and she didn't try, but it came anyway, a small little twinge with a pleasure all its own, like smelling brandy in another room.

Then he was through. He rolled onto his side of the bed, and she felt his sweat cooling on her skin. A good feeling, intimate as a kiss. "Oh, lord," he said, not meaning anything, just breathing the words out. He slid his legs under the covers. He was happy, they were lovers, all was right in the world. They would be sleeping soon.

"David?"

"Yes, light of my life?"

She smiled. "Do you think we're straight?"

He laced his hands behind his head against the pillow. He looked at her sidelong. "Tired of the missionary position?"

"You're such a help. No, I mean it."

He saw that she was serious and shrugged. "I don't know, angel. We're people, that's all. We have a kid and a place in the world. . . . I don't know what that means." He grinned tiredly, then rolled onto his side, throwing one leg over hers. She dimmed the lights with her watchphone. She didn't say anything more, and in a few minutes he was asleep.

The baby woke her, whimpering. This time Laura managed to force herself from bed. David sprawled himself over, into her space. Fine, she thought. Let him sleep in the wet spot.

She got the baby up, changed her diaper. This had to be a sign of something, she thought sourly. Surely avant-garde rebel enemies of the system never had to change diapers.

Laura warmed Loretta's formula and tried to feed her, but she wouldn't be comforted. She was kicking and arching her spine and wadding up her little face. . . . She was a very good-tempered baby, in daylight at least, but if she woke at night she became a bag of nerves.

The sound wasn't her hungry cry, or her lonely cry, but tremulous, high-pitched noises that said she didn't know what to do with herself. Laura decided to take her out on the walkway. That usually calmed her down. It looked like a nice night, anyway. She shrugged into her night-robe.

A three-quarter moon was up. Laura walked barefoot on the damp boards. Moonlight on the surf. It had a numinous look. It was so beautiful that it was almost funny, as if nature had decided to imitate, not Art, but a sofa-sized velvet painting.

She walked back and forth, crooning to Loretta, whose wails had finally died into crotchety whimpers. Laura thought about her mother. Mothers and daughters. This time around it would be different.

A sudden prickling sensation washed over her. Without warning, it turned to fear. She looked up, feeling startled, and saw something she didn't believe.

It perched in midair in the moonlight, humming. An hour-glass, cut by a shimmering disk. Laura shrieked aloud. The apparition hung there for a moment, as if defying her to believe in it. Then it tilted in midair and headed out to sea. In a few moments she had lost it.

The baby was too scared to cry. Laura had crushed her to her breasts in panic, and it seemed to have scared the baby into some primeval reflex. A reflex from cave times when voodoo horrors stalked outside the firelight, things that smelled milk and knew young flesh was tender. A spasm of trembling shook Laura from head to foot.

One of the guest room doors opened. Moonlight glinted on the gray hair of Winston Stubbs. A shaman's dreadlocks. He stepped out onto the boardwalk, wearing only his jeans. His grizzled chest had the sunken look of age, but he was strong. And he was someone else.

"I hear a scream," he said. "What's wrong, daughter?"

"I saw something," Laura said. Her voice shook. "It scared me. I'm sorry."

"I was awake," he said. "I hear the baby outside. Us old people, I-and-I don't sleep much. A prowler, maybe?" He scanned the beach. "I need my glasses."

Shock began seeping out of her. "I saw something in the air," she said, more firmly. "A kind of machine, I think."

"A machine," said Stubbs. "Not a ghost."

"No."

"You look like a duppy come ready to grab your child,

girl,'' Stubbs said. ''A machine, though. . . . I don't like that. There are machines and machines, seen? Could be a spy.''

''A spy,'' Laura said. It was an explanation, and it got her brain working again. ''I don't know. I've seen drone aircraft. People use them to crop-dust. But they have wings. They're not like flying saucers.''

''You saw a flying saucer?'' Stubbs said, impressed. ''Crucial! Where did it go?''

''Let's go in,'' Laura said, shivering. ''You don't want to see it, Mr. Stubbs.''

''But I do see,'' said Stubbs. He pointed. Laura turned to look.

The thing was sweeping toward them, from over the water. It whirred. It swept over the beach at high speed. As it closed on them, it opened fire. A chattering gout of bullets slammed into Stubbs's chest and belly, flinging him against the wall. His body bloomed open under the impact.

The flying thing veered off above the roof, its whine dying as it slipped into darkness. Stubbs slid to the boards of the walkway. His dreadlocks had slipped askew. They were a wig. Below them, his skull was bald.

Laura lifted one hand to her cheek. Something had stung her there. Little bits of sand, she thought vaguely. Little bits of sand that had jumped from those impact holes. Those pockmarks in the wall of her house, where the bullets had passed through the old man. The holes looked dark in the moonlight. They were full of his blood.

3

LAURA watched as they took the body away. The dead Mr. Stubbs. Smiling, cheerful Winston Stubbs, all winking piratical wickedness, now a small bald corpse with its chest smashed open. Laura leaned on the wet walkway railing, watching as the ambulance van cleared the cordon of lights. Unhappy city cops in wet yellow slickers manned the road. It had begun to rain with morning, a bleak September front off the mainland.

Laura turned and pushed through the lobby door. Inside, the Lodge felt empty, a havoc area. All the guests were gone. The Europeans had abandoned their luggage in their panic flight. The Singaporeans, too, had slunk off rapidly during the confusion.

Laura walked upstairs to the tower office. It was just after nine in the morning. Within the office, Debra Emerson prerecorded calls for the Central Committee, her quiet murmur going over the details of the killing for the fourth time. The fax machine whined on copy.

Laura poured herself coffee, slopping some onto the table. She sat down and picked up the terrorists' publicity release. The assassins' statement had come online at the Rizome Lodge only ten minutes after the killing. She had read it three times already, with stunned disbelief. Now she read the statement over one more time. She had to understand. She had to deal with it.

F.A.C.T. DIRECT ACTION BULLETIN—SPECIAL
RELEASE TO AGENCIES OF LAW ENFORCEMENT
At 07:21 GMT September 12, 2023, designated commandos of the Free Army of Counter-Terrorism carried

out sentence on Winston Gamaliel Stubbs, a so-called corporate officer in the piratical and subversive organized-crime unit known as the United Bank of Grenada. The oppressed people of Grenada will rejoice at this long-delayed act of justice against the drug-running crypto-Marxist junta which has usurped the legitimate political aspirations of the island's law-abiding population.

The sentence of execution took place at the Rizome Lodge of Galveston, Texas, U.S.A. (telex GALVEZRIG, ph. (713) 454-9898), where Rizome Industries Group, Inc., an American-based multinational, was engaged in criminal conspiracy with the Grenadian malefactors.

We accuse the aforesaid corporation, Rizome Industries Group, Inc., of attempting to reach a cowardly accommodation with these criminal groups, in an immoral and illegal protection scheme which deserves the harshest condemnation from state, national, and international law enforcement agencies. With this act of short-sighted greed, Rizome Industries Group, Inc., has cynically betrayed the efforts of legitimate institutions, both private and public, to contain the menace of criminally supported state terrorism.

It is the long-sustained policy of the Free Army of Counter-Terrorism (FACT) to strike without mercy at the cryptototalitarian vermin who pervert doctrines of national sovereignty. Behind its mask of national legality, the Grenada United Bank has provided financial, data, and intelligence support to a nexus of pariah organizations. The executed felon, Winston Stubbs, has in particular maintained close personal involvement with such notorious groups as the Tanzanian Knights of Jah, the Inadin Cultural Revolution, and the Cuban Capitalist Cells.

In eliminating this menace to the international order, FACT has performed a valuable service to the true cause of law enforcement and global justice. We pledge to maintain our course of direct military action against the economic, political, and human resources of the so-called United Bank of Grenada until this antihuman and oppressive institution is entirely and permanently liquidated.

A further intelligence dossier on the crimes of the deceased, Winston Stubbs, may be accessed within the files of the United Bank itself: Direct-dial (033) 75664543, Account ID: FR2774. Trapdoor: 23555AK. Password: FREEDOM.

So flat, Laura thought, setting the printout aside. It read like computer-generated prose, long, obsessive streams of clauses . . . Stalinist. No grace or fire in it, just steam-driven robot pounding. Any pro in P.R. could have done better—she could have done better. She could have done a lot better in making her company, and her home, and her people, and herself, look like garbage. . . . She felt a sudden surge of helpless rage, so powerful that tears came. Laura fought them back. She peeled away the printout's perforated strip and rolled it between her fingers, staring at nothing.

"Laura?" David emerged from downstairs, carrying the baby. The mayor of Galveston followed him.

Laura stood up jerkily. "Mr. Mayor! Good morning."

Mayor Alfred A. Magruder nodded. "Laura." He was a hefty Anglo in his sixties, his barrel paunch wrapped in a garish tropical dashiki. He wore sandals and jeans and had a long Santa Claus beard. Magruder's face was flushed and his blue eyes in their little pockets of suntanned fat had the rigid look of contained fury. He waded into the room and flung his briefcase onto the table.

Laura spoke quickly. "Mr. Mayor, this is our security coordinator, Debra Emerson. Ms. Emerson, this is Alfred Magruder, Galveston's mayor."

Emerson rose from the console. She and Magruder looked each other up and down. They summed each other up with slight involuntary winces of distaste. Neither offered to shake hands. Bad vibes, Laura thought shakily, echoes from some long-buried social civil war. Already things were out of control.

"There's some heavy heat coming down here soon," Magruder announced, looking at Laura. "And now your old man here tells me that your pirate friends are at large on my island."

"It was quite impossible for us to stop them," Emerson said. Her voice had the infuriating calmness of a grade school teacher.

Laura cut in. "The Lodge was strafed by a machine gun, Mr. Mayor. It woke the whole staff—threw us into panic. And the—the guests—were up and out of here before the rest of us could think of anything. We called the police—"

"And your corporate headquarters," Magruder said. He paused. "I want a record of all the calls in and out of this place."

Laura and Emerson spoke at once.

"Well of course I called Atlanta—"

"That will need a warrant—"

Magruder cut them off. "The Vienna Convention heat will seize your records anyway. Don't screw me around on technicalities, okay? We're all walking fast and loose here, that's the point of Fun City. But y'all have gone way over the line this time. And someone's ass is gonna fry, okay?"

He glanced at David. David nodded once, his face frozen in a bogus look of chipper nice-guy alertness.

Magruder plunged on. "Now who's it gonna be? Is it gonna be me?" He thumbed his baggy shirt, prodding a splashy yellow azalea. "Is it gonna be you? Or is it gonna be these pirate assholes from off-the-island?" He drew a breath. "This is a terrorist action, *comprende?* That kind of crap isn't supposed to come down anymore."

Debra Emerson was all strained politeness. "It still does, Mr. Mayor."

"Maybe in Africa," Magruder grunted. "Not here!"

"The point is to cut the feedback relationship between terrorism and the global media," Emerson said. "So you needn't worry about bad publicity. The Vienna Convention specifies—"

"Look," Magruder said, turning the full force of his glare on Emerson. "You're not dealing with some cracker hippie here, okay? When this blows over you can sneak back to your spook warren in Atlanta, but I'll still be down here trying to make a go of a city on the fucking ropes! It's not the press that scares me—it's the cops! Global cops, too—not the locals, I can deal with them. I don't want to go down on their bad-boy list with the data-haven mafiosi. So do I need you using my island for your clapped-out shenanigans? No, ma'am, I don't."

Rage boiled up in Laura. "What the hell is this? Did we shoot him? We got shot at, Your Honor, okay? Go outside and look at my house."

They stared at her, shocked at her outburst. "They could have killed us. They could have blown the whole Lodge up." She snatched up the printout and shook it at Magruder. "They even wrote directly to us and taunted us! The F.A.C.T. —whoever they are—they're the killers, what about them?"

The baby's face clouded up and she tried a tentative sob. David rocked her in his arms, half turning away. Laura lowered her voice. "Mr. Mayor, I see what you're getting at. And I guess I'm sorry about this, or whatever the hell you want me to say. But we have to face the truth. These data-haven people are professionals, they're long gone. Except maybe the other Grenadian, Sticky Thompson. I think I know where Thompson is. He's gone underground here in Galveston, with the Church girl. I mean your friends here in the Church of Ishtar, Mr. Mayor."

She shot a quick look at David. David's face had thawed, he was with her. He looked encouragement: *go on, babe.* "And we don't want them looking at the Church, do we? They're all webbed together, these fringe groups. Pull one thread and the whole thing comes apart."

"And we end up bare-ass naked," David put in. "All of us."

The mayor grimaced, then shrugged. "But that's exactly what I was saying."

"Damage limitation," Emerson said.

"Right, that's it."

Emerson smiled. "Well, now we're getting somewhere."

Laura's watchphone beeped. She glanced at the board. It was a priority call. "I'll take it downstairs and let y'all talk," she said.

David followed her downstairs, with Loretta in the crook of his arm. "Those two old boomers," he muttered.

"Yeah." She paused as they stepped into the dining room.

"You were great," he said.

"Thanks."

"Are you okay?"

"Yeah, I'm okay. Now." The Lodge staff, red-eyed with lack of sleep, sat around the largest table, taking in Spanish.

They were disheveled and shaky. The gunfire had jolted them out of bed at two in the morning. David stopped with them.

Laura took her call in the little downstairs office. It was Emily Donato, calling from Atlanta. "I just heard," Emily said. She was pale. "Are you all right?"

"They shot up the Lodge," Laura said. "They killed him. The old Rastaman, I was standing right next to him." She paused. "I was scared of the spy machine. He came out to protect me. But they were waiting for him, and they shot him dead right there."

"You're not hurt, though."

"No, it was the walls, y'know, concretized sand. The bullets sank right in. No ricochets." Laura paused again and ran her fingers through her hair. "I can't believe I'm saying this."

"I just wanted to say. . . . Well, I'm with you all the way on this one. You and David. All the way." She held up two fingers, pressed together. "Solidarity, okay?"

Laura smiled for the first time in hours. "Thanks, Em." She looked at her friend's face gratefully. Emily's video makeup looked off; too much blusher, eyeliner shaky. Laura touched her own bare cheek. "I forgot my vid makeup," Laura blurted, realizing it for the first time. She felt a sudden unreasoning surge of panic. Of all the days—a day when she'd be on the Net all the time.

There was noise in the lobby. Laura glanced through the open door of the office and past the front desk. A woman in uniform had just pushed through the lobby door from outside. A black woman. Short hair, military blouse, big leather gun belt, cowboy hat in her hand. A Texas Ranger.

"Oh, Jesus, the Rangers are here," Laura said.

Emily nodded, her eyes wide. "I'm loggin' off, I know you have your hands full."

"Okay, bye." Laura hung up. She hurried past the desk into the lobby. A blond man in civvies followed the Ranger into the Lodge. He wore a charcoal-gray tailored suit vented at the waist, wide, flamboyant tie in computer-paisley. . . . He had dark glasses and had a suitcase terminal in his hand. The Vienna heat.

"I'm Laura Webster," Laura told the Ranger. "The Lodge

coordinator." She offered her hand. The Ranger ignored it, giving her a look of blank hostility.

The Vienna spook set down his portable terminal, took Laura's hand, and smiled sweetly. He was very handsome, with an almost feminine look—high Slavic cheekbones, a long, smooth swoop of blond hair over one ear, a film-star mole dotting his right cheekbone. He released her hand reluctantly, as if tempted to kiss it. "Sorry to greet you in such circumstances, Ms. Webster. I am Voroshilov. This is my local liaison, Captain Baster."

"Baxter," the Ranger said.

"You witnessed the attack, I understand," Voroshilov said.

"Yes."

"Excellent. I must interview you." He paused and touched a small stud on the corner of his dark glasses. A long fiber-optic cord trailed from the earpiece down into the vest of his suit. Laura saw now that the sunglasses were videocams, the new bit-mapped kind with a million little pixel lenses. He was filming her. "The terms of the Vienna Convention require me to tell you of your legal position. First, your speech is being recorded and you are being filmed. Your statements will be kept on file by various agencies of Vienna Convention signatory governments. I am not required to specify these agencies or the amount or location of the data from this investigation. Vienna treaty investigation are not subject to freedom-of-information or privacy laws. You have no right to an attorney. Investigations under the convention have global priority over the laws of your nation and state."

Laura nodded, barely following this burst of rote. She had heard it all before, on television shows. TV thrillers were very big on the Vienna heat. Guys showing up, flicking hologram ID cards, overriding the programming on taxis and zooming around on manual, chasing baddies. They never forgot their video makeup, either. "I understand, Comrade Voroshilov."

Voroshilov lifted his head. "What an interesting smell. I do admire regional cooking."

Laura started. "Can I offer you something?"

"Some mint tea would be very fine. Oh, just tea, if you have no mint."

"Something for you, Captain Baxter?"

Baxter glared. "Where was he killed?"

"My husband can help you with that. . . ." She touched her watchphone. "David?"

David looked into the lobby through the dining room door. He saw the police, turned, and shot some quick, urgent border-Spanish over his shoulder at the staff. All Laura caught was *los Rinches,* the Rangers, but chairs scraped and Mrs. Delrosario appeared in a hurry.

Laura made introductions. Voroshilov turned the intimidating videoglasses on everyone in turn. They were creepy-looking things—at a certain angle Laura could see a fine-etched golden spiderwebbing in the opaque lenses. No moving parts. David left with the Ranger.

Laura found herself sipping tea with the Vienna spook in the downstairs office. "Remarkable decor," Voroshilov observed, easing back in the vinyl car seat and shooting an inch of creamy-looking shirtcuff through his charcoal-gray coat sleeves.

"Thank you, Comrade."

Voroshilov lifted his videoglasses with a practiced gesture, favoring her with a long stare from velvety blue pop-star eyes. "You're a Marxist?"

"Economic democrat," Laura said. Voroshilov rolled his eyes in brief involuntary derision and set the glasses back onto his nose. "Have you heard from the F.A.C.T. before today?"

"Never," Laura said. "Never heard of them."

"The statement makes no mention of the groups from Europe and Singapore."

"I don't think they knew the others were here," Laura said. "We—Rizome, I mean—we were very careful on security. Ms. Emerson, our secrity person, can tell you more about that."

Voroshilov smiled. "The American notion of 'careful security.' I'm touched." He paused. "Why are you involved in this? It's not your business."

"It is now," Laura said. "Who is this F.A.C.T.? Can you help us against them?"

"They don't exist," Voroshilov said. "Oh, they did once.

Years ago. All those millions your American government spent, little groups here, little groups there. Ugly little spin-offs from the Old Cold Days. But F.A.C.T. is just a front now, a fairy story. F.A.C.T. is a mask the data havens hide behind to shoot at each other.'' He made a pistol-pointing gesture. "Like the old Red Brigades, pop-pop-pop against NATO. Angolan UNITA, pop-pop-pop against the Cubans.'' He smiled. "So here we are, yes, we sit in these nice chairs, we drink this nice tea like civilized people. Because you stepped into the rubbish left over because your grandfather didn't like mine.''

"What do you plan to do?''

"I ought to scold you,'' Voroshilov said. "But I'm going to scold your ex-CIA commissar upstairs. And my Ranger friend will scold too. My Ranger friend doesn't care for the nasty mess you make of the nice reputation of Texas.'' He flipped up the screen of his terminal and keyed in commands. "You saw the flying drone that did the shooting.''

"Yes.''

"Tell me if you see it here.''

Images flashed by, four-second bursts of nicely shaded computer graphics. Stubby-winged aircraft with blind fuse-lages—no cockpit, they were radio controlled. Some were spattered in camouflage. Others showed ID numbers in sten-ciled Cyrillic or Hebrew. "No, not like that,'' Laura said.

Voroshilov shrugged and touched the keys. Odder-looking craft appeared: two little blimps. Then a skeletal thing, like a collision between a helicopter and a child's tricycle. Then a kind of double-rotored golfball. Then an orange peanut. "Hold it,'' Laura said.

Voroshilov froze the image. "That's it,'' Laura said. "That landing gear—like a barbecue pit.'' She stared at it. The narrow waist of the peanut had two broad counterrotating helicopter blades. "When the blades move, they catch the light, and it looks like a saucer,'' she said aloud. "A flying saucer with big bumps on the top and the bottom.''

Voroshilov examined the screen. "You saw a Canadair CL-227 VTOL RPV. Vertical Take-Off and Landing, Re-motely Piloted Vehicle. It has a range of thirty miles—miles, what a silly measurement. . . .'' He typed a note on his

Cyrillic keyboard. "It was probably launched somewhere on this island by the assassins . . . or perhaps from a ship. Easy to launch, this thing. No runway."

"The one I saw was a different color. Bare metal, I think."

"And equipped with a machine gun," Voroshilov said. "Not standard issue. But an old craft like this has been on the black arms markets for many, many years. Cheap to buy if you have the contacts."

"Then you can't trace the owners?"

He looked at her pityingly.

Voroshilov's watchphone beeped. It was the Ranger. "I'm out here on the walkway," she said. "I have one of the slugs."

"Let me guess," Voroshilov said. "Standard NATO 35 millimeter."

"Affirmative, yes."

"Think of those millions and millions of unfired NATO bullets," mused Voroshilov. "Too many even for the African market, eh? An unfired bullet has a kind of evil pressure in it, don't you think? Something in it wants to be fired. . . ." He paused, his blank lenses fixed on Laura. "You're not following me."

"Sorry, I thought you were talking to her." Laura paused. "Can't you do anything?"

"The situation seems clear," he said. "An 'inside job,' as they say. One of the pirate groups had collaborators on this island. Probably the Singapore Islamic Bank, famous for treachery. They had the chance to kill Stubbs and took it." He shut down the screen. "During my flight into Galveston, I accessed the file in Grenada, on Stubbs, that was mentioned in the FACT communiqué. Very interesting to read. The killers exploited the nature of data-haven banking—that the coded files are totally secure, even against the haven pirates themselves. Only a haven would turn a haven's strength against itself in this humiliating way."

"You must be able to help us, though."

Voroshilov shrugged. "The local police can carry out certain actions. Tracing the local ships, for instance—see if any were close offshore, and who hired them. But I am glad to say that this was not an act of politically motivated terrorism. I would classify this as a gangster killing. The FACT communiqué is only an attempt to muddy the waters. A Vienna Convention case has certain publicity restrictions that they find useful.''

"But a man was killed here!"

"It was a murder, yes. But not a threat to the political order of the Vienna Convention signatories.''

Laura was shocked. "Then what good are you?"

Voroshilov looked hurt. "Oh, we are very much good at easing international tension. But we are not a global police force." He emptied his teacup and set it aside. "Oh, Moscow has been pressing for a true global police force for many years now. But Washington stands in the way. Always trifling about Big Brother, civil liberties, privacy laws. It's an old story.''

"You can't help us at all."

Voroshilov stood up. "Ms. Webster, you invited these gangsters into your home, I didn't. If you had called us first we would have urged you against it in the strongest possible terms." He hefted his terminal. "I need to interview your husband next. Thank you for the tea.''

Laura left him and went upstairs to the telecom office. Emerson and the mayor were sitting together on one of the rattan couches, with the satisfied look of people who had beaten a debate into submission. Magruder was forking his way through a belated Tex-Mex breakfast of migas and refried beans.

Laura sat down in a chair across the table and leaned forward, vibrating with anger. "Well, you two look comfortable.''

"You've been talking to the Vienna representative," Emerson said.

"He's no goddamn use at all."

"KGB," Emerson sniffed.

"He says it's not political, not their jurisdiction."

Emerson looked surprised. "Hmmph. That's a first for them."

Laura stared at her. "Well, what do we do about it?"

Magruder set down a glass of milk. "We're shutting you down, Laura."

"Just for a while," Emerson added.

Laura's jaw dropped. "Shutting down my Lodge? Why? Why?"

"It's all worked out," Magruder said. "See, if it's criminal, then the media get to swarm all over us. They'd play it up big, and it'd be worse for tourism than a shark scare. But if we shut you down, then it looks like spook business. Classified. And nobody looks too deep when Vienna comes calling." He shrugged. "I mean, they'll figure it eventually, but by then it'd be old news.. And the damage is limited." He stood up. "I need to talk to that Ranger. You know. Assure her that the city of Galveston will cooperate in every way possible." He picked up his briefcase and lumbered down the stairs.

Laura glared at Emerson. "So that's it? You shut down the scandal, and David and I pay the price?"

Emerson smiled gently. "Don't be impatient, dear. Our project isn't over because of this one attack. Don't forget—it's because of attacks like this that the pirates agreed to meet in the first place."

Laura was surprised. She sat down. Hope appeared amidst her confusion. "So you're still pursuing that? Despite all this?"

"Of course, Laura. The problem has scarcely gone away, has it? No, it's closer to us than ever before. We're lucky we didn't lose you—you, a very valued associate."

Laura looked up, surprised. Debra Emerson's face was set quite calmly—the face of a woman simply relaying the truth. Not flattery—a fact. Laura sat up straighter. "Well, it was an attack on Rizome, wasn't it? A direct attack on our company."

"Yes. They found a weakness in us—the F.A.C.T. did, or the people behind that alias." Emerson looked grave. "There must have been a security leak. That deadly aircraft—I suspect it's been waiting in ambush for days. Someone knew of the meeting and was watching this place."

"A security leak within Rizome?"

"We mustn't jump to conclusions. But we will have to find out the truth. It's more important than this Lodge, Laura. Much more important." She paused. "We can come to terms with the Vienna investigators. We can come to terms with the city of Galveston. But that's not the hardest part. We promised safety to the people at this conference, and we failed. Now we need someone to smooth the waters. In Grenada.''

Rizome's Chattahoochee Retreat was in the foothills of the Smokies, about sixty miles northeast of Atlanta. Eight hundred acres of wooded hills in a valley with a white stony creek that was dry this year. Chattahoochee was a favorite of the Central Committee; it was close enough to the city for convenience, and boondocky enough for people to stay out of the Committee's collective face.

New recruits were often brought here—in fact this was where Emily had first introduced her to David Webster. Back in the old stone farmhouse, the one without the geodesics. Laura couldn't look at these Chattahoochee hills without remembering that night: David, a stranger, tall and thin and elegant in midnight blue, with a drink in his hand and black hair streaming down his back.

In fact everybody in that party, all the sharper recruits anyway, had gone out of their way to dress in penthouse elegance. To go against the grain a bit, to show they weren't going to be socialized all that easily, thank you. But here they were, years later, out in the Georgia woods with the Central Committee, not new recruits but full-fledged associates, playing for keeps.

Of course the Committee personnel were all different now, but certain traditions persisted.

You could tell the importance of this meeting by the elaborate informality of their dress. Normal problems they would have run through in Atlanta, standard boardroom stuff, but this Grenada situation was a genuine crisis. Therefore, the whole Committee were wearing their Back-slapping Hick look, a kind of Honest Abe the Rail-Splitter image. Frayed denim jeans, flannel work shirts rolled up to the elbow. . . . Garcia-Meza, a hefty Mexican industrialist who looked like he could bite tenpenny nails in half, was carrying a big straw picnic basket.

It was funny to think of Charlie Cullen being CEO. Laura hadn't met Cullen face to face since his appointment, though she'd networked with him a little when they were building the

Lodge. Cullen was a biochemist, in construction plastics mostly, a nice enough guy. He was a great caretaker Rizome CEO, because you trusted him instinctively—but he didn't much come across as an alley fighter. Since his appointment he'd taken to wearing a gray fedora perched on the back of his head. Less like a hat than a halo or crown. It was funny how authority affected people.

Cullen's whole face had changed. With his square chin and broad nose, and mouth gone a little severe, he was starting to look like a black George Washington. The original, primeval George Washington, not the recent black president by the same name.

Then there were the others. Sharon McIntyre, Emily Donato's mentor on the Committee, and Emily herself, her ringleted hair caught under a scarf so that she looked like she'd just been cleaning a stove. Kaufmann, the realpolitik European, managing to look refined and natty even in jeans and knapsack. De Valera, self-styled firebrand of the Committee, who tended to grandstand, but was always coming up with the bright idea. The professorial Gauss, and the cozy-conciliatory Raduga. And bringing up the rear of the group, the ancient Mr. Saito. Saito was wearing a kind of Ben Franklin fur hat and bifocals, but he leaned on a tall knotted staff, like some hybridized Taoist hermit.

Then there were herself, and David, and Debra Emerson. Not Committee members, but witnesses.

Cullen crunched to a stop in a leaf-strewn autumn glade. They were meeting far from wires for security reasons. They'd even left their watchphones behind, in one of the farmhouses.

McIntyre and Raduga spread a large checkered picnic cloth. Everyone shuffled into a circle and sat. They joined hands and sang a Rizome anthem. Then they ate.

It was fascinating to watch. The Committee really worked at it, that sense of community. They'd made a practice of living together for weeks on end. Doing each other's laundry, tending each other's kids. It was policy. They were elected, but once in power they were given wide authority and expected to get on with it. For Rizome, getting on with it meant a more or less open, small-scale conspiracy.

Of course the fashion for *gemeineschaft* intensity came and went. Years ago, during Saito's period as CEO, there had been a legendary time when he'd taken the whole Committee to Hokkaido. When they rose before dawn to bathe naked in freezing waterfalls. And ate brown rice and, if rumor were true, had killed, butchered, and eaten a deer while living for three days in a cave. No one on the Committee had ever talked much about the experience afterward, but there was no denying that they'd become one hell of a group.

Of course that was the sort of bullshit half-legendry that clumped around any center of corporate power, but the Committee fed the mystique. And Rizome instinctively fell back on gut-level solidarity in times of trouble.

It was far from perfect. You could see it by the way they were acting—the way, for instance, that de Valera and Kaufmann made an unnecessarily big deal over who was going to cut and serve the bread. But you could see that it worked, too. Rizome association was a lot more than a job. It was tribal. You could live and die for it.

It was a simple meal. Apples, bread, cheese, some "ham spread" that was obviously tailored scop. And mineral water. Then they got to business—not calling anybody to order, but drifting into it, bit by bit.

They started with the F.A.C.T. They were more afraid of them than of Grenada. The Grenadians were thieving pirates, but at least they'd stayed in deep background, whereas the F.A.C.T., whoever they were, had seriously embarrassed the company. Thanks to that, they had Vienna to worry about now, though Vienna was vacillating. Even more than usual.

Rizome was determined to track down the F.A.C.T. They didn't expect that it would be simple or easy, but Rizome was a major multinational with thousands of associates and outposts on five continents. They had contacts throughout the Net and a tradition of patience. Sooner or later they would get at the truth. No matter who was hiding it.

The immediate target of suspicion was Singapore, either the Islamic Bank or the Singapore Government, though the lines between the two were blurry. No one doubted Singapore was capable of carrying out the killing in Galveston. Singapore had never signed the Vienna Convention, and they boasted openly of the reach of their military and intelligence services.

It was hard to understand, though, why they would pick a fight with Grenada, after agreeing to negotiate. Especially a rash provocation like the Stubbs killing, guaranteed to enrage Grenada without doing real strategic damage. Singapore was arrogant, and technologically reckless, but no one had ever said they were stupid.

So the Committee agreed to suspend judgment while awaiting further evidence. There were too many possibilities at present, and to try to cover every contingency would only bring paralysis. In the meantime they would move with the initiative, ignoring the terrorist communiqué.

FACT was obviously a threat, assuming FACT had a separate existence from the people they were already dealing with. But they'd had a clear chance to kill a Rizome associate—Laura—and had chosen not to take it. That was some small comfort.

The discussion moved to the Grenada situation.

"I don't see what we can do on the ground in Grenada that we can't manage over the Net," Raduga said.

"It's time we stopped making that false distinction!" de Valera said. "With our newest online stuff—the tech Vienna uses—we *are* the Net. I mean—in MacLuhanesque terms—a Rizome associate in videoshades can be a *cognitive spearhead* for the entire company. . . ."

"We're not Vienna," Kaufmann said. "It does not mean it will work for us."

"We're in a one-down situation with Grenada now," said Cullen. "We're not in a position to talk media invasion."

"Yes, Charlie," de Valera said, "but don't you see, that's exactly why it will *work*. We go in apologizing, but we come out indoctrinating."

Cullen frowned. "We're responsible for the death of one of their top people. This Winston Stubbs. It's as if one of us had been killed. Like we'd lost Mr. Saito."

Simple words, but Laura could see it hit them. Cullen had a knack for pulling things down to human scale. They were wincing.

"That is why *I* should go to Grenada," Saito said. He never said much. He didn't need to.

"I don't like it," said Garcia-Meza. "Why make this an

eye-for-eye situation? It's not our fault that the pirates have enemies. We didn't shoot them. And we are not one down, because they were never up on our level." Garcia-Meza was the hard-liner of the group. "I think this diplomatic approach was a mistake. You don't stop thieves by kissing them." He paused. "But I agree that we can't back out now. Our credibility's at stake."

"We can't allow this to degenerate into a gangster power struggle," Gauss declared. "We have to restore the trust that we went to such pains to establish. So we must convince Grenada of three things: that it was not our doing, that we are still trustworthy, and that they can gain from cooperation with us. Not from confrontation."

That kind of plonking summation was typical of Gauss. He had killed the conversation. "I think Heinrich has hit it on the head," Cullen said at last. "But we can't do any of that convincing by remote control. We need to send people in who can press the flesh and get right on the Grenadians, hand to hand. Show them what we're made of, how we operate."

"All right," David said sharply. Laura was surprised. She'd felt the pressure building, but she'd assumed he would let her pick the moment. "It's obvious," he said. "Laura and I are the ones you need. Grenada knows us already, they've got dossiers on us a foot thick. And we were there when Stubbs was killed. If you *don't* send us—the eyewitnesses—they're bound to wonder why not."

The Committee members were silent a moment—either wondering at his tone, or maybe appreciating the sacrifice. "David and I feel responsible," Laura added. "Our luck's been bad so far, but we're willing to see the project through. And we have no other assignments, since Galveston shut our Lodge down."

Cullen looked unhappy. Not with them—with the situation. "David, Laura, I appreciate that correct attitude. It's very courageous. I know you're aware of the danger. Better than we are, since you've seen it personally."

David shrugged it off. He never reacted well to praise. "Frankly, I'm less afraid of the Grenadians than the people who shot them."

"An excellent point. I also note that the terrorists shot

them in America," Gauss said. "Not in Grenada, where the security is much stronger."

"I should go," Saito objected. "Not because I would be better at it." A polite lie. "But I am an old man. I have little to lose."

"And I'll go with him," said Debra Emerson, speaking for the first time. "If there's any blame in this security debacle, it's certainly not the Websters'. It's my own. I was also at the Lodge. I can testify as well as Laura can."

"We can't go into this expecting that our people will be shot!" de Valera said passionately. "We must arrange things so they never even *think* we might be prey. Either that, or not go in at all. Because if that confidence fails, it's gonna be war, and we'll have to become gangland sodiers. Not economic democrats."

"No guns," Cullen agreed. "But we do have armor, at least. We can give our diplomats the armor of the Net. Whoever goes will be online twenty-four hours. We'll know exactly where they are, exactly what they're doing. Everything they see and hear will be taped and distributed. All of Rizome will be behind them, a media ghost on their shoulder. Grenada will respect that. They've already agreed to those terms."

"I think Charlie's right," Garcia-Meza said, unexpectedly. "They won't harm our diplomats. What's the point? If they want to savage Rizome, they won't start with the Websters just because they are close at hand. They are not so naive. If they shoot us, they will shoot for the head. They will go for us—the Committee."

"Jesus," de Valera said.

"We are feasting with tigers here," Garcia-Meza insisted. "This is a vital operation and we'll have to watch each step. So I'm glad we have those Vienna glasses. We'll need them."

"Let me go," Ms. Emerson begged. "They're young and they have a baby."

"Actually," de Valera said, "I think that's the Websters' major advantage as candidates. I think the Websters should go, and I think they should take their baby with them." He smiled at the circle, enjoying the stir he'd created. "Look, think about it. A peaceable young married couple, with a baby. It's a perfect diplomatic image for our company, because it's *true*. It's what they *are*, isn't it? It may sound cold-blooded, but it's a perfect psychological defense."

"Well," said Garcia-Meza, "I don't often agree with de Valera, but that's clever. These pirates are macho. They would be ashamed to fight with babies."

Kaufmann spoke heavily. "I did not want to mention this. But Debra's background in American intelligence . . . that is simply not something that a Third World country like Grenada will accept. And I do *not* want to send a Committee member, because, frankly, such a target is too tempting." He turned to them. "I hope you understand, David and Laura, that I mean no reflection on your own high value as associates."

"I just don't like it," Cullen said. "Maybe there's no other choice, but I don't like risking company people."

"We're all in danger now," Garcia-Meza said darkly. "No matter what choices we make."

"I believe in this initiative!" de Valera declared. "I pushed for this from the beginning. I know the consequences. I truly believe the Grenadians will go for this—they're not barbarians, and they know their own best interests. If our diplomats are hurt on duty, I'll take the heat and resign my post."

Emily was annoyed by this grab for the limelight. "Don't be non-R, de Valera! That won't do *them* much good."

De Valera shrugged off the accusation. "David, Laura, I hope you understand my offer in the meaning I intended. We're associates, not bosses and pawns. If you're hurt, I won't walk from that. Solidarity."

"None of us will walk," Cullen said. "We don't have that luxury. Laura, David, you realize what's at stake. If we fail to smooth things with Grenada, it could plunge us into disaster. We're asking you to risk yourselves—but we're giving you the power to risk all of us. And that kind of power is very rare in this company."

Laura felt the weight of it. They wanted an answer. They were looking to the two of them. There was no one else for them to look to.

She and David had already talked it out, privately. They knew they could duck this assignment, without blame. But they had lost their home, and it would leave all their plans floundering. It seemed better to seize the risk, go with the flow of the crisis, and depend on their own abilities to deal with it. Better that than to sit back like victims and let terrorists trample their lives with impunity. Their minds were made up.

"We can do it," Laura said. "If you back us."

"It's settled then." And that was that. They all rose and folded up the picnic. And went back to the farmhouses.

Laura and David began training immediately with the videoglasses. They were the first the company had bought, and they were grotesquely expensive. She'd never realized it before, but each set cost as much as a small house.

They looked it, too—at close range they had the strange aura of scientific instruments. Nonconsumer items, very specialized, very clean. Heavy, too—a skin of tough black plastic, but packed tight with pricy superconductive circuitry. They had no real lenses in them—just thousands of bit-mapped light detectors. The raw output was a prismatic blur—visual software handled all the imagery, depth of focus, and so on. Little invisible beams measured the position of the user's eyeballs. The operator, back at his screen, didn't have to depend on the user's gaze, though. With software he could examine anything in the entire field of vision.

You could see right through them, even though they were opaque from outside. They could even be set to adjust for astigmatism or what have you.

They made custom-fitted foam earpieces for both of them. No problem there, that was old tech.

Chattahoochee Retreat had a telecom room that made the Galveston Lodge's look premillennial. They did a crash course in videoglass technique. Strictly hands-on, typical Rizome training. The two of them took turns wandering over the grounds, scanning things at random, refining their skills. A lot to look at: greenhouses, aquaculture ponds, peach orchards, windmills. A day-care crèche where a Retreat staffer was baby-sitting Loretta. Rizome had given the crèche system a shot, years ago, but people hadn't liked it—too kibbutzish, never caught on.

The Retreat had been a working farm once, before single-cell protein came in and kicked the props out of agriculture. It was a bit Marie Antoinette now, like a lot of modern farms. Specialty crops, greenhouse stuff. A lot of that commercial greenhouse work was in the cities now, where the markets were.

Then they would go inside, and watch their tapes, and get vertigo. And then try it again, but with books balanced on their heads. And then take turns, one monitoring the screen and the other out walking and taking instruction and bitching cheerfully about how tough it was. It was good to be working at something. They felt more in control.

It was going to work, Laura decided. They were going to run a propaganda number on the Grenadians and let the Grenadians run a propaganda number on them, and that would be it. A risk, yes—but also the widest exposure they'd ever had within the company, and that meant plenty in itself. The Committee hadn't been crass enough to talk directly about reward, but they didn't have to; that wasn't how things were done in Rizome. It was all understood.

Dangerous, yes. But the bastards had shot up her house. She'd given up the illusion that anyplace would be truly safe anymore. She knew it wouldn't. Not until this was all over.

They had a two-hour layover in Havana. Laura fed the baby. David stretched out in his blue plastic seat, propping his sandaled feet one atop the other. Crude overhead speakers piped twinkling Russian pop music. No robot trolleys here— porters with handcarts, instead. Old janitors, too, who pushed brooms like they'd been born pushing them. In the next row of plastic seats, a bored Cuban kid dropped an empty soft-drink carton and stomped it. Laura watched dully as the mashed carton started to melt. "Let's get plastered," David said suddenly.

"What?"

David tucked his videoglasses into the pocket of his suit, careful not to smudge the lenses. "I look at it this way. We're gonna be online the whole time in Grenada. No time to relax, no time for ourselves. But we got an eight-hour flight coming up. Eight hours in a goddamn airplane, right? That's free license to puke all over ourselves if we want. The stews'll take care of us. Let's get wasted."

Laura examined her husband. His face looked brittle. She felt the same way. These last days had been hell. "Okay," she said. David smiled.

He picked up the baby's tote and they trudged to the nearest duty-free shop, a little cubbyhole full of cheap straw hats and goofy-looking heads carved from coconuts. David bought a liter flask of brown Cuban rum. He paid with cash. The Committee had warned them against using plastic. Too easy to trace. Data havens were all over the electric money business.

The Cuban shopgirl kept the paper money in a locked drawer. David handed her a 100-ecu bill. She handed over his paper change with a sloe-eyed smile at David—she was dressed in red, chewing gum and listening to samba music over headphones. Little hip-swaying motions. David said something witty in Spanish and she smiled at him.

The ground wouldn't settle under Laura's shoes. The ground in airports wasn't part of the world. It had its own logic— Airport Culture. Global islands in a net of airline flight paths. A nowhere node of sweat and jet lag with the smell of luggage.

They boarded their flight at Gate Diez-y-seis. Aero Cubana. Cheapest in the Caribbean, because the Cuban government was subsidizing flights. The Cubans were still touchy about their Cold War decades of enforced isolation.

David ordered Cokes whenever the stewardess came by and topped them off with deadly layers of pungent rum. Long flight to Grenada. Distances were huge out here. The Caribbean was flecked with cloud, far-down fractal wrinkles of greenish ocean surge. The stews showed a dubbed Russian film, some hot pop-music thing from Leningrad with lots of dance sequences, all hairdos and strobe lights. David watched it on headphones, humming and bouncing Loretta on his knee. Loretta was stupefied with travel—her eyes bulged and her sweet little face was blank as a kachina doll's.

The rum hit Laura like warm narcotic tar. The world became exotic. Businessmen in the aisles ahead had plugged their decks into the dataports overhead, next to the air vents. Cruising forty thousand feet over Caribbean nowhere, but still plugged into the Net. Fiber-optics dangled like intravenous drips.

Laura leaned her seat back and adjusted the blower to puff her face. Airsickness lurked down there somewhere below the alcoholic numbness. She sank into a stunned doze. She dreamed. . . . She was wearing one of those Aero Cubana stewardess outfits, nifty blue numbers, kind of paramilitary 1940s with chunky shoulders and a pleated skirt, hauling her trolley down the aisle. Giving everyone little plastic tumblers full of something . . . milk. . . . They were all reaching out demanding this milk with looks of parched desperation and pathetic gratitude. They were so glad she was there and really wanted her help—they knew she could make things better. . . . They all looked frightened, rubbing their sweating chests like something hurt there. . . .

A lurch woke her up. Night had fallen. David sat in a pool of light from the overhead, staring at his keyboard screen. For a moment Laura was totally disoriented, legs cramped, back aching, her cheek sticky with spit. . . . Someone, David probably, had put a blanket over her. "My Optimal Persona," she muttered. The plane jumped three or four times.

"You awake?" David said, plucking out his Rizome earplug. "Hitting a little rough weather."

"Yeah?"

"September in the Caribbean." Hurricane season, she thought—he didn't have to say it. He checked his new, elaborate watchphone. "We're still an hour out." On the screen, a Rizome associate in a cowboy hat gestured eloquently at the camera, a mountain range looming behind him. David froze the image with a keytouch.

"You're answering mail?"

"No, too drunk," David said. "Just looking at it. This guy Anderson in Wyoming—he's a drip." David winked the screen's image off. "There's all kinds of bullshit—oh, sorry, I mean *democratic input*— pilin' up for us in Atlanta. Just thought I'd get it down on disk before we leave the plane."

Laura sat up scrunchily. "I'm glad you're here with me, David."

He looked amused and touched. "Where else would I be?" He squeezed her hand.

The baby was asleep in the seat between them, in a collapsible bassinet of chromed wire and padded yellow synthetic. It looked like something a high-tech Alpine climber would haul oxygen in. Laura touched the baby's cheek. "She all right?"

"Sure. I fed her some rum, she'll be sleeping for hours."

Laura stopped in mid-yawn. "You fed her—" He was kidding. "So you've come to that," Laura said. "Doping our innocent child." His joke had forced her awake. "Is there no limit? To your depravity?"

"All kinds of limits—while I'm online," David said. "As we're about to be, for God knows how many days. Gonna cramp our style, babe."

"Mmmm." Laura touched her face, reminded. No video makeup. She hauled her cosmetics kit from the depths of her shoulder bag and stood up. "Gotta get our vid stuff on before we land."

"Wanna try a quickie in the bathroom, standing up?"

"Probably bugged in there," Laura said, half stumbling past him into the aisle.

He whispered up at her, holding her wrist. "They say Grenada has scuba diving, maybe we can mess around under water. Where no one can tape us."

She stared down at his tousled head. "Did you drink all that rum?"

"No use wasting it," he said.

"Oh, boy," she said. She used the bathroom, dabbed on makeup before the harsh steel mirror. By the time she returned to her seat they were starting their descent.

4

A stewardess thanked them as they stepped over the threshold. Down the scruffy carpeted runway into Point Salines Airport. "Who's online?" Laura murmured.

["Emily,"] came the voice in her earplug. ["Right with you."] David stopped struggling with the baby's tote and reached up to adjust his volume. His eyes, like hers, hidden behind the gold-fretted videoshades. Laura felt nervously for her passport card, wondering what customs would be like. Airport hallway hung with dusty posters of white Grenadian beaches, ngratiating grinning locals in fashion colors ten years old, splashy holiday captions in Cyrillic and Japanese katakana.

A young, dark-skinned soldier leaned out from against the wall as they approached. "Webster party?"

"Yes?" Laura framed him with her videoglasses, then scanned him up and down. He wore a khaki shirt and trousers, a webbing belt with holstered gun, a starred beret, sunglasses after dark. Rolled-up sleeves revealed gleaming ebony biceps.

He fell into stride ahead of them, legs swinging in black lace-up combat boots. "This way." They paced rapidly across the clearing area, heads down, ignored by a sprinkling of fatigue-glazed travelers. At customs their escort flashed an ID card and they breezed through without stopping.

"They be bringin' you luggage later," the escort muttered. "Got a car waiting." They ducked out a fire exit and down a flight of rusting stairs. For a brief blessed moment they touched actual soil, breathed actual air. Damp and dark; it had rained. The car was a white Hyundai Luxury Saloon with one-way mirrored windows. Its doors popped open as they approached.

Their escort slid into the front seat; Laura and David hustled in back with the baby. The doors thunked shut like armored tank hatches and the car slid into motion. Its suspension whirled them with oily ease across the pitted and weedy tarmac. Laura glanced back at the airport as they left—pools of light over a dozen pedicabs and rust-riddled manual taxis.

The saloon's frigid AC wrapped them in antiseptic chill. "Online, can you hear us in here?" Laura said.

["A little image static, but audio's fine,"] Emily whispered. ["Nice car, eh?"]

"Yeah," David said. Outside the airport grounds, they turned north onto a palm-bordered highway. David leaned forward toward their escort in the front seat. "Where we going, *amigo?*"

"Takin' you to a safehouse," said their escort. He turned in his seat, throwing one elbow over the back. "Maybe ten mile. Sit back, relax, seen? Twiddle you big Yankee thumbs, try and look harmless." He took off his dark glasses.

"Hey!" David said. "It's Sticky!"

Sticky smirked. " 'Captain Thompson' to you, Bwana."

Sticky's skin was now much darker than it had been in Galveston. Some kind of skin dye, Laura thought. Disguise, maybe. It seemed best to say nothing about it. "I'm glad to see you safe," she said. Sticky grunted.

"We never had a chance to tell you," Laura said. "How sorry we are about Mr. Stubbs."

"I was busy," Sticky said. "Trackin' those boys from Singapore." He stared into the lenses of Laura's glasses, visibly gathering himself up, talking through her to the Rizome videotapes spooling in Atlanta. "This, while our Rizome security still dancin' like a chicken with its head lick off, mind. The Singapore gang ran off first thing after the killing. So I track 'em in darkness. They run maybe half a mile south down the coast, then wade out to a smart yacht, waitin', so cozy, right offshore. A good-size ketch; two other men aboard. I get the registry number." He snorted. "Rented by Mr. Lao Binh Huynh, a so-call 'prominent Viet-American businessman,' live in Houston. Rich man this Huynh—run half a dozen groceries, a hotel, a truckin' business."

["Tell him we'll get right on that,"] Emily's whisper urged.

"We'll get right on that," David said.

"You a little late, Bwana Dave. Mr. Huynh vanish some days back. Somebody snatch him out of his car."

"Jesus," David said.

Sticky stared moodily out the window. Rambling white-walled houses emerged from darkness in the Hyundai's headlights, the walls gleaming like shellac. A lone drunk scurried off the road when the car honked once, sharply. A deserted marketplace; tin roofs, bare flagpole, a colonial statue, bits of trampled straw basket. Four tethered goats—their eyes shone red in the headlights like something out of a nightmare. "None of that proves anything against the Singapore Bank," Laura said.

Sticky was annoyed; his accent faltered. "What proof? You think we're planning to *sue* them? We're talking *war!*" He paused. "Too funny, Yankees asking for proof, these days! Somebody blow up your battleship *Maine,* seen—two months later wicked Uncle Sam invade Cuba. No proof at all."

"Well, that goes to show you how we've learned our lesson," David said mildly. "The invasion of Cuba, it failed really badly. Bay of Pork—Bay of Pigs, I mean. A big humiliation for imperial Yankeedom."

Sticky looked at him with amazed contempt. "I'm talking eighteen ninety-eight, mon!"

David looked startled. "Eighteen ninety-eight? But that was the Stone Age."

"We don't forget." Sticky gazed out the window. "You in the capital now. Saint George."

Multistory tenements, again with that strange plastic-looking whitewash sheen. Dim greenish bursts of foliage clustered the rising hillside, shaggy jagged-edged palms like dreadlocked Rasta heads. Satellite dishes and skeletal TV antennas ridged the tenement rooftops. Old dead dishes stood face-up on the trampled lawns—birdbaths? Laura wondered. "These are the government yards," Sticky said. "Public housing." He pointed away from the harbor, up the rising hillside. "That's Fort George on the hill—the prime minister live up there."

Behind the fort, a trio of tall radio antennas flashed their aircraft warning lights in sync. Red blips raced from ground to sky, seeming to fling themselves upward, into stellar blackness. Laura leaned to peer through David's window. The dim bulk of Fort George's battlements, framed against the racing lights, gave her a buzz of unease.

Laura had been briefed about Grenada's prime minister. His name was Eric Louison and his "New Millennium Movement" ruled Grenada as a one-party state. Louison was in his eighties now, rarely seen outside his secretive cabinet of data pirates. Years ago, after first seizing power, Louison had made a passionate speech in Vienna, demanding investigation of the "Optimal Persona phenomenon." It had earned him a lot of uneasy derision.

Louison was in the unhappy Afro-Caribbean tradition of ruler-patriarchs with heavy voodoo. Guys who were all Papa Docs and Steppin' Razors and Whippin' Sticks. Looking up the hill, Laura had a sudden clear mental image of old Louison. Skinny, yellow-nailed geezer, tottering sleepless through the fort's torchlit dungeons. In a gold-braided jacket, sipping hot goat blood, his naked feet stuck in a couple of Kleenex boxes . . .

The Hyundai cruised through town under amber streetlights. They passed a few Brazilian three-wheelers, little wasplike buggies in yellow and black, chugging on alcohol. Saint George had the sleepy look of a town where they roll up the pavements on week nights. By modern Third World standards it was a small city—maybe a hundred thousand people. Half a dozen high-rises loomed downtown, in the old and ugly International Style, their monotonous walls stippled with glowing windows. A fine old colonial church with a tall square clock tower. Idle construction cranes jutted over the geodesic skeleton of a new stadium. "Where's the Bank?" David said.

Sticky shrugged. "Everywhere. Wherever the wires are."

"Good-lookin' town," David said. "No shantytowns, nobody camping under the overpasses. You could teach Mexico City something." No response. "Kingston, too."

"Gonna teach *Atlanta* something," Sticky retorted. "Our Bank—you think we're thieves. No so, mon. It's *your* banks what been sucking these people's blood for four hundred years. Shoe on the other foot, now."

The lights of the capital receded. Loretta stirred in her tote, waved her arms, and noisily filled her diaper. "Uh-oh," David said. He opened the window. The wet-dust smell of hot tropic rain filled the car. Another aroma crept under it, spicy, pungent, haunting. A kitchen smell. Nutmeg, Laura realized. Half the world's nutmeg came out of Grenada. Real natural nutmeg, off trees. They rounded a bay—lights glittered from an offshore station, lights on still water, industrial glare on gray clouds overhead.

Sticky wrinkled his nose and looked at Loretta as if she were a bag of garbage. "Why bring that baby? It's dangerous here."

Laura frowned, and reached for a fresh diaper. David said, "We're not soldiers. We don't pretend to be fair targets."

"That's a funny way to think," Sticky said.

"Maybe you think she'd be safer at our home," Laura said. "You know, the place that got machine-gunned."

"Okay," Sticky shrugged. "Maybe we can cut it a bullet-proof bib."

Emily spoke online. ["Oh, he's funny. They're wasting him here, he ought to be in network comedy."]

Sticky noticed their silence. "Don't worry, Atlanta," he said loudly. "We be takin' better care of these guests than you did of ours."

["Ouch,"] the whisper said.

They covered more miles in silence. ["Look,"] Emily said, ["y'all shouldn't waste this time so I'm going to play you selected highlights of the Committee campaign speeches . . ."] Laura listened intently; David played with the baby and looked out the window.

Then the Hyundai slid west off the highway, onto a graveled track. Emily cut off a speech about Rizome's Pacific Rim holdings in lumber and microchips. The car cruised uphill, through thick stands of casuarina trees. It stopped in darkness.

"Car, honk," Sticky told the Hyundai, and it did. Arc lights flashed on from two iron poles at the gates of a plantation estate. The tops of the compound's fortress walls gleamed wickedly with embedded broken glass.

A guard hustled up belatedly, a rumpled-looking teenage

militiaman with a blunderbuss tangle-gun slung on his back. Sticky left the car. The guard looked jolted from sleep and guilty about it. As the gates swung open, Sticky pulled rank and hassled the kid. "Hey, check this cheap-shot fascist shit," David muttered, just for the record.

The car rolled into a graveled courtyard with a dead marble fountain and wet, weed-choked rosebushes. The distant gate lights showed low whitewashed stairs up to a long screened verandah. Above the verandah, windows glowed in a pair of goofy-looking turrets. Some Victorian colonial's idea of class. ["Check it out!"] Emily commented.

"A Queen Anne mansion!" David said.

The car stopped at the stairs and its doors swung open. They stepped out into rich-smelling tropic dampness, hauling the baby and their carry-ons. Sticky rejoined them, pulling a key card.

"Whose place is this?" David said.

"Yours, for now." Sticky motioned them up the stairs and across the dark, open porch. They passed a flat, dust-shrouded table. A ping-Pong ball glanced off David's foot, tick-ticking off into darkness and the skeletal gleam of aluminum lounge chairs. Sticky slid his key card into double doors of brass-studded rosewood.

The doors opened; hall lights flashed on. David was surprised. "This old place has a house system installed."

"Sure," sniffed Sticky. "It belong to Bank brass once— old Mr. Gelli. He fix it up." The voices of strangers echoed down the hall. They entered a living room: flocked velvet wallpaper, flower-printed couch and two matching recliners, kidney-shaped coffee table, wall-to-wall carpet in a purulent shade of maroon.

Two men and a woman, dressed in servants' whites, knelt beside a toppled drinks trolley. They stood up hastily, looking flustered.

"She not workin'," the taller man said sullenly. "Been chasin' us around all day."

"This is your staff," Sticky said. "Jimmy, Rajiv, and Rita. The place a little musty now, but they'll make you cozy."

Laura looked them over. Jimmy and Rajiv looked like

pickpockets and Rita had eyes like hot black marbles—she looked at little Loretta as if wondering how she'd go in a broth with carrots and onions. "Are we doing entertaining?" Laura said.

Sticky looked puzzled. "No."

"I'm sure Jimmy, Rajiv, and Rita are very capable," Laura said carefully. "But unless there's a pressing need for staff, I think we'd be cozier on our own."

"You had servants in Galveston," Sticky said.

Laura gritted her teeth. "The Lodge staff are *Rizome associates*. Our *coworkers*."

"The Bank picked these people for you," Sticky said. "They had good reason." He shepherded Laura and David toward another door. "Master bedroom in here."

They followed Sticky into a room with a massive canopied waterbed and closet-lined walls. The bed was freshly made. Gardenia incense smoldered atop an old mahogany bureau. Sticky closed the door behind them.

"Your servants protect you from spies," Sticky told them with an air of put-upon patience. "From people, and things too, things with wings and cameras, seen? We don't want them wondering what you are, why you here." He paused to let that sink in. "So this the plan: we pass you off for mad doctors."

David said, "For what?"

"Techies, Bwana. Hired consultants. High-technocrats, the Grenada upper crust." Sticky paused. "Don't you see it? How do you think we run this island? We got mad doctors all points round in Grenada. Yankees, Europeans, Russians, they come here for perks, like this place, seen? Big houses, with servants." He winked deliberately. "Plus other tasty things."

"That's just great," David said. "Do we get field hands, too?"

Sticky grinned. "You a sweet pair, you really are."

"Why not pass us off for tourists, instead?" Laura said. "You must get *some*, right?"

"Lady, this is the Caribbean," Sticky said. "America's backyard, seen? We're used to seeing Yankees runnin' round without their pants. It nah shock us, any." He paused, considering, or pretending to. "Except that retrovirus—fancy Yank V.D.—it do take a toll on the workin' girls."

Laura throttled her temper. "Those perks don't tempt us, Captain."

"Oh, sorry," Sticky said. "I forgot you were online back to Atlanta. You under heavy manners, must nah talk rude . . . while they can hear."

["Oh,"] Emily whispered suddenly, ["if y'all are hypocrites, that means he has a right to be an asshole."]

"You want to prove that we're hypocrites," David said. "Because that makes it right to insult us." Caught off guard, Sticky hesitated. "Look," David soothed. "We're your guests. If you want to surround us with these so-called 'servants,' that's your decision."

Laura caught on. "Maybe you don't trust us?" She pretended to think it over. "Good idea to have some houseboys watching us, just in case we decide to swim back to Galveston."

"We'll think about it," Sticky said grudgingly. The doorbell sounded, the bell plonking out the first verse of an old pop song. "I'm dream-ing of a White Christ-mas," David chanted, recognizing it. They hurried to the door, but the servants had beaten them there. Their luggage had arrived. Rajiv and Jimmy were already hauling bags from the van.

"I can take the baby, madam," Rita volunteered at Laura's elbow. Laura pretended not to hear her, staring through the verandah screen. Two new guards lurked under the arc lights at the gate.

Sticky handed them matched key cards. "I'm going—got business elsewhere tonight. You make yourselves real cozy. Take what you want, use what you want, the place is yours. Old Mr. Gelli, he won't be complaining."

"When do we meet with the Bank?" Laura said.

"Soon come," Sticky said meaninglessly. He rambled down the steps; the Hyundai opened and he slipped in without breaking stride. The car took off.

They rejoined the servants in the living room and stood about uncomfortably in a knot of unresolved tension. "A little supper, sir, madam?" Rajiv suggested.

"No, thank you, Rajiv." She didn't know the proper term for Rajiv's ethnic background. Indo-Caribbean? Hindu-Grenadian?

"Draw madam a bath?"

Laura shook her head. "You could start by calling us David and Laura," she suggested. The three Grenadians looked back stonily.

Loretta adroitly chose this moment to burst into sobs. "We're all a bit tired from the trip," David said loudly. "I think we'll, uh, retire to the bedroom. So we won't need you tonight, thanks." There was a brief struggle over the bags, which Rajiv and Jimmy won. They triumphantly carried the luggage into the master bedroom. "We unpack for you," Rajiv announced.

"Thank you, no!" David spread his arms and herded them through the bedroom door. He locked it behind them.

"We be upstairs if you need us, madam," Jimmy shouted through the door. "The intercom nah work, so yell real good!"

David plucked Loretta from her tote and set about fixing her formula. Laura fell backward onto the bed, feeling a sapping rush of stress fatigue. "Alone at last," she said.

"If you don't count thousands of Rizome associates," David said from the bathroom. He emerged and set the baby on the bed. Laura roused herself to one elbow and held Loretta's bottle.

David checked all the closets. "Seems safe enough in this bedroom. No other ways in or out—this is great old woodwork, too." He pulled his earpiece loose with a wince, then set his videoglasses on a bedside table. He aimed them carefully at the door.

["Don't mind me,"] Emily said in Laura's ear. ["If David wants to sleep in the raw, I'll edit it."]

Laura laughed, sitting up. "You two and your in-jokes," David said.

Laura changed the baby and got her into her paper pajamas. She was doped with food, sleepy and content, her eyes rolling under half-shut flickering lids. Sweet little hand-clenching motions, like she was trying to hold on to wakefulness but couldn't quite remember where she put it. It was funny how much she looked like David when she slept.

They undressed, and he hung his clothes in the closet. "They still got the old guy's wardrobe here," he said. He showed her a tangle of leather. "Nice tailor, huh?"

"What the hell is that? Bondage gear?"

"Shoulder holster," David said. "Macho bang-bang stuff."

"Terrific," Laura said. More goddamned guns. Tired as she was, she dreaded sleep; she could smell another nightmare waiting. She plugged her gear into a clockphone from the biggest bag. "How's that?"

["It ought to do."] Emily's voice came loudly from the clockphone's speakers. ["I'm logging off, but the night shift will watch over you."]

"Good night." Laura slid under the sheets. They nestled the baby between them. Tomorrow they'd look for a crib. "Lights, turn off."

Laura came sluggishly out of sleep. David was already wearing jeans, an unbuttoned tropical shirt, and his videoglasses. "The doorbell," he explained. It rang again, plonking through its antique melody.

"Oh." She looked gummy-eyed at the bedside clock. Eight A.M. "Who's online?"

["It's me, Laura,"] the clock said. ["Alma Rodriguez."]

"Oh, Mrs. Rodriguez," Laura said to the clock. "Um, how are you?"

["Oh, the old man, his bursitis pretty bad today."]

"Sorry to hear that," Laura muttered. She struggled to sit up, the waterbed rippling queasily.

["This Lodge, it's pretty empty without you or the guests,"] Mrs. Rodriguez said brightly. ["Mrs. Delrosario, she says her two girls are running around downtown like wild animals."]

"Well, why don't you tell her that, uh . . ." Laura stopped, suddenly stunned by culture shock. "I don't know where the hell I am."

["Are you all right, Laurita?"]

"Sure, I guess. . . ." She looked wildly around the strange bedroom, located the bathroom door. That would help.

When she returned she dressed quickly, then slipped on the shades. ["Ay, it's strange when the picture moves like that,"] Mrs. Rodriguez said from Laura's earplug. ["Makes me seasick!"]

"You and me both," Laura said. "Who's David talking to out there? The so-called servants?"

["You won't like it,"] Mrs. Rodriguez said drily. ["It's the witch girl. Carlotta."]

"Jesus, now what?" Laura said. She picked up the squirming, bright-eyed baby and carried her into the living room. Carlotta sat on the couch; she had brought a wicker basket full of groceries. "Chow," she announced, nodding at the food.

"Good," Laura said. "How are you, Carlotta?"

"I'm jus' fine," Carlotta said sunnily. "Welcome to Grenada! Real nice place you have here, I was just telling your mister."

"Carlotta gets to be our liaison today," David said.

"I don't mind, since Sticky's pretty busy," Carlotta said. "Besides, I know the island, so I can tour y'all around. You want some papaya juice, Laura?"

"Okay," Laura said. She took the other armchair, feeling restless, wanting to run on the beach. No chance for that though, not here. She balanced Loretta on her knee. "So the Bank trusts you to show us around?"

"I'm wired for sound," Carlotta said, pouring. A light pair of earphones circled her neck, trailing wire to a telephone on her studded belt. She wore a short-sleeved cotton top, with eight inches of bare freckled stomach between it and her red leather miniskirt. "Y'all gotta be a little careful of the food around here," Carlotta said. "They got *houngans* on this island that can really fuck you up."

" 'Houngans?' " David said. "You mean those designer drug people?"

"Yeah, them. They got voodoo poisons here that can do stuff to your CNS that I wouldn't do to a Pentagon Chief of Staff! They ship those mad doctors in, high bio-techies, and kind of crossbreed 'em with those old blowfish-poison zombie masters, and they come out mean as a junkyard dog!" She passed Laura a glass of juice. "If I was in Singapore right now, I'd be burnin' joss!"

Laura stared unhappily into her glass. "Oh, you're fine and safe with me," Carlotta said. "I bought all this in the market myself."

"Thanks, that's very thoughtful," David said.

"Well, us Texans gotta stick together!" Carlotta reached

for the basket. "Y'all can try some of these little tamale things, 'pastels' they call 'em. They're like little curries in pastry. Indian food. East Indians I mean, they snuffed all the local Indians a long time ago."

["Don't eat it!"] Mrs. Rodriquez protested. Laura ignored her. "They're good," she said, munching.

"Yeah, they chased 'em off Sauteur's Point, Leaper's Point that means," Carlotta said to David. "The Carib Indians. They knew the Grenada settlers had their number, so they all jumped off a cliff into the sea together, and died. That's where we're going today—Sauteur's point. I got a car outside."

After breakfast they took Carlotta's car. It was a longer, truck version of the Brazilian three-wheelers, with a kind of motorcycle grip for manual driving. "I like manual driving," Carlotta confessed as they got in. "High speed, that's a big premillennium kick." She beeped merrily with a thumb button as they rolled past the guards at the gate. The guards waved; they seemed to know her. Carlotta gunned her engine, spraying gravel down the weaving hillside road, until they hit the highway.

"You think it's safe to leave the household slaveys with our gear?" Laura asked David.

David shrugged. "I woke 'em up and put 'em to work. Rita's weeding the roses, Jimmy's cleaning the pool, and Rajiv gets to strip the fountain pump."

Laura laughed.

David cracked his knuckles, his eyes clouded with anticipation. "When we get back, we can hit it a lick ourselves."

"You want to work on the house?"

David looked surprised. "A great old place like that? Hell, yes! Can't just let it rot!"

The highway was busier in daylight, lots of rusting old Toyotas and Datsuns. Cars inched past a construction bottleneck, where a pick-and-shovel crew were killing time, sitting in the shade of their steamroller. The crew stared at Carlotta, grinning, as she inched the three-wheeler past. "Hey darleeng!" one of them crowed, waving.

Suddenly a canvas-topped military truck appeared from the north. The crew grabbed their picks and shovels and set to with a will. The truck rumbled past them on the road's shoulder—it was full of bored-looking NMM militia.

A mile later, they passed a town called Grand Roy. "I stay at the Church here," Carlotta said, waving her arm as the engine sputtered wildly. "It's a nice little temple, local girls, they have funny ideas about the Goddess but we're bringin' 'em around."

Cane fields, nutmeg orchards, blue mountains off to the west whose volcanic peaks cut a surf of cloud. They passed two more towns, bigger ones: Gouyave, Victoria. Crowded sidewalks with black women in garish tropical prints, a few women in Indian saris; the ethnic groups didn't seem to mix much. Not many children, but lots of khaki-clad militia. In Victoria they drove past a bazaar, where weird choking music gushed from chest-high sidewalk speakers, their owners sitting behind fiberboard tables stacked high with tapes and videos. Shoppers jostled coconut vendors and old men shoving popsicle carts. High on the walls, out of reach of scribblers, old AIDS posters warned against deviant sex-acts in stiffly accurate health-agency prose.

After Victoria they turned west, circling the shoreline at the northern tip of the island. The land began to rise.

Red loading cranes sketched the horizon over Point Sauteur, like skeletal, sky-etching filigree. Laura thought again of the red radio towers with their eerie leaping lights. . . . She reached for David's hand. He squeezed it and smiled at her, below the glasses; but she couldn't meet his eyes.

Then they were over a hill and suddenly they could see all of it. A vast maritime complex sprawled offshore, like a steel magnate's version of Venice, all sharp metallic angles and rising fretworks and greenish water webbed with floating cables. . . . Long protective jetties of white jumbled boulders, stretching north for miles, spray leaping here and there against their length, the inner waters calmed by fields of orange wave-breaker buoys. . . .

"Mrs. Rodriguez," David said calmly. "We need an oceaneering tech online. Tell Atlanta."

["Okay David, right away."]

Laura counted thirty major installations standing offshore. They were full of people. Most of them were old jackup oil-drilling rigs, their fretted legs standing twenty stories tall, their five-story bases towering high above the water. Martian giants, their knees surrounded by loading docks and small moored barges. Grenada's tropic sunlight gleamed fitfully from aluminum sleeping cabins the size and shape of mobile homes, seeming as small as toys aboard their rigs.

A pair of round, massive OTECS chugged placidly, sucking hot seawater to power their ammonia boilers. Octopus nests of floating cables led from the power stations to rigs piled high with green-and-yellow tangles of hydraulics.

They pulled off the highway. Carlotta pointed: "That's where they jumped!" The cliffs of Point Sauteur were only forty feet high, but the rocks below them looked nasty enough. They would have looked better with raging romantic breakers, but the jetties and wave baffles had turned this stretch of sea into a mud-colored simmering soup. "On a clear day you can see Carriacou from the cliffs," Carlotta said. "Lot of amazing stuff out on that little island—it's part of Grenada, too."

She parked the three-wheeler on a strip of white gravel beside a drydock. Inside the drydock, blue-white arc welders spat brilliance. They left the car.

A sea breeze crept onshore, stinking of ammonia and urea. Carlotta threw her arms back and inhaled hugely. "Fertilizer plants," Carlotta said. "Like the old days on the Gulf Coast, huh?"

"My granddad used to work in those," David said. "The old refinery complexes . . . you remember those, Carlotta?"

"*Remember* 'em?" She laughed. "These *are* them, I reckon. They got all this dead tech dirt cheap—bought it, abandoned in place." She slipped on her earphones and listened. "Andrei's waiting . . . he can explain for y'all. C'mon."

They walked under the shadows of towering cranes, up the limestone steps of a seawall, down to the waterfront. A deeply tanned blond man sat on the stone dock, drinking coffee with a pair of Grenadian longshoremen. All three men wore loose cotton blouses, multipocketed jeans, hard hats, and steel-toed deck shoes.

"At last, here they are," said the blond man, rising. "Hello, Carlotta. Hello, Mr. and Mrs. Webster. And this must be your little baby. What a cute little chicken.'' He touched the baby's nose with a grease-stained forefinger. The baby gurgled at him and gave him her best toothless smile.

"My name is Andrei Tarkovsky," the technician said. "I was from Poland." He looked at his dirty hands apologetically. "Forgive me for not shaking."

"S'okay," David said.

"They have asked me to show you some of what we do here." He waved at the end of the pier. "I have a boat."

The boat was a twelve-foot swamp runner with a blunt prow and a water-jet outboard. Andrei handed them life jackets, including a small one for the baby. They belted up. Loretta, amazingly, took it cheerfully. They climbed down a short ladder onto the boat.

David sat in the stern. Laura and the baby took the bow, facing backward, sitting on a padded thwart. Carlotta sprawled in the bottom. Andrei shoved off and thumbed the engine on. They scudded north over the slimy water.

David turned to Andrei and said something about catalytic cracking units. At that moment a new voice came online. ["Hello Rizome-Grenada, this is Eric King in San Diego. . . . Could you give me another look at that distillation unit. . . . No, you, Laura, look at the big yellow thing—"]

"I'll take it," Laura shouted to David, putting her hand over her ear. "Eric, where is it you want me to look?"

["To your left—yeah—jeez, I haven't seen one like that in twenty years. . . . Could you give me just a straight, slow scan from right to left. . . . Yeah, that's great."] He fell silent as Laura panned across the horizon.

Andrei and David were already arguing. "Yes, but you pay for feedstocks," Andrei told David passionately. "Here we have power from ocean thermals"—he waved at a chugging OTEC—"which is free. Ammonia is NH3. Nitrogen from the air, which is free. Hydrogen from the seawater, which is free. All it costs is capital investment."

["Yeah, and maintenance,"] Eric King said sourly. "Yeah, and maintenance," Laura said loudly.

"Is not a problem, with the modern polymers," Andrei said smoothly. "Inert resins . . . we paint them on . . . reduce corrosion almost to nothing. You must be familiar with these."

"Expensive," David said.

"Not for us," Andrei said. "We manufacture them."

He piloted them below a jackleg rig. When they crossed the sharp demarcation of its shadow, Andrei cut the engine. They drifted on; the rig's flat, two-acre flooring, riddled with baroque plumbing, rose twenty feet above the shadowed water. At a sea-level floating dock, a dreadlocked longshoreman looked them over coolly, his face framed in headphones.

Andrei guided them to one of the rig's four legs. Laura could see the thick painted sheen of polymer on the great load-bearing pipes and struts. There were no barnacles at the waterline. No seaweed, no slime. Nothing grew on this structure. It was slick as ice.

David turned to Andrei, waving his hands animately. Carlotta slouched in the bottom of the boat and dangled her feet over the side, smiling up at the bottom of the rig.

["I wanted to mention that my brother, Michael King, stayed in your Lodge last year,"] King said online. ["He spoke really highly of it."]

"Thanks, that's nice to know," Laura said into the air. David was talking to Andrei, something about copper poisoning and embedded biocides. He ignored King, turning down the volume on his earpiece.

["I've been following this Grenadian affair. Under the awful circumstances, you've been doing well."]

"We appreciate that support and solidarity, Eric."

["My wife agrees with me on this—though she thinks the Committee could have managed better. . . . You're supporting the Indonesian, right? Suvendra?"]

Laura paused. She hadn't thought of the Committee elections in a while. Emily supported Suvendra. "Yeah, that's right."

["What about Pereira?"]

"I like Pereira, but I'm not sure he has the stuff," Laura said. Carlotta grinned to see her, like an idiot, muttering into midair at an unseen presence. Schizoid. Laura frowned. Too much input at once. With her eyes and ears wired on separate realities, her brain felt divided on invisible seams, everything going slightly waxy and unreal. She was getting Net-burned.

["Okay, I know Pereira blew it in Brasilia, but he's honest.

What about Suvendra and this Islamic Bank business? That doesn't bother you?"]

David, still rapt in conversation with the emigré Pole, stopped suddenly and put his hand to his ear. "Islamic Bank business," Laura thought, with a little cold qualm. Of course. Someone from Rizome was negotiating with the Singapore data pirates. And of course, it would be Suvendra. It fell neatly into place: Ms. Emerson, and Suvendra, and Emily Donato. The Rizome old girls' network in action.

"Um . . . Eric," David said aloud. "This is not a private line."

["Oh,"] King said in a small, now-I've-done-it voice.

"We'd be glad to have your input, if you could write it up and send e-mail. Atlanta can encrypt it for you."

["Yeah, sure,"] King said. ["Stupid of me . . . my apologies."] Laura felt sorry for him. She was glad David had gotten him off her back, but she didn't like the way it sounded. The guy was being frank and up-front, in very Rizome-correct fashion, and here they were telling him to mind his manners because they were on spook business. How would it look?

David glanced at her and jerkily spread his hands, frowning. He looked frustrated.

Television. A kind of shellac of television surrounded and shielded both of them. It was like reaching out to touch someone's face, but feeling your fingers hit cold glass instead.

Andrei fired up the engine again. They picked up speed, scudding out to sea. Laura settled her videoglasses back carefully, blinking as her hair whipped around her head.

Caribbean water, smiling tropical sun, the cool, gleaming rush of speed below the bows. Intricate chunks of heavy industry loomed above the polluted shallows, huge, peculiar, ambitious . . . full of insistent thereness. Laura closed her eyes. Grenada! What in hell was she doing here? She felt dazed, culture-shocked. A garbled crackling of talk from Eric King. Suddenly the distant Net seemed to be digging into Laura's head like an earwig. She felt a quick impulse to strip off the glasses and fling them into the sea.

Loretta squirmed in her arms and tugged her blouse in a tight little fist. Laura forced her eyes open. Loretta was reality, she thought, hugging her. Her unfailing little guide. Real life was where the baby was.

Carlotta edged closer across the damp bottom of the boat. She waved her arm around her head. "Laura, you know why, all this?"

Laura shook her head.

"It's practice, that's what. Any one of these rigs—it could hold the whole Grenada Bank!" Carlotta pointed at a bizarre structure off to starboard—a flattened geodesic egg surrounded by buttressed pontoons. It looked like a fat soccer ball on bright orange spider's legs. "Maybe the Bank's computers are in there," Carlotta insinuated. "Even if the Man comes down on Grenada, the Bank can just duck aside, like electric judo! All this ocean tech—they can jackleg way out into international waters, where the Man just can't reach."

"The 'Man'?" Laura said.

"The Man, the Combine, the Conspiracy. You know. The Patriarchy. The Law, the Heat, the Straights. The Net. Them."

"Oh," Laura said. "You mean 'us.' "

Carlotta laughed.

Eric King broke in incredulously. ["Who is this strange woman? Can you give me another scan of that geodesic station? Thanks, uh, David . . . wild! You know what it looks like? It looks like your Lodge!"]

"I was just thinking that!" David said loudly, cupping his earphone. His eyes were riveted on the station and he was half leaning over the gunwale. "Can we cruise by it, Andrei?"

Andrei shook his head.

The stations fell behind them, their angular derricks framed against the curdled tropical green of the shoreline. The water grew choppier. The boat began to rock, its flat prow spanking each surge and flicking Laura's back with spray.

Andrei shouted and pointed off the port bow. Laura turned to look. He was pointing at a long, gray-black dike, a sea-wall. A four-story office building stood near one end of it. The installation was huge—the black dike was at least sixty feet high. Maybe a quarter mile long.

Andrei headed for it, and as they drew nearer, Laura saw little white spires scratching the skyline above the dike—tall street lights. Bicyclists rolled along the roadbed like gnats on wheels. And the office building looked more and more peculiar as they drew near—each story smaller than the last, stacked on a slant, with long metal stairs on the outside. And on its roof, a lot of tech busywork—satellite dishes, a radar mast.

The top story was round and painted nautical white. Like a smokestack.

It *was* a smokestack.

["That's a U.L.C.C.!"] Eric King said.

"A what, Eric?" Laura said.

["Ultra-Large Crude Carrier. A supertanker. Biggest ships ever built. Used to make the Persian Gulf run all the time, back in the old days."] King laughed. ["Grenada has supertankers! I wondered where they'd ended up."]

"You mean it floats?" Laura said. "That seawall is a ship? The whole thing moves?"

"It can load half a million tons," Carlotta said, luxuriating in Laura's surprise. "Like a skyscraper full of crude. It's bigger than the Empire State Building. Lots bigger." She laughed. "Course they don't have no crude in it, now. It's a righteous city now. One big factory."

They cruised toward it at full speed. Laura saw surface surges cresting against its bulk, whacking against it like a cliffside. The supertanker didn't show the slightest movement in response. It was far, far too big for that. It wasn't like any kind of ship she'd ever imagined. It was like someone had cut off part of downtown Houston and welded it to the horizon.

And on the closer edge of the mighty deck she could see—what? Mango trees, lines of flapping laundry, people clustered at the long, long railing. . . . Hundreds of them. Far more than anybody could need for a crew. She spoke to Carlotta. "They live there, don't they."

Carlotta nodded. "A lot goes on in these ships."

"You mean there's more than one?"

Carlotta shrugged. "Maybe." She tapped her own eyelid, indicating Laura's videoglasses. "Let's just say Grenada makes a pretty good flag of convenience."

Laura stared at the supertanker, scanning its length carefully for the sake of Atlanta's tapes. "Even if the Bank bought it for junk—that's a lot of steel. Must have cost millions."

Carlotta snickered. "You're not too hip about black markets, huh? The problem's always cash. What to do with it, I mean. Grenada's rich, Laura. And gettin' richer all the time."

"But why buy ships?"

"Now you're getting into ideology," Carlotta told her. "Have to ask ol' Andrei about that."

Now Laura could see how old the monster was. Its sides were blotted with great caking masses of rust, sealed shut under layers of modern high-tech shellac. The shellac clung, but badly; in places it had the wrinkled look of failing plastic wrap. The ship's endless sheet-iron hull had flexed from heat and cold and loading stress, and even the enormous strength of modern bonded plastics couldn't hold. Laura saw stretch marks, and broken-edged blisters of "boat pox," and patches of cracked alligatoring where the plastic had popped loose in plates, like dried mud. All this covered with patches of new glue and big slathery drips of badly cured gunk. A hundred shades of black and gray and rust. Here and there, work gangs had spray-bombed the hull of the supertanker with intricate colored graffiti. "TANKERSKANKERS," "MONGOOSE CREW—WE OPTIMAL," "CHARLIE NOGUES BATALLION."

They tied up at a floating sea-level dock. The dock was like a flattened squid of bright yellow rubber, with radiating walkways and a floating bladder-head in the center. A birdcage elevator slid down the dock's moored cable from a deck-level gantry seventy feet up. They followed Andrei into the cage and it rose, jerkily. David, who enjoyed heights, watched avidly through the bars as the sea shrank below them. Below his dark glasses, he grinned like a ten-year-old. He was really enjoying this, Laura realized as she clutched the baby's tote, white-knuckled. It was all right up his alley.

The gantry swung them over the deck. Laura saw the gantry's operator as they passed—she was an old black woman in dreadlocks, shuffling her knobbed gearshifts and rhythmically chewing gum. Below them, the monstrous deck stretched like an airport runway, broken with odd-looking functional clusters: dogged hatches, ridged metal vents, fireplugs, foam tanks, foil-wrapped hydraulic lines bent in reverse U's over the bicycle paths. Long tents, too, and patches of garden: trees in tubs, stretched greenhouse sheets of plastic over rows of citrus. And neatly stacked mountains of stuffed burlap bags.

They descended over a taped X on the deck and settled with a bump. "Everybody off," Andrei said. They stepped out and the elevator rose at once. Laura sniffed the air. A familiar scent under the rust and brine and plastic. A wet, fermenting smell, like tofu.

"Scop!" David said, delighted. "Single-cell protein!"

"Yes," Andrei said. "The *Charles Nogues* is a food ship."

"Who's this 'Nogues'?" David asked him.

"He was a native hero," Andrei said, his face solemn.

Carlotta nodded at David. "Charles Nogues threw himself off a cliff."

"What?" David said. "He was one of those Carib Indians?"

"No, he was a Free Coloured. They came later, they were anti-slavery. But the Redcoat army showed up, and they died fighting." Carlotta paused. "It's an awful fuckin' mess, Grenada history. I learned all this from Sticky."

"The crew of this ship are the vanguard of the New Millennium Movement," Andrei declared. The four of them followed his lead, strolling toward the distant, looming high-rise of the ship's super-structure. It was hard not to see it as some peculiar office complex, because the ship itself felt so city-solid underfoot. Traffic passed them on the bicycle paths, men pedaling loaded cargo-rickshaws. "Trusted party cadres," said blond, Polish Andrei. "Our *nomenklatura*."

Laura fell a step behind, hefting the baby in her tote, while David and Andrei walked forward, shoulder to shoulder. "It's starting to make a certain conceptual sense," David told him. "This time, if you get chased off your own island like Nogues and the Caribs, you'll have a nice place to jump to. Right?" He waved at the ship around them.

Andrei nodded soberly. "Grenada remembers her many invasions. Her people are very brave, and visionaries too, but she's a small country. But the ideas here today are big, David. Bigger than boundaries."

David looked Andrei up and down, taking his measure. "What the hell is a guy from Gdansk doing here, anyway?"

"Life is dull in the Socialist Bloc," Andrei told him airily. "All consumer socialism, no spiritual values. I wanted to be with the action. And the action is South, these days. The North, our developed world—it is boring. Predictable. This is the edge that cuts."

"So you're not one of those 'mad-doctor' types, huh?"

Andrei was contemptuous. "Such people are useful, only. We buy them, but they have no true role in the New Millennium Movement. They don't understand people's Tech." Laura could hear the capital letters in his emphasis. She didn't like the way this was going at all.

She spoke up. "Sounds very nice. How do you square that with dope factories and data piracy?"

"All information should be free," Andrei told her, slowing his walk. "As for drugs—" He reached into a side pocket in his jeans. He produced a flat roll of shiny paper and handed it to her.

Laura looked it over. Little peel-off rectangles of sticky-backed paper. It looked like a blank roll of address labels. "So?"

"You paste them on," Andrei said patiently. "The glue has an agent, which carries the drug through the skin. The drug came from a wetware lab, it is synthetic THC, the active part of marijuana. Your little roll of paper is the same, you see, as many kilograms of hashish. It is worth about twenty ecu. Very little." He paused. "Not so thrilling, so romantic, eh? Not so much to get excited about."

"Christ," Laura said. She tried to hand it back.

"Please keep it, it means very little."

Carlotta spoke up. "She can't hold this, Andrei. Come on, they're online and the bosses are lookin'." She stuffed the roll of paper into her purse, grinning at Laura. "You know, Laura, if you'd point those glasses over there to starboard, I can slap a little of this crystal on the back of your neck, and nobody in Atlanta will ever know. You can rush like Niagara on this stuff. Crystal THC, girl! The Goddess was cruisin' when She invented that one."

"Those are *mind-altering drugs*," Laura protested. She

sounded stuffy and virtuous, even to herself. Andrei smiled indulgently, and Carlotta laughed aloud. "They're dangerous," Laura said.

"Maybe you think it will jump off the paper and bite you," Andrei said. He waved politely at a passing Rastaman.

"You know what I mean," Laura said.

"Oh, yes"—Andrei yawned—"you never use drugs yourself, but what about the effect on people who are stupider and weaker than you, eh? You are patronizing other people. Invading their freedoms."

They walked past a huge electric anchor winch, and a giant pump assembly, with two-story painted tanks in a jungle of pipes. Rastas with hard hats and clipboards paced the catwalks over the pipes.

"You're not being fair," David said. "Drugs can trap people."

"Maybe," Andrei said. "If they have nothing better in their lives. But look at the crew on this ship. Do they seem like drugged wreckage to you? If America suffers from drugs, perhaps you should ask what America is lacking."

["What an asshole,"] Eric King commented suddenly. They ignored him.

Andrei led them up three flights of perforated iron stairs, bracketed to the portholed superstructure of the *Charles Nogues*. There was an intermittent flow of locals up and down the stairs, with chatting crowds on the landings. Everyone wore the same pocketed jeans and the standard-issue cotton blouses. But a chosen few had plastic shirtpocket protectors, with pens. Two pens, or three pens, or even four. One guy, a beer-bellied Rasta with a frown and bald spot, had half a dozen gold-plated fibertips. He was followed by a crowd of flunkies. "Whoopee, real Socialism," Laura muttered at Carlotta.

"I can take the baby if you want." Carlotta said, not hearing her. "You must be getting tired."

Laura hesitated. "Okay." Carlotta smiled as Laura handed her the tote. She slung its strap over her shoulder. "Hello, Loretta," she cooed, poking at the baby. Loretta looked up at her doubtfully and decided to let it pass.

They stepped through a hatch door, with rounded corners

and a rubber seal, into the fluorescent lights of a hall. Lots of old scratched teak, scuffed linoleum. The walls were hung with stuff—"People's Art," Laura guessed, lots of child-bright tropical reds and golds and greens, dreadlocked men and women reaching toward a slogan-strewn blue sky. . . .

"This is the bridge," Andrei announced. It looked like a television studio, dozens of monitor screens, assorted cryptic banks of knobs and switches, a navigator's table with elbowed lamps and cradled telephones. Through a glassed-in wall above the monitors, the deck of the ship stretched out like a twenty-four-lane highway. There were little patches of ocean, way, way down there, looking too distant to matter much. Glancing through the windows, Laura saw that there were a pair of big cargo barges on the supertanker's port side. They'd been completely hidden before, by the sheer rising bulk of the ship. The barges pumped their loads aboard through massive ribbed pipelines. There was a kind of uneasy nastiness to the sight, vaguely obscene, like the parasitic sexuality of certain deep-sea fish.

"Don't you wanna look?" Carlotta asked her, swinging the baby back and forth at her hip. Andrei and David were already deeply engrossed, examining gauges and talking a mile a minute. Really absorbing topics, too, like protein fractionation and slipstream turbulence. A ship's officer was helping explain, one of the bigwigs with multiple pens. He looked weird: velvety black skin and straight blond flaxen hair. "This is more David's sort of thing," Laura said.

"Well, could you go offline for a second, then?"

"Huh?" Laura paused. "Anything you want to tell me, you ought to be able to tell Atlanta."

"You gotta be kidding," Carlotta said, rolling her eyes. "What's the deal, Laura? We talked private all the time at the Lodge, and nobody bothered us then."

Laura considered. "What do you think, online?"

["Well, hell, I trust you,"] King said. ["Go for it! You're in no danger that I can see."]

"Well . . . okay, as long as David's here to watch over me." Laura stepped to the navigator's table, took off her videoglasses and earplug, and set them down. She backed away and rejoined Carlotta, careful to stay in view of the glasses. "There. Okay?"

"You've got really strange eyes, Laura," Carlotta murmured. "Kind of yellow-green. . . . I'd forgotten how they looked. It's easier to talk to you when you don't have that rig on—kinda makes you look like a bug."

"Thanks a lot," Laura said. "Maybe you ought to take it a little easy on the hallucinogens."

"What's this high-and-mighty stuff?" Carlotta said. "This grandmother of yours, Loretta Day, that you think so much of—she got busted for drugs once. Didn't she?"

Laura was startled. "What's my grandmother got to do with it?"

"Only that she raised you, and looked after you, not like your real mother. And I know you thought a lot of old granny." Carlotta tossed her hair, pleased at Laura's look of shock. "We know all about you . . . and her . . . and David. . . . The farther you go back, the easier it is to sneak the records out. 'Cause no one's keeping guard on all the data. There's just too much of it to watch, and no one really cares! But the Bank does—so they've got it all."

Carlotta narrowed her eyes. "Marriage certificates—divorces —charge cards, names, addresses, phones. . . . Newspapers, scanned over twenty, thirty years, by computers, for every single mention of your name. . . . I've seen their dossier on you. On Laura Webster. All kinds of photos, tapes, hundreds of thousands of words." Carlotta paused. "It's really weird. . . . I know you so well, I feel like I'm inside your head, in a way. Sometimes I know what you'll say even before you say it, and it makes me laugh."

Laura felt herself flush. "I can't stop you from invading my privacy. Maybe that gives you an unfair advantage over me. But I don't make final decisions—I'm only representing my people." A group of officers broke up around one of the screens, leaving the bridge with looks of stern devotion to duty. "Why are you telling me this, Carlotta?"

"I'm not sure . . ." Carlotta said, looking genuinely puzzled, even a little hurt. "I guess it's cause I don't want to see you walk blind into what's coming down for you. You think you're safe cause you work for the Man, but the Man's had his day. The real future's here, in this place.'' Carlotta lowered her voice and stepped closer; she was serious. ''You're on the wrong side, Laura. The losin' side, in the long run. These people have hold of things that the Man don't want trifled with. But there's not a thing the Man can do about it, really. Cause they got his number. And they can do things here that straights are scared to even think about.''

Laura rubbed her left ear, a little sore from its plug-in phone. ''You're really impressed by that black market tech, Carlotta?''

''Sure, there's that,'' Carlotta said, shaking her tousled head. ''But they got Louison, the Prime Minister. He can raise up his Optimals. He can call 'em out, Laura—his Personas, understand? They walk around in broad daylight, while he never leaves that old fort. I've seen 'em . . . walkin' the streets of the capital . . . little old men.'' Carlotta shivered.

Laura stared at Carlotta with mixed annoyance and pity. ''What's that supposed to mean?''

''Don't you know what an Optimal Persona is? It's got no substance, time and distance mean nothing to it. It can look and listen . . . spy on you. . . . Or maybe walk right through your body! And two days later you drop dead without a mark on you.''

Laura sighed; Carlotta had had her going for a moment there. She could understand outlaw tech; but mystic bullshit had never done much for her. David and the Polish emigré were going over a CADCAM readout, all smiles. ''Does Andrei believe all this?''

Carlotta shrugged, her face closing up, becoming distant again. ''Andrei's a political. We get all kinds in Grenada. . . . But it all adds up in the end.''

''Maybe it does . . . if you're batshit.''

Carlotta gave her a look of pious sorrow. ''I better put my rig back on,'' Laura said.

They had lunch with the ship's captain. He was the potbellied character with the six gold pens. His name was Blaize. Nineteen of the ship's other commissars joined him in the supertanker's cavernous dining room, with its hinged chandeliers and oak wainscoting. They dined off old gold-rimmed china with the insignia of the P&O Shipping Line and were served by teenage waiters in uniform, hauling big steel tureens. They ate scop. Various hideous forms of it. Soups. Nutmeg-flavored mock chicken breast. Little fricasseed things with toothpicks in them.

Eric King didn't wait through lunch. He signed offline, leaving them with Mrs. Rodriguez.

"We are by no means up to capacity," Captain Blaize announced in a clipped Caribbean drawl. "But we come, by and by, a little closer to the production quotas each and every month. By this action, we relieve the strain on Grenada's productive soil . . . and its erosion . . . and the overcrowding as well, you understand, Mr. Webster. . . ." Blaize's voice drifted through a singsong cadence, causing strange waves of glazed ennui to course through Laura's brain. "Imagine, Mr. Webster, what a fleet of ships, like this, could do, for the plight of Mother Africa."

"Yeah. I mean, I grasp the implications," David said, digging into his scop with gusto.

Light background music was playing. Laura listened with half an ear. Some kind of slick premillennium crooner on vocals, lots of syrupy strings and jazzy razzing saxophones . . ."(something something) for you, dear . . . buh buh buh boooh . . ." She could almost identify the singer . . . from old movies. Cosby, that was it. Bing Cosby.

Now digitizing effects started creeping in and something awful began to happen. Suddenly a bandersnatch had jumped into Cosby's throat. His jovial white-guy Anglo good vibes stretched like electric taffy—*arrooooh,* werewolf noises. Now Bing was making ghastly *hub hub hub* backward croonings, like a sucking chest wound. The demented noise was filtering around the diners but no one was paying attention.

Laura turned to the young three-pen cadre on her left. The guy was waving his fingers over Loretta's tote and looked up guiltily when she asked. "The music? We call it didge-Ital . . . dig-ital, seen, D.J.-Ital. . . . Mash it up right on the ship." Yeah. They were doing something awful to poor old Bing while he wasn't looking. He sounded like his head was made of sheet metal.

Now Blaize and Andrei were lecturing David about money.

The Grenadian rouble. Grenada had a closed, cash-free economy; everybody on the island had personal credit cards, drawn on the bank. This policy kept that "evil global currency," the ecu, out of local circulation. And that "razored off the creeping tentacles" of the Net's "financial and cultural imperialism."

Laura listened to their crude P.R. with sour amusement. They wouldn't crank out this level of rhetoric unless they were trying to hide a real weakness, she thought. It was clear that the Bank kept the whole population's credit transactions on file, just so they could look over everybody's shoulders. But that was Orwell stuff. Even bad old Mao and Stalin couldn't make that kind of crap work out.

David raised his brows innocently and asked about "left-hand payments," an old tag line from East Bloc premillennium days. Andrei got a stiff and virtuous look on his face. Laura hid her smile with a forkful of mock carrots. She'd bet anything that a wad of paper ecu, under the table, would buy the average Grenadian body and soul. Yeah, it was just like those old-time Russki hustlers, who used to pester tourists in Moscow for dollars, back when there were dollars. Big fleas had little fleas, big black markets had little black markets. Funny!

Laura felt pleased, sure she was on to something. Tonight she'd have to write Debra Emerson in Atlanta, on an encrypted line, and tell her: yeah, Debra, here's a place to stick a crowbar. Debra'd know how, too: it was just like bad old CIA work before the Abolition. . . . What did they used to call it? Destabilization.

"It's not like the Warsaw Pact, before openness," continued Andrei, shaking his handsome blond head. "Our island is more like little OPEC country—Kuwait, Abu Dhabi. . . . Too much easy money eats the social values, makes life like Disneyland, all fat Cadillacs and the cartoon mouses . . . empty, meaningless."

Blaize smiled a little, his eyes half closed, like a dreadlocked Buddha. "Without Movement discipline," he rumbled smoothly, "our money would flow back, like water downhill . . . from the Third World periphery, down to the centers of the Net. Your 'free market' cheats us; it's a Babylon slave market in truth! Babylon would drain away our best people, too . . . they would go to where the phones already work, where the streets are already paved. They want the infrastructure, where the Net is woven thickest, and it's easiest to prosper. It is a vicious cycle, making Third World sufferation.''

''But today the adventure is here!'' Andrei broke in, leaning forward. ''No more frontiers in your America, David, my friend! Today it's all lawyers and bureaucrats and 'social impact statements'. . . .''

Andrei sneered and slapped his fork on the tabletop. ''Huge prison walls of paperwork to crush the life and hope from modern pioneers! Just as ugly, just such a crime, as the old Berlin Wall, David. Only more clever, with better public relations.'' He glanced at Laura, sidelong. ''Scientists and engineers, and architects, too, yes—we brothers, David, who do the world's true work—where is our freedom? Where, eh?''

Andrei paused, tossing his head to flick back a loose wing of blond hair. Suddenly he had the dramatic look of an orator on a roll, a man drawing inspiration from deep wells of sincerity. ''We have no freedom! We cannot follow our dreams, our visions. Governments and corporations break us to their harness! For them, we make only colored toothpaste, softer toilet paper, bigger TVs to stupefy the masses!'' He chopped air with his hands. ''It's an old man's world today, with old man's values! With soft, cozy padding on all the sharp corners, with ambulances always standing by. Life is more than this, David. Life has to be more than this!''

The ship's officers had stopped to listen. As Andrei paused, they nodded among themselves. ''I-rey, mon, star righteous. . . .'' Laura watched them trade sturdy looks of macho comradeship. The air felt syrup-thick with their ship crew's *gemeineschaft*, reinforced by the Party line. It felt familiar to Laura, like the good community feeling at a Rizome meeting, but stronger, less rational. Militant—and scary, because it felt so good. It tempted her.

She sat quietly, trying to relax, to see through their eyes and feel and understand. Andrei blazed on, hitting his stride now, preaching about the Genuine Needs of the People, the social role of the Committed Technician. It was a mishmash:

Food, and Liberty, and Meaningful Work. And the New Man and New Woman, with their hearts with the people, but their eyes on the stars. . . . Laura watched the crew. What must they be feeling? Young, most of them; the committed Movement elite, taken from those sleepy little island towns into a place like this. She imagined them running up and down the deck stairs of their strange steel world, hot and fervid, like hopped-up lab rats. Sealed in a bottle and drifting away from the Net's laws and rules and standards.

Yeah. So many changes, so many shocks and novelties; they broke people up inside. Dazzled by potential, they longed to throw out the rules and limits, all the checks and balances— all discredited now, all lies of the old order. Sure, Laura thought. This was why Grenada's cadres could chop genes like confetti, rip off data for their Big Brother dossiers, and never think twice. When the People march in one direction, it only hurts to ask awkward questions.

Revolutions. New Orders. For Laura the words had the cobwebby taste of twentieth-century thinking. Visionary mass movements were all over the 1900s, and whenever they broke through, blood followed in buckets. Grenada could be 1920s Russia, 1940s Germany, 1980s Iran. All it would take was a war.

Of course it wouldn't be a big war, not nowadays. But even a little terror war could turn things septic in a little place like Grenada. Just enough killing to raise the level of hysteria and make every dissident a traitor. A little war, she thought, like the one beginning to seethe already. . . .

Andrei stopped. David smiled at him uneasily. "I can see you've given this speech before."

"You are skeptical about talk," Andrei said, throwing down his napkin. "That's only wise. But we can show you the facts and the practice." He paused. "Unless you want to wait for dessert."

David looked at Laura and Carlotta. "Let's go," Laura said. Sweetened scop was nothing to linger for.

They nodded at the crew, thanked the captain politely, left the table. They exited the dining room by another hallway and stopped by a pair of elevators. Andrei punched a button and they stepped in; the doors slid shut behind them.

Static roared in Laura's head. "Jesus Christ!" David said, clutching his earpiece. "We just went offline!"

Andrei glanced once, over his shoulder, skeptically. "Relax, yes? It's only a moment. We can't wire everything."

"Oh," David said. He glanced at Laura. Laura stood clutching the tote as the elevator descended. Yeah, they'd lost the armor of television, and here they stood helpless: Andrei and Carlotta could jump them . . . jab them with knockout needles. . . . They'd wake up somewhere strapped to tables with dope-crazed voodoo doctors sewing little poisoned time bombs into their brains. . . .

Andrei and Carlotta stood flat-footed, with the patient, bovine look of people in elevators. Nothing whatever happened.

The doors slid open. Laura and David rushed out into the corridor, clutching their headsets. Long, long seconds of crackling static. Then a quick staccato whine of datapulse. Finally, high-pitched anxious shouting in Spanish.

"We're fine, fine, just a little break," Laura told Mrs. Rodriguez. David reassured her at length, in Spanish. Laura missed the words, but not the distant tone of voice: frantic little-old-lady fear, sounding weak and tremulous. Of course, good old Mrs. Rodriguez, she was only worried for them; but despite herself, Laura felt annoyed. She adjusted her glasses and straightened self-consciously.

Andrei was waiting for them, suffering fools gladly, holding a side door. Beyond it was a scrubbing room, with shower stalls and stainless-steel sinks under harsh blue light, and air that smelled of soap and ozone. Andrei yanked open a rubber-sealed locker. Its shelves were stacked with fresh-pressed scrub garments in surgical green: tunics, drawstring pants, hairnets and surgical masks, even little crinkly, tie-on galoshes.

"Mrs. Rodriguez," David said, excited. "Looks like we need a Rizome bio-tech online."

Andrei stretched over a sink, catching an automatic drip feed of pink disinfectant. He lathered up vigorously. Beside him, Carlotta caught water in a sterile paper cup. Laura saw her palm a red Romance pill from her purse. She knocked it back with the ease of long practice.

From within her tote, Loretta wrinkled up her little eyes.

She didn't like the scrub room's light, or maybe it was the smell. She whimpered rhythmically, then began screaming. Her yells echoed harshly from the walls and scared her into new convulsions of effort. "Oh, Loretta," Laura chided her. "And you've been so good lately, too." She kicked down the tote's wire rocker stand and rocked it on the floor; but Loretta only turned tomato-red and flung her chubby arms wildly. Laura checked her diaper and sighed. "Can I change her in here, Andrei?"

Andrei was rinsing his neck; he pointed with his elbow at a disposal chute. Laura dug in the back of the tote and unrolled the changing pad from its tube. "That's cute," Carlotta said, crowding up and peering over her shoulder. "Like a window shade."

"Yeah," Laura said. "See, you press this button on the side, and little bubble-cell padding pops up." She spread the pad over a laminated counter and set Loretta on it. The baby wailed in existential terror.

Her little kicking rump was caked with shit. By this time, Laura had learned to look at it without really seeing it. She cleaned it deftly with an oiled napkin, not saying anything.

Carlotta was squeamish and looked away, at the tote. "Wow! This thing is really intricate! Hey look, these flaps pop out and you can make it into a baby bath . . ."

"Hand me the powder, Carlotta." Laura puffed dry spray on the baby's rump and sealed her in a new diaper. Loretta howled like a lost soul.

David came up. "You get scrubbed, I'll take her." Loretta had one look at her father's surgical mask and screamed in anguish. "For heaven's sake," David said.

["You shouldn't take your baby into a bio-hazard zone,"] said a new voice online.

"You don't think so?" David shouted. "She won't like wearing the mask, that's for sure."

Carlotta looked up. "I could take her," she said meekly.

["Don't trust her,"] online said at once.

"We can't let the baby out of our sight," David told Carlotta. "You understand."

"Well," Carlotta said practically, "I could wear Laura's

headset. And that way, Atlanta could watch everything I did. And meanwhile Laura would be safe with you.''

Laura hesitated. "My earplug's custom-made."

"It's flexible, I could wear it for a while. C'mon, I can do it, I'd like to.''

"What do you think, online?" David said.

["It's me, Millie Syers, from Raleigh,"] online told them. ["You remember. John and I and our boys were in your Lodge, last May.''

"Oh, hello," Laura said. "How are you, Professor Syers?"

["Well, I got over my sunburn."] Millie Syers laughed. ["And please don't call me Professor, it's very non-R. Anyway, if you want my advice, I wouldn't leave any baby of mine with some data pirate dressed like a hooker.''

"She *is* a hooker," David said. Carlotta smiled.

["Well! I guess that explains it. Must not see many babies in her line of work. . . . Hmmm, if she wore Laura's rig, I suppose I could watch what she did, and if she tries anything I could scream. But what's to keep her from dropping the glasses and running off with the baby?''

"We're in the middle of a supertanker, Millie," David said. "We got about three thousand Grenadians all around us.''

Andrei looked up from tying his galoshes. "Five thousand, David," he said, over the baby's piercing sobs. "Are you not sure you are both carrying this a bit far? All these little quibbles of security?''

"I promise she'll be all right," Carlotta said. She raised her right hand, with the center finger bent down into the palm. "I swear it by the Goddess.''

["Good heavens, she's one of—"] said Millie Syers, but Laura lost the rest as she stripped off her rig. It felt glorious to have it out of her head. She felt free and clean for the first time in ages; a weird feeling, with the sudden strange urge to jump in a shower stall and soap down.

She locked eyes with Carlotta. "All right, Carlotta. I'm trusting you, with what I love best in the world. You understand that, don't you? I don't have to say anything more.''

Carlotta nodded soberly, then shook her head.

Laura scrubbed and got quickly into the gear. The baby's howling was driving them out of the room.

Andrei ushered them to another elevator, at the back of the scrub room. She looked back one last time at the door and saw Carlotta walking back and forth with the baby, singing.

Andrei stepped in after them, turned his back, and pushed the button. "We're losing the signal again," David warned. The steel doors slid shut.

They descended slowly. Suddenly Laura was shocked to feel David tenderly pat her ass. She jumped and stared at him.

"Hey, babe," he murmured. "We're offline. Wow."

He was starved for privacy.

And here they had almost thirty seconds of it. As long as Andrei didn't turn and look.

She glanced at David in frustration, wanting to tell him . . . what? To reassure him that it wasn't so bad. And that she felt it, too. And that they could tough it out together, but he'd better behave himself. And yeah, that it was a funny thing to do, and she was sorry she was jumpy.

But absolutely none of it could get across to him. With the surgical mask and the gold-etched glasses, David's face had turned totally alien. No human contact.

The doors opened; there was a sudden rush of air and their ears popped. They turned left into another hall. "It's okay, Millie," David said distractedly. "We're fine, leave Carlotta alone. . . ."

He kept mumbling from behind his mask, shaking his head and talking into the air. Like a madman. It was odd how peculiar it looked when you weren't doing it yourself. This hall looked peculiar, too: strangely funky and makeshift, the ceiling tilted, the walls out of true. It was *cardboard,* that was it—brown cardboard and thin wire mesh, but all of it lacquered over with a thick, steel-hard ooze of translucent plastic. The lights overhead were wired with extension cord, cheap old household extension cord, all stapled to the ceiling and sealed under thick lacquered gunk. It was all stapled, there wasn't a nail in it anywhere. Laura touched the wall, wondering. It was quality plastic, slick and hard as porcelain, and she knew from the feel of it that a strong man couldn't dent it with an axe.

But there was so much of it—and it cost so much to make!

Yeah, but maybe not so much—if you didn't pay insurance, or worker's comp, and never shut down for safety inspections, and didn't build failsafes and crashproof control systems and log every modification in triplicate. Sure; even nuclear power was cheap if you played fast and loose.

But bio-safety rules were ten times as strict, or supposed to be. Maybe plutonium was bad, but at least it couldn't jump out of a tank and grow by itself.

"This hall is made of *cardboard!*" David said.

"No, it's thermal epoxy over cardboard," Andrei told him. "You see that plug? Live steam. We can boil this entire hall at any moment. Not that we would need to, of course."

At the hall's end, they stopped by a tall sealed hatchway. It had the international symbol of bio-hazard: the black-and-yellow, triple-horned circle. Good graphic design, Laura thought as Andrei worked the hatch wheel; as frightening in its elegant way as a skull and crossbones.

They stepped through.

They emerged on a landing of lacquered bamboo. It stood forty feet in the air, overlooking a steel cavern the size of an aircraft hangar. They'd reached a section of the supertanker's hold; its floor—the steel hull—was gently curved. And littered with surreal machinery, like the careless toys of some giant ten-year-old with a taste for chemistry sets.

The cardboard corridor, and their bamboo landing, and its sloping, spidery catwalks, were all bolted to a monster bulkhead at their backs. The hangar's far bulkhead rose in the distance, a great gray wall of girder-stiffened steel—this one spread with a giant polychrome mural. A mural of men and women in berets and fatigue shirts, marching under banners, their pie-cut painted eyes as big as basketballs, fixed in midair . . . their brown arms rounded and monolithic, gleaming like wax in a strange underwater glare.

The hangar's eerie lighting flowed from liquid chandeliers. They were glass-bottomed steel tubs, big as children's wading pools, full of cool and oozy radiance. Thick, white, luminescent goo. It threw weird shadows on the dents and ripples of the cardboard ceiling.

It was loud here: industrial chugging and gurgling, with the busy whir of loaded motors and the thrum and squeal of plumbing. The warm, moist air smelled bland and pleasant, like boiled rice. With strange reeks cutting through—the chemical tang of acid, a chalk-dust whiff of lime. A plumber's dope dream: great towers of ribbed stainless steel, jutting three stories tall, their knobby bases snaked with tubing. Indicator lights in Christmas-tree red and green, glossy readout panels shining like cheap jewelry. . . . Scores of crew people in white paper overalls—checking readouts, leaning over long, glass-topped troughs full of steamy, roiling oatmeal . . .

They followed Andrei down the stairs, David carefully scanning everything and mumbling into his set. "Why aren't they wearing scrub gear?" Laura asked.

"*We* wear the scrub gear," Andrei said. "It's clean down here. But we have wild bugs on our skin." He laughed. "Don't sneeze or touch things."

Three flights down, still above the hull, they detoured onto a catwalk. It led to glass-fronted offices, which overlooked the plant from a bamboo pier.

Andrei led them inside. It was quiet and cool in the offices, with filtered air and electric lights. There were desks, phones, office calendars, a fridge beside stacked cartons of canned Pepsi-Cola. Like an office back in the States, Laura thought, looking around. Maybe twenty years behind the times . . .

A door marked "PRIVATE" opened suddenly, and an Anglo man backed through it. He was working a pump-piston aerosol spray. He turned and noticed them. "Oh! Hi, uh, Andrei. . . ."

"Hello," Laura said. "I'm Laura Webster, this is David, my husband. . . ."

"Oh, it's you folks! Where's your baby?" Unlike everyone they'd seen so far, the stranger wore a suit and tie. It was an old suit, in the flashy "Taipan" style that had been all the rage, ten years ago. "Didn't want to bring the little guy down here, huh? Well it's perfectly safe, you needn't have worried." He peered at them; light gleamed from his glasses. "You can take off those masks, it's okay inside here. . . . You don't have, like, flu or anything?"

Laura pulled her mask below her chin. "No."

"I'll have to ask you not to use the, um, toilets." He paused. "It's all linked together down here, see—all sealed tight and recycled. Water, oxygen, the works! Just like a space station.'' He smiled.

"This is Dr. Prentis,'' Andrei told them.

"Oh!'' Prentis said. "Yeah. I'm kind of the head honcho down here, as you must've guessed. . . . You're Americans, right? Call me Brian.''

"A pleasure, Brian.'' David offered his hand.

Prentis winced. "Sorry, now, that's not kosher, either. . . . You guys want a Pepsi?'' He set his sprayer on a desk and opened the fridge. "Got some Doo-Dads, Twinkies, beef jerky . . .''

"Uh, we just ate. . . .'' David was listening to something online. "Thanks anyway.''

"All plastic-sealed, all perfectly safe! Right out of the carton! You're sure? Laura?'' Prentis popped a Pepsi. "Oh, well, all the more for me.''

"My contact online,'' David said. "She wants to know if you're the Brian Prentis who did the paper on . . . I'm sorry, I didn't quite catch that—polysaccharide something.''

Prentis nodded, shortly. "Yeah. I did that.''

"Reception's a little scratchy down here,'' David apologized.

"At Ohio State. Long time ago,'' Prentis said. "Who is this person? Somebody from your Rizome, right?''

"Professor Millie Syers, a Rizome Fellow at North Carolina State . . .''

"Never heard of her,'' Prentis said. "So! What's new Stateside, huh? How about that 'L.A. Live' comedy show? I never miss an episode.''

"They say it's very funny,'' Laura said. She never watched it.

"Those guys who do the 'Breadhead Brothers,' they slay me.'' Prentis paused. "We can get everything down here, y'know. Anything that hits the Net—not just American! Those Stateside cable companies, they edit out a lot. Brazilian exotics . . .'' He winked clumsily. "And that Japanese blue stuff—whew!''

"Porn doesn't sell like it used to,'' Laura said.

"Yeah, they're stuffy, they're uptight,'' Prentis nodded. "I don't hold with that. I believe in total openness . . . honesty, y'know? People shouldn't go through life with blinders on.''

"Can you tell us what you do here?" Laura said.

"Oh. Surely. We use auxotrophic *E. coli,* they're homoserine auxotrophs mostly, though we use double auxotrophy if we're trying anything ticklish. . . . And the fermenters, the tower rigs, those are saccharomyces. . . . It's a standard strain, Pruteen copyright, nothing very advanced, just tried-and-true scop technology. At eighty percent capacity, we pump about fifteen metric tons per rig per day, dry weight. . . . Of course we don't leave it raw, though. We do a lot of what they call cosmetics—palate work."

Prentis walked toward the windows. "Those smaller troughs are bell-and-whistle rigs. Texture, flavoring, secondary fermentation . . ." He smiled at Laura, glassily. "It's very much the normal things that any housewife might do in the comfort of her own kitchen! Blenders, microwaves, eggbeaters; just a little scaled up, that's all."

Prentis glanced at David and away; the dark glasses bothered him. He looked to Laura, gazing raptly at her bustline. "It's not so new, really. If you've ever eaten bread or cheese or beer, you're eating molds and yeasts. All that stuff: tofu, soy sauce; you'd be amazed what they have to go through to make soy sauce. And believe it or not, it's far safer than so-called natural foods. Fresh vegetables!" Prentis barked with laughter. "They're chock-full of natural poisons! There are cases on record where people have died outright from eating potatoes!"

"Hey," David said, "you're preaching to the converted, amigo."

Laura turned away toward the windows. "This isn't exactly new to us, Dr. Prentis. Rizome has a synthetic foods division. . . . I did some P.R. for them once."

"But that's good, that's good!" Prentis said, nodding in surprise. "People have, you know, absurd prejudices. . . . About 'eating germs.' "

"Maybe they did years ago," Laura said. "But nowadays it's mostly a class thing—that it's poor people's food. Cattle feed."

Andrei folded his arms. "A bourgeois Yankee notion . . ."

"Well, it's a marketing problem," Laura said. "But I agree with you. Rizome sees nothing wrong with feeding hungry people. We have our own expertise in this—and it's the kind of technology transfer that might be very helpful to a developing industry. . . ." She paused. "I heard your speech upstairs, Andrei, and there's more common ground between us than you may think."

David chimed in, nodding. "There's a game in the States now called Worldrun. I play it a lot, it's very popular. . . . Protein tech, like this, is one of your major tools for world stability. Without it, there are food riots, cities crumble, governments go down. . . . And not just in Africa, either."

"This is work," Andrei said. "Not a game."

"We don't make that distinction," David told him seriously. "We don't have 'work' in Rizome—just things to do, and people to do them." He smiled winningly. "For us, play is learning . . . you play Worldrun, and you learn that you can't sit on your ass and let things go to hell. You can't just take a salary, make a profit, be a dead weight in the system. In Rizome, we know this—hell, that's why we came to Grenada."

He turned to Prentis. "I got a copy on my rig—call me up, I can download it for you. You too, Andrei."

Prentis snickered. "Uh, I can access the Bank from here, David. . . . Computer games, they've got a couple hundred thousand on file, all kinds, all languages. . . ."

"Pirated?" Laura said.

Prentis ignored her. "But Worldrun, I'll give it a shot, could be fun, I like to keep up with what's new. . . ."

David touched his earpiece. "How long have you been in Grenada, Dr. Prentis?"

"Ten years four months," Prentis said. "And very rewarding work, too." He gestured out at the thudding rigs outside the glass. "You look at this and you may think: secondhand plant, jury-rig, corner cutting. . . . But we got something they'll never match Stateside. We got the True Entrepreneurial Spirit. . . ." Prentis stepped behind the desk and yanked open a bottom drawer.

He started piling things on the scarred tabletop: pipe cleaners, X-acto knives, a magnifying glass, a stack of tape cassettes held with a rubber band. "We'll tackle anything here, shake it, turn it upside down, look at any angle . . . you can blue-sky it, brainstorm. . . . The money boys here, they're not like those jaspers back Stateside; once they trust you, well, it's just like a block grant, only better. You get True Intellectual Freedom. . . .''

More crap hit the desk: rubber stamps, paperweights, molecular tinker toys. ''And they know how to party, too! You might not think so to see those Movement cadres up-deck, but you never seen a carnival fête in Grenada. . . . They go ape! They really know how to get loose. . . . Oh, here it is.'' He pulled out an unmarked tube; it looked like toothpaste. ''Now this is something!''

''What is it?'' David said.

''What? Just the greatest suntan lotion ever made, that's all!'' He tossed it to David. ''We invented this right here in Grenada. It's not just sunscreens and emollients. Hell, that old crap just layers the epidermis. But this soaks right into the cells, changes the reaction structure. . . .''

David unscrewed the cap. A sharp, minty reek filled the room. ''Whew!'' He recapped it.

''No, keep it.''

David stuck the tube in his pocket. ''I haven't seen this on the market. . . .''

''Hell, no, you haven't. And you know why? 'Cause the Yankee health feds flunked it, that's why. A 'mutagen risk.' 'Carcinogenic.' In a pig's eye, brother!'' Prentis slammed the drawer shut. ''Raw sunlight! Now *that's* a *real* cancer risk. But no, they'll let that go, won't they? 'Cause it's 'natural.' '' Prentis sneered. ''Sure, you use that lotion every day for forty years, maybe you get a little problem. Or maybe you already got gastric ulcers from booze! That'll wreck you from top to bottom, but you don't see them banning alcohol, do you? Goddamn hypocrites.''

''I take your point,'' Laura said. ''But look what's been done about cigarettes. Alcohol's a drug too, and people's attitudes—''

Prentis stiffened. ''You're not gonna start in on that, are you? Drugs?'' He glared at Andrei.

''The *Charles Nogues* is a food ship,'' Andrei said. ''I have told them this already.''

''I don't make dope!'' Prentis said. ''You believe that?''

"Sure," David said, surprised.

"People come down here, they try and hit off me," Prentis complained. "They say, 'Hey Brian, pal, bet you got tons of syncoke, never miss a couple teaspoons for us, huh?'" He glared. "Well, I'm off that. Totally."

Laura blinked. "We weren't trying to imply—"

Prentis pointed angrily at David. "Look, he's listening. What are they telling you on the Net, huh? All about me, I bet. Jesus Christ." Prentis stamped out from behind the desk.

"They never forget, do they? Sure, I'm famous! I did it—the Prentis Polysaccharide Process—man, I made millions for Biogen. And they had me on hot proteins, too. . . ." He held up thumb and finger. "I was that far from the Nobel, maybe! But that was live bioactives, Type Three Security. So they made me piss in a cup." He glared at Laura. "You know what that means."

"Drug tests," Laura said. "Like for airline pilots. . . ."

"I had this girl friend," Prentis said slowly. "Kind of a live wire. Not one of those Goddess types, but, you know, a party girl. . . . 'Brian,' she says, 'you'll make it really smooth, behind a couple lines.' And she was right!" He whipped off his glasses. "Goddamn it, she was the most fun I ever had."

"I'm sorry," Laura said in the sudden embarrassed silence. "Did they fire you?"

"Not at first. But they took me off everything important, wanted to give me to their goddamn shrinks. . . . A lab like that, it's like a fuckin' monastery. 'Cause what if you crack, y'know, what if you run out with some Jell-O in your pocket . . . dangerous Jell-O . . . *patented* Jell-O."

"Yeah, it's tough," David told him. "I guess they pretty much run your social life."

"Well, more fools they," Prentis said, a little calmer now. "Guys with imagination . . . visionaries . . . we need elbow room. Space to relax. An outfit like Biogen, it ends up with bureaucrats. Drones. That's why they're not getting anywhere." He put his glasses back on. Then he sat on the desk, swinging his feet. "A conspiracy, that's what it is. All those Net multinationals, they're in each other's pockets. It's a closed market, no real competition. That's why they're fat and lazy. But not here."

"But if it's dangerous . . ." Laura began.

"Dangerous? Hell, I'll show you *dangerous.*" Prentis brightened. "Stay here, I'll be back, you gotta see this. Everybody oughta see this."

He hopped down and vanished into his back office.

Laura and David traded uneasy glances. They looked at Andrei. Andrei nodded. "He's right, you know."

Prentis emerged. He was brandishing a yard-long scimitar.

"Jesus Christ!" David said.

"It's from Singapore," Prentis said. "They make 'em for the Third World market. You ever see one of these?" He waved it. David stepped backward. "It's a machete," Prentis said impatiently. "You're a Texan, right? You must have seen a machete before."

"Yeah," David said. "For clearing brush . . ."

Prentis slammed the machete down, overhand. It hit the desk with a shriek. The desk's corner flew off and hit the floor, spinning.

The machete blade had sheared completely through the wooden desk. It had sliced off an eight-inch triangle of tabletop, including two sections of desk wall and the back of a drawer.

Prentis picked up the severed chunk and set it on the desk like a little wooden pyramid. "Not a splinter! You want to give it a try, Dave?"

"No thanks," David said.

Prentis grinned. "Go ahead! I can superglue it right back; I do this all the time. You're sure?" He held the machete loosely, at arm's length, and let it fall. It sank half an inch into the desktop.

"A wicked knife," Prentis said, dusting his hands. "Maybe you think that's dangerous, but you don't see it all, yet. You know what that is? That's peasant technology, brother. It's slash-and-burn agriculture. You know what that might do to what's left of the planet's tropical forests? It'll make every straw-hat Brazilian into Paul Bunyan, that's what. The most dangerous bio-tech in the world is a guy with a goat and an axe."

"Ax, hell," David blurted, "that thing's a monster! It can't be legal!" He leaned toward the desk and scanned it with his glasses. "I can see I never thought this through . . . I know we use ceramic blades in machine-tools . . . but that's in factory settings, with safety standards! You can't just sell 'em to all and sundry—it's like handing out personal flame-throwers!"

Andrei spoke up. "Don't tell us, David—tell Singapore. They are radical technical capitalists. They don't care about forests—they have no forests to lose."

Laura nodded. "That's not farming, it's mass destruction. That'll have to be stopped," she said.

Prentis shook his head. "We got one chance to stop it, and that's to put every goddamn farmer in the world out of business." He paused. "Yeah, honest old Mr. Yeoman Farmer, and the wife, and his million goddamn kids. They're eating the planet alive."

Prentis reached absently through the hole in the desk and pulled out a tube of glue. "That's all that matters. Sure, maybe we've cooked a little dope in Grenada, liberated a few programs, but that's just for start-up money. We make food. And we make jobs to make food. See all those people working down there? You wouldn't see 'em in a Stateside plant. The way we do it here, it's labor-intensive—people who might have been farmers, making their own food, for their own country. Not just handouts, dumped from some charity plane by rich nations."

"We have no quarrel with that," Laura said.

"Sure you do," Prentis said. "You don't want it stripped down and cheap. You want it expensive, and controlled, and totally safe. You don't want peasants and slum kids with that kind of technical power. You're afraid of it." He pointed to the machete. "But you can't have it both ways. All tech is dangerous—even with no moving parts."

Long silence. Laura turned to Andrei. "Thanks for bringing us down here. You've brought us in touch with a genuine problem." She turned to Prentis. "Thank you, Brian."

"Sure," said Prentis. His gaze flickered upward from her breasts. She tried to smile at him.

Prentis set the glue down carefully. "You want to tour the plant?"

"I'd love to," David said.

They left the office, reassuming their masks. They went down among the workers. The crew didn't look much like "slum kids"—they were mostly middle-aged cadres, most of them women. They wore hair nets and their paper overalls had the shiny look of old bakery bags. They worked in twenty-four-hour shifts—a third of the crew was asleep, in soundproof acoustic cubicles, clustered under the giant mural like Styrofoam barnacles.

Backed by Millie Syers, David asked alert questions about the equipment. Any containment spills? No. Souring trouble? Just the usual throwbacks to the wild state—tailored bacteria did tend to revert, after millions of generations. And wild bugs wouldn't produce—they just ate goop and freeloaded. Left to multiply at the expense of the worthy, these backsliders would soon take over, so they were scorched from the tanks without mercy.

What about the rest of the *Charles Nogues,* beyond the bulkheads? Why, she was full of factories like this from bow to stern, all safety-sealed so spoiling couldn't spread. Lots of careful slurry-pumping back and forth between units—they used the old tanker pumps, still in fine condition. The ship's containment systems, built to prevent petroleum gas explosions, were ideal for bio-hazard work.

Laura quizzed some of the women. Did they like the work? Of course—they had all kinds of special perks, credit-card boosts whenever they beat the quotas, TV links with their families, special rewards for successful new recipes. . . . Didn't they feel cooped up down here? Heavens no, not compared to the crowded government yards down-the-island. A whole month vacation time, too. Of course, it did itch a bit when you got that skin bacteria back. . . .

They toured the plant for over an hour, climbing bamboo stiles over the hull's six-foot reinforcement girders. David spoke to Prentis. "You said something about bathrooms?"

"Yeah, sorry. *E. coli,* that's a native gut bacterium. . . . If it gets loose, we have a lot of trouble."

David shrugged, embarrassed. "The food upstairs was good, I ate a lot. Uh, my compliments to the chef."

"Thanks," Prentis said.

David touched his glasses. "I think I've scanned pretty

much everything. . . . If Atlanta has questions, could we get in touch?''

"Uhmmm . . .'' Prentis said. Andrei broke in. "That's a bit difficult, David.'' He didn't elaborate.

David forgot and offered to shake hands again. When they left, they could see Prentis stalking behind the office glass, pumping his spray gun.

They retraced their steps up the catwalk. Andrei was pleased. "I'm glad you met Dr. Prentis. He's very dedicated. But he does get a bit lonely for his native countrymen.''

"He does seem to lack a few of the amenities,'' David said.

"Yeah,'' Laura said. "Like a girl friend.''

Andrei was surprised. "Oh, Dr. Prentis is married. To a Grenadian worker.''

"Oh,'' Laura said, feeling the gaffe. "That must be wonderful. . . . How about you, Andrei? Are you married?''

"Only to the Movement,'' Andrei said. He wasn't kidding.

The sun was setting by the time they returned to their safehouse. It had been a long day. "You must be tired, Carlotta,'' Laura said as they climbed stiffly from the three-wheeler. "Why don't you come in and have supper with us?''

"It's nice to ask,'' Carlotta said, smiling sweetly. Her eyes glistened and there was a soft rosy glow to her cheeks. "But I can't make it tonight. I have Communion.''

"You're sure?'' Laura said. "Tonight's good for us.''

"I can come by later this week. And bring my date, maybe.''

Laura frowned. "I might be testifying then.''

Carlotta shook her head. "No, you won't. I haven't even testified yet.'' She reached from the driver's seat and patted the baby's tote. "Bye, little one. Bye, y'all. I'll call or something.'' She gunned the engine, kicking gravel, and drove through the gates.

"Typical,'' Laura said.

They walked up onto the porch. David pulled his key card. "Well, Communion, that sounds pretty important—''

"Not Carlotta, she's just a klutz. I mean the Bank. It's a ploy, don't you see? They're gonna make us cool our heels here in this big old barn, instead of letting me make my case. And they're calling Carlotta to testify first, just to rub it in.''

David paused. ''You think so, huh?''

''Sure. That's why Sticky was giving us the runaround earlier.'' She followed him into the mansion. ''They're working on us, David; this is all part of a plan. That tour, everything. . . . What smells so good?''

Rita had dinner waiting. It was stuffed pork with peppers and parsley, Creole ratatouille, hot baked bread and chilled rum soufflé for dessert. In a candlelit dining room with fresh linen and flowers. It was impossible to refuse. Not without offending Rita. Someone they had to share the house with, after all. . . . At the very least, they had to try a few bites, just for politeness sake. . . . And after all that nasty scop, too. . . . It was all so delicious it stung. Laura ate like a wolverine.

And no dishes to wash. The servants cleared everything, stacking it onto little rosewood trolleys. They brought brandy and offered Cuban cigars. And they wanted to take the baby too. Laura wouldn't let them.

There was a study upstairs. It wasn't much of a study—no books—just hundreds of videotapes and old-fashioned plastic records, but they retired to the study with their brandies anyway. It seemed the proper thing to do, somehow.

Lots of old framed photos on the study's walls. Laura looked them over while David shuffled curiously through the tapes. It was clear who Mr. Gelli, the former owner, was. He was the puffy-faced hustler throwing a good-buddy arm over vaguely familiar, vaguely repulsive Vegas show-biz types. . . . Here he was toadying up to some snake-eyed goofball in a long white dress—with a start, Laura realized it was the Pope.

David loaded a tape. He sat on the couch—an overstuffed monster in purple velour—and fired up the TV with a clunky remote. Laura joined him. ''Find something?''

''Home movies, I think. He's got lots—I picked out the most recent.''

A party at the mansion. Big ugly cake in the dining room, smorgasbord groaning with food. ''I shouldn't have eaten so much,'' Laura said.

"Look at that jerk in the party hat," David said. "That's a mad doctor, for sure. Can you see that, Atlanta?"

Faint squeaking came from Laura's earpiece; she was wearing it loose, and it dangled. She felt a little funny about having shared the earpiece with Carlotta; kind of like sharing a toothbrush, or like sharing a . . . well, best not to think about that one. "Why don't you take that off, David?" She removed her own glasses and pointed them at the door, guarding them from intruders. "We're safe here, right? No worse than the bedroom."

"Well . . ." David froze the tape and got up. He punched an intercom button by the door. "Hello. Um, Jimmy? Yeah, I want you to bring us that plug-in clock by the bedside. Right away. Thanks." He returned to the couch.

"You shouldn't do that," Laura said.

"You mean order them around like they were servants? Yeah, I know. Very non-R. I got some ideas though—I want to talk to Personnel about it, tomorrow. . . ." Discreet knock at the door. David took the clock from Jimmy. "No, nothing else . . . okay, go ahead, bring the bottle." He plugged his headset into the clock. "How's that, Atlanta?"

["You might as well point one set at the TV,"] the clock told him loudly. ["Watching that door's pretty boring."] Laura didn't recognize the guy's voice; some Rizomian on the night shift, she'd given up caring at this point.

The tape spooled on; David had muted the sound. "Lotta Anglos at this gig," David commented. "I miss the Rastas."

Laura sipped her brandy. It wrapped her mouth in molten gold. "Yeah," she said, inhaling over the glass. "There's a lot of different factions on this island, and I don't think they get along too well. There's the Movement revolutionaries . . . and the Voodoo mystics . . . and the high-techies . . . and the low-techies . . ."

"And the street poor, just looking for food and a roof . . ." Knock knock knock; the brandy had arrived. David brought it to the couch. "You realize this could be poisoning us." He refilled their snifters.

"Yeah, but I felt worse when I left Loretta behind with Carlotta, she's been so good since then, I was afraid Carlotta'd slipped her some kind of happy-pill. . . ." She kicked off her shoes and curled her legs beneath her. "David, these people know what they're doing. If they want to poison us they could do it with some speck of something we would never even see."

"Yeah, I kept telling myself that, while I ate the ratatouille." Some rich drunk had collared the cameraman and was shouting gleefully into the lens. "Look at this clown! I forgot to mention the local faction of pure criminal sleazebags. . . . Takes all kinds to make a data haven, I guess."

"It doesn't add up," Laura said, sinking easily into brandy-fueled meditation. "It's like beachcombing after a storm, all kinds of Net flotsam thrown up on the golden Grenadian shore. . . . So if you push on these people, maybe they go neatly to pieces, if you hit the right flaw. But too much pressure, and it all welds together and you got a monster on your hands. I was thinking today—the old Nazis, they used to believe in the Hollow Earth and all kinds of mystical crap. . . . But their trains ran on time and their state cops were efficient as hell. . . ."

David took her hand, looking at her curiously. "You're really into this, aren't you?"

"It's important, David. The most important thing we've ever done. You bet I'm involved. All the way."

He nodded. "I noticed you seemed a little tense when I grabbed your ass in the elevator."

She laughed, briefly. "I was nervous . . . it's good to relax here, just us." Some moron in a bow tie was singing on a makeshift stage, some slick-haired creep pausing to make wisecracks and snappy in-joke banter. . . . Camera kept moving to men in the audience, Big Operators laughing at themselves with the bogus joviality of Big Operators laughing at themselves. . . .

David put his arm around her. She leaned her head onto his shoulder. He wasn't taking this as seriously as she did, she thought. Maybe because he hadn't been standing there with Winston Stubbs . . .

She cut off that ugly thought and had more brandy. "You should have picked an earlier tape," she told him. "Maybe we could get a look at the place before old Gelli brought his decorators in."

"Yeah, I haven't seen our pal Gelli in any of this. Must be his nephew's party, or something. . . . Whoa!"

The tape had switched scenes. It was later now, outside, by the pool. A late-night swim party, lots of torches, towels . . . and opulent young women in bikini bottoms. "Holy cow," David said in his comedian's voice. "Naked broads! Man, this guy really knows how to live!"

A crowd of young women, next to nude. Sipping drinks, combing wet hair with long, sensuous strokes and their elbows out. Lying full length, drowsy or stoned, as if expecting a tan by torchlight. A full-color assortment of them, too. "Good to see some black people have finally shown up," Laura said sourly.

"Those girls must have crashed the gig," David said. "No room in that gear for invites."

"Are they hookers?"

"Gotta be."

Laura paused. "I hope this isn't going to turn into an orgy or anything."

"No," David said callously, "look at the way the camera follows their tits. He wouldn't be getting this excited if there was anything hot and heavy coming up." He set his empty glass down. "Hey, you can see part of the old back garden in that shot—" He froze the image.

["Hey,"] the clock protested.

"Sorry," David said. The tape kept rolling. Men enjoyed seeing women this way—rolling hips, jiggle, that soft acreage of tinted female skin. Laura thought about it, the brandy hitting her. It didn't do much for her. But despite David's pretended nonchalance she could feel him reacting a little. And in some odd, vicarious way that itself was a little exciting.

For once there was no one looking at them, she thought wickedly. Maybe if they curled up on the couch and were very, very quiet . . .

A slim brown girl with ankle bracelets mounted the diving board. She sauntered to the end, bent gracefully, and went into a hand-stand. She held it for five long seconds, then plunged head-first. . . . "Jesus Christ!" David said. He froze it in mid-splash.

Laura blinked. "What's so special about—"

"Not her, babe. Look." He ran it backward; the girl flew up feet-first, then grabbed the board. She bent at the waist, strolled backward . . . She froze again. "There," David said. "There to the far right, by the water. It's Gelli. Lying in that lawn chair."

Laura stared. "It sure is . . . he looks thinner."

"Look at him move. . . ." The girl walked the board . . . and Gelli's head was wobbling. A spastic movement, compulsive, with his chin rolling in a ragged figure eight, and his eyes fixed on nothing at all. And then he stopped the wobbling, caught it somehow, leering with the pain of effort. And his hand came up, a wizened hand like a bundle of sticks, bent down acutely at the wrist.

In the foreground, the girl balanced gracefully, slim legs held straight, toes pointed like a gymnast. And behind her Gelli went touch-touch-touch, three little dabs of movement to his face—fast, jerky, totally ritualized. Then the girl plunged, and the camera slid away. And Gelli vanished.

"What's wrong with him?" Laura whispered.

David was pale, his mouth tight-set. "I don't know. Some nerve disorder, obviously."

"Parkinson's disease?"

"Maybe. Or maybe something we don't even have a name for."

David killed the television. He stood up and unplugged the clock. He put on his glasses, carefully. "I'm gonna go answer some mail, Laura."

I'll come with you." She didn't sleep for a long time. And there were nightmares, too.

Next morning, they inspected the foundations for settling and dry rot. They opened every window, making note of cracked glass and warped lintels. They checked the attic for drooping joists and moldy insulation, checked the stairs for springy boards, measured the slopes of the floor, cataloged the multitude of cracks and bulges in the walls.

The servants watched them with growing anxiety. At lunch they had a little discussion. Jimmy, it transpired, considered himself a "butler," while Rajiv was a "majordomo" and Rita a "cook" and "nanny." They weren't a construction crew. To David this sounded ludicrously old-fashioned; things needed doing, so why not do them? What was the problem?

They responded with wounded pride. They were skilled house staff, not no-account rudies from the government yards. They had certain places to fill and certain work that came with the places. Everybody knew this. It had always been so.

David laughed. They were acting like nineteenth-century colonials, he said; what about Grenada's high-tech, anti-imperialist revolution? Surprisingly, this argument failed to move them. Fine, David said at last. If they didn't want to help, it was no problem of his. They could prop up their feet and drink piña coladas.

Or maybe they could watch some television, Laura suggested. As it happened, she had some Rizome recruiting tapes that might help explain how Rizome felt about things. . . .

After lunch Laura and David continued their inspection remorselessly. They climbed up into the turrets, where the servants had their quarters. The floors were splintery, the roofs leaked, and the intercoms had shorted out. Before they left Laura and David deliberately made all the beds.

During the afternoon David caught some sun in the bottom of the dead pool. Laura played with the baby. Later David checked the electrical system while she answered the mail. Supper was fantastic, again. They were tired and made an early night of it.

The Bank was ignoring them. They returned the favor.

Next day David got out his tool chest. He made a little unconscious ritual of it, like a duke inspecting his emeralds. The toolbox weighed fifteen pounds, was the size of a large breadbox, and had been lovingly assembled by Rizome craftsmen in Kyoto. Looking inside, with the gleam of chromed ceramic and neat foam sockets for everything, you could get a kind of mental picture of the guys who had made it—white-robed Zen priests of the overhead lathe, guys who lived on brown rice and machine oil. . . .

Pry bar, tin snips, cute little propane torch; plumbing snake, pipe wrench, telescoping auger; ohm meter, wire stripper, needlenose pliers . . . Ribbed ebony handles that popped off and reattached to push drills and screwdriver bits . . . David's tool set was by far the most expensive possession they owned.

They worked on the plumbing all morning—starting on the servants' bathroom. Hard, filthy work, with lots of creeping about on one's back. After his afternoon sun worship David stayed outside. He'd found some gardening tools in a shed and tackled the front acreage, stripped to the waist and wearing his videoshades. Laura saw that he had fast-talked the two gate guards into helping him. They were trimming wild ivy and pruning dead branches and joking together.

She had nothing to report to Atlanta, so she spent her time catching flack. Unsurprisingly, there was plenty of gratuitous advice from every corner of the compass. Several idiots expressed grave disappointment that they had not yet toured a secret Grenadian drug lab. A Rizome graphics program was showing up as a pirate knock-off in Cuba—was the Bank involved? Rizome had contacted the Polish government— Warsaw said Andrei Tarkovsky was a black-market operator, wanted for forging false passports.

The Rizome elections were heating up. It looked like the Suvendra race was going to be close. Pereira—Mr. Nice Guy—was making a surprisingly strong showing.

David came in to shower for supper. "You're gonna burn up out there," she told him.

"No, I won't, smell." He reeked of rank male sweat with an undertone of mint. His skin looked waxed.

"Oh no!" she said. "You haven't been using that tube stuff, have you?"

"Sure," David said, surprised. "Prentis claimed it was the best ever—you don't expect me to take that on faith, surely." He examined his forearms. "I used it yesterday, too. I'd swear I'm darker already, and no burn either."

"David, you're hopeless. . . ."

He only smiled. "I think I may have a cigar tonight!"

They had supper. The servants were upset by the recruiting tapes. They wanted to know how much of it was true. All of it, Laura said innocently.

As they lay in bed, she got Atlanta to slot her a Japanese-language tape—mystery stories of Edogawa Rampo. David fell asleep at once, lulled by the meaningless polysyllables. Laura listened as she drifted off, letting the alien grammar soak in to those odd itchy places where the brain stored language. She like Rampo's straight journalistic Japanese, none of those involved circumlocutions and maddening veiled allusions. . . .

Hours later she was shaken awake in darkness. Harsh babble of English. "Babe, wake up, it's news. . . ."

Emily Donato spoke out of the darkness. ["Laura, it's me."]

Laura twisted in the lurching waterbed. The room was dim purples and grays. "Lights, turn on!" she croaked. Flash of overhead glare. She winced at the clock. Two A.M. "What is it, Emily?"

["We got the fact,"] the clock proclaimed, in Emily's familiar voice.

Laura felt a pang of headache. "What fact?"

["The F.A.C.T., Laura. We know who's behind them. Who they really are. It's Molly."]

"Oh, the terrorists," Laura said. A little jolt of shock and fear coursed through her. Now she was awake. "Molly? Molly who?"

["The *government* of Molly,"] Emily said.

"It's a country in North Africa," David said from his side of the bed. "The Republic of Mali. Capital Bamako, main export cotton, population rate two percent." David, the Worldrun player.

"Mali." The name sounded only vaguely familiar. "What do they have to do with anything?"

["We're working on that. Mali's one of those Sahara famine countries, with an army regime, it's nasty there. . . . The F.A.C.T. is their front group. We've got it from three different sources."]

"Who?" Laura said.

["Kymera, I. G. Farben, and the Algerian State Department."]

"Sounds good," Laura said. She trusted Kymera Corporation —the Japanese didn't throw accusations lightly. "What does the Vienna heat say?"

["Nothing. To butt out. They're covering something up, I think. Mali never signed the Vienna Convention. . . ."] Emily paused. ["The Central Committee meets tomorrow. Some people from Kymera and Farben are flying in. We all think it smells."]

"What do you want us to do?" Laura said.

["Tell the Bank when you testify. It wasn't Singapore that killed their man. Or the European Commerzbank either. It was the secret police in Mali."]

"Jesus," Laura said. "Okay . . ."

["I'm sending you some backup data on a coded line. . . . Good night, Laura. I'm up late, too, if it helps."]

Emily signed off.

"Wow . . ." Laura shook her head, clearing the last cobwebs. "Things are really moving. . . ." She turned to her husband—"Yike!"

"Yeah," David said. He stretched out one arm, showing it to her. "I'm, uh, black."

"David . . . you're black!" Laura yanked the sheet back, revealing his bare chest and stomach. She could feel her neck bristle in astonishment. "David, look at you. Your skin is black! All over!"

"Yeah . . . I was sunbathing nude in the pool." He shrugged sheepishly, his shoulders dark against the crisp white pillow. "You remember that ship's officer—a blond, black guy—back on the *Charles Nogues?* I wondered, when I saw him . . ."

Laura blinked, trying to think back. "The blond black man . . . Yeah, but I thought he'd dyed his hair . . ."

"His hair was natural, but he'd changed his skin. It's that suntan oil Prentis gave me. It affects the skin pigment, the melanin, I guess. It's a little patchy down here by my, uh, crotch . . . like I got very dark freckles, but big, kinda splotchy. . . . I should've asked how it works."

"It's obvious how it works, David—it makes you black!" Laura began laughing, her mind pinched between the shocking and the ridiculous. He looked so different. . . . "Do you feel all right, sweetheart?"

"I feel fine," he said coolly. "How do you feel about it?"

"Let me look at you. . . ." She sneaked a look at his crotch and began giggling helplessly. "Oh . . . It's not that funny but . . . Oh, David, you look like a horny giraffe." She rubbed his shoulder, hard, with her thumb. "It's not coming off, is it. . . . Honey, you've really done it this time."

"This is revolutionary," he said soberly.

A fit of laughter seized her.

"I mean it, Laura. You can be black, from a tube. Don't you see what that means?"

She bit her knuckle until she got control of herself. "David, people don't want to risk skin cancer, just so they can be black."

"Why not? I would. We live under a hard Texas sun. All Texans ought to be black. In that kind of climate, it's best for you. Sensible."

She stared at him, biting her lip. "This is just too, too weird. . . . You're not really black, David. You've got an Anglo nose, and Anglo mouth. Oh look, here's a patch on your ear that you missed!" She shrieked with laughter.

"Stop that, Laura, you're making me mad." He sat up straighter. "Okay, maybe I'm not black, up close. . . . But in a crowd, I'm a black man. Same in a car, or walking on the street. Or at a political meeting. That could change everything."

His passion surprised her. "Not everything, David, come on. Rizome's CEO is black. America's had a black president, even."

"Bullshit, Laura, don't pretend racism's a dead issue, why do you think Africa's in the mess it's in? Goddamn it, these Grenadians have really got something! I'd heard rumors of stuff like this, but the way they painted it, it was some kind of risky freak experiment. . . . But it's *easy!* I wonder how much they've made? Pounds? Tons?"

David's eyes were full of visionary fire. "I'm gonna walk up to the first Third Worlder I see, and say, 'Hi! I'm a white American imperial exploiter, and I'm black as the ace of spades, compadre.' This is the greatest thing I've ever heard of."

Laura frowned a little. "It's just color. It doesn't change how you feel about yourself, inside. Or the way you act, either."

"The hell you say. Even a new haircut can do that much." He leaned back against the pillow, cradling his head. His armpits were splotchy. "I gotta get more of this stuff."

Now he was involved. At last. It had taken something very weird to jolt him, but now he was with her all the way. He'd found something to galvanize him, and he was off and running. He had that look in his eyes again. Just like when they were first married, back when they were planning the Lodge together. She felt glad.

She reached across his chest, admiring the svelte contrast of her arm against his dark ribs. "You look good, David, really. . . . It suits you somehow. . . . I guess I never told you this, but I always had a kind of minor thing for black guys." She kissed his shoulder. "I knew this guy in high school, he and I—"

David clambered suddenly out of bed. "Atlanta, who's online?"

["Uh, the name's Nash, Thomas Nash, you don't know me . . ."]

"Tom, I want you to get a look at this." David picked up his glasses and scanned himself head to foot. "What do you think of that?"

["Um, seem to be having some trouble with brightness levels, Rizome Grenada. Also, you're not wearing clothes. Right?"]

Laura waited for David to come back to bed. Instead he started calling people. She fell asleep again while he was still ranting.

5

THEY were under the mansion's foundations with a hydraulic jack when they heard Sticky calling. "Yo Bwana, Blondie! You be comin' out now, time to face the music. . . ."

They wormed their way back into afternoon sunlight. Laura hauled herself through the foundation's concrete crawl hole and got to her feet. "Hello, Captain." She picked at her hair, and came away with strings of cobweb.

David crawled out after her. His jeans and denim work shirt were caked at the knees and elbows with stale mud. Sticky Thompson grinned at David's darkened face. "You datin' locals now, Blondie? Where's the Great White Hunter?"

"Very funny," David said.

Sticky led them back around the mansion's west wing. As they walked under newly pruned ylang-ylang trees, David juggled his glasses and jammed the earplug in. "Who's online? Oh. Hi. What? Hell, I got mud on my lenses." He cleaned them with his shirt tail, ruefully.

Two military jeeps were waiting on the gravel drive—olive-drab hardtops with silvered windows. Three uniformed militiamen sat on the flat, square bumpers, sipping soft drinks from paper cartons. Sticky whistled sharply; the skinniest guard leapt to attention and opened one door. A colored decal flashed on the door panel: garish red, gold, and green—the Grenadian flag. "Truth-tellin' time, Mrs. Webster. We ready when you are."

"She'll need to change—" David said.

"No, I won't," Laura broke in. "I'm ready at any time. Unless your Bank thinks I'll soil their upholstery." She pulled her glasses from a buttoned shirt pocket.

Sticky turned to David, pointing to the second jeep. "We got a special tourist show for you, today. This other jeep be escort duty for you, they driving you down to the beach. We got some very special building projects. You be loving this one, Dave."

"Okay," David told him. "But I gotta finish some bracing work under the house first, or the kitchen falls in." He gave Laura a sudden hard hug. "Looks like I'm taking the baby today." He whispered into her ear. "Luck, babe. Give 'em hell." She kissed him hard. The soldiers grinned at them.

Laura climbed up into the jeep's front passenger seat. One of the soldiers got in back, his assault rifle clattering. Sticky lingered outside. He had slipped on a pair of polarized glasses. He scanned the sky carefully, shading his eyes with both hands. Satisfied, he vaulted into the driver's seat and slammed the door.

Sticky fired the engine with an old-fashioned ignition key. He took the estate's winding curves at hair-raising speed, driving loosely, easily, one dark hand on the steering wheel. Laura understood now why his skin color had varied. It wasn't makeup, but chameleon technical tricks, right down in the cells. Lots of changes—maybe too many. The little half-moons of his fingernails looked oddly yellowish. He'd been gnawing them, too.

He grinned at her breezily—now that he was driving, he seemed elated, high. Stimulants, Laura thought darkly. "Aren't you a sight," Sticky told her. "I can't believe you didn't call time for pattin' on a little rouge."

Laura touched her cheek involuntarily. "You mean video makeup, Captain? I understood this was to be a closed hearing."

"Oooh," Sticky said, amused at her formality. "That's seen, now. Long as the camera not lookin', you can run around in you grubbies, play dress-up all workin' class, huh?" He laughed. "What if you college-girl pal see you? The one what dress up all southern belle slavery drag? Emily Donato?"

"Emily's my closest friend," Laura told him tightly. "She's seen me a lot worse than this, believe me."

Sticky raised his brows. He spoke lightly. "You ever

wonder about this Donato and your husband? She knew him before you did. Introduced you, even.''

Laura throttled her instant spurt of anger. She waited a moment. ''You been having fun, Sticky? Running barefoot through my personnel file? I'll bet that gives you a real feeling of power, huh? Kind of like bullying teenage guards in this toy militia of yours.''

Sticky glanced sharply at the rearview mirror. The guard in the back pretended not to have heard.

They took the highway south. The sky was leaden with overcast, the greenish mounds of trees gone dusky and strange on misty volcanic slopes. ''You think I don't know what you up to?'' Sticky said. ''All this workin' on the house? For no pay—just to make an impression. Giving the servants propaganda tapes. . . . Tryin' to bribe our people.''

''A position in Rizome is hardly bribery,'' Laura said coolly. ''If they work with us, they deserve a place with us.'' They passed an abandoned sugar factory. ''It's tough on them, doing our housework and moonlighting as your domestic spies.''

Sticky glared at her. ''Those bloodclot fuckin' glasses,'' he hissed suddenly.

''Atlanta, I'm going offline,'' Laura said. She ripped off her rig and yanked open the map compartment. A cardboard egg carton of tanglegun ammo fell on her foot. She ignored it and stuffed the rig in—it was squawking—and slammed the little steel door.

Sticky sneered. ''That'll be trouble for you. You'd better put them back on.''

''Fuck it,'' Laura told him. ''It's worth it just to hear you cut that goddamn accent.'' She grinned at him humorlessly. ''C'mon, soldier. Let's have it out. I'm not gonna have you pick on me all the way to the Bank, just to psych me out, or whatever the hell it is you think you're doing.''

Sticky flexed his muscular hands on the steering wheel. ''Aren't you afraid to be alone with me? Now you're off the Net, you're kind of soft and helpless, aren't you?'' He gave her a sudden poke in the ribs with his finger, like testing a side of beef. ''What if I drive off into those trees and get rude with your body?''

"Jesus." That had never even occurred to her. "I dunno, Captain. I guess I tear your goddamned eyes out."

"Oh, tough!" He didn't look at her—he was watching the road, driving fast—but his right hand darted out with unbelievable quickness and caught her wrist with a slap of skin on skin. Her hand went funny-bone numb and a rolling pain shot up her arm. "Pull free," he told her. "Try."

She tugged, feeling the first surge of real fear. It was like pulling on a bench vise. He didn't even quiver. He didn't look that strong, but his bare brown arm had locked like cast iron. Unnatural. "You're hurting me," she said, trying for calmness. A hateful little tremor in her voice.

Sticky laughed triumphantly. "Now, you listen to me, girl. All this time, you—"

Laura sank suddenly in her seat and stamped the brake. The jeep skidded wildly; the soldier in the back cried out. Sticky let her go as if scalded; his hands slapped the wheel with panic speed. They swerved, hit potholes in the road shoulder. Their heads banged the hard ceiling. Two seconds of lurching chaos. Then they were back on the road, weaving.

Safe. Sticky drew a long breath.

Laura sat up and rubbed her wrist silently.

Something truly nasty had happened between them. She felt no fear yet, even though they'd almost died together. She hadn't known it would be so bad—a manual jeep—she'd just done it. On impulse. Rage that had boiled up suddenly, when their inhibitions had vanished, gone with the glass eye of the Net's TV.

Both acting like raging drunks when the Net was gone.

It was over now. The soldier—the boy—in the back seat was gripping his rifle in panic. He hadn't been feeling the Net—it was all a mystery to him, that sudden gust of violence, like a hurricane wind. There for no reason, gone for no reason . . . he didn't even know it was over yet.

Sticky drove on, his jaw set, his eyes straight ahead. "Winston Stubbs," he said at last. "He was my father."

Laura nodded. Sticky had told her this for a reason—it was the only way he knew how to apologize. The news didn't surprise her much, but for a moment she felt her eyes stinging. She leaned back against the seat, relaxing, breathing.

She had to be careful with him. People should be careful with each other. . . .

"You must have been very proud of him," she said. Gently, tentatively. "He was a special kind of man." No answer. "From the way he looked at you, I know that—"

"I failed him," Sticky said. "I was his warrior and the enemy took him."

"We know who did it now," Laura told him. "It wasn't Singapore. It was an African regime—the secret police in the Republic of Mali."

Sticky stared at her as if she'd gone insane. His polarized shades had bounced off during the near wreck and his yellowish eyes gleamed like a weasel's. "Mali's an *African* country," he said.

"Why should that make a difference?"

"We're fighting for African people! Mali . . . they're not even a data haven. They a sufferation country. They have no reason." He blinked. "They're lying to you if they tell you that."

"We know that Mali is the F.A.C.T.," Laura said.

Sticky shrugged. "Anyone can use those letters. They're asking shakedown money, and we know where that's going. To Singapore." He shook his head slowly. "War's coming, Laura. Very bad times. You should never have come to this island."

"We had to come," Laura said. "We were witnesses."

"Witnesses," Sticky said with contempt. "We know what happened in Galveston, we never needed you for that. You're hostages, Laura. You, your man, even the lickle baby. Hostages for Rizome. Your company is in the middle, and if they favor Singapore against us, the Bank will kill you."

Laura licked her lips. She straightened in her seat. "If it comes to war, a lot of innocent people are going to die."

"They've played you for a fool. Your company. They sent you here, and they knew!"

"Wars kill people," Laura said. "David and I are not as innocent as some."

He slammed the wheel with his hand. "Aren't you afraid, girl?"

"Are you, Captain?"

"I'm a soldier."

Laura forced a shrug. "What does that mean in a terror war? They murdered a guest in my house. In front of me and my baby. I'm going to do what I can to get them. I know it's dangerous."

"You're a brave enemy," Sticky said. He pulled onto a secondary road, through a wretched little village of red dirt and rusted tin. They began winding uphill, into the interior. The sun split the clouds for a moment and branches dappled the windshield.

From a hairpin turn high on a hillside, Laura saw the distant clustered harbor of colonial Grand Roy—sleepy red roofs, little white porch-pillars, crooked, sloping streets. A drill rig crouched offshore like a spider from Mars.

"You're a fool," Sticky told her. "You're trying to push some propaganda bullshit that you think will make everybody play nice. But this isn't some mama-papa Yankee shopping mall where you can sell everybody peace like Coca-Cola. It nah going to work. . . . But I don't think you ought to die for tryin'. It's not righteous."

He snapped orders. The militiaman reached behind him and passed Laura a flak jacket and a black, hooded robe. "Put these on," Sticky said.

"All right." Laura buckled the bulky jacket over her work shirt. "What's this bathrobe?"

"It's a *chador*. Islamic women wear them. Real modest . . . and it'll hide that blond hair. There been spy planes where we're going. I don't want 'em seeing you."

Laura tunneled into the robe and pulled the hood over her head. Once inside the baggy thing, she caught a lingering whiff of its previous user—scented cigarettes and attar of roses. "It wasn't the Islamic Bank—"

"We know it's the Bank. They been running spy planes in every day, puddle-jumping over from Trinidad. We know the plantation they're using, everything. We have our own sources—we don't need you to tell us anything." He nodded at the map compartment. "You might as well put on your TV rig. I've said everything I'm saying."

"We don't mean to hurt you or your people, Sticky. We don't mean you anything but good—"

He sighed. "Just do it."

She pulled the glasses out. Emily screeched into her ear. ["What are you doing!? Are you all right?"]

"I'm fine, Emily. Cut me some slack."

["Don't be stupid, Laura. You're gonna damage our credibility in this. No secret negotiations! It looks bad—like they might be getting at you. It's bad enough now, without people thinking that you're going through back channels offline."]

"We be goin' to Fedon's Camp," Sticky said loudly, liltingly. "You listenin', Atlanta? Julian Fedon, he was a Free Coloured. His time was the French Revolution and he preach the Rights of Man. The French smuggle him guns, and he take over plantations, free the slaves, and arm them. He burned out the baccra slaveocrats with righteous fire. And he fight with a gun in his hand when the Redcoats invade . . . it took an army months to break his fort."

They had come into a broken bowl of hills—ragged, volcanic wilderness. A tropical paradise, dotted with tall watchtowers. At first sight they looked blankly harmless, like water towers. But the rounded storage tanks were armored pillboxes, ridged with slotted gun slits. Their gleaming sides were pocked with searchlights and radar blisters, and their tops were flattened for helicopter pads. Thick elevator taproots plunged deep into the earth—no doors were visible anywhere.

They drove uphill on a tall stone roadway of hard, black blasted rock. Excavation rubble. There were mounds of it everywhere, leg-breaking dykes of sharp-edged boulders, half hidden under bird-twittery flowering vines and scrub. . . .

Fedon's Camp was a new kind of fortress. There were no sandbags, no barbed wire, no gates or guards. Just the ranked towers rising mutely from the quiet green earth like deadly mushrooms of ceramic and steel. Towers watching each other, watching the hills, watching the sky.

Tunnels, Laura thought. There must be underground tunnels linking those death towers together—and storage rooms full of ammunition. Everything underground, the towers mushrooming from under the surface in a geometry of strategic fire zones.

What would it be like to attack this place? Laura could imagine angry, hungry rioters with their pathetic torches and

Molotov cocktails—wandering under those towers like mice under furniture. Unable to find anything their own size— anything they could touch or hurt. Growing frightened as their yells were answered by silence—beginning to creep, in muttering groups, into the false protection of the rocks and trees.. While every footstep sounded loud as drumbeats on buried microphones, while their bodies glowed like human candles on some gunner's infrared screens. . . .

The road simply ended, in a half-acre expanse of weedy tarmac. Sticky killed the engine and found his polarized glasses. He peered through the windshield. "Over there, Laura. See?" He pointed into the sky. "By that gray cloud, shaped like a wolf's head . . ."

She couldn't see anything. Not even a speck. "A spy plane?"

"Yeah. From here, they can count your teeth on telephoto. Just the right size, too. . . . Too small for a stupid missile to find, and the smart ones cost more than it does." A rhythmic thudding above them. Laura winced. A skeletal shadow crossed the tarmac. A cargo helicopter was hovering overhead.

Sticky left the jeep. She saw the shadow drop a line, heard it clunk as it hit the hard top of the jeep. Latches clacked shut and Sticky climbed back in. In a moment they were soaring upward. Jeep and all.

The ground fell dizzily. "Hold tight," Sticky said. He sounded bored. The chopper lowered them atop the nearest tower, into a broad yellow net. The net's arms creaked on heavy springs, the whole jeep listing drunkenly; then the arms lowered and they settled to the deck.

Laura climbed out, shaking. The air smelled like dawn in Eden. All around them mountainsides too steep for farming: green-choked hills wreathed with ink-gray mist like a Chinese landscape. The other towers were like this one: their tops ringed by low ceramic parapets. On the nearest tower, fifty yards away, half-naked soldiers were playing volleyball.

The chopper landed, stuttering, on the black trefoil of its pad nearby. Rotor wind whipped Laura's hair. "What do you do during hurricanes?" she shouted.

Sticky took her elbow and led her toward a hatchway. "There are ways in, besides choppers," he said. "But none you need to know about.'' He yanked the twin hatch covers open, revealing a short flight of stairs to an elevator.

["Hold it,"] came an unfamiliar voice in her ear. ["I can't handle both of you at once, and I'm not a military architect. This seaside stuff is weird enough. . . . David, do you know of anyone in Rizome who can handle military? I didn't think so. . . . Laura, could you kill about twenty minutes?"]

Laura stopped short. Sticky looked impatient. ''You won't be seeing much, if that's what's stopping you. We goin' down fast.''

''Another elevator,'' Laura told Atlanta. ''I'll be going off-line.''

''It's wired,'' Sticky assured her. ''They knew you were coming.''

They dropped six stories, fast. They emerged into a striated stone tunnel the size of a two-lane highway. She saw military storage boxes stenciled in old Warsaw Pact Cyrillic. Sagging tarps over vast knobby heaps of God-knew-what. Sticky ambled forward, his hands in his pockets. ''You know the Channel Tunnel? From Britain to France?''

It was cold. She hugged her arms through the *chador*'s baggy sleeves. ''Yeah?''

''They learned a lot about tunnel making. All on open databases, too. Handy.'' His words echoed eerily. Ceiling lights flickered on overhead as they walked and died as they moved on. They were walking the length of the tunnel in a moving pool of light. ''You ever see the Maginot Line?''

''What's that?'' Laura asked.

''Big line of forts the French dug ninety years ago. Against the Germans. I saw it once. Winston took me.'' He adjusted his beret. ''Big old steel domes still rusting in the middle of pastures. There are railroad tunnels underneath. Sometimes tourists ride 'em.'' He shrugged. ''That's all they're good for. This place, too, someday.''

''What do you mean?''

''The tankers are better. They move.''

Laura matched his stride. She felt spooked. ''It reeks down here, Sticky. Like the tankers . . .''

''That's tangle-gun plastic,'' Sticky told her. ''From war-game drills. You get hit by a tangle-gun, there's a funny stink while the plastic sets. Then it's like you're wrapped in barbed wire. . . ."

He was lying. There were labs down here somewhere. Somewhere off in the fungal darkness. She could feel it. That faint acid reek . . .

"These are the killing grounds," he said. "Where the invaders will pay. Not that we can stop them, any more than Fedon did. But they'll pay blood. These tunnels, they're full of things to jump you out of darkness. . . ." He sniffed. "Don't worry, not your Yankees. Yankees nah have much nerve these days. But whoever. Babylon."

" 'The Man,' " Laura said.

Sticky grinned.

The Bank's Directors were waiting for her. They were simply there, in the tunnel, under a pool of light. They had a long, rectangular meeting table and some comfortable leather chairs. Coffee thermoses, ashtrays, some keypads and pencils. They were chatting with each other. Smiling. Little curls of cigarette smoke rising under the light.

They rose when they saw her. Five black men. Four in well-tailored suits; one was wearing a uniform with starred shoulder boards. Three sat on the table's left, two on the right.

The chair at the head of the table was empty. So was the chair at its right-hand side. Sticky escorted her to the seat at the table's foot.

The general spoke. "That will be all, Captain." Sticky saluted sharply and turned on his heel. She heard his boots ring as he marched off into darkness.

"Welcome to Grenada, Mrs. Webster. Please be seated." Everyone sat, with squeaks of leather. They all had brass nameplates, thoughtfully turned her way. DR. CASTLEMAN. MR. RAINEY. MR. GOULD. GEN. CREFT. MR. GELLI. Mr. Gelli was the youngest man among them. He looked about forty; he was Italian, and his skin was black. The empty seats had nameplates, too. MR. STUBBS. And P.M. ERIC LOUISON . . .

"My name is Mr. Gould," Mr. Gould announced. He was a heavyset, black-skinned Anglo, about sixty-five, wearing video rouge and a wiry toupee. "I'm acting as chairman for this special panel of inquiry, examining the circumstances of the death of a Grenadian citizen, Mr. Winston Stubbs. We are not a court and cannot decide legal issues, though we can offer advice and counsel to the prime minister. Under Grenadian law, Mrs. Webster, you are not entitled to counsel before a special panel of this kind; however, false testimony carries the penalty of perjury. Mr. Gelli will administer your oath. Mr. Gelli?''

Mr. Gelli rose quickly to his feet. "Raise your right hand, please. Do you solemnly swear, or affirm . . .'' He read her the whole thing.

"I do,'' Laura said. Castleman was the weirdest of the lot. He was grossly fat and had shoulder-length hair and a scraggly beard; he was smoking a cigarillo down to the filter. His eyes were blue and spacy. He tapped left-handed at a little keyboard deck.

Rainey was bored. He was doodling at his paper and touching his large black Anglo nose as if it ached. He had an emerald earring and a bracelet of heavy gold link. General Creft looked like he might be a genuine black person, though his cream-and-coffee skin was the lightest of the lot. He had the unblinking eyes of a crocodile and a street brawler's scar-knuckled hands. Hands that would look natural clutching pliers or a rubber hose.

They quizzed her for an hour and a half. They were polite, low-key. Gould did most of the talking, pausing to page through notes on his deck. Rainey didn't care—the thrill level here was obviously too low for him; he would have been happier running speedboats past the Florida Coast Guard. Creft took center stage when they asked about the killer drone. Creft had a whole portfolio of printout photos of the Canadair CL-227—the orange peanut refitted with a dreadful variety of strafing guns, napalm squirters, gas dispensers. . . . She pointed out the model that looked closest to the profile she remembered. Creft passed it silently down the row. They all nodded. . . .

Gelli didn't say much. He was the junior partner. The older model of Gelli obviously hadn't kept up with the times. Somebody had scrapped him. . . .

She waited for the right moment to spring her news about the F.A.C.T. She called her deck back in the mansion, downloaded the evidence Emily had sent her, and spilled it in their laps. They looked it over, hemming and hawing. (Castleman zipped through it at 2400 baud, his fat-shrouded eyes devouring whole paragraphs at once.)

They were polite. They were skeptical. The president of Mali, one Moussa Diokité, was a personal friend of Prime Minister Louison. The two countries shared fraternal bonds and had contemplated cultural-exchange missions. Unfortunately, plans for peaceful exchange had fallen through, because of the constant state of crisis in all the Sahara countries. Mali had nothing at all to gain from an attack on Grenada; Mali was desperately poor and racked by civil disorder.

And the evidence was bad. Algeria and Mali had a long-standing border dispute; Algeria's State Department would say anything. I. G. Farben's list of F.A.C.T. terrorist actions in Turkish Cyprus was impressive and useful, but proved nothing. Kymera Corporation were paranoid, always blaming foreigners for the actions of Japanese yakuza crime gangs. Blaming Mali was a wild flight of fancy, when the Singaporeans were clearly the aggressors.

"How do you know it's Singapore?" Laura asked. "Can you prove that Singapore killed Mr. Stubbs? Did Singapore attack the Rizome Lodge in Galveston? If you can prove that you dealt faithfully, while the Islamic Bank broke the terms, I promise that I'll support your grievances in every way I can."

"We appreciate your position," said Mr. Gould. "Legal proof in a murder committed by remote control is, of course, rather difficult. . . . Have you ever been to Singapore?"

"No. Rizome has an office there, but . . ."

"You've had a chance to see what we do here, on our own island. I think you understand now that we're not the monsters we've been painted."

General Creft's lean face creased with a gleam of fangs. He was smiling at her, or trying to. Castleman stirred with a grunt and began hitting function keys.

"A trip to Singapore might enlighten you," Gould said. "Would you be interested in going there?"

Laura paused. "In what capacity?"

"As our negotiator. As an officer in the United Bank of Grenada." Mr. Gould tapped at his deck. "Let me point out," he said, watching the screen, "that Rizome operates under severe legal strictures. Very likely the Vienna Convention will soon shut down Rizome's investigations entirely." He glanced up at her. "Unless you join us, Mrs. Webster, you will never learn the truth about who attacked you. You will have to go back to that bullet-riddled Lodge of yours, never knowing who your enemy was, or when they will strike again. . . ."

Mr. Rainey spoke up. He had the drawl of an old-time Florida cracker. "I reckon you know that we have a lot of data on you and your husband. This is no sudden decision on our part, Mrs. Webster. We know your abilities—we've even seen the work you did, on that safehouse where we've been protecting you." He smiled. "We like your attitude. To put it short, we believe in you. We know how you had to fight within Rizome, to get a chance to build your Lodge and put your ideas into practice. With us, you'd have no such fight. We know how to leave creative people to their work."

Laura touched her earphone. There was dead silence on the line. "You've cut me off the Net," she said.

Rainey spread his hands, his gold wristlet catching the light. "It did seem wisest."

"You want me to defect from my company."

"Defect—my, that's an ugly word! We want you to join us. Your husband, David, too. We can promise you both a level of support that might surprise you." Rainey nodded at the deck screen before her. A financial spreadsheet was coming up. "Of course, we know about your personal financial worth. We were surprised to see that, without Rizome, you scarcely own anything! Sure, you've got shares, but the things you've built don't belong to you—you just run them for your corporation. I've known plumbers with bigger salaries than you have! But things are different here. We know how to be generous."

"You seem to enjoy the plantation house," Gould said. "It's yours—we could sign over title today. You can hire your own staff, of course. Transportation's no problem—we'll put a chopper and pilot at your disposal. And I can assure you that you'll be better protected under Bank security than you could ever be back in the States."

Laura glanced at the screen before her. A sudden shock—they were talking *millions*. Millions of Grenadian roubles, she realized. Funny money. "I don't have anything to offer you that's worth this amount," she said.

"We have an unfortunate public image," Gould said sadly. "We've turned our back on the Net, and we've been vilified for it. Repairing that damage would be your job in the long run, Mrs. Webster—it should suit your skills. In the short run, we have this Singapore crisis. There's no love lost between us and our rival bank. But escalating warfare doesn't suit either of us. And you are a perfect candidate for conveying a peace proposal."

"Pure as the driven snow," murmured Mr. Castleman. He was gazing at the shiny surface of his gold cigarillo case. He popped it open and fired up another.

"You do have a credibility with Singapore that our own ambassadors lack," Mr. Gould said. A little twitch of irritation had passed his face at Castleman's indiscretion.

"I can't possibly give you an answer without checking with my company," Laura said. "And my husband."

"Your husband seems to like the idea," Gould said. "Of course we broached the idea to him already. Does that affect your thinking?"

"My company is going to be very upset that you've cut me offline," Laura said. "That wasn't in our agreement."

"We haven't exactly cut you off," Castleman said. "The line's still up, but we're feeding it a simulation. . . ." His pudgy fingers flickered in midair. "An easy graphics job—no backgrounds, just light, darkness, a tabletop and talking heads. None of this exists, you see. We haven't been existing for some time now."

Gelli laughed nervously.

"Then I'm closing this meeting of our investigative panel," said Mr. Gould. "You could have told me, Castleman."

"Sorry," Castleman said lazily.

"I mean that I would have officially closed the investigation, even before we went offline for the recruitment effort."

"I'm sorry, Gould, really," Castleman said. "You know I don't have your flair for this sort of thing."

"But now we can reason together," Rainey said, with an

air of relief. He bent and reached beneath the table. He rose
clutching a Rastafarian hookah of speckled bamboo, with a
bowl of curving ramshorn, burnt sticky-black with resin. It
looked a thousand years old, mummy-wrapped in antique
leather thongs and crude dangling beads. "Will His Excel-
lency join us?" Rainey asked.

"I'll check," Castleman said. He tapped rapidly at his
keyboard. The lights dimmed to a mellow glow.

Rainey slapped a leather bag onto the tabletop and pulled
its drawstring with a hiss. "Lamb's *bread!*" he exulted,
pulling a handful of chopped green weed. He began stuffing
the pipe with deft, flashy gestures.

The prime minister was sitting at the head of the table. A
little black man wearing dark shades and a high-collared
military jacket. He'd materialized out of nowhere.

"Welcome to Grenada," he said.

Laura stared.

"Please don't be alarmed, Mrs. Webster," said Prime
Minister Louison. "This is not a formal proceeding. We often
reason together in this manner. In the sacrament of meditation."

Rainey slid the pipe across the table. Louison took it and
fired it with a chrome lighter, puffing loudly. The marijuana
ignited with an angry hiss and bluish flames danced above the
bowl.

"Burn the Pope!" said General Creft.

Louison's head was wreathed in smog. He blew a stream to
his right, across Stubbs's empty chair. "In memory of a good
friend." He passed the pipe to Rainey. Rainey sucked loudly—
the pipe bubbled. "Fire and water," he said, giving it to
Gelli.

Gelli huffed enthusiastically and leaned back in his chair.
He slid it to Laura. "Don't be scared," Gelli said. "None of
this is happening, really."

Laura slid the pipe toward General Creft. The air was
growing blue with sweetish smoke. Creft puffed and blew
with great hyperventilating wheezes.

Laura sat tensely on the edge of her seat. "I'm sorry I can't
join your ceremony," she said. "It would discredit me as a
bargaining partner. In the eyes of my company."

Rainey cawed with laughter. They chuckled all around.

"They won't know," Gelli told her.

"They won't understand," Castleman said, breathing smoke.

"They won't believe," said Gould.

The prime minister leaned forward, his shades gleaming. His medals glistened in the light. "Some mon deal with information," he told her. "And some mon deal with the concept of truth. But some mon deal with *magic*. Information flow around ya. And truth flow right at ya. But magic—*it flow right through ya.*"

"These are tricks," Laura said. She gripped the table. "You want me to join you—how can I trust you? I'm not a magician. . . ."

"We know what you are," Gould said, as if talking to a child. "We know all about you. You, your Rizome, your Net—you think that your world encompasses ours. But it doesn't. Your world is a subset of our world." He slapped the table with his open palm—a gunshot bang of noise. "You see, we know everything about you. But you know *nothing at all* about us."

"You have a little spark, maybe," Rainey said. He was leaning back in his chair, steepling his fingertips, his eyes slitted, and already reddening. "But you'll never see the future—the *real* future—until you learn to open up your mind. To see all the levels . . ."

"All the levels under the world," Castleman said. " 'Tricks,' you call it. Reality's nothing but levels and levels of tricks. Take that stupid black glass off your eyes, and we can show you . . . so many things. . . ."

Laura jumped to her feet. "Put me back on the Net! You have no right to do this. Put me back at once."

The prime minister laughed. A dry little wizened chuckle. He set the fuming pipe under the table. Then he sat back up, lifted both hands theatrically, and vaporized.

The Bank's Directors stood in a body, shoving their chairs back. They were laughing and shaking their heads. And ignoring her.

They strolled off together, chuckling, muttering, into the pitch blackness of the tunnel. Leaving Laura alone under the pool of light, with the glowing decks and cooling mugs of coffee. Castleman had forgotten his cigarette case. . . .

["Oh my God,"] came a quiet voice in her ear. ["They all vanished! Laura, are you there? Are you all right?"]

Laura's knees buckled. She half fell backward into her chair. "Ms. Emerson," she said. "Is that you?"

["Yes, dear. How did they do that?"]

"I'm not sure," Laura said. Her throat was sandpaper dry. She poured herself some coffee, shakily, not caring what might be in it. "What exactly did you see them do?"

["Well . . . it seemed quite a reasonable discussion. . . . They said that they appreciate our mediation, and don't blame us for Stubbs's death. . . . Then suddenly this. You're alone. One moment they were sitting and talking, and the next, the chairs were empty and the air was full of smoke."] Ms. Emerson paused. ["Like a video special effect. Is that what you saw, Laura?"]

"A special effect," Laura said. She gulped warm coffee. "Yes . . . they chose this meeting ground, didn't they? I'm sure they could rig it somehow."

Ms. Emerson laughed quietly. ["Yes, of course. It did give me a turn. . . . For a moment I was afraid you'd tell me they were all Optimal Personas. Ha ha. What a cheap stunt."]

Laura set her mug down carefully. "How did I, uh, do?"

["Oh, very well, dear. You were quite your usual self. I did offer a few minor suggestions online, but you seemed distracted. . . . Not surprising, in such an important meeting. . . . Anyway, you did well."]

"Oh. Good," Laura said. She gazed upward. "I'm sure if I could reach that ceiling and dig around behind those lights, I'd find holograms or something."

["Why waste your time?"] Ms. Emerson chuckled. ["And spoil their harmless little touch of drama. . . . I notice that David has also had a very interesting time. . . . They tried to recruit him! We've been expecting that."]

"What did he say?"

["He was very polite. He did well, too."]

She heard footsteps. Sticky ambled out of the darkness. "So," he said. "You sittin' here talkin' to thin air again." He sprawled carelessly into Gelli's chair. "You okay? You look a lickle pale." He glanced curiously at one of the screens. "They give you a hard time?"

"They're a hard bunch," Laura told him. "Your bosses."

"Well it's a hard world," Sticky shrugged. "You'll be wanting to get back to that baby of yours. . . . I got the jeep waitin' up on the roof. . . . Let's move."

The swaying descent from the tower turned her stomach. She felt greenish and clammy as they took the winding road back to the coast. He drove far too fast, the steep, romantic hills lurching and dipping with the shocks, like cheap backstage scenery. "Slow down, Sticky," she said. "I'll throw up if you don't."

Sticky looked alarmed. "Why you nah tell me? Hell, we'll stop." He bounced off the road into the shelter of some trees, then killed the engine. "You stay here," he told the soldier.

He helped Laura out of her seat. She hung on his arm. "If I could just walk a little," she said. Sticky led her away from the jeep, checking the sky again, by reflex.

A light pattering of rain rustled the leaves overhead. "What's this?" he said. "You hanging all over me. You been taking Carlotta's pills or something?"

She let him go reluctantly. He felt warm and solid. Made of human flesh. Sticky laughed to see her swaying there flat-footed. "What's the matter? Uncle Dave not givin' you any?"

Laura flushed. "Didn't your mother teach you not to be such a fucking chauvinist? I can't believe this."

"Hey," Sticky said mildly. "My mother was just one of Winston's gals. When he snap a finger, she jump like a gunshot. Not everyone touchy like you, you know." He squatted beneath a tree, bracing his back, and picked up a long twig. "So. They give you a scare, do they?" He juggled the twig between his fingers. "Tell you anything about the war?"

"Some," Laura said. "Why?"

"Militia's been on full alert for three days," Sticky said. "Barracks talk says the terries gave the Bank an ultimatum. Threaten brimstone fire. But we through payin' shakedown money. So looks like we gonna start poppin' caps."

"Barracks talk," Laura said. Suddenly she felt stifled in the long black *chador*. She stripped it over her head.

"Better keep the flak jacket," Sticky told her. There was a gleam in his eyes. He liked seeing her throw clothes off. "Lickle gift from me to you."

She looked around herself, breathing hard. The fine wet smell of tropic woods. Bird calls. Rain. The world was still here. No matter what went on in people's heads. . . .

Sticky jabbed at a termite nest in the tree's roots, waiting for her.

She felt better now. She understood Sticky. The vicious fight they'd had earlier seemed almost comfortable now—like a necessary thing. Now he was giving her a look—not like a side of beef or an enemy, but a kind of look she was used to getting from men. He wasn't so different from other young men. Kind of a jerk maybe, but a human being. She felt a sudden gush of comradely human feeling for him—almost felt she could hug him. Or at least invite him to dinner.

Sticky looked down at his boots. "Did they say you a hostage?" he said tightly. "Say they were gonna shoot you?"

"No," Laura said. "They want to hire us. To work for Grenada."

Sticky began laughing. "That's good. That's real good. That's funny." He stood up loosely, happily, as if shrugging off a weight. "You gonna do it?"

"No."

"I nah think so." He paused. "You ought to, though."

"Why don't you have dinner with us tonight?" Laura said. "Maybe Carlotta can come. We'll have a good talk together. The four of us."

"I have to watch what I eat," Sticky said. Meaningless. But it meant something to him.

Sticky left her at the mansion. David arrived an hour later. He kicked open the door and came down the hall whooping, banging the baby on his hip. "Home again, home again . . ." Loretta was crowing with excitement.

Laura was waiting in the hideous living room, nursing her second rum punch. "Mother of my child!" David said. "Where are the diapers, and how was your day?"

"They're supposed to be in the tote."

"I used all of those. God, what smells so good? And what are you drinking?"

"Rita made planter's punch."

"Well, pour me some." He vanished with the baby and brought her back freshly changed, with her bottle.

Laura sighed. "You had a good time, David, didn't you?"

"You wouldn't believe what they have out there," David said, sprawling onto the couch with the baby in his lap. "I met another one of the Andreis. I mean his name's not Andrei, but he acted just like him. Korean guy. Big Buckminster Fuller fan. They're making massive arcologies out of nothing! For nothing! Concretized sand and seastone. . . . They sink these iron grates into the ocean, run some voltage through, and get this: solids begin to accrete . . . calcium carbonate, right? Like seashells! They're growing buildings offshore. Out of this 'seastone.' And no building permits . . . no impact statements . . . nothing."

He gulped three inches of cloudy rum and lime, then shuddered. "Man! I could do with another of these. . . . Laura, it was the hottest thing I ever saw. People are *living* in 'em. Some of them are *under water* . . . you can't tell where the walls end and the coral starts."

Little Loretta grabbed her bottle avidly. "And get this—I was walking around in my work clothes and *nobody paid any attention.* Just another black guy, right? Even with old uhmm . . . Jesus, I forgot his name already, the Korean Andrei. . . . He was giving me the tour, but it was really low-key, I got to see everything."

"They want you to work on it?" Laura said.

"More than that! Hell, they offered me a fifteen-million-rouble budget and carte blanche to get on with whatever I like." He took off his glasses and set them on the arm of the couch. "Of course I said no dice—no way I'm staying here without my wife and kid—but if we could work out some kind of co-op thing with Rizome, hell, yes, I'd do it. I'd do it tomorrow."

"They want me to work for them, too," Laura said. "They're worried about their public image."

David stared at her and burst into laughter. "Well of

course they are. Of course. Well, hell, pour me another one. Tell me all about the meeting.''

''It was bizarre,'' Laura said.

''Well, I believe that! Hell, you ought to see what they're up to out on the coast. They've got ten-year-old kids out there who were born—I mean literally born—in seawater. They have these *maternity tanks*. . . . They have women at term, right . . . they take 'em out into these birthing tanks. . . . Did I mention the dolphins?'' He sipped his drink.

''Dolphins.''

''You ever hear of laser acupuncture? I mean right here along the spine. . . .'' He leaned forward, jostling the baby. ''Oh, sorry, Loretta.'' He switched arms. ''Anyway, I can tell you all that later. So, you testified, huh? Were they tough?''

''Not tough exactly. . . .''

''If they want us to defect, it can't have been that bad.''

''Well . . .'' Laura said. It was all slipping away from her. She was feeling increasingly hopeless. There was no way she could tell him what had really happened . . . what she thought had happened . . . especially not online, in front of Atlanta's cameras. There'd be a better time later. Surely. ''If we could only talk privately . . .''

David smirked. ''Yeah, it's a bitch, online. . . . Well, I can have Atlanta send us back the tapes of your testimony. We'll look over 'em together, you can tell me all about it.'' Silence. ''Unless there's something you have to tell me right now.''

''No . . .''

''Well, I have something to tell you.'' He finished his drink. ''I was gonna wait till after supper, but I just can't hold it.'' He grinned. ''Carlotta made a pass at me.''

''Carlotta?'' Laura said, shocked. ''She did what?'' She sat up straighter.

''Yeah. She was there. We were offline together for just a second in one of the aquaculture rooms. It wasn't wired, see. And she kind of sways over, slips her hand up under my shirt, and says . . . I don't remember exactly, but it was something like: 'Ever wonder what it would be like? We know a lot of things Laura doesn't.' ''

Laura turned livid. "What was that?" she demanded. "What about her hand?"

David blinked, his smile fading. "She just ran her hand over my ribs. To show she meant business, I guess." He was already defensive. "Don't blame me. I wasn't asking for it."

"I'm not blaming you, but I'm the one that means your business," Laura told him. Long silence. "And I kind of wish you weren't so gleeful about it."

David could not hide his grin. "Well . . . I guess it was kind of flattering. I mean, everybody we know, knows we have a solid thing together, so it's not like the woods are full of women flinging themselves at me. . . . Y'know, it wasn't even so much that Carlotta herself was making a pass. . . . It was sort of a generic hooker pass. Like a business proposition."

He let Loretta grip his fingers. "Don't think too much of it. You were right when you said they were trying to get at us. It's like, they use whatever they can. Drugs—we don't go for that. Money—well, we're not breadheads. . . . Sex—I think they just told Carlotta to try it, and she said she would. None of that means much. But man—*creative potential*—I'm not ashamed to say that got me where I lived."

"What a shitty thing to do," Laura said. "At the very least, she could have sent some other Church girl."

"Yeah," he mused, "but maybe another girl would have looked better. . . . Oh, sorry. Forget I said that. I'm drunk."

She forced herself to think about it. Maybe he'd been offline for just five minutes in that offline netherworld they had here, and maybe, just maybe, he'd done it. Maybe he'd slept with Carlotta. She could feel her world cracking at the thought, like ice over deep black water.

David played with the baby, a harmless tra-la-la expression on his face. No. No way he could have done it. She'd never even doubted him before. Never like this.

It was like a dozen years of confident adulthood had split open in black crevasses. Way down there, raw scars of the world-eating fear she'd felt, when she was nine years old and her parents broke up. Rum soured in her stomach, and she felt a sudden cramping pang.

It was another ploy, she thought grimly. They weren't going to do this to her. Everyone had insecurities. They knew about hers—they knew her personal history. But they weren't going to play on her private feelings of dread and make her start doubting reality. She wouldn't let them. No. No more weaknesses. Nothing but stern resolve. Until she'd put an end to this.

She stood up and walked quickly through the bedroom, to the bath. She threw off her filthy clothes. There was a stain. Her period had started. The first she'd had since the pregnancy. "Oh, fuck," she said, and burst into tears. She got into the shower and let the needle-thin gush of odd-smelling water blast her face.

The weeping helped. She flushed the weakness out like poison in her tears. Then she put on mascara and eye shadow, so he wouldn't see the redness. And she wore a dress for dinner.

David was still full of the things he'd seen, so she let him talk, and just smiled and nodded, in Rita's candlelight.

He was serious about staying in Grenada. "The tech is more important than the politics," he told her blithely. "That crap never lasts, but a real innovation's like a permanent infrastructural asset!" The two of them could form a real 'Rizome Grenada'—it would be like arranging the Lodge, but on a scale twenty times bigger, and with *free money*. They would show them what a Rizome architect could do—and it'd be a foothold for some sane social values. Sooner or later the Net would civilize the place—wean them away from their crazy piracy bullshit. Grenada didn't need dope, it needed food and shelter.

They went to bed, and David reached for her. And she had to tell him she had her period. He was surprised, and glad. "I thought you were looking a little stressed," he said. "It's been a whole year, hasn't it? Must feel pretty weird to have it back."

"No," she said, "it's just . . . natural. You get used to it."

"You haven't said much tonight," he said. He rubbed her stomach gently. "Kind of mysterious."

"I'm just tired," she said. "I can't really talk about it just now."

"Don't let 'em get you down. Those Bank creeps aren't so much," he said. "I hope we get a chance to meet old

Louison, the prime minister. Down in the projects, people were talking about him like these Bank hustlers were just his errand boys.'' He hesitated. ''I don't like the way they talked about Louison. Like they were really scared.''

''Sticky told me there's a lot of war talk,'' Laura told him. ''The army's on alert. People are tense.''

''*You're* tense,'' he said, rubbing her. ''Your shoulders are like wood.'' He yawned. ''You know you can tell me anything, Laura. We don't keep secrets, you know that.''

''I want to see the tapes tomorrow,'' she said. ''We'll go over 'em together, like you said.'' There was bound to be a flaw in them, she thought. Somewhere, a little flicker, or a misplaced chunk of pixels. Something that would prove that they were faked, and that she wasn't crazy. She couldn't have people thinking she was cracking up. It would ruin everything.

She was unable to sleep. The day tossed through her mind, over and over. And the cramps were bad. At half past midnight she gave up and put on a robe.

David had made Loretta a crib—a little square corral, padded all around with blankets. Laura looked over her little girl and cradled her with a glance. Then back at David. It was funny how much they looked alike when they slept. Father and daughter. Some strange human vitality that had passed through her, that she'd nurtured within herself. Wonderful, painful, eerie. The house was still as death.

She heard distant thunder. From the north. Hollow, repeated booms. It was going to rain. That would be nice. A little tropic rain to soothe her nerves.

She walked silently through the living room onto the porch. She and David had cleared the junk away and swept the place; it was comfortable there now. She swung out the arms of an old Morris chair and reclined in it, propping up her tired legs. Warm garden air with the heavy-lidded perfume reek of ylang-ylang. No rain yet. The air was full of tension.

The distant lights at the gate flashed on. Laura winced and lifted her head. The two night guards—she didn't know their names yet—had come out and were conferring over their belt phones.

She heard a pop overhead. Very quiet, unobtrusive, like a

rafter settling. Then another one: a faint metallic bonk, and a rustle. Very quiet, like birds landing.

Something had dropped onto the roof. Something had hit the top of one of the turrets—bonked off its tin roof onto the shingles.

White glare sheeted over the yard, silently. White glare from the top of the mansion. The guards looked up, startled. They flung their arms up in surprise, like bad actors.

The roof began crackling.

Laura stood up and screamed at the top of her lungs.

She dashed through the darkened house to the bedroom. The baby had jerked awake and was howling in fear. David was sitting up in bed, dazed. "We're on fire," she told him.

He catapulted out of bed and stumbled into his pants. "Where?"

"The roof. In two places. Fire bombs, I think."

"Oh, Jesus," he said. "You grab Loretta and I'll get the others."

She strapped Loretta into her tote and tossed their decks into a suitcase. She could smell smoke by the time she'd finished. And there was a steady crackling roar.

She hauled the baby and the suitcase out into the yard. She left Loretta in her tote, behind the fountain, then turned to look. One of the turrets was wrapped in flames. A leaping ulcer of fire spread over the west wing.

Rajiv and Jimmy came out, half carrying a coughing, weeping Rita. Laura ran to them. She sank her nails into Rajiv's naked arm. "Where's my husband, you stupid bastard!"

"Very sorry, madam," Rajiv whimpered. He tugged nervously at his drooping pants. "Sorry, madam, very sorry . . ."

She shoved him aside so hard that he spun and fell. She vaulted the stairs and rushed back in, ignoring their yells.

David was in the bedroom. He was crouched almost double, with a wet washcloth pressed to his face. He was wearing his videoglasses, and had hers propped on his head. The bedside clock was clamped under his armpit. "Just a sec," he muttered, fixing her with blank, gold-etched eyes. "Gotta find my toolbox."

"Fuck it, David, go!" She hauled at his arm. He went reluctantly, stumbling.

Once outside, they had to back away from the heat. One by one, the upper rooms were beginning to explode. David dropped his washcloth, numbly. "Flashover," he said, staring.

A fist of dirty flame punched out an upstairs window. Shards of glass fountained across the lawn. "The heat builds up," David muttered clinically. "The whole room ignites at once. And the gas pressure just blows the walls out."

The soldiers pushed them back, holding their stupid, useless tangle-guns at chest level, like police batons. David went reluctantly, hypnotized by destruction. "I've run simulations of this, but I've never seen it happen," he said, to no one in particular. "Jesus, what a sight!"

Laura shoved one of the teenage soldiers as he trampled her bare foot. "Some help you are, asshole! Where in hell is the fire department or whatever you use in this godforsaken place?"

The boy backed off, trembling, and dropped his gun. "Look at the sky!" He pointed northeast.

Low scud of burning clouds on the northern horizon. Lit like dawn with ugly, burning amber. "What the hell," David said, marveling. "That's miles away. . . . Laura, that's Point Sauteur. It's the whole fucking complex off there. That's a refinery fire!"

"Brimstone fire," the soldier wailed. He started sobbing, dabbing at his face. The other soldier, a bigger man, kicked him hard in the leg. "Pick up you weapon, bloodclot!"

A distant dirty flash lit the clouds. "Man, I hope they haven't hit the tankers," David said. "Man, I hope the poor bastards on those rigs have lifeboats." He tugged at his earpiece. "You getting all this, Atlanta?"

Laura pulled her own rig off his head. She backed away and fetched Loretta in her tote. She pulled the screaming baby free of the thing and cradled her against her chest, rocking her and murmuring.

Then she put the glasses on.

Now she could watch it without hurting so much.

The mansion burned to the ground. It took all night. Their little group huddled together in the guardhouse, listening to tales of disaster on the phones.

Around seven A.M., a spidery military chopper arrived and set down by the fountain.

Andrei, the Polish emigré, hopped out. He took a large box from the pilot and joined them at the gates.

Andrei's left arm was wrapped in medicinal gauze, and he stank of chemical soot. "I have brought shoes and uniforms for all survivors," he announced. The box was full of flat, plastic-wrapped packs: the standard cadre's jeans and short-sleeved shirts. "Very sorry to be such bad hosts," Andrei told them somberly. "The Grenadian People apologize to you."

"At least we survived," Laura told him. She slipped her bare feet gratefully into the soft deck shoes. "Who took credit?"

"The malefactors of the F.A.C.T. have broken all civilized bounds."

"I figured," Laura said, taking the box. "We'll take turns changing inside the guardhouse. David and I will go first." Inside, she shucked out of her flimsy nightrobe and buttoned on the stiff, fresh shirt and heavy jeans. David put on a shirt and shoes.

They stepped out and Rita went in, shivering. "Now, you will please join me in the helicopter," Andrei said. "The world must know of this atrocity. . . ."

"All right," Laura said. "Who's online?"

["Practically everybody,"] Emily told her. ["We got you on a live feed throughout the company, and to a couple of news services. Vienna's gonna have a hard time holding this one. . . . It's just too big."]

Andrei paused at the chopper's hatchway. "Can you leave the baby?"

"No way," David said flatly. They climbed into two crash couches in the back, and David held Loretta's tote in his lap. Andrei took the copilot's seat and they buckled in.

Up and away in a quiet hiss of rotor blades.

David glanced out the bulletproof window at the mansion's black wreckage. "Any idea what hit our house?"

"Yes. There were many of them. Very small, cheap planes—paper and bamboo, like children's kites. Radar-transparent. Many have crashed now, but not before they dropped their many bombs. Little thermite sticks with flaming jelly.''

"Were they hitting us in particular? Rizome, I mean?''

Andrei shrugged in his shoulder harness. "It is hard to say. Many such houses have burned. The communiqué does mention you. . . . I have it here." He passed them a printout. Laura glanced at it: date and tag line, and block after block of the usual Stalinist garbage. "Do you have a casualty count?''

"Seven hundred so far. It is rising. They are still pulling bodies from the offshore rigs. They hit us with antiship missiles.''

"Good God," David said.

"Those were heavy armaments. We have choppers out looking for ships. There may have been several. But there are many ships in the Caribbean, and missiles have a long range." He reached into his shirt pocket. "Have you seen these before?''

Laura took the object from his fingers. It looked like a big plastic paper clip. It was speckled camo-green and brown, and weighed almost nothing. "No.''

"This one is defused—it is plastic explosive. A mine. It can blow the tire off a truck. Or the leg off a woman or child." His voice was cold. "The small planes scattered many, many hundreds of them. You will not be traveling by the road anymore. And we will not set foot around the complex.''

"What kind of crazy bastard—" David said.

"They mean to deny us our own country," Andrei said. "These devices will shed our blood for months to come.''

Land slid below them; suddenly they were over the Caribbean. The chopper wheeled. "Do not fly into the smoke," Andrei told the pilot. "It is toxic.''

Smoke still billowed from two of the offshore rigs. They resembled giant tabletops piled high with burning cars. A pair of fire barges spewed long, feathered plumes of chemical foam over them.

The jackleg rigs had cranked themselves down to the surface; their ornate hydraulics were awash with saltwater. The water was full of blackened flotsam—blobs of fabric, writhing plastic snakes of cable. And stiff-armed floating things that looked like dummies. Laura looked away with a gasp of pain.

"No, look very well," Andrei told her. "They never even showed us a face. . . . Let these people have faces, at least."

"I can't look," she said tightly.

"Then close your eyes behind the glasses."

"All right." She pressed her blind face to the window. "Andrei. What are you going to do?"

"You are leaving this afternoon," he said. "As you see, we can no longer guarantee your safety. You will leave as soon as the airport is swept for mines." He paused. "These will be the last flights out. We want no more foreigners. No prying journalists. And none of the vermin from the Vienna Convention. We are sealing our borders."

She opened her eyes. They were hovering over the shoreline. Half-naked Rastas were pulling corpses up onto the docks. A dead little girl, limp clothes sheeting water. Laura bit back a shriek, grabbing David's arm. Her gorge rose. She slumped back into the seat, fighting her stomach.

"Can't you see my wife is sick?" David said sharply. "This is enough."

"No," Laura said shakily. "Andrei's right. . . . Andrei, listen. There's no way that Singapore could have done this. That's not gang war. This is atrocity."

"They tell us the same," Andrei admitted. "I think they are afraid. This morning, we captured their agents in Trinidad. It seems they have been playing with toy planes and matches."

"You can't attack Singapore!" Laura said. "More killing can't help you!"

"We are not Christs or Gandhis," Andrei said. He spoke slowly, carefully. "This is terrorism. But there is a deeper kind of terror than this . . . a fear far older and darker. You could tell Singapore about that terror. You know something about it, Laura, I think."

"You want me to go to Singapore?" Laura said. "Yes. I'll go there. If it'll stop this."

"They need not fear little toy planes," Andrei said. "But you can tell them to be afraid of the dark. To be afraid of food—and air—and water—and their own shadows."

David looked at Andrei, his jaw dropping.

Andrei sighed. "If they are innocent of this, then they must prove it and join us immediately."

"Yes, of course," Laura said quickly. "You have to make common cause. Together. Rizome can help."

"Otherwise I pity Singapore," Andrei said. He had a look in his eyes that she had never seen in a human face. It was the farthest thing from pity.

Andrei left them at the little military airstrip at Pearls. But the evacuation flight he'd promised never showed—some kind of foulup. Eventually, after dark, a cargo chopper ferried Laura and David to the civilian airport at Point Salines.

The night was pierced with headlights and the airport road was snarled with traffic. A company of mechanized infantry had seized the airport gates. A blasted truck on the roadside smoldered gently—it had wandered through a scattering of paper-clip mines.

Their chopper carried them smoothly over the fence. Inside, the airport was a jumble of luxury saloons and limos.

Militia in flak jackets and riot helmets were beating the airport bounds with long bamboo poles. Minesweepers. As the chopper settled to the weedy tarmac, Laura heard a sharp crack and flash as a pole connected.

"Watch you step," the pilot said cheerily, flinging open the hatch. A militia kid in camo, about nineteen—he looked excited by the night's action. Any kind of destruction was thrilling—it didn't seem to matter that it was his own people. Laura and David decamped onto the tarmac, carrying the sleeping baby in her tote.

The chopper lifted silently. A little baggage cart scurried past them in the darkness. Someone had crudely wired a pair of push brooms to the cart's front. Laura and David shuffled carefully toward the lights of the terminal. It was only thirty yards away. Surely somebody had swept it for mines already. . . . They eased their way around a mauve sports car. Two fat men, wearing elaborate video makeup, were asleep or drunk in the car's plush bucket seats.

Soldiers yelled at them, beckoning. " 'Ey! Get away! You people! No robbin', no lootin'!"

They stepped into the long floodlit portico of the terminal. Some of the glass frontage had been smashed or blown out; inside, the place was crammed. Excited crowd noise, waft of body heat, popping, scuffling. A Cuban airliner lifted off, its graceful hiss of takeoff drowned by the crowd.

A soldier in shoulder bars grabbed David's arm. "Papers. Passport card."

"Don't have 'em," David said. "We were burned out."

"No reservation, no tickets?" the colonel said. "Can nah come in without tickets." He examined their cadre's uniforms, puzzled. "Where you get those telly-glasses?"

"Gould and Castleman sent us," Laura lied smoothly. She touched her glasses. "Havana's just a stopover for us. We're witnesses. Outside contacts. You understand."

"Yah," the colonel said, flinching. He waved them inside.

They filtered quickly into the crowd. "That was brilliant!" David told her. "But we still got no tickets."

["We can handle that,"] Emerson said. ["We have the Cuban airline online now. They're running the evacuation—we can get you the next flight."]

"Great."

["You're almost back—try not to worry."]

"Thanks, Atlanta. Solidarity." David scanned the crowd. At least three hundred of them. "Man, it's a mad doctor's convention. . . ."

Like kicking over a rotten log, Laura thought. The airport was crawling with tight-faced Anglos and Europeans—they seemed split pretty evenly between well-dressed gangster exiles and vice-dazzled techies gone native. Dozens of refugees sprawled on the floor, nervously clutching their loot. Laura stepped over the feet of a slim black woman passed out on a heap of designer luggage, a dope sticker glued to her neck. Half a dozen hustlers in Trinidadian shirts were shooting craps on the floor, shouting excitedly in some East European language. Two screaming ten-year-olds chased each other through a group of men methodically smashing tape cassettes.

"Look," David said, pointing. A group of white-clad women stood at the edge of the crowd. Faint looks of disdain on their faces. Nurses, Laura thought. Or nuns.

"Church hookers!" David said. "Look, that's Carlotta!"

They shouldered their way through, skidding on trash. Suddenly a scream erupted to their left. "What do you mean, you can't change it?" The shouter was waving a Grenadian credit card in the face of a militia captain. "There's fucking millions on this card, asshole!" A portly Anglo in a suit and jogging shoes—the shoes flickered with readouts. "You'd better call your fucking boss, Jack!"

"Sit down," the captain ordered. He gave the man a shove.

"Okay," the man said, not sitting. He stuffed the card inside his lapel. "Okay. I changed my mind. I'm choosing the tunnels instead. Take me back to the tunnels, pal." No response. "Don't you know who you're fucking talking to?" He grabbed the captain's sleeve.

The captain knocked the grasping hand loose with a quick chop to the arm. Then he kicked the man's feet out from under him. The complainer fell heavily on his ass. He lurched back to his feet, his fists clenching.

The captain shrugged his tangle-gun free and shot the man pointblank. A high-speed splattering punch of wet plastic. A serpent's nest of stinking ribbon flew over the Anglo's chest, trapping his arms, his neck, his face, and a nearby piece of luggage. He hit the floor squalling.

A roar of alarm from the crowd. Three militia privates rushed to their captain's aid, guns drawn. "Sit down!" the captain shouted, pumping another round into the chamber. "Everyone! Down, now!" The tangle-victim started to choke.

People sat. Laura and David, too. people sat in a spreading wave, like a sporting event. Some laced their hands behind their heads, as if by reflex. The captain grinned and brandished his gun over them. "Better." He kicked the man, casually.

Suddenly the nuns approached in a body. Their leader was a black woman; she pulled back her wimple, revealing gray hair, a lined face. "Captain," she said calmly. "This man is choking."

"He a t'ief, Sister," the captain said.

"That may be, Captain, but he still needs to breathe." Three of the Church women knelt by the victim, tugging at the strands around his throat. The old woman—an Abbess,

Laura thought unwillingly—turned to the crowd and spread her hands in the crook-fingered Church blessing. "Violence serves no one," she said. "Please be silent."

She walked away, her sisters following without a word. They left the tangle-victim where he lay, wheezing quietly. The captain shrugged, and slung his gun again, and turned away, gesturing to his men. After a moment people began to stand up.

["That was well done,"] Emerson said.

David helped Laura to her feet and picked up the baby's tote. "Hey! Carlotta!" They followed her.

Carlotta spoke briefly to the Abbess, pulled her wimple back, and stepped away from her sisters.

"Hello," she said. Her frizzy mane of hair was pulled back. Her sharp-cheeked face looked naked and bleak. It was the first time they'd ever seen Carlotta without makeup.

"I'm surprised to see you leaving," Laura told her.

Carlotta shook her head. "They hit our temple. A temporary setback."

"Sorry," David said. "We were burned out, too."

"We'll be back," Carlotta shrugged. "Where there's war, there's whores."

The speakers crackled into life—a Cuban stewardess speaking Spanish. "Hey, that's us," David said suddenly. "They want us at the desk." He paused. "You hold Loretta, I'll go." He hurried off.

Laura and Carlotta stared at each other.

"He told me what you did," Laura said. "In case you were wondering."

Carlotta half smirked. "Orders, Laura."

"I thought we were friends."

"Friends maybe. But not Sisters," Carlotta said. "I know where my loyalties lie. Just as well as you do."

Laura hefted Loretta's tote and slipped its strap onto her shoulder. "Loyalty doesn't give you the right to trash my family life."

Carlotta blinked. "Family, huh? If family meant so much to you, you'd be taking care of your man and baby in Texas, not dragging them here into the line of fire."

"How dare you," Laura said. "David believes in this as much as I do."

"No, he doesn't. You hustled him into this so you could crawl up your company hierarchy." She raised a hand. "Laura, he's just a man. You need to get him away from the guns. The old evil's loose again. Men are full of war poison."

"That's *craziness!*"

Carlotta shook her head. "You're out of your league, Laura. Are you willing to put your body between a gun and a victim? I am. But you're not, are you? You don't have faith."

"I'm faithful to David," Laura said tightly. "I'm faithful to my company. What about you? What about faithful old Sticky?"

"Sticky's a buffalo soldier," Carlotta said. "Cannon fodder, full of war evil."

"So that's it?" Laura said, amazed. "You just drop him? Write him off, just like that?"

"I'm off Romance now," Carlotta said, as if that explained everything. She reached into her robes and handed Laura a vial of red pills. "Look, take these, I don't need 'em now—and stop being so stupid. All that crap you think is so important—two of these'll put it all out of your mind. Go back to Galveston, Laura, check into a hotel somewhere, and fuck David's brains out. Snuggle up under the covers and stay out of the way where you won't get hurt."

Carlotta folded her arms and refused to take the vial back. Laura stuffed it angrily into her jeans pocket. "So it really was completely artificial," she said. "You never felt anything genuine for Sticky at all."

"I was watching him for the Church," she said. "He kills people."

"I can't believe this," Laura said, staring at her. "I don't much like Sticky, but I accept him. As a person. Not a monster."

"He's a professional hit man," Carlotta said. "He's killed over a dozen people."

"I don't believe you."

"What did you expect—that he'd carry an axe and drool? Captain Thompson doesn't follow your rules. The *houngans* have been workin' on him for years. He's not an 'acceptable person'—he's like an armed warhead! You wondered about drug factories—Sticky Thompson *is* a drug factory."

"What's that supposed to mean?" Laura said.

"I mean his guts are full of bacteria. Special ones—little drug factories. Where do you think he got that nickname—Sticky? He can eat a carton of yogurt and it turns him into a killing machine."

"A killing machine?" Laura said. "A *carton* of *yogurt?*"

"It's the enzymes. The bugs eat 'em. Make him fast—strong—feeling no pain, no doubt at all. They're gonna sic him on Singapore, and wow, I feel sorry for that little island."

Sticky Thompson—a drug-crazed assassin. She still couldn't believe it. But what did hit men look like, anyway? Laura's head spun. "Why didn't you tell me all this before?"

Carlotta looked at her pityingly. "Because you're a straight, Laura."

"Stop calling me that!" Laura said. "What makes you so different?"

"Look at you," Carlotta said. "You're educated. You're smart. You're beautiful. You're married to a goddamn architect. You have a wonderful baby and friends in high places."

Her eyes narrowed; she began to hiss. "Then look at me. I'm a cracker. Ugly. No family. Daddy used to beat me up. I never finished school—I can't hardly read and write. I'm diselxic, or whatever they call it. You ever wonder what happens to people who can't read and write? In your fucking beautiful Net world with all its fucking data? No, you never thought of that, did you? If I found a place for myself, it was in the teeth of people like you."

She pulled her wimple back over her head. "And getting older, too. I bet you never even wondered what happens to old Church girls. When we can't work that old black magic on your precious husbands. Well, don't worry about me, Mrs. Webster. Our Goddess stands by Her own. Our Church runs hospitals, clinics, rest homes—we take care of people. The Goddess gave me my life, not you or your Net. So I don't owe you nothing!" She looked ready to spit. "Never forget that."

David came up with the tickets. "It's all set. We're out of

here. Thank God.'' The speaker announced a flight—the crowd broke into hubbub. The baby began whimpering. David took her tote. ''You okay, Carlotta?''

''I'm jus' fine,'' Carlotta said, smiling on him sunnily. ''Y'all come visit me in Galveston, won't y'all? Our Reverend Morgan just won a seat on the City Council. We got big plans for Galveston.''

''This is our flight,'' David said. ''Good thing we don't have any luggage—but man, I'm gonna miss that toolbox.''

6

*I*T was a nightmarish flight—like a cattle car. Luggage crammed everywhere, every seat taken, and refugees crouching in the aisles. Nothing to eat or drink. An instant black market, packed into a flying aluminum jail.

There were five armed Cuban flight marshals onboard. They kept fending back entrepreneurs—sweaty hustlers trying to scrape together some global cash. Their tinker-toy Grenadian roubles were meaningless now; they needed ecu and were selling anything—pinky rings, strips of drug stickers, sisters if they had them. . . . Cut off from the world, thirty thousand feet above the Caribbean, but still going through the ritual motions. But faster now, senselessly, jumping and flickering . . .

"Like a lizard throwing off its tail," Laura said. "That's what the Bank did with these people. Let the Net have 'em, let the Vienna heat work 'em over. To distract attention."

"You told Andrei you'd go to Singapore," David said.

"Yeah."

"No way," David said. In his toughest voice.

"We're in too deep to back out now."

"The hell," he said. "We could have been killed today. This isn't our problem—not anymore. It's way too big for us."

"So what do we do? Go back to our Lodge and hope they forget all about us?"

"There's lots of other Lodges," David said. "We could go into a Retreat. You and I, we could do with a good Retreat sabbatical. Relax a little, get away from the televisions. Get our thoughts together."

A Retreat. Laura didn't like the idea. Retreats were for Rizome's retired people, or failures, or blunderers. A place to rusticate while other people made the decisions. "That won't wash," she said. "It would discredit Rizome's attempt to negotiate. But we were right to try it. We have to do something. It's coming to a head—this proves it.

"Then it should be the U.S. State Department," David said. "Or the Vienna heat—somebody global. Not our company."

"Rizome is global! Besides, Grenada would shoot a Yankee diplomat on sight. State Department—come on, David, you might as well send in guys with big placards around their neck that say 'hostage.' " She sniffed. "Besides, the Feds don't have any clout."

"This is a war. Governments run wars. Not corporations."

"That's premillennium talk," Laura said. "The world's different now."

"You could have been one of those dead bodies in the water. Or me, or the baby. Don't your realize that?"

"I know it better than you," she said grimly. "You weren't standing next to me when they killed Stubbs."

David flushed. "That's a shitty thing to say. I'm standing next to you now, aren't I?"

"Are you?"

His jaw muscles clenched and he stared at his hands as if willing them not to punch her. "Well, I guess that depends, doesn't it? On what you think you're doing."

"I know my long-term goals," Laura said. "Which is more than you can say." She touched the baby's cheek. "What kind of world will she live in? That's what's at stake."

"That sounds really noble," he said. "And just a hair away from megalomania. The world's bigger than the two of us. We don't live in the 'globe,' Laura. We live with each other. And our child."

He took a deep breath, let it out. "I've had it, that's all. Maybe my number came up once—okay, I'll stand in the front lines for Rizome. I'll do one tour of duty. I'll watch dead bodies, I'll have my house burned over my head. But they don't pay me enough to die."

"Nobody's ever paid that much," Laura said. "But we can't watch people be murdered, and say it's fine and dandy and none of our business."

"We're not indispensable. Let somebody else have a shot at playing Joan of Arc."

"But I know what's happening," she said. "That makes me valuable. I've seen things other people didn't. Even you, David."

"Oh, great," David said. "So now you're going to start in on how I walk through life in a fog. Listen, *Mrs. Webster*, I saw more of the real Grenada than you ever did. The *real* things—not this trivial power-play bullshit that you run with your old girls' network. Goddamn it, Laura! You've got to learn to take some setbacks and accept your limits!"

"You mean *your* limits," Laura said.

He stared. "Sure. If you want to see it that way. My limits. I've reached them. That's it. End of discussion."

She sank back into her seat, raging. Fine. He'd given up listening. Let's see how some silence suited him.

After a few hours of silence she realized she'd made a mistake. But it was too late to go back then.

Police boarded the plane at Havana Airport. The passengers were marched off—not exactly at gunpoint, but close enough not to matter much. It was dark and raining. Behind a distant line of striped sawhorses, the Spanish-language press lifted cameras and shouted questions. One exile tried to wander in their direction, waving his arms—he was quickly herded back.

They entered a wing of the terminal, surrounded by jeeps. It was crawling with customs men. And the Vienna heat—exquisitely dressed plainclothesmen with their portable terminals and speckled glasses.

Police began hustling the refugees into ragged lines. Cuban cops, locals, demanding ID. They escorted a group of triumphantly grinning techs past the glowering Viennese. Law-enforcement turf battles. Cuba had never been all that hot about the Convention.

Someone called out in Japanese. *"Laura-san ni o-banashi shitai no desu ga!"*

"Koko desu," she answered. She spotted them—a young Japanese couple, standing near an exit door beside a uniformed Cuban cop. "C'mon," she told David—her first word

to him in hours—and walked toward them. *"Donata ni goyo desu ka?"*

The woman smiled shyly, bowing, "Rara Rebsta?"

"Hai," Laura said. "That's me." She gestured at David. *"Kore wa David Webster to iu mono desu."*

The woman reached for Loretta's tote. Surprised, David let her take it. The woman wrinkled her nose. *"O-mutsu o torikaetea hoga iito omoimasu."*

"Yeah, we ran out of them," Laura said. Blank looks. "Diapers. *Eigo wa shabere masuka?"* They shook their heads glumly. "They don't speak English," she told David.

"¿Qué tal?" David said. *"Yo no hablo japones—un poquito solo. Uhh . . . ¿quien es Ustedes? ¿Y su amigo interesante?"*

"Somos de Kymera Havana," the man said happily. He bowed and shook David's hand. *"Bienvenidos a Cuba, Señor Rebsta! Soy Yoshio, y mi esposa, Mika. Y el Capitan Reyes, del Habana Securidad . . ."*

"It's Kymera Corporation," David said.

"Yeah, I know."

"Looks like they've made some kind of arrangement with the local police." He paused. "Kymera—they're with us, right? Economic democrats."

"Solidaridad," Yoshio told him, holding up two fingers. He winked and opened the door.

Kymera had a car waiting.

Kymera was very well prepared. They had everything. New passports for them—legal ones. New decks. Diapers and baby formula. A change of clothes that almost fit, or would have if they hadn't been eating Rita's banquets. And they'd cooled things with the Cuban police. Laura thought it was best not to ask how.

They spent a quiet evening in miraculous, cozy safety at one of Kymera's Havana compounds. And off the Net, in privacy—a kind of ecstasy, like getting over an illness. Their rooms were smaller and everything was closer to the floor, but otherwise it was like old home week in a Rizome Lodge. They chatted in Japanese and Spanish over seafood and sake, and met the Takedas' adorable four-year-old.

"Rizome has shown us some of your tapes," Yoshio said,

pausing for translations. "We are coordinating. Putting all cards on the table between us."

"You saw the terrorist attack, then," Laura said.

Yoshio nodded. "Mali has gone too far."

"You're sure it's Mali?"

"We know," Yoshio said. "We used to hire them."

Laura was stunned. "Kymera hired the F.A.C.T.?"

Yoshio looked sheepish, but determined to have it out. "We suffered much from piracy. The 'Army of Counter-Terrorism' offered us their services. To frighten the pirates, discourage them. Yes, even kill them. They were efficient. We paid them secretly for years. So did many other companies. It seemed better than making armies of our own people."

David and Laura conferred. David was scandalized. "The Japanese hired terrorist mercenaries?"

Yoshio looked impatient. "We're not Japanese! Kymera is incorporated in Mexico."

"Oh."

"You know how things are in Japan," Yoshio scoffed. "Fat! Lazy! Full of elderly people, far behind the times . . ." He tapped his cup and Mika poured him sake. "Too much success in Japan! It's Japanese politics that created this world crisis. Too much behind the scenes. Too many polite lies— *hipokurasi . . .*" He used the English word. The Japanese terms for the word *hypocrisy* sounded too much like compliments.

"We thought the Free Army was a necessary evil," he continued. "We never knew they were so ambitious. So smart, so fast. The Free Army is the dark side of our own conglomerates—our *keiretsu.*"

"But what does Mali have to gain?"

"Nothing! The Free Army owns that country. They conquered it while it was weak with famine. They've grown stronger and stronger, while we quietly paid them and pretended not to know that they existed. They used to hide, like a rat—now they are grown large, like a tiger."

More translations. "What are you saying?" David said.

"I say the Net has too many holes. All these criminals— Singapore, Cyprus, Grenada, even Mali itself, which we creaed—must be crushed. It had to happen. It is happening today. The Third World War is here."

Mika giggled.

"It is a little war," Yoshio admitted. "Does not live up to its press, eh? Small, quiet, run by remote control. Fighting in places where no one looks, like Africa. Places we neglected, because we could not make profit there. Now we must stop being so blind."

"Is this Kymera's official policy line these days?" Laura said.

"Not just ours," Yoshio said. "Talk is spreading fast, since the attack. We were prepared for something like this. Kymera is launching a diplomatic offensive. We are taking our case to many other multinationals. East, West, South, North. If we can act in concert, our power is very great.'

"You're proposing some kind of global security cartel?" Laura said.

"Global Co-Prosperity Sphere!" Mika said. "How does that sound?"

"Uhmm," David mused. "In America, that's known as 'conspiracy in restraint of trade.' "

"What is your loyalty?" Yoshio asked soberly. "America or Rizome?"

Laura and David exchanged glances. "Surely it wouldn't come to that," Laura said.

"Do you think America can set things to rights? Rearm, invade the data havens, and impose peace?"

"No way," David said. "The other Vienna signatories would be all over us. . . . 'Imperial America'—Christ, it wouldn't be six months before people were car-bombing us all over the world." He prodded glumly with his chopsticks at a lump of sukiyaki. "And *ay de mi, los Rusos*—not that the Soviets amount to much these days, but would they ever be pissed. . . . Look, the real agency to handle these matters is the Vienna Convention. The Vienna spooks are licensed to stop terrorism—that's their job."

"Then why aren't they doing it?" Yoshio said.

"Well," David said uneasily, "I guess it's like the U.N. used to be. A good idea, but when it comes down to it, no sovereign government really wants to—"

"*Exactamente*," Yoshio said. "No *government*. But *we* could be very happy with a global police force. And Vienna is global. *Un grupo nuevo-millennario*. Just like a modern *keiretsu*.''

Laura shoved her plate away, struggling with her Japanese. "Vienna exists to protect 'the political order.' To protect governments. They don't belong to us. Corporations can't sign diplomatic treaties.''

"Why not?" Yoshio said bluntly. "A treaty is only a contract. You're talking like my grandmother. It's our world now. Now there's a tiger loose in it! A tiger we made—because we foolishly paid other people to be the claws and teeth of our corporations.''

"Who bells the cat?" said Mika in English. She poured fresh sake into the little electric kettle.

Yoshio laughed at them. "Such long faces. Why be so shocked? You were acting as Rizome diplomats already—subverting Grenada for your corporate politics. Don't be so—what's the word? Inscrutable! Be more modern!" He stretched out his kimono'd arms. "Grab the problem with both hands.''

"I don't see how that's possible," Laura said.

"It's very possible," Yoshio said. "Kymera and Farben have studied this problem. With help from other allies, such as your Rizome, we could multiply Vienna's budget many times, quickly. We could hire many mercenaries and put them under Vienna's command. We could launch a sudden attack on Mali and kill the tiger immediately.''

"Is that legal?" David said.

Yoshio shrugged. "Who do you ask? Who makes that decision? Governments like America? Or Japan? Or Mali or Grenada? Or do we decide, instead? Let's vote." He raised his hand. "I say it's legal.''

Mika raised her hand. "Me too.''

"How long can we wait?" Yoshio said. "The Free Army attacked a little island, but it could have been Manhattan Island. Should we wait for that?''

"But you're talking about bribing the global police," Laura said. "That sounds like a coup d'état!''

" 'Kudetah?' " Yoshio said, blinking. He shrugged. "Why work through governments anymore? Let us cut out the middleman.''

"But Vienna would never agree. Would they?''

"Why not? Without us, they will never be a true global army."

"Let me get this straight," Laura said. "You're talking about a corporate army, without any legal national backing, invading sovereign nations?"

"A revolution is not a dinner party," Mika said. She rose gracefully and began clearing dinner away.

Yoshio smiled. "Modern governments are weak. We have *made* them weak. Why pretend otherwise? We can play them against one another. They need us worse than we need them."

"Traicion," David said. "Treason."

"Call it a labor strike," Yoshio suggested.

"But by the time you got all your corporations together," Laura said, "government police would be arresting your conspirators right and left."

"It is a little race, isn't it?" Yoshio observed brightly. "But let us see who controls the Vienna police. They will do much arresting before this is over. The bureaucrats call us 'traitors'? We can call them 'terrorist sympathizers.' "

"But you're talking global revolution!"

"Call it 'rationalization,' " Yoshio suggested, handing Mika a plate. "It sounds nicer. We remove unnecessary barriers in the flow of the global Net. Barriers that happen to be governments."

"But what kind of world would that give us?"

"It would depend on who made the new rules," Yoshio said. "If you join the winning side, you get to vote. If not, well . . ." He shrugged.

"Yeah? What if your side loses?"

"Then the nations get to fight over us, to try us for treason," Mika said. "The courts could sort it out. In fifty years maybe."

"I think I'd burn my Japanese passport and become a Mexican citizen," Yoshio mused. "Maybe all of us could become Mexican citizens. Mexico wouldn't complain. Or we could try Grenada! We could try a new country every year."

"Don't betray your *own* government," Mika suggested. "Just betray *everyone else's* government. No one ever called *that* treason."

"Rizome elections are coming up soon," Yoshio said.

"You say you're economic democrats. If you believe in the Net—if you believe your own morality—you cannot escape this issue. Why not put it to a vote?"

Even at Atlanta's airport, Laura felt that hemmed-in, antsy feeling the city always gave her. The megalopolis, that edgy tempo . . . So many Americans, with their clean, expensive clothes and bulging luggage. Milling under the giant, slanting openwork of multimillion-ecu geodesics, sleek designer geometries of light and space. Rose-pink abstract mobiles, reacting to the crowd flow, dipped and whirled slowly overhead. Like exploded cybernetic flocks of flamingos . . .

"Wow," David said, nudging her with the baby's tote. "Who's the fox with Emily?"

Two women approaching. One, short and round-faced, in long skirt and frilled blouse: Emily Donato. Laura felt a surge of pleasure and relief. Emily was here, Rizome's cavalry. Laura waved.

And Emily's companion: a tall black woman with a lovely machine-curled mane of auburn hair, carrying herself like a runway model. Lean and elegant, with coffee-colored skin and cheekbones to die for. "Whoa," Laura said. "That's— what's her name—Arbright something."

"Dianne Arbright on cable news," David said, gawking. "A media talking head. Look, she's got legs just like a real human being!"

David gave Emily a hard, crunching hug, lifting her off the floor. Emily laughed at him and kissed his cheeks. "Hi," Laura said to the TV journalist. She shook Arbright's cool, muscular hand. "I suppose this means we're famous."

"Yeah, this crowd's full of journos," Arbright told her. She flicked the lapel of her saffron silk business vest. "I'm wired for sound, by the way."

"So are we, I think," Laura said. "I got a telly-rig in my carry-on."

"I'll pool my data with the other correspondents," Arbright said. There was the faintest beading of sweat on her upper lip, below the sleek mocha perfection of her video makeup. "Not that we can air it, but . . . we network behind the scenes." She glanced at Emily. "Y'all know how it is."

Laura watched Arbright with an eerie sense of dislocation. Meeting Dianne Arbright in person was a bit like seeing the "real" Mona Lisa—some essential reality leached out by too many reproductions. "Is it Vienna?" she said.

Arbright allowed herself a grimace. "We ran some of Rizome's disaster footage two days ago. We know how bad it is there—the casualty counts, the forms of attack. But since then, Grenada's sealed its borders. And Vienna censors everything we air."

"But this is too big to contain," Emily said. "And everybody knows it. This goes way past the limits—somebody just trashed an entire country, for Christ's sake."

"It's the biggest terrie operation since Santa Vicenza," Arbright said.

"What happened there?" David asked innocently.

Arbright gave David the blank look one gives to the terminally out-of-it. "Maybe you can tell me exactly what happened at your Lodge in Galveston," Arbright said at last.

"Oh," David said. "I, uh, guess I see what you mean."

" 'Damage limitation,' " Laura said. "That's what happened in Galveston."

"And in a lot of other places—for years," Arbright said. "So you two are nonpeople, deep-background, off the record. Kinda tough on the good old First Amendment . . ." Arbright flashed some high sign at a brown-suited stranger in the crowd, who grinned and nodded at her. "But Vienna can't stop us from discovering the truth—just from publicizing it."

They filtered toward one of the exists. Arbright tapped her platinum watchphone. "I got a limo waiting. . . ."

"The Vienna heat's here!" David said.

Arbright glanced up placidly. "Nah. It's just some guy wearin' viddies."

"How can you tell?" David said.

"He's got the wrong vibe for Vienna," Arbright told him patiently. "Viddies don't mean much—I wear 'em myself sometimes."

"We've been wearing viddies for days," Laura said.

Arbright perked up. "You mean you've got it all? Your whole tour of Grenada? On tape?"

"Every minute," David told her. "Damn near."

"It's worth plenty," Arbright said.

"Oughta be," David grumbled. "It was a living hell."

"Emily," Arbright said, "who owns the rights, and what are you asking?"

"Rizome doesn't peddle news for money," Emily said virtuously. "That's *gesellschaft* stuff. . . . Besides, there's the little matter of explaining what Rizome personnel were doing in a pirate data haven."

"Mmm," Arbright said. "Yeah, that's a tough angle."

Glass double doors hissed open and shut for them, and Arbright's stretch limo flung its door over the curb, amid a line of taxis. The limo had mirrored windows and a set of microwave beamers in its roof that looked like water-cooled ray guns. They jumped in, following Arbright's lead. The limo slid away.

"Now we're cool," Arbright announced. She popped down a sliding cabinet door and checked her makeup in a stage mirror. "My people have worked this limo over—it's surveillance-tight."

They headed down a curving access ramp. It was an ugly day, gray September overcast cutting across the Atlanta skyline. A mountain range of skyscrapers: postmodern, neo-Gothic, Organic Baroque, even a few boxy premillennium relics, dwarfed by their weird progeny. "Three cars are following us," Emily said.

"Jealous of my sources." Arbright smiled, her eyes lighting up to television wattage. David turned to look.

"They're tracking all of us," Emily said. "The whole Rizome committee. Got our apartments staked out—and I think Vienna's tapping our lines." She rubbed her eyelids. "Dianne—you got a wet bar in this thing?"

Arbright picked up an eyebrow pencil. "Just tell the machine."

"Car, make me a Dirty Kimono," Emily commanded. She rubbed her neck, mashing curls. "Not much sleep lately—I'm a little wired."

"They're really after us? Vienna?" David said.

"They're after everybody. Like an anthill jabbed with a stick." The car gave Emily a cloudy mix that reeked of sake. "This meeting we held with Kymera and Farben—'summit,' they called it. . . ." She blinked and sipped her drink. "Laura, I missed you."

"Getting crazy," Laura said. An old tag line from their college days together. How tired Emily looked—crow's feet in the fine-boned hollow of her temples, more gray threading in her hair—tired hell, why mince words, Laura thought, they were both in their thirties now. Not college kids. Old. An impulse struck her, and she rubbed Emily's shoulders. Emily almost dropped her glass in gratification. "Yeah," she said.

"Who are you with?" David asked Arbright.

"You mean my company?"

"I mean your basic loyalties."

"Oh," Arbright said. "I'm a professional. An American journalist."

David looked tentative. " 'American?' "

"I don't believe in Vienna," Arbright declared. "Spooks and censors telling Americans what we can and can't say. Cover-ups to deny the terries publicity—that was always a half-assed idea." She tossed her head. "Now the whole system, the whole political structure . . . is gonna blow to hell!" She slapped the seat with the flat of her hand. "I've been waiting for this for *years!* Man, I'm as happy about it as a cutworm in corn!" She looked surprised at herself. "As my granddad used to say . . ."

"Sounds kind of anarchical. . . ." David rocked the tote on his knees. Little Loretta didn't like the sound of political stridency. Her face was clouding up.

"Americans used to live like that all the time! We called it 'freedom.' "

David looked dubious. "I meant, realistically speaking . . . the global information structure . . ." He let Loretta grip his fingers and tried to shush her.

"I'm saying we need to pull the masks off and tackle our problems head-on," Arbright said. "Okay, Singapore's a pariah state, they just trashed their rivals—fine. Let 'em pay the price for aggression."

"Singapore?" David said. "You think Singapore is the F.A.C.T.?"

Arbright leaned back in her seat and looked at all three of

them. "Well. I see the Rizome contingent has another opinion." A dangerous lightness in her voice.

Laura had heard that tone before. During interviews, just before Arbright was about to nail some poor bastard.

The baby wailed aloud.

"Don't all speak up at once," Arbright said.

"How do you know it's Singapore?" Laura said.

"How? Okay. I'll tell you." Arbright shoved her makeup cabinet shut with the toe of her Italian boot. "I know it because the pirate databanks in Singapore are full of it. Y'know, we journos—we need a place to trade information, where Vienna can't get on our case. That's why every damned one of us worth his salt is a data pirate."

"Oh . . ."

"And they're laughing about it in Singapore. Bragging. It's all over the boards." She looked at them. "All right. I've told you. Now you tell me."

Emily spoke up. "The F.A.C.T. is the secret police of the Republic of Mali."

"Not that again," Arbright said, crestfallen. "Look, you hear ugly rumors about Mali all the time. It's nothing new. Mali's a starvation regime, full of mercenaries, and their reputation stinks. But they wouldn't dare try a stunt as huge and flagrant as FACT's attack on Grenada. Mali, defying Vienna with an international terror atrocity? It doesn't make sense."

"Why not?" Laura said.

"Because Vienna could knock over Mali tomorrow—there's nothing to stop them. Another coup in Africa wouldn't even make the midnight news. If FACT were Mali, Vienna would've wiped them out long ago. But Singapore—well! Have you ever *seen* Singapore?"

"No, but—"

"Singapore hates Grenada. And they loathe Vienna. They hate the whole idea of a global political order—unless they're running it. They're fast and strong and reckless, and they've got a lot of nerve. They make those little Grenadian Rastas look like Bill Cosby."

"Who?" David broke in. "You mean 'Bing' Cosby?"

Arbright stared at him for a moment. "You're not really black, are you? Either that, or that's not really your baby, fella."

"Huh?" David said. "Actually, uh, there's this, uh, suntan lotion. . . ."

Arbright cut the air with her hand. "It's okay, I've been to Africa, and they tell me I look French. But Mali—that's just disinformation. They've got no money and no motive, and it's an old rumor. . . ." The limo came to a stop and interrupted her.

"Oxford Towers, Miss Arbright."

"That's our stop," Emily said, putting her drink aside. "We'll get back to you, Dianne."

Arbright sagged back into the cushions. "Look. I want those Grenada tapes."

"I know."

"And they won't be worth as much if Vienna makes a major move. That'll crowd everything else off the wires."

"Car, open the door." Emily got out. Laura and David hustled after her. "Thanks for the lift, Dianne."

"Stay in touch." The limo's doors slammed.

The bottom floor of Oxford Towers was a minor city. Healthy-looking fake sunlight poured from fluorescents over the little gourmet groceries and discreet boutiques. Private security dressed like Keystone Kops, cute tall hats and brass-buttoned coats. Meek-looking teenagers on recliner bikes cruised the pastel storefronts.

They ducked into a grocery for diapers and baby food and put it on Emily's card. They joined a group of two dozen bored tenants waiting on curved hardwood benches. An elevator arrived, and everyone shuffled aboard it and took a pew. Floors zipped past in ghastly mag-lev silence with only the occasional sniffle or rustle of newsprint.

They got off on Emily's floor and their ears popped. The air smelled just the least bit fried and stuffy here, fifty floors up. Arcane color-coded maps on the walls. They caught a hall bus. Crabbed little nooks and crannies branched off, leading into patios—what the sociologists called "defensible space." Emily led them off the bus and up a nook. A security mouse scuttled along the floor—nasty-looking little microbot with fretted eyes and a muzzle clotted with dirt. Emily carded the door open.

Three-room place—stark Art Deco black-and-white. David

took the baby into the bathroom, while Emily stepped into the little open kitchen. "Wow," Laura said. "You sure have changed the place."

"This isn't mine," Emily said. "It's Arthur's. You know, the photographer."

"That guy you were dating?" The walls were hung with Arthur's blowups: moody landscape studies, bare trees, a round-faced model in Garbo black-and-white with a cat-eating-cream look on her face . . . "Whoa," Laura half laughed, pointing. "That's you! Hey! Nice."

"You like it?" Emily said. "Me too. Almost unretouched— okay, a little digitizer work." She peered into the freezer. "We got chicken almondine—catfish—Rajaratnam's Ready-2-Eat Lamb Curry . . ."

"Something bland and American," Laura suggested. "Last thing I heard you and Arthur were on the outs."

"Now we're on the very heavy ins," Emily said smugly. "Sorry the food's not better, but Arthur and I, we don't do much *cooking* in here. . . . Y'know, they got my place staked out, but it's eight floors down—and in a rat nest like Oxford Towers, that might as well be in Dallas. . . . This place is as good a safehouse as anywhere. Arthur's cool about it—I think he's a little thrilled by all the hubbub, actually." She grinned. "I'm his mystery woman."

"Do I get to meet him?"

"He's out of town right now, but I hope so." Emily slotted trays into the microwave. "I have a lot of hopes these days. . . . I'm thinking maybe I finally got it figured. The method of modern romance."

Laura laughed. "Yeah?"

"Better living through chemistry," Emily said, and blushed. "Romance. Did I tell you about it?"

"Oh, Em, no." Laura reached into her jeans pocket, past a wad of change and some salted airline peanuts. "You mean these?"

Emily stared at the plastic vial. "Jesus! You mean you walked through Customs with a pocketful of Red-Hots?"

Laura winced. "They're not illegal, are they? I forgot all about them."

"Where'd you get 'em?"

"In Grenada. From a hooker."

Emily's jaw dropped. "Is this the Laura Webster I know? You're not high on those, are you?"

"Well, have *you* been taking them?"

"Just a couple of times. . . . Can I see that?" Emily shook the little vial. "Boy, these look like megadosage. . . . I dunno, I took 'em, they kind of made an idiot of me. . . . I guess you'd say I went crawling back to Arthur, after that fight we had, but it seemed to do us both good. I mean, maybe it's wrong to be too proud. Take one of those, and it makes the other stuff, the problems, feel kind of pointless. . . . You and David aren't having trouble, are you?"

"No . . ." Laura hedged. David emerged from the bathroom carrying the freshly changed baby. Emily quickly swept the vial into a kitchen drawer.

"What's up?" David said. "You two have that in-joke look again."

"Just saying how y'all have changed," Emily told him. "You know something, Dave? Black suits you. You look really good."

"I put on some weight in Grenada," David said.

"On you it looks fine."

He half smiled. "That's it, flatter the moron. . . . You two talking company politics, right? Might as well let me hear the worst." He sat on a black-and-chrome counter stool. "Assuming it's safe to talk in here . . ."

"Everyone's talking about y'all," Emily said. "You Websters earned *beaucoup* brownie points on this one."

"Good. Maybe we can coast a little now."

"I dunno," Emily said. "Frankly, you're gonna be in pretty heavy demand. The Committee wants you for a council session. You're our situation experts now! And then there's Singapore."

"The hell," David said.

"Singapore's Parliament is holding open hearings on their data-haven policy. Suvendra's there right now. She's been our contact with the Islamic Bank, and she's going to testify." Emily paused. "It's kind of complicated."

"Suvendra can handle that," David said.

"Sure," Emily said, "but if she handles it *really well*, her Committee election's a shoe-in."

David's eyes widened. "Wait a minute—"

"You don't know how this has been playing Stateside," Emily told him. "A month ago it was a side show, but now it's a major crisis. You heard how Dianne Arbright was talking. A month ago a top-rank journo like Arbright wouldn't have given me the time of day, but now suddenly we're sisters, very heavy solidarity." Emily held up two fingers. "Something's gonna give, and soon. You can smell it coming. It's gonna be like Paris '68, or early Gorbachev. But global." She was serious. "And we can be right on top of it."

"We can be six feet fucking under it!" David shouted. "What are you up to? You been talking to those crackpots from Kymera?"

Emily flinched. "Kymera . . . That corpocracy stuff doesn't cut much ice with us, but it sure bears watching. . . . Vienna's acting screwy."

"Vienna knows what it's doing," David said.

"Maybe, but is it what we want?" Emily pulled plates and plasticware. "I think Vienna's waiting. They're gonna let it get bad this time—until somebody, somewhere, gives them political carte blanche. To clean house, globally. A new world order, and a new world army."

"I don't like it," David said.

"It's what we have now, but without the ratholes."

"I like ratholes."

"In that case, you'd better go talk some sense to Singapore." The microwave dinged. "It's only for a few days, David. And Singapore's got a real government, not some goofy criminal front like Grenada's. Your testimony to their Parliament could make a major difference in their policy. Suvendra says—"

David's face turned leaden. "We're gonna get killed," he said. "Don't you understand that yet? All the little ratholes are gonna be battle zones. There are people out there who would kill us for nothing at all, and if they can kill us for *profit*, they're *thrilled!* And *they know who we are*, that's what scares me. We're *valuable* now. . . ."

He rubbed his stubbled cheek. "We're getting the hell out of here, into a Lodge or a Retreat, and if you want to take care of Singapore, Emily, well, call Vienna and finance Rizome's Fightin' Armor Division. 'Cause they mean business these pirates and we're never gonna sweet-talk 'em into anything! Not till we put a tank on every fucking street corner! Until we find the sons-of-bitches who pressed the buttons that killed those drowned little kids in Grenada. But not my kid! Never again!''

Laura punctured the foil over her steaming chicken almondine. She felt no appetite. Those drowned bodies . . . stiff and dead and moving on dark currents . . . dark currents of rage. "He's right," she said. "Not my Loretta. But one of us has to go. To Singapore.''

David gaped. *"Why?"*

"Because we're needed there, that's why. Because it has what we want," she said. "Power to control our own lives. And the real answers. The truth!''

David stared at her. "The truth. You think you can get it? You think you're that important?''

"I'm not important," Laura said. "I know I'm nothing much now—the sort of person who gets pushed around, insulted, and has her house shot up. But I might make myself important, if I worked at it. It could happen. If Suvendra needs me, I'm going.''

"You don't even know Suvendra!''

"I know she's Rizome, and I know she's fighting for us. We can't turn our backs on an associate. And whoever shot up our Lodge is going to pay for it.''

The baby started to whimper. David slumped in his chair. He spoke very quietly. "What about us, Laura—you and me and Loretta? You could die over there.''

"This isn't just for the company—it's for us! Running away can't make us safe.''

"Then what am I supposed to do?" David said. "Stand on the dock and blow kisses? While you sail off to make the world safe for democracy?''

"So what? Women always did that in wartime!" Laura struggled to lower her voice. "You're needed here anyway, to counsel the Committee. I'll go to Singapore.''

"I don't want you to go." He was trying to be curt and tough, lay it down in front of Emily like an ultimatum, but all the force was out of it. He was afraid for her, and it was half a plea.

"I'll come back and I'll be fine," she said. The words sounded like a reassurance, instead of a refusal. But he wasn't any less hurt.

Taut silence. Emily looked wretched. "Maybe this isn't the time to talk about it. You've both been under a lot of strain. No one says you're acting non-R."

"They wouldn't have to say it," Laura said. "We know how to feel it without any words."

David spoke up. "You're going to do it no matter what I say to you, aren't you."

It was no use hesitating now. Better to get it over with. "Yes. I have to," she told him. "It's gotten to me now. It's inside me, David. I've seen too much of it. If I don't work through this somehow, I'll never really sleep again."

"Well," he said. "Then it's no use arguing, is it? This is where I beat you into submission, or threaten divorce." He got off his barstool, jerkily, and began pacing. Wired with tension, his feet sluffing the carpet. Somehow she forced herself to stay quiet and let him struggle with himself.

At last he spoke aloud. "I guess we're in the thick of it now, whether we like it or not. Hell, for all we know, half of Rizome's on some terrorists' hit list, just because we took a stand. If we cower to criminals, we'll never live it down." He stopped and looked at her.

She'd won. She felt her face, set stiff and stubbornly, break into a smile. Helpless and radiant, a smile for him. She was very proud of him. Proud just because of what he was; and proud, too, that Emily had seen it.

He sat on his barstool again and locked eyes with her. "But you're not going," he told her. "I am."

She took his hand and looked at it, held it in her fingers. Good, strong, warm hand. "That's not how it works with us," she told him gently. "You're the idea man, David. I'm the one who hustles people."

"Let me get shot," he said. "I couldn't stand it if anything happened to you. I mean that."

She hugged him hard. "Nothing will happen, sweetheart.

I'll just do the goddamned job. And I'll come back. Covered with glory.''

He broke away from her, got to his feet. "You won't even give me that much, will you?'' He headed for the door. "I'm going out.''

Emily opened her mouth. Laura grabbed her arm. David left the apartment.

"Let him go,'' Laura said. "He's like that when we fight. He needs it.''

"I'm sorry,'' she said.

Laura felt close to tears. "It's been real bad for us. All that time online. He has to blow off some steam.''

"You're just jet-lagged. And Net-burned. I'll get you some Kleenex.''

"I'm better with him, usually.'' She forced a smile. "But right now I'm on-rag.''

"Oh, gosh.'' Emily gave her a tissue. "No wonder.''

"Sorry.''

Emily touched her shoulder gently. "I always hassle you with my problems, Laura. But you never lean on me. Always so controlled. Everyone says so.'' She hesitated. "You and David need some time together.''

"We'll have all the time in the world when I get back.''

"Maybe you ought to think it over.''

"It's no use, Emily. We can't get away from it.'' She wiped her eyes. "It was something Stubbs told me, before they killed him. One world means there's no place to hide.'' She shook her head, tossed her hair back, forced the sting in her eyes to fade. "Hell, Singapore's just a phone call away. I'll call David from there every day. Make it up to him.''

Singapore.

7

SINGAPORE. Hot tropic light slanted through brown wooden shutters. A ceiling fan creaked and wobbled, creaked and wobbled, and dust motes did a slow atomic dance above her head.

She was on a cot, in an upstairs room, in an elderly waterfront barn. Rizome's HQ in Singapore—the Rizome godown.

Laura sat up, reluctantly, blinking. Thin wood-grain linoleum, cool and tacky under her sweating feet. The siesta had made her head hurt.

Massive steel I-beams pierced through floor and ceiling, their whitewash peeling over lichen patches of rust. The walls around her were piled high with bright, unstable heaps of crates and cardboard boxes. Canned hairspray that was bad for the atmosphere. Ladies' beauty soap full of broad-spectrum antibiotics. Quack tonics of zinc and ginseng that claimed to cure impotence and clarify the spleen. All this evil crap had come with the place when the previous owners went bankrupt. Suvendra's Rizome crew refused to market it.

Sooner or later they would toss it out and take the loss, but in the meantime a clan of geckos had set up housekeeping in the nooks and crannies. Geckos—wall-walking lizards with pale, translucent skins, and slitted eyes, and swollen-fingered paws. Here came one now, picking its way stealthily across the water-stained ceiling. It was the big matronly-looking one that liked to crouch overhead by the light fixture. "Hello, Gwyneth," Laura called to it, and yawned.

She checked her wrist. Four P.M. She was still far behind on her sleep, hurry and worry and jet lag, but it was time to get up and get back after it.

She stepped into her jeans, straightened her T-shirt. Her deck sat on a small folding table, behind a big woven basket of paper flowers. Some Singapore politico had sent Laura the bouquet as a welcome gift. Customary. She'd kept it, though, because she'd never seen paper flowers like they made here in Singapore. They were extremely elegant, almost scary looking in their museum-replica perfection. Red hibiscus, white chrysanthemum, Singapore's national colors. Beautiful and perfect and unreal. They smelled like French cologne.

She sat, and turned the deck on, and loaded data. Poptopped a jug of mineral water and poured it in a dragongirdled teacup. She sipped, and studied her screen, and was absorbed.

The world around her faded. Into black glass, green lettering. The inner world of the Net.

PARLIAMENT OF THE REPUBLIC OF SINGAPORE
Select Committee on Information Policy
Public hearings, October 9, 2023

COMMITTEE CHAIR
S. P. Jeyaratnam, M.P. (Jurong), P.I.P.

VICE-CHAIR
Y. H. Leong, M.P. (Moulmein), P.I.P.

A. bin Awang, M.P. (Bras Basah), P.I.P.
T. B. Pang, M.P. (Queenstown), P.I.P.
C. H. Quah, M.P. (Telok Blangah), P.I.P.
Dr. R. Razak, M.P. (Anson), Anti-Labour Party

Transcript of Testimony

MR. JEYARATNAM: . . . accusations scarcely less than libelous!

MRS. WEBSTER: I'm well aware of the flexibility of the local laws of libel.

MR. JEYARATNAM: Are you slurring the integrity of our legal system?

MRS. WEBSTER: Amnesty International has a list of eighteen

local political activists, bankrupted or jailed through your Government's libel actions.

MR. JEYARATNAM: This committee will not be used as a globalist soapbox! Could you apply such high standards to your good friends in Grenada?

MRS. WEBSTER: Grenada is an autocratic dictatorship practicing political torture and murder, Mr. Chairman.

MR. JEYARATNAM: Indeed. But this has not prevented you Americans from cosying up to them. Or from attacking us: a fellow industrial democracy.

MRS. WEBSTER: I'm not a United States diplomat, I'm a Rizome associate. My direct concern is with your corporate policies. Singapore's information laws promote industrial piracy and invasion of privacy. Your Yung Soo Chim Islamic Bank may have a better screen of legality, but it's damaged my company's interests as badly as the United Bank of Grenada. If not more so. We don't want to offend your pride or your sovereignty or whatever, but we want those policies changed. That's why I came here.

MR. JEYARATNAM: You equate our democratic government with a terrorist regime.

MRS. WEBSTER: I don't equate you, because I can't believe that Singapore is responsible for the vicious attack that I saw. But Grenadians do believe it, because they know full well that you and they are rivals in piracy, and so you have a motive. And for revenge, I think . . . I *know,* that they are capable of almost anything.

MR. JEYARATNAM: Anything? How many battalions does this witch doctor have?

MRS. WEBSTER: I can only tell you what they told me. Just before I left, a Grenadian cadre named Andrei Tarkovsky gave me a message for you. *(Mrs. Webster's testimony deleted)*

MR. JEYARATNAM: Order, please! This is rank terrorist propaganda. . . . Chair recognizes Mr. Pang for a motion.

MR. PANG: I move that the subversive terrorist message be stricken from the record.

MRS. QUAH: Second the motion.

MR. JEYARATNAM: It is so ordered.

DR. RAZAK: Mr. Chairman, I wish to be recorded as objecting to this foolish act of censorship.

MRS. WEBSTER: Singapore could be next! I saw it happen! Legalisms—that won't help you if they sow mines through your city and firebomb it!

MR. JEYARATNAM: Order! Order, please, ladies and gentlemen.

DR. RAZAK: . . . a kind of innkeeper?

MRS. WEBSTER: We in Rizome don't have "jobs," Dr. Razak. Just things to do and people to do them.

DR. RAZAK: My esteemed colleagues of the People's Innovation Party might call that "inefficient."

MRS. WEBSTER: Well, our idea of efficiency has more to do with personal fulfillment than, uh, material possessions.

DR. RAZAK: I understand that large numbers of Rizome employees do no work at all.

MRS. WEBSTER: Well, we take care of our own. Of course a lot of that activity is outside the money economy. An invisible economy that isn't quantifiable in dollars.

DR. RAZAK: In ecu, you mean.

MRS. WEBSTER: Yes, sorry. Like housework: you don't get any money for doing it, but that's how your family survives, isn't it? Just because it's not in a bank doesn't mean it doesn't exist. Incidentally, we're not "employees," but "associates."

DR. RAZAK: In other words, your bottom line is ludic joy rather than profit. You have replaced "labour," the humiliating specter of "forced production," with a series of varied, playlike pastimes. And replaced the greed motive with a web of social ties, reinforced by an elective power structure.

MRS. WEBSTER: Yes, I think so . . . if I understand your definitions.

DR. RAZAK: How long before you can dispose of "work" entirely?

Singha Pura meant "Lion City." But there had never been lions on Singapore island.

The name had to make some kind of sense, though. So local legend said the "lion" had been a sea monster.

On the opposite side of Singapore's National Stadium, a human sea lifted their flash cards and showed Laura their monster. The Singapore "merlion," in a bright mosaic of cardboard squares.

Loud, patriotic applause from a packed crowd of sixty thousand.

The merlion had a fish's long, scaled body and the lion head of the old British Empire. They had a statue of it in Merlion Park at the mouth of the Singapore River. The thing was thirty feet high, a genuinely monstrous hybrid.

East and West—like cats and fishes—never the twain shall meet. Until some bright soul had simply chopped the fish's head off and stuck the lion's on. And there you had it: Singapore.

Now there were four million of them and they had the biggest goddamn skyscrapers in the world.

Suvendra, sitting next to Laura in the bleachers, offered her a paper bag of banana chips. Laura took a handful and knocked back more lemon squash. The stadium hawkers were selling the best fast food she'd ever eaten.

Back across the field there was another practiced flurry. A big grinning face this time, flash-card pixels too big and crude, like bad computer graphics.

"It is the specimen they are showing," Suvendra said helpfully. Tiny little Malay woman in her fifties, with oily hair in a chignon and frail, protuberant ears. Wearing a yellow sundress, tennis hat, and a Rizome neck scarf. Next to her a beefy Eurasian man chewed sunflower seeds and carefully spat the hulls into a small plastic trash bag.

"The what?" Laura said.

"Spaceman. Their cosmonaut."

"Oh, right." So that was Singapore's astronaut, grinning from his space helmet. It looked like a severed head stuck in a television.

A roar from the western twilight. Laura cringed. Six matte-black pterodactyls buzzed the stadium. Nasty-looking things. Combat jets from the Singapore Air Force, the precision flyers, Chrome Angels or whatever they called themselves.

The jets spat corkscrewed plumes of orange smoke from their canted wing tips. The crowd jumped gleefully to their feet, whooping and brandishing their programs.

The Boys and Girls Brigades poured onto the soccer field, in red-and-white T-shirts and little billed caps. They assumed formation, twirling long, ribbony streamers from broomsticks. Antiseptic marching school kids, of every race and creed, though you wouldn't guess it to look at them.

"They are very well trained, isn't it?" Suvendra said.

"Yeah."

A video scoreboard towered at the eastern end of the field. It showed a live feed of the televised coverage from the Singapore Broadcasting Service. The screen flashed a closeup from within the stadium's celebrity box. The local bigwigs, watching the kids with that beaming, sentimental look that politicos reserved for voters' children.

Laura studied them. The guy in the linen suit was S. P. Jeyaratnam, Singapore's communications czar. A spiky-eyebrowed Tamil with the vaguely unctuous look of a sacred Thuggee strangler. Jeyaratnam was formerly a journalist, now chief hatchet man for the People's Innovation Party. He had a talent for invective. Laura hadn't liked tangling with him.

Singapore's prime minister noticed the camera. He tipped his goldbridged sunglasses down his nose and peered at the lens. He winked.

The crowd elbowed each other and squirmed with delight.

Chuckling amiably, the P.M. murmured to the woman beside him, a young Chinese actress with high-piled hair and a gold chiton. The girl laughed with practiced charisma. The P.M. flicked back the smooth, dark wing of hair across his forehead. Gleam of strong, young teeth.

The video board left the celebs and switched to the plunging, bootclad legs of a majorette.

The kids left the stadium to fond applause, and two long lines of military police marched in. White chin-strapped helmets, white Sam Browne belts, pressed khakis, spit-polished boots. The soldiers faced the stands and began a complex rifle drill. Snappy over-the-shoulder high toss, in a precisely timed cascade.

"Kim looks good today," Suvendra said. Everybody in

Singapore called the prime minister by his first name. His name was Kim Swee Lok—or Lok Kim Swee, to his fellow ethnic Chinese.

"Mmm," Laura said.

"You are quiet this evening." Suvendra put a butterfly touch on Laura's forearm. "Still tired from testimony, isn't it?"

"He reminds me of my husband," Laura blurted.

Suvendra smiled. "He's a good-looking bloke, your husband."

Laura felt a tingle of unease. She'd flown around the world with such bruising speed—the culture shock had odd side effects. Some pattern-seeking side of her brain had gone into overdrive. She'd seen Singapore store clerks with the faces of pop stars, and street cops who looked like presidents. Even Suvendra herself reminded Laura somehow of Grace Webster, her mother-in-law. No physical resemblance, but the vibe was there. Laura had always gotten on very well with Grace.

Kim's practiced appeal made Laura feel truly peculiar. His influence over this little city-state had a personal intimacy that was almost erotic. It was as if Singapore had married him. His People's Innovation Party had annihilated the opposition parties at the ballot box. Democratically, legally—but the Republic of Singapore was now essentially a one-party state.

The whole little republic, with its swarming traffic and cheerful, disciplined populace, was now in the hands of a thirty-two-year-old visionary genius. Since his election to Parliament at twenty-three, Kim Lok had reformed the civil service, masterminded a vast urban development scheme, and revitalized the army. And while carrying on a series of highly public love affairs, he had somehow managed to pick up advanced degrees in engineering and political science. His rise to power had been unstoppable, buoyed by a strange mix of menace and playboy appeal.

The soldiers finished with a flourish, then snapped to attention, saluting. The crowd rose to sing the national anthem: a ringing ditty called "Count On Me, Singapore." Thousands of smiling, neatly dressed Chinese and Malays and Tamils—all singing in English.

The crowd resumed their bleacher seats with that loud, peculiar rustle emitted by tons of moving human flesh. They smelled of sassafras and suntan oil and snow cones. Suvendra lifted her binoculars, scanning the bulletproof glass of the celebrity box. "Now comes the big speech," she told Laura. "He may start with the space launch, but shall end with the Grenada crisis, as usual. You could be taking the measure of this fellow."

"Right." Laura clicked on her little tape deck.

They turned and stared expectantly at the video screen.

The prime minister rose, carelessly tucking his shades into his suit pocket. He gripped the edge of the podium with both hands, leaning forward, chin tilted, shoulders tense.

A tight, attentive silence seized the crowd. The woman next to Laura, a Chinese matron in stretch pants and straw hat, clamped her knees together nervously and jammed her hands in her lap. The guy eating sunflower seeds set his bag between his feet.

Closeup. The prime minister's head and shoulders loomed thirty feet high on the video board. A silkily amplified voice, smooth and intimate, rang from the elaborate P.A. system.

"My dear fellow citizens," Kim said.

Suvendra whispered hastily. "This shall be major, eh, definitely!" Sunflower Seeds hissed for silence.

"In the days of our grandparents," Kim intoned, "Americans visited the moon. At this moment, an antique space station from the Socialist Bloc still circles our Earth.

"Yet until today, the greatest adventure of humanity has languished. The power brokers outside our borders are no longer interested in new frontiers. The globalists have stifled these ideals. Their clumsy, ancient space rockets still mimic the nuclear missiles with which they once threatened the planet.

"But ladies and gentlemen—fellow citizens—today I can stand before you and tell you that the world did not reckon with the vision of Singapore!"

(Frantic applause. The prime minister waited, smiling. He lifted a hand. Silence.)

"The orbital flight of Captain Yong-Joo is the greatest space achievement of our era. His feat proves to all that our republic now owns the most advanced launch technology on Earth. Technology that is clean, swift, and efficient—based on modern breakthroughs in superconductivity and tunable lasers. Innovations that other nations seem unable to achieve—or even to imagine."

(Wry smile from Kim. Fierce cries of glee from the sixty thousand.)

"Today, men and women around the world turn their eyes to Singapore. They are bewildered by the magnitude of our achievement—a cold fact that puts the lie to years of globalist slander. They wonder how our city of four million souls has triumphed where continental nations have failed.

"But our success is not a secret. It was inherent in our very destiny as a nation. Our island is lovely—but cannot feed us. For two centuries, we of the Lion City have earned every mouthful of rice by our own wits."

(A stern frown on the enormous video-board face. Excited ripples through the crowd.)

"This struggle gave us strength. Harsh necessity forced Singapore to shoulder the burden of excellence. Since Merdeka, we have matched the achievements of the developed world—and surpassed them. There has never been room here for sloth or corruption. Yet while we forged ahead, those vices have eaten into the very core of global culture."

(A gleam of teeth—almost a sneer.)

"Today the American giant slumbers—its Government reduced to a televised parody. Today, the Socialist Bloc pursues its hollow dreams of consumer avarice. Even the once-mighty Japanese have grown cautious and soft.

"Today, under the malignant spell of the Vienna Convention, the world slides steadily toward gray mediocrity.

"But the flight of Captain Yong-Joo marks a turning point. Today our historic struggle enters a new phase—for stakes higher than any we have faced before.

"Empires have always sought to dominate this island. We fought Japanese oppressors through three merciless years of occupation. We sent the British imperialists packing, back to their European decay. Chinese communism, and Malaysian treachery, sought to subvert us, without success.

"And today, at this very moment, the globalist media net seethes with propaganda, targeted against our island."

(Laura shivered in the balmy tropic air.)

"Tariffs are raised—export quotas imposed on our products—conspiracies launched against our pioneering industries by foreign multinationals. Why? What have we done to deserve such treatment?

"The answer is simple. We have beaten them on their own ground. We have succeeded where the globalists have failed!"

(His hand cut the air with a sudden flash of cuff link.)

"Travel through any other developed nation in the world today! You will find laziness, decay, and cynicism. Everywhere, an abdication of the pioneering spirit. Streets littered with trash, factories eaten by rust. Men and women abandoned to useless lives on the dole queue. Artists and intellectuals, without goals or purpose, playing empty games of listless alienation. And everywhere the numbing web of one-world propaganda.

"The regime of Gray Culture stops at nothing to defend, and extend, its status quo. Gray Culture cannot fairly match the unleashed vigor of Singapore's free competition. So they pretend to despise our genius, our daring. We live in a world of Luddites, who give billions to preserve ugly jungle wilderness—but nothing for the highest aspirations of humanity.

"Lulled by the empty promise of security, the world outside our borders is falling asleep.

"It is an ugly prospect. Yet there is hope. For Singapore today is alive and awake as no society has ever been before.

"My fellow citizens—Singapore will no longer accept an imposed and minor role in the world's periphery. Our Lion City is no one's backyard, no one's puppet state! This is an Information Era, and our lack of territory—mere topsoil—no longer restrains us. In a world slipping into medieval slumber, our Singapore is the potential center of a renaissance!"

(The woman in stretch pants clutched her husband's hand.)

"I have risen before you today to tell you that a battle is coming—a struggle for the soul of civilization. Our Singapore will lead that battle! And we will win it!"

(Frenzied applause. Throughout the stadium, men and women—Party cadres perhaps?—leapt to their feet. Catching the cue, the entire crowd rose in surges. Laura and Suvendra stood, not wanting to be conspicuous. Shouts died down, and the stadium rang with cadenced applause.)

("He's nasty," Laura muttered. Suvendra nodded, pretending to clap.)

"Dear ladies and gentlemen," the prime minister murmured. (The crowd settled back like angry surf.)

"We have never been a people of complacency. We Singaporeans have never abandoned our wise tradition of universal military service. Today we profit by that long sacrifice of time and effort. Our small but highly advanced armed forces now rank with the finest in the modern world. Our adversaries have threatened and blustered for years, but they dare not trifle with Fortress Singapore. They know very well that our Rapid Deployment Forces can carry swift, surgical retribution to any corner of the globe!

"So the battle we face will be subtle, without clear boundaries. It will challenge our will, our independence, our traditions—our very survival as a people.

"The first skirmish is already upon us. I refer to the recent terrorist atrocity against the Caribbean island of Grenada.

"The Grenadian government—I use the term loosely . . ."

(A tension-relieving burst of laughter.)

"Grenada has publicly alleged that certain elements in Singapore bear responsibility for this attack. I have called on Parliament to conduct a thorough and public investigation of the affair. At present, dear ladies and gentlemen, I cannot comment on this matter fully. I will not prejudice the investigation, nor will I endanger our vital intelligence sources. However—I can tell you that Grenada's enemies may have used Singapore's commercial conduits as a blind.

"If this is true, I pledge to you today that the parties responsible will pay a heavy price."

(Look of grim sincerity. Laura checked the faces of the crowd. They sat on the edges of their seats, looking serious and glowing and ennobled.)

"Dear ladies and gentlemen, we of this island bear no ill will toward the suffering people of Grenada. Through diplomatic channels, we have already reached out to them, offering them medical and technical assistance in their time of crisis.

"These acts of goodwill have been rejected. Stunned by the cruel attack, their government is in shambles, and their rhetoric is scarcely rational. Until the crisis settles, we must stand firm against acts of provocation. We must have patience. Let us remember that the Grenadians have never been a disciplined people. We must hope that when their panic fades they will come to their senses."

(Kim released his white-knuckled grip on the podium and brushed the smooth lock of hair from his eyes. He paused a moment, working his fingers as if they itched.)

"In the meantime, however, they continue to utter belligerent threats. Grenadia has failed to recognize our basic commonality of interest."

(Laura blinked. "Grenadia?")

"An attack on Grenadia's sovereignty is a potential threat to our own. We must recognize the possibility—the probability—of a covert divide-and-conquer strategy at work. Happening . . . today . . ."

(Kim glanced away from the camera. There were sudden beads of sweat on his powdered forehead—on the giant screen, they looked as big as soccer balls. Long seconds passed. Little knots of anxious murmuring rose among the crowd.)

"Today—tomorrow—I will be declaring a state of emergency—granting the executive . . . power. Necessary to protect our citizenry from possible subversion . . . from attack. By either the Gray globalists, or the blacks. The Gremadies. The . . . Negro niggers!"

(Kim lurched from the podium, half reeling. He glanced to his left again, dizzily, searching for support. Someone off-camera murmured drowned words, anxiously. Kim muttered aloud.)

"What did I say?"

He tugged at his pocket kerchief, and his shades clattered to the floor. He mopped his forehead, his neck. Then a sudden convulsion seized him. He stumbled forward, slapping his podium. His face congested and he screamed into the microphones.

"Dogs fucked Vienna! Ladies and gentlemen, I . . . I'm afraid I'm sorry that the pariah dump-dogs fucked the Ayatollah! Lick my ass! You should—shit on the Space Captain fucking laser launch—"

Horrified screams. A roar and rustle as the crowd of thousands rose in bewilderment.

Kim slumped and fell behind the podium.

Suddenly he vaulted up again, like a puppet. He opened his mouth.

Suddenly, hellishly, he vomited blood and fire. A torrent of livid flame gushed from his mouth and eyes. In seconds his giant video face was blackening with impossible heat. A deafening agonized scream shook the stadium. A sound like damned souls and sheet metal torn apart.

His hair flared like a candle, his skin crisped. He clawed at his burning eyes. The air became a hurricane of obscene metallic noise.

Suddenly, people from the lower stands were scrambling onto the soccer field. Vaulting, stumbling, clambering over the rails, over each other. Sweeping the white helmets of police away, like buoys in a tidal wave.

The noise went on and on.

There was a hard tug at Laura's knee. It was Suvendra. She was crouching low beneath the bleacher, hunkered on knees and elbows. She shouted something impossible to hear. Then gestured—get down!

Laura hesitated, looked up, and suddenly the crowd was all over her.

It poured down the slope like a juggernaut. Elbows, knees, shoulders, murderous stampeding feet. A sudden slamming body block, and Laura tumbled backward, downhill, over the bleacher. She slammed down into something that buckled spongily—a human body.

Concrete rose and smacked her face. She was down and trampled—a crushing blow across her back that drove the air from her lungs. Winded, blinded. Dying!

Raw seconds of black panic. Then she found herself scrambling. Squirming, like Suvendra, under a denting, rocking bleacher. People pouring over her now. An endless, mad threshing engine of pistoning legs. A sandaled foot mashed her fingers and she snatched her hand back.

A little boy spun past her headlong. His shoulder smashed against the hard edge of a bleacher, and he was down.

Shadows and rising heat and the stink of fear and noise, bodies falling, scrambling—

Laura clenched her teeth and lunged out into a beating. She grabbed the boy's waist and hauled him back with her. She wrapped her arms around him, huddled him under her.

He buried his face against her shoulder, clutching her so hard it hurt. Concrete trembled under her, the stadium quaking to the avalanche of human meat.

Suddenly the hellish racket from the speakers vanished. Laura's ears rang. With shocking suddenness, she could hear the boy sobbing. Wails of shock and pain bloomed in the sudden silence.

The soccer field was awash with the mob. The bleachers around her were littered with abandoned trash: shoes, hats, splattered dripping drinks. Down at the railing, the dazed and wounded staggered like drunks. Some knelt, sobbing. Others lay sprawled and broken.

Laura sat up slowly onto the bleacher, holding the boy on her lap. He hid his face against her shoulder.

Streaks of television static hissed soundlessly on the giant display board. She breathed hard, trembling. As long as it had lasted, there had been no time, just a maddened, deafening eternity. Madness had streaked through the crowd like a tornado. Now it was gone.

It had lasted maybe forty seconds.

An elderly turbanned Sikh limped past her, his white beard dripping blood.

Down in the soccer field the crowd was milling, slowly. The police had rallied here and there, clumps of white helmets. They were trying to make people sit. Some were doing it, but most were shying away, dumb and reluctant, like cattle.

Laura sucked her mashed knuckles and gazed down in wonder.

It was all for *nothing*. Sensible, civilized people had boiled out of their seats and trampled each other to death. For no sane reason at all. Now that it was over, they weren't even trying to leave the stadium. Some of them were even *returning to their seats in the bleachers*. Faces drained, legs rubbery—the look of zombies.

At the far end of Laura's bleacher, a fat woman in a flowered sari was shaking and screaming. She was hitting her husband with her floppy straw hat, over and over again.

There was a touch on Laura's shoulder. Suvendra sat beside her, her binoculars in her hand. "You are all right?"

"Mama," the little boy begged. He was about six. He had a gold ID bracelet and a T-shirt with a bust of Socrates.

"I hid. Like you did," Laura told Suvendra. She cleared her throat shakily. "That was smart."

"I have seen such troubles before, in Djakarta," Suvendra said.

"What the hell happened?"

Suvendra tapped her binoculars and pointed at the celebrity box. "I have spotted Kim there. He is alive."

"Kim! But I saw him die. . . ."

"You saw a dirty trick," Suvendra said soberly. "What you saw was not possible. Even Kim Swee Lok cannot spit fire and explode." Suvendra winced a little, sourly. "They knew he was scheduled to speak today. They had time to prepare. The terrorists."

Laura knotted her hands. "Oh, Jesus."

Suvendra nodded at the static-laden screen. "The authorities have shut it down, now. Because it was sabotaged, yes? Someone pirated that screen and put on a nightmare. To frighten the city."

"But what about that weird, vile stuff Kim was babbling. . . . He looked doped!" Laura smoothed the boy's hair absently. "But that had to be faked, too. It was all a faked tape. Right? So Kim's all right, really."

Suvendra touched her binoculars. "No, I saw him. They were carrying him. . . . I'm afraid the celebrity box was booby-trapped. Kim fell into a trap."

"You mean all that really happened? Kim actually *said* that? All about dogs and . . . oh, God, no."

"To drug a man so to play a fool, then make him seem to burn alive—that might seem pleasant—to a voodoo man." Suvendra stood up, tying the ribbons of her sun hat under her chin.

"But Kim . . . he said he wanted peace with Grenada."

"Hurting Kim is a stupid blunder. We could have worked

things out sensibly," Suvendra said. "But then, we are not terrorists." She opened her purse and dug out a cigarette.

A woman in a torn satin blouse limped up the aisle, screaming for someone named Lee.

"You can't smoke in public," Laura said blankly. "It's illegal here."

Suvendra smiled. "Rizome must help these poor mad people. I hope you are remembering your first-aid training."

Laura lay in her Rizome camp bed, feeling like shredded confetti. She touched her wrist. Three A.M. Singapore time, Friday, October 13. The window glowed palely with the bluish light of arc lamps from the wharfs of East Lagoon. Longshore robots on big lugged tires rolled unerringly through patches of darkness. A skeletal crane dipped into the holds of a Rumanian cargo clipper, the vast iron arm moving with mindless persistence, shuffling giant cargo containers like alphabet blocks.

A television flickered at the foot of Laura's cot, its sound off. Some local newsman, a government-approved flunky like all the newsmen here in Singapore . . . like newsmen everywhere, when you came right down to it. Reporting from the hospitals . . .

When Laura closed her eyes, she could still see chests laboring beneath torn shirts and the gloved, probing fingers of the paramedics. Somehow the screams had been the worst, more unnerving than the sight of blood. That nerve-shredding din of pain, the animal sounds people made when their dignity was ripped away . . .

Eleven dead. Only eleven, a miracle. Before this day she'd never known how tough the human body was, that flesh and blood were like rubber, full of unexpected elasticity. Women, little old ladies, had been at the bottom of massive, scrambling pileups and somehow come out alive. Like the little Chinese granny with her ribs cracked and her wig knocked off, who had thanked Laura over and over with apologetic nods of her threadbare head, like the riot was all her own fault.

Laura couldn't sleep, still dully tingling with an alchemy of horror and elation. Once again the black water of her nightmares had broken into her life. But she was *getting better at it*. This time she had actually saved someone. She had jumped out into the middle of it and rescued someone, a random statistic: little Geoffrey Yong. Little Geoffrey, who lived in Bukit Timah district and was in first grade and took violin lessons. She'd given him back, alive and whole, to his mother.

"I have a little girl myself," Laura had told her. Mrs. Yong had given her an unforgettable spirit-lifting look of vast and mystical gratitude. Battlefield gallantry, from sister-soldiers in the Army of Motherhood.

She checked her watchphone again. Just now noon, in Georgia. She could phone David again, at his hideout at a Rizome Retreat. It would be great to hear his voice again. They missed each other terribly, but at least he was there on the phone, to give her the view from the outside world and tell her she was doing well. It made all the difference, took the weight off. She needed desperately to talk about what had happened. To hear the baby's sweet little voice. And to make arrangements to get the hell out of this no-neck town and back where she belonged.

She tapped numbers. Dial tone. Then nothing. Damned thing was broken or something. Cracked in the crush.

She sat up in bed and tried some functions. Still had all her appointment notes, and the list of tourist data they'd given her at customs. . . . Maybe the signal was bad, too much steel in the walls of this stupid barn. She'd slept in some dumps in her day, but this retro-fitted godown was pushing it, even for Rizome.

A flicker on the television. Laura glanced down.

Four kids in white karate outfits—no, Greek tunics—had rushed the reporter. They had him down on the pavement outside the hospital, and they were methodically kicking and punching him. Young guys, students maybe. Striped bandannas hid their mouths and noses. One of them batted at the camera with a protest sign in hasty, splattered Chinese.

The scene blinked away to an anchor room where a middle-aged Eurasian woman was staring at her monitor aghast.

Laura quickly turned up the sound. The anchor woman jerkily grabbed a sheaf of printout. She began speaking Chinese.

"Damn!" Laura switched channels.

Press conference. Chinese guy in medical whites. He had that weird, repulsive look common to some older Singaporeans —the richer ones. A tightened vampire face, sleek, ageless skin. Part hair dye, part face-lift, part monkey glands maybe, or weekly blood changes tapped from teenage Third Worlders . . .

". . . full function, yes," Dr. Vampire said. "Today, many people with Tourette's Syndrome can live quite normal lives."

Mumble mumble mumble from the floor. This thing looked taped. Laura wasn't sure why. Somehow it lacked that fresh feeling.

"After the attack, Miss Ting held the prime minister's hands," said Dr. Vamp. "Because of this, the transfer agent contaminated her fingers also. Of course, the drug dosage was much lower than that received by the prime minister. We still have Miss Ting under observation. But the convulsions and so forth were, ah, never in question in her case."

Laura felt a surge of shock and loathing. That poor little actress. They got Kim through something he touched, and she held his hands. Holding the hands of her country's leader while he was foaming and screaming like some rabid baboon. Oh, Christ. What did Miss Ting think when she realized she was getting it, too? Laura missed the next question. Mumble mumble Grenada mumble.

Frown, dismissive wave. "The use of biomedicine for political terrorism is . . . horrifying. It violates every conceivable ethical code."

"You fucking hypocrite!" Laura shouted at the box.

Light rap at her door. Laura started, then tugged her cotton T-shirt lower, over her underwear. "Come in?"

Suvendra's husband peeked around the door, a natty little man wearing a hair net and paper pajamas. "I am hearing you awake," he said politely. His accent was even less comprehensible than Suvendra's. "There is a messenger at loading gate. He ask for you!"

"Oh. Okay. Be right down." He left and Laura jumped into her jeans. Grenadian cadre jeans—now that she'd broken them in, she liked them. She kicked on cheap foam sandals she'd bought locally for the price of a pack of gum.

Out the room, up the hall, down the catwalk stairs, under

the arching girders and the dusty arc-lit glass. Walls lined with domino stacks of container shipping, socketed steel boxes the size of mobile homes. A dock robot sprawled wheelless on a hydraulic lift. Smell of rice and grease and coffee beans and rubber.

Outside the godown, at the truck dock, one of Suvendra's Rizome crew was talking with the messenger. They spotted her, and there was a quick flare of red as the Rizome kid stomped out a cigarette.

The messenger's sandaled feet were propped on the handle-bars of his rickshaw, an elegant, springy tricycle framed in lacquered bamboo and piano wire.

The boy leapt from his seat with easy, balletic grace. He wore a white muscle shirt and cheap paper slacks. He looked about seventeen, a Malay kid with brown shoe-button eyes and arms like a gymnast. "Good evening, madam."

"Hi," Laura said. They shook hands, and he stuck his knuckle into her palm. A secret-society shake.

"He is 'lazy' and 'stupid,' " the Rizome kid hinted. Like the rest of Suvendra's local crew, the Rizome kid was not Singaporean, but a Maphilindonesian, from Djakarta. His name was Ali.

"Huh?" Laura said.

"I am 'unfit for conventional employment,' " the messenger said, meaningfully.

"Oh. Right," Laura said, realizing. The kid was from the local opposition. The Anti-Labour Party.

Suvendra had scraped up a little solidarity with the leader of the Anti-Labourites. His name was Razak. Like Suvendra, Razak was a Malay, a minority group in a city 80 percent Chinese. He had managed to cobble together a fragile local mandate: part ethnic, part classbased, but mostly pure lunatic fringe.

Razak's political philosophy was bizarre, but he had held out stubbornly against the assaults of Kim's ruling party. Therefore, he was now in a position to raise embarrassing questions on the floor of Parliament. His interests partly coincided with Rizome's, so they were allies.

And the Anti-Labourites made full use of the alliance, too. Ragged bands of them hung out at the Rizome godown, cadging handouts, using the phones and bathroom, running off peculiar handbills on the company Xerox. In the mornings they grouped together in the city parks, eating protein paste and practicing martial arts in their torn paper pants. People gathered to laugh at them.

Laura gave the kid her best conspiratorial glance. "Thanks for coming so late. I appreciate your, uh, dedication."

The boy shrugged. "No problem, madam. I am the observer for your civil rights."

Laura glanced at Ali. "What?"

"He is staying this place all night," Ali said. "He is observing for our civil rights."

"Oh. Thank you," Laura said vaguely. It seemed as good an excuse to loiter as any. "We could send down some food or something."

"I eat only scop," the boy said. He plucked a crumpled envelope from a hidden slot under his rickshaw seat. Parliamentary stationery.: THE HONORABLE DR. ROBERT RAZAK, M.P. (Anson).

"It's from Bob," Laura told them, hoping to retrieve some lost prestige. She opened it.

A hasty scrawl of red ink above a printout.

Despite our well-founded ideological opposition we of the Anti-Labour Party do of course maintain files in the Yung Soo Chim Islamic Bank, and this message arrived at 2150 hrs local time, tagged for you. If reply is necessary, do not use local phone system. Wishing you the best of luck in these difficult times. Message follows: YDOOL EQKOF UHFNH HEBSG HNDGH QNOQP LUDOO. JKEIL KIFUL FKEIP POLKS DOLFU JENHF HFGSE! IHFUE KYFEN KUBES KUVNE KNESE NHWQQ KVNEI? JEUNF HFENA OBGHE BHSIF WHIBE. QHIRS QIFES BEHSE IPHES HBESA HFIEW HBEIA!

DAVID

"It's from David," Laura blurted. "My husband."

"Husband," the Party kid mused. He seemed sorry to hear that she had one.

"Why this? Why didn't he just phone me?" Laura said.

"The phones being out of order," the boy said. "Full of spooks."

"Spooks?" Laura said. "You mean spies?"

The boy muttered something in Malay. "He means demons," Ali translated. "Evil spirits."

"You kidding?" Laura said.

"It tell me they are evil spirits," said the boy calmly. " 'Uttering terrorist threats intended to sow panic and dissension.' A felony under Article 15, Section 3." He frowned. "But only in English, madam! It did not use Malay language although use of Malay is officially mandated in Singapore Constitution."

"What did the demon say?" Laura demanded.

" 'The enemies of the righteous to burn with brimstone fire,' " the boy quoted. " 'Jah Whirlwind to smite the oppressor.' Much else in similar bloody vein. It call me by name." He shrugged. "My mother cried."

"His mother thinks he should get a job," Ali confided.

"The future belong to the stupid and lazy," the boy declared. He doubled up his legs and perched expertly on the bamboo strut of his rickshaw.

Ali rubbed his chin. "Chinese and Tamil languages—were these also neglected?"

A gust of wind blew in from offshore. Laura rubbed her arms. She wondered if she should tip the kid. No, she remembered—the A-L.P. had some kind of strange phobia against touching money. "I'm going back inside."

The boy examined the sky. "Sumatra monsoon coming, madam." He popped hinges and pulled up the accordioned canopy of his rickshaw. The white nylon was painted in red, black, and yellow: a Laughing Buddha, crowned with thorns.

Inside the godown, Mr. Suvendra squatted on a quilted gray loading mat under the watery light of the geodesics. He had a television and a pot of coffee. Laura joined him, sitting cross-legged. "I am not like this graveyard shift," he said. "Your message, it is saying?"

"What do you make of this? It's from my husband."

He examined the paper. "Not English. . . . A computer cipher."

A dock robot rolled in with a shipping container on its

back. It stacked the box with a powerful wheeze of hydraulics. Mr. Suvendra ignored it. "You and husband have a cipher, yes? A code. For hiding the meaning, and showing the message is truly from him."

"We never used anything like that! That's Triad stuff."

"Triad, tong." Suvendra smiled. "Like us, good *gemeineschaft*."

"Now I'm worried! I've got to call David right now!"

Suvendra shook his head. "The telly say the phones are bloody down. Subversives."

Laura thought it over. "Look, I can take a taxi across the causeway and call from a phone in Johore. That's Malaysian territory. Maphilindonesian, I mean."

"In the morning," Suvendra said.

"No! David could be hurt. Shot! Dying! Or maybe our baby . . ." She felt a racing jolt of guilt and fear. "I'm calling a taxi right now." She accessed the tourist data on her watchphone.

"Taxis," the phone announced tinnily. "Singapore has over twelve thousand automated taxis, over eight thousand of them air-conditioned. Starting fare is two ecu for the first fifteen hundred meters or part thereof . . ."

"Get on with it," Laura grated.

". . . hailed in the street or called by telephone: 452-5555 . . ."

"Right." Laura punched numbers. Nothing happened. "Shit!"

"Have some coffee," Suvendra offered.

"They've killed the phones!" she said, realizing it again, but with a real pang this time. "The Net's down! I can't get on the goddamn Net!"

Suvendra stroked his pencil mustache. "So very important, is it? In your America."

She slapped her own wrist, hard enough to hurt. "David should be talking here right now! What kind of jerkwater place is this?" No access. Suddenly it seemed hard to breathe. "Look, you must have another line out, right? Fax machine or telex or something."

"No, sorry. Is a bit rough and ready here in Rizome Singapore. Just lately we move into this wonderful palace." Suvendra waved his arm. "Very difficult for us." He shrugged.

"You are relaxing, having some coffee, Laura. Could be message is nothing. A trick by the Bank."

Laura smacked her forehead. "I bet that Bank has a line out. Sure. Guarded fiber-optics! Even Vienna can't crack them. And they're right downtown on Bencoolen Street."

"Oh, dear me," said Suvendra. "Very bad idea."

"Look, I know people there. Old Mr. Shaw, a couple of his guards. They were my house guests. They owe me."

"No, no." He put a hand to his mouth.

"They owe me. Stupid bastards, what else are they good for? What are they going to do, shoot me? That'd look great in Parliament, wouldn't it? Hell, I'm not afraid of them—I'm going down there right now." Laura stood up.

"It's very late," Suvendra said timidly.

"They're a bank, aren't they? Banks are open twenty-four hours."

He looked up at her. "Are they all like you, in Texas?"

Laura frowned. "What's that supposed to mean?"

"Can't call taxi," he said practically. "Can't walk in rain. Catching cold." He stood up. "You are waiting here, I get my wife." He left.

Laura went outside. Ali and the Party kid were sitting together in the back seat of the rickshaw, under the canopy, holding hands. Didn't mean anything. Different culture. Probably not, anyway . . .

"Hi," she said. "Ummm . . . I didn't catch your name."

"Thirty-six," the boy said.

"Oh. . . . Is there a taxi stand near here? I need one."

"A taxi, is it," Thirty-six said blankly.

"For the Yung Soo Chim Bank. On Bencoolen Street?"

Agent Thirty-six hissed a little between his teeth. Ali dug out a cigarette.

"Can I have one of those?" Laura said.

Ali lit it and handed it to her, grinning. She took a puff. It tasted like clove-scented burning garbage. She felt her taste buds dying under a lacquer of cancerous spit. Ali was pleased.

"Okay, madam," said Thirty-six, with a fatalist's shrug. "I am taking you." He elbowed Ali out of the rickshaw's back seat, then gestured to Laura. "Get on, madam. Start pedaling."

She pedaled briskly out of the docks and a kilometer up Trafalgar Street. Then the skies opened up like a water balloon, and rain came down in unbelievable pounding torrents. She stopped and bought a nickel raincoat from a street-corner vending machine.

She turned up Anson Road, pedaling hard, steaming inside her cheap plastic. Rain sheeted from the wheels and steamed off the sidewalks and gushed down the spotless, trashless gutters.

There were a few old colonial-vintage piles by the docklands: white columns, verandahs, and railings. But as they neared downtown the city began to soar. Anson Road became a narrow defile into a mountain range of steel and concrete and ceramic.

It was like downtown Houston. But more like Houston than even Houston had ever had the nerve to become. It was an anthill, a brutal assault against any sane sense of scale. Nightmarishly vast spires whose bulging foundations covered whole city blocks. Their upper reaches were pocked like waffle irons with triangular bracing. Buttresses, glass-covered superhighways, soared half a mile above sea level.

Story after story rose silent and dreamlike, buildings so unspeakably huge that they lost all sense of weight; they hung above the earth like Euclidean thunderheads, their summits lost in sheets of steel-gray rain.

Here and there the rounded tunnels of Singapore's mag-lev trains; she saw one flit silently above Tanjong Pagar, wheelless and bright, the carriages gleaming in Singapore's Coca-Cola white-and-red.

Agent Thirty-six guided her off the street through the automatic doors of a mall. Air conditioning gripped her wet shins. Soon she was pedaling past rank after silent rank of clothing stores, video places, creepy-looking health centers offering cut-rate blood fractionation.

They drove on for over a mile, through ceramic halls thick with garish, brain-damaging ads. Meandering up and down empty ramps, pausing once to enter an elevator. Thirty-six casually popped the rickshaw onto its rear wheels, telescoped the front, and walked it along behind him like a luggage tote.

The malls were almost deserted; an occasional all-night

eatery or coffee bar, its sober, well-groomed customers quietly munching their salads under vivid, spiritless murals of daisies and seagulls. Once they saw some cops, Singapore's finest, in neatly pressed blue Gurkha shorts, with tangle-guns and yard-long lathi sticks.

She no longer knew where the ground was. It didn't seem to mean much here.

They cruised a walkway. Below them lurked a teenage cycle gang: well-dressed Chinese boys with oiled quiffs, crisp white silk shirts, and gleaming chromed recliner bikes. Thirty-six, who had been lounging in the back with his feet up, sat up and yelled. He shot the boys a series of cryptic gestures, the last unmistakably obscene.

He leaned back again. "Pedal fast," he urged Laura. The boys downstairs hastily split up into hunting packs.

"Let me pedal," Thirty-six said. Laura jumped panting into the back. Thirty-six stood on his pedals and the trike took off like a scalded ape. They took corners on two wheels, his hard, plunging legs rasping in their paper trousers.

They crossed the Singapore River half a mile above the ground, inside a glassed-in archway offering snack stands and rented telescopes. Swollen with tropical rain, the little river surged hopelessly in its neatly managed concrete culvert. Something about the sight depressed her enormously.

The rain had stopped by the time they reached Bencoolen Street. Tropical dawn the color of hibiscus was touching the highest steel peaks downtown.

The Yung Soo Chim Islamic Bank was a modest little place, 1990s vintage, a mirror-glass office carton, sixty stories high.

There was a line of people outside it a block long. Agent Thirty-six cruised by silently, languidly dodging the automatic taxis. "Wait a minute," Laura muttered into empty air. "I *know* these people."

She'd seen them all before. In the Grenada airport, just after the attack. The vibe was uncanny. The same people—only instead of Yanks and Europeans and South Americans, these were Japanese, Koreans, Southeast Asians. The same mix though—seedy-looking techies, and hustlers with vacant money-eyes, and nasty-looking bullshit artists in wrinkled tropical suits. That same jittery, verminous look of people native to the woodwork and very unhappy outside of it . . .

Yeah. It was like the world had sloughed off a layer of crime in a bathtub, and this city block was its sink trap, full of suds and hair.

Flotsam, floating garbage, to be racked up and tidied away. Suddenly she imagined the quiet and itchy-looking line of people all lined up and shot. The image gave her a rush of ugly joy. She felt bad. Losing control here. Bad vibrations . . .

"Stop," she said. She jumped out of the rickshaw and dodged across the street. She walked deliberately toward the front of the line: a pair of nervous Japanese techs. *"Konnichiwa!"* The two men looked at her sullenly. She smiled. *"Denwa wa doko ni arimasu ka?"*

"If we had a telephone we'd be using it right now," said the taller Japanese. "And you can knock it off with the high-school *nihongo;* I'm from Los Angeles."

"Really?" Laura said. "I'm from Texas."

"Texas—" His eyes widened. "Jesus, Harvey, look. It's her. What's-her-face."

"Webster," Harvey said. "Barbara Webster. What the fuck happened to you, girlie? You look like a drowned fucking rat." He looked over the rickshaw and laughed. "Did you ride here on that little fucking bike?"

"How do I cut through this crap and get to the Net?" she said.

"Why should we tell you?" Los Angeles smirked. "You crucified us in Parliament. You oughta break your goddamn legs."

"I'm not the Bank's enemy," Laura said. "I'm an integrationist. I thought I made that clear in my testimony."

"Bullshit," Harvey said. "You telling me there's room in your little Rizome for guys who do *musketeer chips?* Fuck it! Are you as straight as you act? Or were you turned, in Grenada? Me, I figure you're turned! 'Cause I don't see how any mama-papa bourgeois democrat is gonna fuck with the P.I.P. out of *principle."*

Thirty-six had now successfully crossed the street, towing his folded rickshaw. "You could being more polite to madam," he suggested.

Los Angeles examined the kid. "Don't tell me you're hanging with these little fuckers. . . ." Suddenly he shrieked and grabbed at his thigh. "God*damn* it! There it is again! Something fucking bit me, man!"

Thirty-six laughed at him. Los Angeles's face clouded instantly. He aimed a shove at the kid. Thirty-six twisted aside easily. With a muted clack, Thirty-six yanked one of the rickshaw's lacquered bracing bars from its sockets. He gripped it and smiled, and his shoebutton eyes gleamed like two dollops of axle grease.

Los Angeles stepped backward out of the line and addressed the crowd. "Something stung me!" he screamed. "Like a fucking wasp! And if it was this kid, like I think it was, somebody here ought to break his fucking back! And goddamn it, I've been standing out here all night! How come fucking big shots like this chick here get to go right in and, hey! This is that Webster bitch, everybody! Lauren Webster! Pay attention, goddamn it!"

The crowd ignored him, with the inhuman patience of urbanites ignoring a drunk. Thirty-six quietly juggled his bamboo club.

A Tamil came limping up the pavement. He wore a dhoti, the ethnic skirt of a south Indian. He had a bandage on his bare, dark shin and an ornate walking cane. He gave Harvey a sharp poke with the cane's rubber tip. "Calming your friend down, la!" he advised. "Behaving like civilized fellows!"

"Fuck you, crip!" Harvey offered indifferently.

An automatic taxi pulled up to the curb and flung open its door.

A mad dog leapt out.

It was a big ugly mongrel that looked half Doberman, half hyena. Its hide was wet and slick, with something thick and oily, like vomit or blood. It erupted from the taxi with a frenzied snarl and tore into the crowd as if fired from a cannon.

It bowled into them, raging. Three men fell screaming. The crowd billowed away in terror.

Laura heard the dog's jaws snap like castanets. It tore a chunk from a fat man's forearm, then leapt up with an obscene, desperate wriggle and dashed toward the front of the bank. Great choking barks and shrieks, like some language of the damned. Flesh and shoes slapped damp pavement, the jostle and rush of panic—

The dog leapt six feet into the air, like a hooked marlin. Its fur smoldered. A wedge of flame split it along the spine, bursting its body open.

Flame poured out of it.

It exploded wetly. A grotesque air-burst of steam and stink, spattering the crowd. It flopped to the pavement, dead instantly, a bag of burning flesh. Threads of impossible heat glimmered in it . . .

Laura was running.

The Tamil had her by the wrist. The crowd was running, everywhere, nowhere, into the streets where taxis screeched to sudden halts with robot honks of protest. . . . "In here," the Tamil said helpfully, jumping into a cab.

It was silent inside the cab, air-conditioned. It took a right at the first curb and left the bank behind. The Tamil released her wrist, leaned back, smiled at her.

"Thanks," Laura said, rubbing her arm. "Thanks a lot, sir."

"No problem, la," the Tamil said. "The cab waiting for me." He paused, then tapped his cast with the cane. "My leg, you see."

Laura took a deep breath, shuddered. Half a block passed as she got a grip on herself. The Tamil looked her over, his eyes bright. He'd moved very fast for an injured man—he'd almost sprained her wrist, dragging her. "If you hadn't stopped me, I'd still be running," she told him gratefully. "You're very brave."

"So are you," he said.

"Not me, no way," she said. She was trembling.

The Tamil seemed to think it was funny. He nudged his chin with the head of his cane. A languid, dandyish gesture. "Madam, you were fighting in the street with two big data pirates."

"Oh," she said, surprised. "That. That's nothing." She paused, embarrassed. "Thanks for taking my part, though."

" 'An integrationist,' " the Tamil quoted. He was mimicking her. He looked down deliberately. "Oh, look—the nasty voodoo spoilt your nice coat."

There was a foul splattered blob on Laura's raincoat sleeve. Red, glistening. She gasped in revulsion and tried to shrug her way out of it. Her arms were caught behind her. . . .

"Here," the Tamil said, smiling, as if to help. He held something under her nose. She heard a snap.

A wave of giddy heat touched her face. Then, without warning, she passed out.

A sudden sharp reek dug into Laura's head. Ammonia. Her eyes watered. "Lights . . ." she croaked.

The overheads dimmed to murky amber. She felt old, sick, like hours had marched through her on hangover feet. She was half-buried in something—she struggled, sudden claustrophobic rush . . .

She was lying in a beanbag chair. Like something her grandmother might have owned. The room around her was bluish with the grainy light of televisions.

"You back to the land of the living, Blondie."

Laura shook her head hard. Her nose and throat felt scorched. "I'm . . ." She sneezed, painfully. "Goddamn it!" She got her elbows into the shifting pellets of the beanbag and levered herself up.

The Tamil was sitting in a chair of plastic and tubing, eating Chinese takeout food off a formica table. The smell of it, ginger and prawns, made her stomach tighten painfully. "Is that you?" she said at last.

He looked down at her. "Who you thinkin', eh?"

"Sticky?"

"Yeah," he said, with the chin-swiveling nod of the Tamils. "I and righteous I."

Laura knuckled her eyes. "Sticky, you're really different this time . . . your goddamn *cheeks* are all wrong and your skin . . . your hair. . . . You don't even *sound* the same."

He grunted.

She sat up. "What the hell have they done to you?"

"Trade secrets," Sticky said.

Laura looked around. The room was small and dark, and it stank. Bare plywood shelving weighted down with tape cassettes, canvas bags, frazzled spools of wiring. Heaps of polyurethane sheeting, and styrofoam noodles, and tangled cellulose.

A bolted wall rack held a dozen cheap Chinese televisions, alive with flickering Singapore street scenes. Against the other wall were heaped dozens of eviscerated cardboard boxes: bright commercial colors, American cornflakes, Kleenex, laundry soap. Gallon paint cans, tubing, rolls of duct tape. Someone had tacked swimsuit shots of Miss Ting inside the grimy kitchenette.

It was hot. "Where the hell are we?"

"Don't ask," Sticky said.

"This *is* Singapore, though, right?" She glanced at her bare wrist. "What time is it?"

Sticky held up the smashed wreckage of her watchphone. "Sorry. Nah sure I could trust it." He gestured across the table. "Take a seat, memsahib." He grinned tiredly. "You, I trust."

Laura got to her feet and made it to the second chair. She leaned on the table. "You know something? I'm goddamn glad to see you. I don't know why, but I am."

Sticky shoved her the remnants of his food. "Here, eat. You been out a while." He scrubbed his plastic fork on a paper napkin and gave it to her.

"Thanks. There a ladies' room in this dump?"

"Over there," he nodded. "You feel a sting, back at the Bank? You be sure to check you legs for pinholes in there."

The bathroom was the size of a phone booth. She had wet herself while unconscious—not badly, luckily, and the stains didn't show through her Grenadian jeans. She mopped herself with paper and came back. "No pinholes, Captain."

"Good," he said, "I'm happy I don't have to dig one of those Bulgarian pellets out of you ass. What the fock you doin' in that Bank crowd, anyway?"

"Trying to call David," she said, "after you screwed up the phones."

Sticky laughed. "Why you nah have the sense to stay with your Bwana? He nah as stupid as he look—have the sense not to be here, anyway."

"What are *you* doing here?"

"Having the time of my life," he said. "The last time, maybe." He rubbed his nose—they'd done something to his nostrils, too; they were narrower. "Ten years they train me for something like this. But now I'm here and doin' it, it's . . ."

It seemed to drift away from him then, and he shrugged and waved it past. "I see your testimony, right? Some of it. Too late, but at least you tell them the same things you tell us. Same in Galveston, same in Grenada, same here, same everywhere for you, nah?"

"That's right, Captain."

"That's good," he said vaguely. "Y'know, wartime . . . mostly, you do nothing. Time to think . . . meditate . . . Like down at the Bank, we *know* those fockin' bloodclots hurry down there when the phones shut down, and we *know* they be just like those bloodclots we got, but to *see* them . . . see it happen like that, so predictable . . ."

"Like wind-up toys," Laura said. "Like bugs . . . like they just don't matter at all."

He looked at her, surprised. She felt surprised herself. It had been easy to say, sitting there together with him in the darkness. "Yeah," he said. "Like toys. Like wind-up toys pretending to have souls. . . . It's a wind-up city, this place. Full of lying and chatter and bluff, and cash registers ringin' round the clock. It's Babylon. If there ever was a Babylon, it's here."

"I thought *we* were Babylon," Laura said. "The Net, I mean."

Sticky shook his head. "These people are more like you than you ever were."

"Oh," Laura said slowly. "Thanks, I guess."

"You wouldn't do what they did to Grenada," he said.

"No. But I don't think it was them, Sticky."

"Maybe it wasn't," he said. "But I don't care. I hate them. For what they are, for what they want to be. For what they want to make of the world."

Sticky's accent had wavered, from Tamil to Islands patois. Now it vanished completely into flat Net English. "You can burn down a country with toys, if you know how. It shouldn't be true, but it is. You can knock the heart and soul out of people. We know it in Grenada, as well as they do here. We know it better."

He paused. "All that Movement talk your David thought

was cute, cadres and feed the people. . . . Come the War, it's gone. Just like that. In that madhouse under Fedon's Camp, they're all chewing on each other's guts. I know I'm getting my orders from that fucker Castleman. That fat hacker, who's got no real-life at all—just a *screen*. It's all *principles* now. Tactics and strategy. Like someone *has* to do this, doesn't matter where or who, just to prove it's possible. . . .''

He bent in his chair and rubbed his bare leg, briefly. The cast was gone now, but there were buckle marks on his shin. ''They planned this thing in Fedon's Camp,'' he said. ''This demon thing, DemonStration Project. . . . They been working under there for twenty years, Laura, they've got tech like . . . *not human*. I didn't know about it—*nobody* knew about it. I can do things to this city—me, just a few brother soldiers smuggled in, not many—things you can't *imagine*.''

''Voodoo,'' Laura said.

''That's right. With the tech they gave us, I can do things you can't tell from magic.''

''What are your orders?''

He stood up suddenly. ''You're not in them.'' He walked into the kitchenette and opened the rust-spotted refrigerator.

There was a book on the table, a thick looseleaf pamphlet. No spine, no title. Laura picked it up and opened it. Page after page of smudgy Xerox: *The Lawrence Doctrine and Postindustrial Insurgency* by Colonel Jonathan Gresham.

''Who's Jonathan Gresham?'' she said.

''He's a genius,'' Sticky said. He came back to the table with a carton of yogurt. ''That's not for you to read. Don't even look. If Vienna knew you'd touched that book, you'd never see daylight again.''

She set it down carefully. ''It's just a book.''

Sticky barked with laughter. He started shoveling yogurt into his mouth with the pinched look of a little boy eating medicine. ''You see Carlotta lately?''

''Not since the airport in Grenada.''

''You gonna leave this place? Go back home?''

''I sure as hell want to. Officially, I'm not through testifying in Parliament. I want to know their decision on information policy. . . .''

He shook his head. ''We'll take care of Singapore.''

"No, you won't," she said. "No matter what you can do, you'll only drive the data bankers underground. I want them out in the open—everything out in the open. Where everyone can deal with it honestly."

Sticky said nothing. He was breathing hard suddenly, looking greenish. Then he belched and opened his eyes. "You and your people—you're staying on the waterfront, in Anson District."

"That's right."

"Where that Anti-Labour fool, Rashak . . ."

"Dr. Razak, yes, that's his electoral district."

"Okay," he said. "Razak's people, we can let them alone. Let him run this town, if there's anything left of it. Stay there and you'll be safe. Understand?"

Laura thought it over. "What is it you want from me?"

"Nothing. Just go home. If they'll let you."

There was a moment of silence. "You gonna eat that, or what?" Sticky said at last. Laura realized that she had picked up the plastic fork. She'd been bending it in her fingers, over and over, as if it were glued to her hand.

She set it down. "What's a 'Bulgarian pebble,' Sticky?"

" 'Pellet,' " Sticky said. "Old Bulgarian KGB use 'em long ago. Tiny lickle piece of steel, holes drilled in, and sealed with wax. Stick it in a man, wax melts from his body heat, poison inside, ricin mostly, good strong venom. . . . Not what we use."

"What?" Laura said.

"Carboline. Wait." He left the table, opened a kitchen cabinet, and pulled out a sealed bubble pack. Inside it was a flat black plastic cartridge. "Here."

She looked it over. "What's this? A printer ribbon?"

"We wire 'em up to the taxis," Sticky said. "Has a spring gun inside, twenty, thirty pellets of carboline. When the taxi spots a man in the street, sometimes the gun fires. An unmanned taxi is easy to steal and rig. The taxis outside that bank were full of these toys. Carboline is a brain drug, it makes *terror*. Terror in his blood, slow, steady leak, to last for days and days! Why work to terrorize some fool when you can just *terrorize* him, simple and sweet?"

Sticky laughed. He was beginning to talk a little faster

now. "That Yankee Jap in the line ahead of you, he's gonna toss, and turn, and sweat, and dream bad dreams. I could have killed him, just as easy, with venom. He could be dead right now, but why kill a flesh, when I can touch a soul? For everyone around him now, he'll talk dread and fear, dread and fear, just like burning meat stinks."

"You shouldn't tell me this," Laura said.

"Because you have to go tell the government, don't you?" Sticky sneered. "You do that for me, go ahead! There are twelve thousand taxis in Singapore, and after you tell it, they have to search every damn one! Too much work to wreck their transport system, when we can get they own cops to do it for us! Don't forget to say this too: we rig their magnet trains. And we got plenty more such lickle guns left."

She set it down on the table. Carefully. As if it were made from spun glass.

The words began to tumble from him. "By now they know that sticky gum their boss man, Kim, touched." He pointed. "You see those paint cans?" He laughed. "Evening gloves comin' back to fashion in Singapore! Raincoats and surgery masks, those are smart, too!"

"That's enough!"

"You don't want to hear about the paper-clip mines?" Sticky demanded. "How cheap they are, to blow a fockin' leg off at the knee!" He slammed his fist into the table. "Don't you cry at me!"

"I'm not crying!"

"What's that on you face then?" He lurched to his feet, kicking back his chair. "Tell me you cry when they haul me out of here dead!"

"Don't!"

"I'm the devil in a cathedral! Stained glass everywhere, but me with lightning under every fingertip! I'm Steppin' Razor, Voice of Destruction, they're gonna bust every black man in this town lookin' for us and they fockin' multiracial social justice, I mean *chaos!*" He was shrieking at her. "Not a stone on a stone! Not a board standing, not a mirror glass that don't cut to the bone!" He danced across the room, flailing his arms, kicking trash underfoot. "Jah fire! Thunder! I can do it, girl! It's *easy!* So easy . . ."

"No! Nobody has to die!"

"It's great! And grand! A great adventure! It's glorious! To have the mighty power in you, and let it run, that's a warrior's life! That's what I have, right now, right here, worth everything, anything!"

"No, it's not!" she screamed at him. "It's craziness! Nothing's easy, you've got to think it through—"

He vanished before her eyes. It was quick, and simple. He gave a sort of sideways jump and wriggle first, as if he'd greased himself to slide through a hole in reality. Gone.

She rose from her chair, legs still a little weak, a pain behind her knees. She looked around herself carefully. Silence, the sound of dust settling, the damp warm smell of garbage. She was alone.

"Sticky?" she said. The words fell on emptiness. "Come back, talk to me."

A rush of human presence. Behind her, at her back. She turned, and there he stood. "You a silly girl," he said, "somebody's *mother*." He snapped his fingers under her nose.

She tried to shove him away. He seized her neck with whiplash speed. "Go on," he crooned, "just breathe."

8

A monsoon breeze whipped at her hair. Laura looked over the city from the roof of the Rizome godown. The Net was a broken spiderweb. No phones at all. Television shut down, except for a single, emergency government channel. Laura felt the dead electric silence in her bones.

The dozen Rizome associates were all on the roof, morosely spooning up breakfasts of seaweed and kashi. Laura rubbed her bare, phoneless wrist, nervously. Below her, three stories down by the loading docks, a gang of Anti-Labourites practiced their morning Tai Chi Chuan. Soft, languorous, hypnotic movements. No one led them, but they moved in unison.

They had barricaded the streets, their bamboo rickshaws laden with stolen sacks of cement and rubber and coffee beans. They were defying the curfew, the government's sudden and draconic declaration of martial law, which lay over Singapore like a blanket of lead. The streets were the army's now. And the skies, too. . . . Tall monsoon clouds over the morning South China Sea, a glamorous tropic gleam like puffed gray silk. Against the clouds, the dragonfly cutouts of police helicopters.

At first, the Anti-Labourites had claimed, as before, that they were "observing for civil rights." But as more and more of them had gathered during the night of the fourteenth, the pretense had faded. They had broken into warehouses and offices, smashing windows, barricading doors. Now the rebels were swarming through the Rizome godown, appropriating anything they felt was useful. . . .

There were hundreds of them, up and down the waterfront, viper-eyed young radicals in blood-red headbands and wrinkled paper clothes, wearing disposable surgical masks to hide their identities from police video. Grouping on street corners, exchanging elaborate ritual handshakes. Some of them muttering into toy walkie-talkies.

They had gathered here deliberately. Some kind of contingency plan. The docklands of East Lagoon were their stronghold, their natural turf.

The docks had been depressed for years, half abandoned from the global embargoes inflicted on Singapore. The powerful Longshoreman's Union had protested to the P.I.P. rulership with increasing bitterness. Until the troublesome union had been simply and efficiently disemployed, as a deliberate act, by a government investment in industrial robots.

But with the embargoes, even the robots were idle much of the time. Which was why Rizome had been able to buy into the shipping business cheaply. It was hard for Singapore to turn down such a sucker bet: even knowing that Rizome's intentions were political, an industrial beachhead.

The P.I.P.'s attack on the union, like most of their actions, was smart and farsighted and ruthless. But none of it had worked out quite the way the Government had planned. The union hadn't broken, but bent, twisted, mutated, and spread. Suddenly they had stopped demanding work at all, and started demanding permanent leisure.

Laura could see them down there now, in the streets. A few were women, a few older men, but mostly classic young troublemakers. She'd read somewhere once that 90 percent of the world's havoc was committed by men between fifteen and twenty-five. They were branding the walls and streets with neat stenciled slogans. "PLAY FOR KEEPS!" . . . "WORKERS OF THE WORLD, RELAX!"

Razak's Rejects, their bellies full of cheap bacterial chow. For years they'd lived for next to nothing, dossing down in abandoned warehouses, drinking from public fountains. Politics filled their days, an elaborate ideology, as convoluted as a religion.

Like most Singaporeans, they were sports nuts. Day after day they gathered in their polite, penniless hordes, keeping fit with healthful exercise. Except in their case it was unarmed combat—a very cheap sport, requiring no equipment but the human body. . . .

You could tell them in the streets by the way they walked. Heads held high, eyes glazed with that calm karate look that came from the knowledge that they could break human bones with their hands. They were worthless and proud, languidly accepting any handout the system offered, but showing nothing even close to gratitude. Legally and constitutionally speaking, it was hard to say why they shouldn't be allowed to do nothing. . . . Except, of course, that it struck at the very heart of the industrial ethic.

Laura left the parapet. Mr. Suvendra had jury-rigged a coat-hanger antenna for his battery-powered TV, and they were struggling to catch a broadcast from Johore. The broadcast flickered on suddenly, and everyone crowded around the television. Laura shouldered her way in between Ali and Suvendra's young niece, Derveet.

Emergency news. The anchorman was a Malay-speaking Maphilindonesian. The image was scratchy. It was hard to tell whether it was a simple TV screwup or deliberate jamming by Singapore.

"Invasion talk," Suvendra translated gloomily. "Vienna are not liking this state of emergency: they call it coup d'état, la!"

A young newswoman in a chiffon Muslim *chador* gestured at a map of the Malay peninsula. Nasty-looking storm fronts showed the potential striking range of Singaporean planes and ships. A weather girl for warfare, Laura thought.

"Definitely, Vienna could not invasion against all that, la. . . ."

"Singapore Air Force are flying up Nauru, to protect the launch sites!"

"I hope their giant lasers are not hitting their own fellow in orbit!"

"Those poor little Pacific Island fellows, they must bitterly regretting the day they started on Singapore client-state!"

Despite its awful news, the television was cheering everyone up. The sense of contact with the Net sent a quick, racing sense of community over them. Half circled, shoulder to shoulder before the TV, they were almost like a Rizome council session. Suvendra felt it, too—she looked up with her first smile in hours.

Laura was discreetly silent. The crew were still chagrined at her for disappearing earlier. She had run off to get in touch with David and had come back unconscious in a cab. She had told them about meeting Sticky. Their first thought was to inform the Government—but the Government had all that news already. The spring guns, the pellets, the mines—the acting prime minister, Jeyaratnam, had announced all that on television. Warned the populace—and shut them up in their own homes.

Suvendra clapped her hands. "Council session?"

A young associate manned the television, off on the corner of the roof. The rest linked hands and briefly sang a Rizome song, in Malay. Amid the city's menacing silence, their raised voices felt good. It almost made Laura forget that Rizome Singapore were now refugees skulking on the roof of their own property. . . .

"For me," Suvendra told them seriously, "I think we have done all we can. The Government is martial law now, isn't it? Violence is coming, isn't it? Do any of us want to fight Government? Hands?"

No one voted for violence. They'd already voted with their feet—by running upstairs to avoid the rebels.

Ali spoke up. "Could we escape the city?"

"Out to sea?" suggested Derveet hopefully.

They looked over the waterfront: the unmanned cargo ships, the giant idle cranes, the loading robots shut down by Anti-Labourite longshoremen who had seized the control systems. Out to sea were the skidding white plumes of navy hydrofoils on patrol.

"This isn't Grenada. They're not letting anyone go," Mr. Suvendra said with finality. "They'd shoot at us."

"I agree," said Suvendra. "But we could demand arrest, la. By the Government."

The others looked gloomy.

"Here we are radicals," Suvendra told them. "We are economic democrats in authoritarian regime. It is Singapore reform we are demanding, but chance is spoilt, now. So the proper place for us in Singapore is jail."

Long, meditative silence. Monsoon thunder rolled in from offshore.

"I like the idea," Laura said meekly.

Ali tugged at his lower lip. "Safe from voodoo terrorists, in jail."

"Also less chance that the fascist Army might accidentally shoot us on purpose, la."

"We must decide for us. We can't ask Atlanta," Suvendra pointed out.

They looked unhappy. Laura had a brainstorm. "Atlanta—it has a famous jail. Martin Luther King stayed there."

They broke into eager discussion.

"But we shan't do any good from jail, la."

"Yes, we can. Embarrass the government! Martial law can't last."

"We do no good here anyway, if Parliament is spoilt."

Distant echoed shouting rose from the streets. "I'll go look," Laura told them, standing up.

She strode across the hot, flat rooftop to the parapet again. The noise grew louder: it was a police bullhorn. For a moment she glimpsed it, two blocks away: a red-and-white police car moving cautiously across a deserted intersection. It stopped before the ragged burlap heap of a street barricade.

Ali joined her. "We voted," he told her. "It's jail."

"Okay. Good."

Ali studied the police car, listening to it. "It's Mr. bin Awang," he said. "Malay M.P. from Bras Basah."

"Oh, yeah," Laura said. "I remember him from the hearings."

"Surrender talk. Go peacefully, back to families, he says."

Rebels emerged from the shadows. They swaggered toward the car, lazily, fearlessly. Laura could see them shouting at the bulletproof glass, gesturing to the cop behind the wheel—turn around, go back. *Verboten.* Liberated territory . . .

The roof-mounted bullhorn bleated arguments.

One of the kids began spray-painting a slogan onto the hood. The prowl car emitted an angry siren wail and began backing up.

Suddenly the kids pulled weapons. Short, heavy swords, hidden in their shirts and pants. They began hacking furiously at the prowl car's tires and door hinges. Unbelievably, the car gave way, with tortured screeches of metal audible for blocks around. . . .

Laura and Ali shouted in astonishment. The rebels were using those deadly ceramic machetes, the same as she'd seen in Grenada. The long high-tech knives that had chopped a desk in half.

The other Rizomians ran up. The rebels hacked the hood off in seconds and efficiently butchered the engine. They wrenched the door off with ear-torturing screeches.

They were pulling the car apart.

They fished out the astonished cops, rabbit-punching them into submission. They got the M.P., too.

But then, suddenly, there was a chopper overhead.

Tear-gas canisters fell, shrouding the scene in up-rushing columns of mist. The rebels scattered. A burly longshoreman, wearing a diving mask, lifted a stolen police blunderbuss and fired tangle-rounds upward. They splattered harmlessly on the chopper's undercarriage in wads of writhing plastic, but it backed off anyway.

More siren howls and three more backup prowl cars rushed into the intersection. They skidded to a halt before the shattered car. Kids were still running from the wreckage, doubled over, clutching stolen tangle-ammo and stenciled canisters. Some wore rubber swim goggles, giving them a weirdly squinty, professorial look. Their surgical masks seemed to help against the tear gas.

Doors flung open and the cops deployed, wearing full riot gear: white helmets, perspex face shields, tangle-guns, and lathi sticks. Kids scuttled for cover into the surrounding buildings. The cops conferred briefly, pointing at a doorway, ready to charge.

There was a sudden feeble *whump* from the wreckage of the prowl car. The car seats belched flame.

In a few moments, a Molotov column of burning upholstery was rising over the waterfront.

Ali yelled in Malay and pointed. Half a dozen rebels had appeared a block away from the fight, hauling an unconscious cop through a rathole in the side of a warehouse. They had chopped their way through the concrete blocks with their machetes.

"They have *parangs!*" Ali said with a kind of horrified glee. "Like magic kung-fu swords, la!"

The cops looked unhappy about charging the doorways. No wonder. Laura could imagine it: dashing bravely forward with tangle-gun drawn . . . only to feel a sudden pain and fall down and find that some rat-faced little anarchist behind the door had just razored your leg off at the knee. . . . Oh, Jesus, those fucking machetes! They were like goddamned *lasers*. . . . What kind of stupid short-term-thinking bastard had invented those?

She felt cold as the implications mounted. . . . All that stupid theatrical kung-fu, the dumbest idea in the world, that silly-ass martial artists with no tanks or guns could resist modern cops or trained soldiers. . . . No, the A-L.P. couldn't fight cops head-on, but room-to-room, with walls riddled with holes, they could sure as hell weasel up from ambush and . . .

People were going to die here, she realized. *They meant it. Razak meant it.* People were going to die. . . .

The cops got back into their prowl cars. They retreated. No one came out to yell or jeer, and somehow it was worse that they didn't. . . .

The rebels were busy elsewhere. Dramatic columns of smoke were rising all along the waterfront. Black, foul, billowing towers, bent like broken fingers by the monsoon breeze. No television, maybe, no phones—but now the whole of Singapore would know that hell was breaking loose. Smoke signals still worked. And their message was obvious.

Down on the docks behind the Rizome godown, three activists sloshed a ribbed jerry can over a heap of stolen truck tires. They stood well back and threw a lit cigarette. The untidy heap went up with a whump, tires jumping like a dropped plate of doughnuts. The tires settled to roast and crackle and spew. . . .

Derveet wiped at her eyes. "It stinks. . . ."

"For me, I like up here better than down in those streets, definitely!"

"We could surrender to a helicopter," Suvendra said practically. "There is room here up on the roof for setdown, and if we signal white flag, they could arrest us, quickly."

"Very good idea, la!"

"Getting a bed sheet if they have left us any. . . ."

Mr. Suvendra and an associate named Bima left for a raid downstairs.

Long, tiring minutes passed. There was no violence for the moment, but the quiet didn't help at all. It only made them feel more paranoiac, more besieged.

Down in the loading docks, groups of rebels clustered around their walkie-talkies. The radios were mass-produced kid's toys, Third World export, costing a few cents. Who the hell needed walkie-talkies when you could carry a telephone on your wrist? But the A-L.P. didn't think like that. . . .

"I don't think the cops can handle this," Laura said. "They'll have to call in the Army."

Mr. Suvendra and Bima returned at last, with wadded bed sheets and a few packs of junk food overlooked by the looters. The rebels hadn't bothered them; they had scarcely seemed to notice.

The crew spread a sheet out on the roof. Kneeling, Suvendra broke open a fibertip pen and smeared a thick black SOS across the fabric. They tore up another sheet for a white flag and white armbands.

"Crude, but efficient," Suvendra said, rising.

"Now we flag up chopper, la. . . ."

The kid monitoring the television yelled. "The Army is in Johore!"

They dropped everything and rushed to the TV.

The Johore announcers were stunned. Singapore's Army had blitzkrieged across the causeway into Johore Bahru. An armored column was racing through the city, meeting no resistance—not that Maphilindonesia could put up much, at the moment. Singapore described it as a "police action."

"Oh, God," Laura said, "how could they be so fucking stupid?"

"They are seizing the reservoirs," said Mr. Suvendra.

"What?"

"Main Singapore water supply on the mainland. Can't defending Singapore with no water."

"They did it before once, during Konfrontation," said Mrs. Suvendra. "Malaysia government very angered at Singapore—try to shut off their water supply."

"What happened then?" Laura said.

"They storm through Johore and head for Kuala Lumpur, the Malaysia capital. . . . Malaysia army runs away, stupid

Malaysia government falls . . . next thing we know, is new Maphilindonesia Federation. New federal government was very nice to Singapore, till they agree to go back in their borders.''

"They learn not to bite the 'Poisonous Shrimp,' " said Mr. Suvendra. "Very hard-working Army in Singapore."

"Singapore Chinese work too hard," said Derveet. "Causing all these troubles, la."

"Now we are enemy aliens, too," said Bima unhappily. "What to do."

They waited for a police chopper. Finding one wasn't difficult. By now a dozen lurked over the waterfront, silent, swaying, dodging the columns of smoke.

The Rizome crew waved their white flag enthusiastically as one cruised nearby, with insolent ease.

The chopper hovered above them, its invisible blades hissing. A cop stuck his helmeted head from the bay, flipping up his face plate.

Confused yelling followed. "Not to worry, Rizome!" shouted the cop at last. "We rescue you, no problem!"

"How many of us?" Suvendra yelled, clamping her sun hat to the top of her head.

"Everyone! Whole thing!"

"In one chopper?" Suvendra shouted, confused. The little police craft might have held three passengers at most.

The chopper made no attempt to land. In a few seconds it rose again, heading north in a smooth, determined arc.

"They could hurry," said Suvendra, glancing at the monsoon front. "Weather turning nasty soon, definitely!"

They wadded up their SOS bed sheet, in case the rebels decided to come up and check on them. Negotiating with the A-L.P. was a possibility, but in council session Rizome had decided not to press them. The rebels had already seized the Rizome godown; they might just as easily seize the Rizome personnel. They'd already kidnapped two cops and a Member of Parliament. The situation's hostage potential was obvious.

Another boring and horrible twenty minutes passed, a tense and morbid silence that fooled nobody. The sun topped the monsoon front, and tropical midmorning blazed over the silent city. So eerie, Laura thought—a blackout of people . . .

Another chopper, larger this time and twin-rotored, buzzed the waterfront. It spun on its axis and hovered momentarily over a corner of the godown. Three black-clad men leapt from the bay doors onto the rooftop. The chopper rose again immediately.

The three men paused a moment, patting gear, then stalked toward them. They wore black fatigues, black combat boots, black webbing belts hung with brass-snapped holsters and utility pouches and ammo kits. They carried short-muzzled, arcane-looking submachine guns.

"Good morning, all!" said their leader cheerfully. He was a big, ruddy-faced Englishman with close-cropped white hair, a veiny nose, and a permanent tropical sunburn. He looked about sixty, but ominously well preserved, for his age. Blood fractionation? Laura thought.

"Morning . . ." someone said dazedly.

"Hotchkiss is the name. Colonel Hotchkiss, Special Weapons and Tactics. This is Officer Lu and Officer Aw. We're here for your safety, ladies and gentlemen. So not to worry, okay?" Hotchkiss showed them a rack of white teeth.

Hotchkiss was huge. Six and a half feet tall, well over two hundred pounds. Arms like tree trunks. She'd almost forgotten how big Caucasians could be. With his thick black boots and heavy, elaborate gear, he was like something from another planet. Hotchkiss nodded at Laura, surprised. "I've seen you on telly, dear."

"The hearings?"

"Yeah. I've—"

There was a sudden bang as the sheet-metal door to the rooftop burst open. A shouting gang of rebels scrambled forward, clutching bamboo clubs.

Hotchkiss spun from the hip and opened up on the doorway with his submachine gun. There was a nerve-shattering racket. Two rebels sprawled, punched backward by impact. The others fled screaming, and suddenly everyone was down, gripping the pebbled surface of the roof in terror.

Lu and Aw kicked the door shut and fired a tangle-round against the jamb, sealing it. They pulled thin loops of plastic from their belts and handcuffed the two fallen, gasping rebels. They sat them up.

"Okay, okay," Hotchkiss told the rest of them, waving his beefy hand. "Only jelly-rounds. See? No problem, la."

The Rizome group rose slowly. As the truth dawned on them, there were nervous, embarrassed titters. The two rebels, teenagers, had been strafed across their chests, tearing gaping holes in their paper shirts. Beneath it, their skins showed fist-sized blotches of indelible purple dye.

Hotchkiss chivalrously helped Laura to her feet. "Jelly bullets don't kill," he announced. "Still pack plenty of sting, however."

"You shot us with a machine gun!" said one of the rebels sullenly.

"Shut up, son," Hotchkiss offered kindly. "Lu, Aw, these two are too small. Throw 'em back, eh?"

"Door is secured, sir," Lu pointed out.

"Use your head, Lu. You have your ropes."

"Yes, sir," Lu said, grinning. He and Officer Aw frog-marched the two boys toward the front of the roof. They began snapping their first captive into a set of chromed rappelling gear. From the loading docks three stories below, furious, bloodthirsty yells rose from the roused A-L.P.

"Well," Hotchkiss said casually. "Seems the rioters have made an operations nexus out of your HQ." Lu kicked one captive over the edge of the roof and paid out rappelling line as the boy hissed helplessly downward.

"But not to worry," Hotchkiss said. "We can break them wherever they stand."

Suvendra winced. "We saw them demolition your squad car. . . ."

"Sending that car in was the politicals' idea," Hotchkiss sniffed. "But now it's our business."

Laura noticed the SWAT leader's complex military watch-phone. "What can you tell us, Colonel? We're starved for news up here. Is the Army really in Johore?"

Hotchkiss smiled at her. "This isn't your Texas, dearie. The Army's just on the other side of the causeway—just a little bridge. A few minutes away." He held up two fingers, an inch apart. "All miniature, you see."

The two Chinese SWAT officers hooked the second rebel to their ropes. Below them, the angry rioters vented howls of frustrated abuse. Flung bricks arched up to crack on the roof. "Throw a few dye-rounds into them," Hotchkiss shouted.

The two Chinese unlimbered their sidearms and cut loose over the parapet. The guns blasted a fearsome racket, spitting spent cartridges. Below them, the crowd shrieked in fear and pain. Laura heard them scatter. She felt a surge of nausea.

Hotchkiss gripped her elbow. "You all right?"

She swallowed hard. "I saw a man killed by a machine gun, once."

"Oh, really?" said Hotchkiss, interested. "You've been to Africa?"

"No—"

"You look a bit young to have seen real action. . . . Oh, Grenada, eh?" He let her go. Frenzied pounding was shaking the roof door. Hotchkiss fired the remaining jelly-rounds of his magazine against it. Brutal pounding and splattering. He flung the empty magazine away, and fitted a second with the casual look of a man chain-smoking cigarettes.

"Isn't this 'real action'?" Laura shouted. Her ears were ringing.

"This is only theater, dearie," Hotchkiss said patiently. "These little parlor radicals don't even have carbines. Try something like this in the bad old days—in Belfast or Beirut— and we'd be lying here with great Armalite sniper holes in us."

" 'Theater.' What's that supposed to mean?" Laura said.

Hotchkiss chuckled. "I've fought real war! Falkland Islands, '82. That was a classic. Scarcely any televisions . . ."

"So you're British, then, Colonel? European?"

"British. I was S.A.S." Hotchkiss wiped sweat. "Europe! What kind of outfit is that, the European Common Army? Bloody joke, is what that is. When we fought for Queen and Country . . . oh, hell, girl, you wouldn't understand anyway." He glanced at his watch. "Okay, here come our boys."

Hotchkiss stalked toward the front of the building. The Rizome crew followed in his wake.

A six-wheeled armored personnel carrier, like some great gray, rubber-wheeled rhinoceros, surged easily over and through the street barricade. Bags burst and squashed aside. Its turret-mounted water cannon swung alertly.

Behind it came two wire-windowed paddy wagons. The wagons flung open rear double doors and cops decamped by the numbers, falling rapidly into disciplined ranks: shields, clubs, helmets.

No one showed to offer resistance. Wisely, because a pair of choppers hung like huge malignant wasps above the street. Their side bays were open and cops crouching inside were manning tear-gas launchers and Gatling tangle-guns.

"Very simple," said Hotchkiss. "No use street-fighting when we can seize the riot's leaders at will. Now we'll grab ourselves a building full of them, and . . . oh, bloody hell."

The entire front of the godown collapsed like cardboard and six giant cargo robots roared into the street.

The cops scattered, stumbling. The robots rushed forward with vim. There was a crude dementia in their actions, the sign of rotten programming. Crude, but efficient. They were built to haul cargo the size of trailers. Now they were grappling wildly at anything remotely the right size.

The paddy wagons toppled over at once, sides denting loudly, tires whirling helplessly at the air. The APC opened up with its water cannon, as three robots tugged and mauled and punched at it with ruthless mechanical stupidity. Finally they levered it over, toppling it stupidly onto the exposed arm of the third robot, which tried to back away, screeching and buckling. The cannon fountained aimlessly, a furious white plume, four stories high.

The rebels were all over the cops. The streets gleamed with water, sloshed under charging feet. Headlong melee, mindless and angry, like a bed of giant ants.

Laura watched in absolute amazement. She could not believe that it had come to this. One of the best-organized cities in the world, and men were beating the shit out of each other in the streets with sticks.

"Oh, Jesus Christ," said Hotchkiss. "We're better armed, but our morale's blown. . . . The air support will tell, though." The copters were firing tangle-rounds at the melee's edges—without much success. Too crowded, too chaotic and slippery. Laura flinched as a skidding dock robot knocked three cops headlong.

Renewed pounding came from the door. Someone had

jammed the ceramic edge of a machete through and was saw-ing vigorously at the tangle-tape. They turned to face it—and saw, beyond it, over the waterfront, one of the loading cranes. The skeletal arm was spinning on its axis, gathering speed with ponderous grace. At the end of its cables was a cargo fridge container, rising high above the docks with centrifugal force.

Suddenly the crane let loose. The heavy cargo box, half the size of a house, spun free and arched dizzily through space. It flew almost gently, arcing and tumbling, like a softball tossed underhand.

Its flight ended suddenly. It slammed, with cybernetic precision, into a black police chopper hovering over the waterfront. There was an explosive burst as the fridge car ruptured, with gaseous jets of frost and the bright cartwheel-ing of hundreds of cardboard boxes. The chopper snapped, buckled, and splashed dramatically into dirty seawater. It lay sprawled amid the floating boxes like a dragonfly crushed by a car grill.

"Mrs. Srivijaya's Frozen Fish Sticks," little Derveet mur-mured, at Laura's elbow. She'd recognized the cargo.

The crane slithered downward, its claws clanking for an-other grab.

"How did they do that?" Hotchkiss demanded.

"It a very smart machine," said Mr. Suvendra.

"I'm getting old," Hotchkiss said sadly. "Where do they control that damned thing?"

"Inside the godown," Mr. Suvendra said. "There are consoles—"

"Fine." Hotchkiss grabbed Mr. Suvendra's skinny wrist. "You take me there. Lu! Aw! We're moving!"

"No," Mr. Suvendra said.

Suvendra grabbed her husband's other arm. Suddenly they were tugging at him like a rag doll. "We don't do violence!" she said.

"You *what?*" Hotchkiss said.

"We don't fight," Suvendra said passionately. "We don't like you! We don't like your government! We don't fight! Arrest us!"

"That bloody crane is going to kill our pilots—"

"Then you stop fighting! Send them away!" Suvendra lifted her voice, shrilly. "Everyone, sit!"

The Rizome crew froze wherever they stood and sat in place, as one person. Mr. Suvendra sat too, though he still dangled by one arm from Hotchkiss's huge, freckled paw.

"You fucking politicals," Hotchkiss said in amazed contempt. "I don't believe this. I'm *ordering* you, as citizens—"

"We're not your citizens," Suvendra said flatly. "We don't obey your illegal martial-law regime, either. Arrest us!"

"I bloody well will arrest you, the lot of you! Hell, you're as bad as they are."

Suvendra nodded, taking a deep breath. "We are nonviolent. But we are your Government's enemies, Colonel, believe it!"

Hotchkiss looked at Laura. "You too, eh?"

Laura glared up at him, angry to see him single her out from her people. "I can't help you," she told him. "I'm a globalist, and you're an arm of the State."

"Oh bloody Christ, you're a sorry bunch of milk-and-water sons-of-bitches," Hotchkiss said mournfully. He looked them over, making a decision. "You," he told Laura.

He pounced on her, handcuffing her arms behind her back.

"He's stealing Laura!" Suvendra yelled, scandalized. "Get in his way!"

Hotchkiss levered Laura to her feet. She didn't want to go, but stumbled up quickly as agonizing pain hit her shoulder sockets. The Rizome crew crowded around him, waving their arms, shouting. Hotchkiss yelled something wordless, kicked Ali in the kneecap, then pulled his tangle-pistol. Ali, and Mr. Suvendra, and Bima went down, clawing at swarming blobs of tape. The others ran.

The rebels were breaking through again. A gap showed at the top of the door. Hotchkiss shouted at Officer Lu, who snatched a black knobby cylinder from his belt and tossed it through.

Two seconds passed. There was a cataclysmic flash from behind the door, a horrific bang, and the door jumped open, gushing smoke. "Go!" Hotchkiss yelled.

The upper stairwell was littered with rebels, deafened, blinded, howling. One was still on his feet, slashing frenziedly at empty air with a ceramic sword and screaming, "Martyr!

Martyr!'' Lu knocked him flat with a burst of jelly-rounds. Then they marched in, firing with their tangle-pistols into the heaving crowd.

Aw tossed another flash-grenade onto the landing below. Another cataclysmic wham. ''Okay,'' Hotchkiss said from behind Laura. ''You wanna play Gandhi, you'll do it with two broken arms. March!'' He shoved her forward through the door.

''I protest!'' Laura shouted, dancing to avoid arms and legs.

Hotchkiss jerked her backward against his chest. ''Look, Yankee,'' he said with chilling sincerity. ''You're a cute little blonde who looks real nice on telly. But if you muck about with me, I'll blow your brains out—and say the rebels did it. Where are the goddamn controls?''

''Ground floor,'' Laura gasped. ''In the back—glassed in.''

''Okay, we're moving. Go! Go!'' Vicious racket as Lu opened up with the gun again. In the enclosed stairwell the hellish noise of it spiked right into her head. Laura felt a sudden burst of sweat drench her from head to foot. Hotchkiss yanked her along, his hand wedged under her armpit. He was crashing down two, three steps at a time, half carrying her. A big man, unbelievably strong—like being dragged by a gorilla.

The throat-catching sting of smoke. Great bubbling spatters on the cheerful pastel walls: purple dye, or smeared blood. Rebels down whimpering, some screaming, hands cupped over eyes or ears. Rebels glued to the stair railings, black-faced and gasping in the grip of tangle-tape. She stumbled on the sprawled legs of a boy, unconscious or dead, his face punched open by a jelly-bullet, blood streaming from a ruined eye. . . .

Then they were down on the first floor, and out the stair-well door. Distant sunlight poured through the smashed-out front of the godown, where the cops and rebels were still in pitched battle, the rebels getting the better of it. Inside the cavernous godown the A-L.P. were frenziedly rallying, machete-slicing tape from some of their tangle-victims, drag-ging captured, handcuffed cops behind a wall of crates. . . . They looked up in surprise, thirty sweat-drenched, blood-smeared, angry men, backlit by the street.

For a moment they all stood in frozen tableau. "Where's the control room?" Hotchkiss whispered.

"I lied," Laura hissed at him. "It's on the second floor."

"You fucking cow," Hotchkiss marveled.

The A-L.P. were edging forward. Some wore stolen police helmets and almost all had riot shields. One of them suddenly fired a tangle-round, which narrowly missed Officer Aw and writhed on the floor like a molten, spastic tumbleweed.

Laura sat down, heavily. Hotchkiss made a grab at her, thought better of it, and began backing up. Suddenly they broke and ran for the back of the godown.

Then it was maelstrom all around her. Men ran after the retreating SWAT team, shouting. Others dashed up the stairs, where Hotchkiss's stunned and blinded victims were moaning, cursing, crying out. Laura drew up her legs, clenched the hands cinched behind her back, tried to make herself small.

Her mind raced wildly. She should go back to the roof, rejoin her people. No—better to help the injured. No—try to escape, to find the police, get arrested. No, she should—

A mustached Malay teenager with a swollen, battered cheek menaced her with a drawn sword. He gestured her up, prodding her with his foot.

"My hands," Laura said.

The boy's eyes widened. He stepped behind her and sawed through the tough plastic strap of her cuffs. Her arms came free with a sudden grating rush of pleasure-pain in her shoulders.

He spat angry Malay at her. She stood up. Suddenly she was a head taller than he was. He backed off a step, hesitated, turned to someone else—

A wind and a sibilant hissing filled the godown. A chopper had dropped to street level—it was looking in on them through the hole in the godown's front wall. Expressionless helmets behind the cockpit glass. An explosive huff as a gun-metal canister jumped loose. It hit the godown floor, rolling, careening, gushing mist. . . .

Oh fuck. Tear gas. A sudden parching, virulent wave of it struck and she could feel the acid grip of it on her eyeballs. Panic hit her then. She scrambled on her hands and knees. Tearblur, savage pain of it in her throat. No air. She bounced off people, blinded and pushing wildly, and suddenly she was running. Running free . . .

Tears, in poisoned torrents, drenched her face. Where they touched her lips she felt a stinging tingle and a taste like kerosene. She kept running, shying away from the gray blur of looming buildings on the side of the street. Her throat and lungs felt full of fish hooks.

She reached the end of her adrenaline. She was too shocked to feel her own fatigue, but her knees began to buckle on their own. She headed for a doorway and collapsed into its recess.

Just then the sky opened up, and it began to rain. Another vertical, bursting monsoon. Wave after wave of it pounded the empty street. Laura crouched miserably in the doorway, catching rain in her cupped hands, bathing her face and the exposed skin of her arms. At first the water seemed to make it worse— a vicious stinging, as if she'd been breathing Tabasco sauce.

She had two plastic bangles now, over the chafed raw skin of her wrists. Her feet were soaked in their cheap, clammy sandals—not from rain, but from the water-cannon puddles in the street outside the godown.

She had run right through the street battle, blind. No one had even touched her. Except—there was a long strip of tangle-tape on her shin, still wriggling feebly, like the shed tail of a lizard. She picked it off her jeans.

She could recognize the area now—she'd run all the way to the Victoria and Albert Docks, just west of East Lagoon. To the north she saw the high-rise of the Tanjong Pagar public-housing complex—bland, dun-colored government bricks.

She sat, breathing shallowly, coughing, spitting every once in a while. She wished she were back with her people in the godown. But there was no way she could reach them again—it was not a sane option.

She'd meet them in jail anyway. Get the hell out of this battle zone and somehow manage to get arrested. Nice quiet jail. Yeah. Sounded good.

She stood up, wiping her mouth. Three cycle-rickshaws raced past her toward East Lagoon, each one crowded with a clinging mass of drenched, staring rebels. They ignored her.

She made a break for it.

There were two wet, unstable street barricades between her

and Tanjong Pagar. She climbed over them in pounding rain. No one showed to stop her.

The glass doors of the Tanjong housing complex had been smashed out of their aluminum frames. Laura ducked into the place, over crunchy heaps of pebbly safety glass. Air conditioning bit into her wet clothes.

She was in a shabby but neat entrance hall. Her foam sandals squelched messily on the scuffed linoleum. The place was deserted, its inhabitants, presumably, respecting the government's curfew and keeping to their rooms upstairs. It was all mom-and-pop shops down here, little bicycle repair places, a fish market, a quack fractionation parlor. Cheerfully lit with fluorescents, ready for business, but all deserted.

She heard the distant murmur of voices. Calm, authoritative tones. She headed for them.

The sounds came from a glass-fronted television store. Cheap low-res sets from Brazil and Maphilindonesia, color gone garish. They'd been turned on all over the store, a few showing the Government channel, others flickering over and over with a convulsive, maladjusted look.

Laura eased through the doorway. A string of brass bells jumped and rang. Inside it reeked of jasmine incense. The shop's walls were papered with smiling, wholesome Singapore pop stars: cool guys in glitter tuxedos and cute babes in straw sun hats and peplums. Laura stepped carefully over a toppled, broken gum machine.

A little old Tamil lady had invaded the place. A wizened granny, white-haired and four feet tall, with a dowager's hump and wrists thin as bird bone. She sat in a canvas director's chair, staring at the empty screens and munching on a mouthful of gum.

"Hello?" Laura said. No response. The old woman looked deaf as a post—senile, even. Laura crept nearer, her shoes squelching moistly. The old woman gave her a sudden startled glance and adjusted her sari, draping the shoulder flap modestly over her head.

Laura combed at her hair with her fingers, feeling rainwater trickle down her neck. "Ma'am, do you speak English?"

The old woman smiled shyly. She pointed at a stack of the canvas chairs, folded against the wall.

Laura fetched one. It had an inscription across the back in wacky-looking Tamil script—something witty and amusing, probably. Laura opened it and sat beside the old woman. "Um, can you hear me at all, or, uh . . ."

The Tamil granny stared straight ahead.

Laura sighed, hard. It felt good to be sitting down.

This poor dazed old woman—ninety if she was a day—had apparently come wandering downstairs, for canary food or something, too deaf or past-it to know about the curfew. To find—Jesus—an empty world.

With a sudden, surreptitious movement the old gal popped a little colored pebble into her mouth. Grape bubble gum. She munched triumphantly.

Laura examined the televisions. The old woman had set them for every possible channel.

Suddenly, on Channel Three, the flickering stabilized.

With the speed of a gunfighter the old woman pulled a remote. The Government spokesman winked out. Channel Three rose to a static-filled roar.

The image was scratchy home video. Laura saw the image bumping as the narrator aimed the camera at his own face. He was a Chinese Singaporean. He looked about twenty-five, chipmunk-cheeked, with thick glasses and a shirt crowded with pens.

Not a bad-looking guy, really, but definitely not TV material. Normal-looking. You wouldn't look twice at him in any street in Singapore.

The guy sat back on his dumpy, overstuffed couch. There was a tacky painting of a seascape behind his head. He sipped from a coffee cup and fiddled with a microphone paper-clipped to his collar. She could hear him swallowing, loudly.

"I think I'm on the air now," he announced.

Laura traded glances with the little old woman. The old gal looked disappointed. Didn't speak English.

"This is my home VCR, la," said Normal Guy. "It always say: 'do not hook to home antenna, can cause broadcast pollution.' Stray signal, you see? So, I did it. I'm broadcasting! I think so, anyway."

He poured himself more coffee, his hand shaking a little. "Today," he said, "my girl and I, I was going to ask to marry. She maybe not such great girl, and I'm not such great fellow either, but we have standard. I think, when a fellow needs to ask to marry, such a thing should at least be possible. Nothing else is civilized.''

He leaned in toward the lens, his head and shoulders swelling. ''But then comes this curfew business. I am not liking this very much, but I am good citizen so I am deciding, okay. Go right ahead Jeyaratnam. Catch the terror rascals, give them what for, definitely. Then, the cops are coming into my building.''

He settled back a little, twitching, a light-trail flickering from his glasses. ''I admire a cop. Cop is a fine, necessary fellow. Cop on the beat, I always say to him, 'Good morning, fellow, good job, keep the peace.' Even ten cops are okay. A hundred cops though, and I am changing mind rapidly. Suddenly my neighborhood very plentiful in cop. Thousands. Have real people outnumbered. Barging into my flat. Search every room, every gracious thing. Take my fingerprints, take my blood sample even.''

He showed a sticking plaster on the ball of his thumb. ''Run me through computer, chop-chop, tell me to clean up that parking ticket. Then off they run, leave door open, no please or thank you, four million others needing botheration also. So I turn on telly for news. One channel only, la. Tell me we have seize Johore reservoir again. If we have so much water, then why is south side of city on fire apparently, la? This I am asking myself.''

He slammed down his coffee cup. ''Can't call girl friend. Can't call mother even. Can't even complain to local politico as Parliament is now all spoilt. What is use of all that voting and stupid campaigns, if it come to this, finish? Is anybody else feeling this way, I am wondering. I am not political, but I am not trusting Government one millimeter. I am small person, but I am not nothing at all.''

Normal Guy looked close to tears suddenly. ''If this is for the good of city then where are citizens? Streets empty! Where is everyone? What kind of city is this become? Where is Vienna police, they the terrorist experts? Why is this happening? Why no one ask me if I think it okay? It not one bit okay to me, definitely! I want to success like everyone, I am working hard and minding business, but this too much. Soon come they arrest me for doing this telly business. Do you feel better off to hear of me? Is better than sit here and rot by myself. . . .''

There was furious pounding on Normal Guy's door. He looked spooked. He leaned forward jerkily and the screen went back to nothingness.

Laura's cheeks were damp. She was crying again. Her eyes felt like they'd been scratched with steel wool. No control. Oh, hell, that poor brave, scared little guy. Goddamn it all anyway. . . .

Someone shouted at the shop's doorway. Laura looked up, startled. It was a tall, tough-looking, turbanned Sikh in a khaki shirt and Gurkha shorts. He had a badge and shoulder patches and he carried a leather-wrapped lathi stick. "What are you doing, madams?"

"Uh . . ." Laura scrambled to her feet. The canvas seat of her chair was soaked through with the rounded wet print of her butt. Her eyes were brimming tears—she felt terrified and deeply, obscurely humiliated.

"Don't . . ." She couldn't think of anything to say.

The Sikh guard looked at her as if she'd dropped from Mars. "You are a tenant here, madam?"

"The riots," Laura said. "I thought there was shelter here."

"Tourist madam? A Yankee!" He stared at her, then pulled black-rimmed glasses from a shirt-pocket case and put them on. "Oh!" He had recognized her.

"All right," Laura said. She stretched out her chafed wrists, still in their severed plastic handcuffs. "Arrest me, officer. Take me into custody."

The Sikh blushed. "Madam, I am only private security. Cannot arrest you." The little old lady got up suddenly and shuffled directly at him. He sidestepped clumsily out of her way at the last moment. She wandered out into the hall. He stared after her meditatively.

"Thought you were looters," he said. "Very sorry."

Laura paused. "Can you take me to a police station?"

"Surely, Mrs. . . . Mrs. Vebbler. Madam, I am not helping to notice that you are all wet."

Laura tried to smile at him. "Rain. Water cannon too, actually."

The Sikh stiffened. "Is a very great sorrow to me that you experience this in our city while a guest of the Singapore government, Mrs. Webber."

"That's okay," Laura muttered. "What's your name, sir?"

"Singh, madam."

All Sikhs were named Singh. Of course. Laura felt like an idiot. "I could kind of use the police, Mr. Singh. I mean some nice calm police, well out of the riot area."

Singh tucked his lathi stick smartly under his arm. "Very well, madam." He was struggling not to salute. "You are following me, please."

They walked together down the empty hall. "Settling you very soon," Singh said encouragingly. "Duty is difficult in these times."

"You said it, Mr. Singh."

They stepped into a cargo elevator and went down a floor into a dusty parking area. Lots of bikes, a few cars, mostly old junkers. Singh pointed with his stick. "You are riding pillion on my motor scooter if agreeable?"

"Sure, okay." Singh unlocked his bike and switched it on. They climbed aboard and drove up an exit ramp with a comical, high-pitched whir. The rain had died down for the moment. Singh eased into the street.

"There are roadblocks," Laura told him.

"Yes, but—" Singh hesitated. He hit the brakes.

One of the cant-winged fighter jets of the Singapore Air Force flew above them with a silken roar. With snaky suddenness, it flickered into a dive, as if sidestepping its own shadow. Real hotdog flying. They watched it open-mouthed.

Something streaked from beneath its wings. A missile. It left a pencil of smoke in the damp air. From the docklands came a sudden violent burst of white-orange fire. Tinkertoy chunks of ruptured loading crane balleted through the air.

Thunder rolled through the empty streets.

Singh swore and turned the bike around. "Enemies attacking! We go back to safety at once!"

They rode back down the ramp. "That was a Singaporean jet, Mr. Singh."

Singh pretended not to hear her. "Duty now is clear. You are coming with me, please."

They took an elevator up to the sixth floor. Singh was silent, his back ramrod-straight. He wouldn't meet her eyes.

He led her down the corridor to a hall apartment and knocked three times.

A plump woman in black slacks and a tunic opened the door. "My wife," said Singh. He gestured Laura inside.

The woman stared in amazement. "Laura Webster!" she said.

"Yes!" Laura said. She felt like hugging the woman.

It was a little three-room place. Very modest. Three bug-cute children bounded into the front room: a boy of nine, a girl, another boy still a toddler. "You have *three* children, Mr. Singh?"

"Yes," Singh said, smiling. He picked up the littlest boy and mussed his hair. "Makes many tax problems. Working two jobs." He and his wife began talking rapidly in Bengali or Hindi maybe, something incomprehensible, but speckled with English loan words. Like *fighter jet* and *television*.

Mrs. Singh, whose name was Aratavari or something vaguely similar, took Laura into the parental bedroom. "We shall get you into some dry clothes," she said. She opened the closet and took a folded square cloth from the top shelf. It was breathtaking: emerald-green silk with gold embroidery. "A sari will fit you," she said, shaking it out briskly. It was obviously her finest garment. It looked like something a rajah's wife would wear for ritual suttee.

Laura toweled her hair and face. "Your English is very good."

"I'm from Manchester," said Mrs. Singh. "Better opportunity here however." She turned her back politely while Laura stripped off her sopping blouse and jeans. She put on a sari blouse too big in the bustline and too tight around the ribs. The sari defeated her. Mrs. Singh helped her pleat and pin it.

Laura combed her hair in the mirror. Her gas-stung eyes looked like cracked marbles. But the beautiful sari gave her a hallucinatory look of exotic Sanskrit majesty. If only David were here. . . . She felt a sudden total rush of culture shock, intense and queasy, like déjà vu with a knife twist.

She followed Mrs. Singh back into the front room, barefoot and rustling. The children laughed, and Singh grinned at her. "Oh. Very good, madam. You would like drinking something?"

"I could sure do with a shot of whiskey."

"No alcohol."

"You got a cigarette?" she blurted. They looked shocked. "Sorry," she muttered, wondering why she'd said it. "Very kind of y'all to put me up and everything."

Mrs. Singh shook her head modestly. "I should take your clothes to the laundry. Only, curfew forbids it." The older boy brought Laura a can of chilled guava juice. It tasted like sugared spit.

They sat on the couch. The Government channel was on, with the sound low. A Chinese anchorman was interviewing the cosmonaut, who was still in orbit. The cosmonaut expressed limitless faith in the authorities. "You like curry?" Mrs. Singh said anxiously.

"I can't stay," Laura said, surprised.

"But you must!"

"No. My company voted. It's a policy matter. We're all going to jail."

The Singhs were not surprised, but they looked unhappy and troubled. She felt genuinely sorry for them. "Why, Laura?" said Mrs. Singh.

"We came here to deal with Parliament. We don't care for this martial law at all. We're enemies of the state now. We can't work with you anymore."

Singh and his wife conversed rapidly while the children sat on the floor, big-eyed and grave. "You stay safely here, madam," Singh said at last. "It's our duty. You are important guest. The Government will understand."

"It's not the same Government," Laura said. "East Lagoon—that whole area's a riot zone now. They're killing each other down there. I saw it happen. The Air Force just fired a missile into our property. Maybe killed some of my people too, I don't know."

Mrs. Singh went pale. "I heard the explosion—but it's not on the television. . . ." She turned to her husband, who stared morosely at the throw rug. They began talking again, and Laura broke in.

"I have no right to get y'all in trouble." She stood up. "Where are my sandals?"

Singh stood up too. "I am escorting you, madam."

"No," Laura said, "you'd better stay here and guard your own home. Look, the doors are broken in downstairs, if you haven't noticed. Those Anti-Labourites took over our godown— they might wander into this place too, any time they like, and take everybody hostage. They mean business, or antibusiness, or whatever the hell they believe in. And they're not afraid to die, either."

"I'm not afraid to die," Singh insisted stoutly. His wife began shouting at him. Laura found her sandals—the toddler was playing with them behind the couch. She slipped them on.

Singh, red-faced, stormed out of the flat. Laura heard him in the hall, shouting and whacking doors with his lathi stick. "What's going on?" she said.

The two older children rushed Mrs. Singh and grabbed her, burying their faces in her tunic. "My husband says, that it was he who rescued you, a famous woman from television, who looked like a lost wet cat. And that you have broken bread in his house. And he will not send a helpless foreign woman to be killed in the streets like some kind of pariah dog."

"He's got quite a way with words, in his own language."

"Maybe that explains it," said Mrs. Singh and smiled.

"I don't think a can of guava juice really qualifies as 'breaking bread.' "

"Not guava. Soursop." She patted her little girl's head. "He's a good man. He's honest, and works very hard, and is not stupid, or mean. And never hits me or the children."

"That's very nice," Laura said.

Mrs. Singh locked eyes with her. "I tell you this, Laura Webster, because I don't want you to throw my man's life away. Just because you're a political, and he doesn't count for much."

"I'm not a political," Laura protested. "I'm just a person, like you."

"If you were like me, you'd be home with your family."

Singh burst in suddenly, grabbed Laura by the arm, and

hauled her out into the hall. Doors were open up and down the corridor, and it was crowded with confused and angry Indian men in their undershirts. When they saw her they roared in amazement.

In seconds they were all around her. *"Namaste, namaste,"* the Indian greeting, nodding over hands pressed together, palm to palm. Some touched the trailing edge of the sari, respectfully. Uproar of voices. "My son, my son," a fat man kept shouting in English. "He's A-L.P., my son!"

The elevator opened and they hustled her inside. They crowded it to the limit, and other men ran for the stairs. The elevator sank slowly, its cables groaning, jammed like an overloaded bus.

Minutes later they had hustled her out into the street. Laura wasn't sure how the decision had been made or even if anyone had consciously made one. Windows had been flung open on every floor and people were shouting up and down in the soggy midafternoon heat. More and more were pouring out—a human tide. Not angry, but manic, like soldiers on furlough, or kids out of school—milling, shouting, slapping each other on the shoulders.

Laura grabbed Singh's khaki sleeve. "Look, I don't need all this—"

"It is the people," Singh mumbled. His eyes looked glazed and ecstatic.

"Let her speak," yelled a guy in a striped jubbah. "Let her speak!"

The shout spread. Two kids rolled a topped trash can into the street and set it down like a pedestal. They raised her onto it. There was frenzied applause. "Quiet, quiet . . ."

Suddenly they were all looking at her.

Laura felt a terror so absolute that she felt like fainting. Say something, idiot—quick, before they kill you. "Thank you for trying to protect me," she squeaked. They cheered, not catching her words, just pleased that she could talk, like a real person.

Her voice came back. "No violence!" she shouted. "Singapore is a modern city." Men around her muttered translations in an undertone. The crowd continued to grow and thicken around her. "Modern people don't kill each other," she shouted. The sari was slipping off her shoulder. She tugged it back into place. They applauded, jostling each other, whites showing around their eyes.

It was the damned sari, she thought dazedly. They loved it. A tall foreign blonde on a pedestal, wrapped in gold and green, some kind of demented Kali juggernaut thing . . .

"I'm just a stupid foreigner!" she screeched. A few moments before they decided to believe her—then they laughed, and clapped. "But I know better than to hurt anyone! So I want to go to jail!"

Blank looks. She had lost them. Inspiration saved her. "Like Gandhi!" she shouted. "The Mahatma. Gandhiji."

A sudden awesome silence.

"So just a few of you, very calmly, please, take me to a jail. Thank you very much." She jumped down.

Singh steadied her. "That was good!"

"You know the way," she said urgently. "You lead us, okay?"

"Okay!" Singh swung his lathi stick over his head. "Everyone, we are marching, la! To the jail!"

He offered Laura his arm. They moved quickly through the crowd, which melted away before them and re-formed behind.

"To the jail!" shouted Striped Jubbah, leaping up and down, striped arms flapping. "To Changi!"

Others took up the yell. "Changi, Changi." The destination seemed to channel their energies. The giddy sense of explosiveness leached out of the situation, like a blowtorch settling to a steady burn. Children ran ahead of them, to turn and marvel at the advancing crowd. They gawked, and capered, and punched each other. People watched from streetside buildings. Windows opened, and doors.

After three blocks, the crowd was still growing. They marched north, onto South Bridge Road. Ahead of them loomed the cyclopean buildings downtown. A lean Chinese with slicked-back hair and a schoolteacherish look appeared at Laura's elbow. "Mrs. Webster?"

"Yes?"

"I am pleased to march with you on Changi! Amnesty International was morally right!"

Laura blinked. "Huh?"

"The political prisoners . . ." The crowd surged suddenly and he was swept away. The crowd had an escort now—two police choppers, hissing above the street. Laura quailed, her eyes burning with remembrance, but the crowd waved and cheered, as if the choppers were some kind of party favor.

It dawned on her, then. She grabbed Singh's elbow. "Hey! I just want to go to a police station. Not march on the goddamned Bastille!"

"What, madam?" Singh shouted, grinning dazedly. "What steel?"

Oh, God. If only she could make a break for it. She looked about wildly, and people waved at her and smiled. What an idiot she'd been to put on this sari. It was like being wrapped in green neon.

Now they were marching through the thick of Singapore's Chinatown. Temple Street, Pagoda Street. The psychedelic, statue-covered stupa of a Hindu temple rose to her left. "Sri Mariamman," it read. Polychrome goddesses leered at each other as if they'd planned all this, just for grins. There were sirens wailing ahead, at a major intersection. The sound of bullhorns. They were going to walk right into it. A thousand angry cops. A massacre.

And then it came into sight. Not cops at all, but another crowd of civilians. Pouring headlong into the intersection, men, women, children. Above them a banner, somebody's bed sheet stretched between bamboo poles. Hasty daubed lettering: LONG LIVE CHANNEL THREE . . .

Laura's crowd emitted an amazing, heartfelt sigh, as if every person in it had spotted a long-lost lover. Suddenly everyone was running, arms outstretched. The two crowds hit, and merged, and mingled. The hair rose on Laura's neck. There was something loose in this crowd, something purely magical—a mystic social electricity. She could feel it in her bones, some kind of glad triumphant opposite to the ugly crowd-madness she'd seen at the stadium. People fell, but they were helping each other up and embracing each other. . . .

She lost Singh. Suddenly she was alone in the crowd, tripping along in the middle of a long fractal swirl of it. She glanced down the street. A block away, another subcrowd, and a cluster of red-and-white police cars.

Her heart leapt. She broke from the crowd and ran toward them.

The cops were surrounded. They were embedded in the crowd, like ham in aspic. People—everyone, anyone—had simply clotted around the police, immobilizing them. The prowl cars' doors were open and the cops were trying to reason with them, without success.

Laura edged up through the crowd. Everyone was shouting, and their hands were full—not with weapons, but with all kinds of strange stuff: bags of bread rolls, transistor radios, even a handful of marigolds snatched from some windowpot. They were thrusting them at the police, begging them to take them. A middle-aged Chinese matron was shouting passionately at a police captain. "You are our brothers! We are all Singaporeans. Singaporeans do not kill each other!"

The police captain couldn't meet the woman's eyes. He sat on the edge of the driver's seat, tight-lipped, in an ecstasy of humiliation. There were three other cops in his car, decked out in full riot gear: helmets, vests, tangle-rifles. They could have flattened the crowd in a few instants, but they looked stunned, nonplussed.

A man in a silk business suit thrust his arm through the open backseat window. "Take my watch, officer! As a souvenir! Please—this is a great day. . . ." The cop shook his head, with a gentle, stunned look. Next to him, his fellow cop munched a rice cake.

Laura tapped the captain's shoulder. He looked up and recognized her. His eyes rolled a little in their sockets, as if she was all that was needed to make his experience complete. "What do you want?"

Laura told him, discreetly. "Arrest you here?" the captain replied. "In front of these people?"

"I can get you away," Laura told him. She clambered onto the hood of the prowl car, stood up, and raised both arms. "Everyone listen! You know me—I'm Laura Webster. Please let us through! We have very important business! Yes, that's right, move back away from the hood, ladies and gentlemen. . . . Thank you very much, you're such good people, I'm so grateful. . . ."

She sat on the hood, propping her feet on the front bumper.

The car crept forward and the crowd peeled away to either side, respectfully. Many of them obviously failed to recognize her. But they reacted instinctively to the totem symbol of a foreign woman in a green sari on the hood of a police car. Laura stretched out her arms and made vague swimming motions. It worked. The crowd moved faster.

They reached the edge of the crowd. Laura wedged herself in the front seat, between the captain and a lieutenant. "Thank God," she said.

"Mrs. Webster," the police captain said. His badge said his name was Hsiu. "You are under arrest for obstruction of justice and incitement to riot."

"Okay," Laura breathed. "Do you know what happened to the rest of my Rizome people?"

"They are also arrested. The helicopters got them."

Laura nodded eagerly, then stopped. "Uhmm . . . they're not in Changi, are they?"

"There's nothing wrong with Changi!" the cop said, nettled. "Don't listen to globalist lies."

They were tooling slowly up Pickering Street, crammed with beauty salons and cosmetic-surgery joints. The sidewalks were crowded with grinning, larking curfew breakers, but they hadn't yet thought to block the street. "You foreigners," the captain said slowly. "You cheated us. Singapore could have built a new world. But you poisoned our leader, and you robbed us. This is it. Enough. All finish."

"Grenada poisoned Kim."

Captain Hsiu shook his head. "I don't believe in Grenada."

"But it's your own people who are doing this," Laura told him. "At least you weren't invaded."

The cop gave her a salt-in-the-wounds look. "We are invaded. Didn't you know?"

She was stunned. "What? Vienna came in?"

"No," said a cop in the back with pessimistic relish. "It's the Red Cross."

For a moment she couldn't place the reference. "The Red Cross," she said. "The health agency?"

"If an army came, we would chop them up," said Captain Hsiu. "But no one shoots the Red Cross. They are already in Ubin and Tekong and Sembawang. Hundreds of them."

"With bandages and medic kits," said the cop eating rice cakes. " 'Civil disaster relief.' " He began laughing.

"Shut up, you," said the captain listlessly. Rice Cakes throttled it down to a snicker.

"I never heard of the Red Cross pulling a stunt like that," Laura said.

"It's the globalist corporations," said Captain Hsiu, darkly. "They wanted to buy Vienna and have us all shot. But it too expensive, and take them too long. So they buy the Red Cross instead—an army with no guns—and kill us with kindness. They just walk in smiling, and never walk out of Singapore again. Dirty cowards."

The police radio squawked wildly. A mob was invading the premises of Channel Four television, at Marina Centre. Captain Hsiu growled something foul in Chinese and turned it off. "I knew they attack the tellies soon or later," he said. "What to do . . ."

"We getting brand-new orders tomorrow," said the lieutenant, speaking for the first time. "Probably big rise in pay, too. For us, plenty busy months ahead."

"Traitor," said Captain Hsiu without passion.

The lieutenant shrugged. "Got to live, la."

"Then we've won," Laura blurted. She was realizing it, in all its scope, for the first time. Ballooning inside her. All that craziness and all that sacrifice—it had worked, somehow. Not quite the way anyone had expected—but that was politics, wasn't it? It was over. The Net had won.

"That's right," said the captain. He turned right, onto Clemenceau Avenue.

"Then I guess there's not much point in arresting me, is there? The protest is meaningless now. And I'll never stand trial for those charges." She laughed happily.

"Maybe we book you just for the fun of it," said the lieutenant. He watched a car full of teenagers zip past, one leaning through the open window, waving a huge Singapore flag.

"Oh, no!" said the captain. "Then we must watch her make more globalist moralizing speeches."

"No way!" Laura said hastily. "I'm getting the hell out of here as soon as I can, back to my husband and baby."

Captain Hsiu paused. "You want to leave the island?"

"More than anything! Believe me."

"Could arrest her anyway," suggested the lieutenant. "Probably take two, three week for the paperwork to find her."

"Especially if we don't file it," said the snickering cop. He started laughing through his nose.

"If you think that scares me, go right ahead," Laura said, bluffing. "Anyway, I couldn't get out now if I tried. There's no way. Martial law closed the airports."

They drove across the Clemenceau Bridge. Tanks guarded it, but they looked abandoned, and the police car cruised past without pause.

"Not to worry," said the captain. "To be rid of Laura Webster? No sacrifice too great!"

And he took her to the Yung Soo Chim Islamic Bank.

It was an eerie reprise. They were all on the top of the bank building—the personnel of Yung Soo Chim. Up there amid the white bristling forests of microwave antennas and fat rain-stained satellite dishes.

Laura wore her sari flap hooded snugly over her head and a pair of cop's mirrorshades that she'd begged from Captain Hsiu. Once past the private security and into the bank building, redolent with the stink of panic and the new-mown-hay aroma of shredded files, the rest had been easy. No one was checking ID—she had none to check, no luggage, either.

No one bothered her—she was passing for somebody's Eurasian mistress, or maybe some exotic tech in high Hindu drag. If the pirates learned she was here among them, they might do almost anything. But Laura knew with thrilling certainty that they'd never touch her. Not here, not now, not after all she'd come through.

She wasn't afraid. She felt bulletproof, invincible, full of electricity. She knew now that she was stronger than they were. Her people were stronger than their people. She could walk in daylight, but they couldn't. They'd thought they had teeth, in all their corner-cutting crime conspiracies, but their bones were made of glass.

The criminal machine just didn't have it—the *gemeineschaft*. They were rip-off artists, flotsam, and there was nothing to hold them together, no basic trust. They'd been hiding under the protective crust of the Singapore Government, and now that it was gone the Bank was wrecked. It would take them years to stick it all back together, even if they were willing to try, and the momentum, the world tide, was against them. This place and its dreams were over—the future was somewhere else.

What a brag session this was going to make. How she'd crept out of Singapore in the very midst of the pirate bankers. A steady procession of twin-rotored Singaporean military choppers was arriving on the plush landing pad on the Bank's roof. Two, three dozen refugees at a time would cram in helter-skelter and vanish into the leaden monsoon sky.

The others waited, perching like crows on the chain-linked parapet and the concrete anchor blocks of the microwave towers. Some clumped moodily around portable televisions: watching Jeyaratnam on Channel Two, weary and beaten and gray-faced, quoting the Constitution and urging the populace back to their homes.

Laura edged around a luggage trolley piled high with bulging ripstop luggage in maroon and yellow synthetic. Three men sat on the far side of it, bent forward attentively with their elbows on their knees. Two Japanese guys and an Anglo, all three in crisp new safari suits and bush hats. They were watching television.

It was Channel Four, "On the Air—For the People," featuring, as a stuttering, blushing anchorwoman, Miss Ting— Kim's old flame.

Laura watched and listened from a discreet distance. She felt a strange sisterhood with Miss Ting, who had obviously been swept into her current situation through some kind of odd synchronistic karma.

It was all like that now, the whole of Singapore, giddy and brittle and suspended in midair. Up here it might be solid gloom, but below them the streets were full of honking cars, one vast street party, the populace out congratulating itself on its heroism. The last billows of smoke were fading in the docklands. Revolutionary Singapore—vomiting out these expensive data pirates, like ambergris from the guts of a convalescent whale.

The smaller Japanese guy lifted his bush hat, and picked at an itchy sales tag inside the brim. "Kiribati," he said.

"If we get the bloody choice we take Nauru," said the Anglo. He was Australian.

The Japanese ripped the tag loose, his face pinched. "Kiribati's nowhere, man. They don't have dedicated landlines."

"The heat will be all over Nauru. They're afraid of those launch sites. . . ."

Nauru and Kiribati, Laura thought—little Pacific island states whose "national sovereignty" could be had for a price. Good dumping grounds for Bank gangsters, obviously. But that was okay by her. Both islands were on the Net, and where there were phones, there was credit. And where there was credit, there were airline tickets. And where there were jets, there was home.

Home, she thought, leaning giddily against the heaped trolley. Not Galveston, not yet. The Lodge would open again sometime, but that wasn't home anyway. Home was David and the baby. Lying in bed with David, in warm tangled sheets, breathing American air, a nice twilight outside maybe. Trees, leaf shadows, red dirt and Georgia kudzu in a safe Rizome Retreat. Little Loretta, her solid little ribs and crooked baby grin. Oh, Lord . . .

The larger Japanese was staring at her. He thought she was drunk. She straightened self-consciously, and he looked away, bored. He muttered something Laura didn't catch.

"Bullshit," the Aussie said. "You think everybody's fire-wired. That 'spontaneous combustion' voodoo bullshit . . . They're good, but they're not *that* good."

The big guy rubbed the back of his neck and shuddered. "They didn't burn that dog on our doorstep for nothing."

"I miss poor Jim Dae Jung," said the little Japanese, sadly. "Burnt feet still in his boots and his skull shrunk as small as an orange. . . ."

The Aussie shook his head. "We don't *know* that he caught fire on his own toilet. Just 'cause we found his feet there. . . ."

"Hey," said the larger Japanese, pointing.

The two others rose eagerly, expecting another chopper flight. But there was something going on in the sky. Against a leaden background of clouds: streaks of blood-colored vapor. Like claw scratches on muddy skin.

Monsoon wind began quickly to distort it. Symbols in red smoke, scrawled against the sky. Letters, numbers:

3 A 3 . . .

"Skywriting," the Aussie said, sitting down again. "Wish we had some binocs. I don't see a plane."

"Very small drone," said the big Japanese. "Or maybe it's made of glass." By now everyone on the roof was looking, pointing, and shading their eyes.

3 A 3 v __ 0\. . .

"It's code," the Aussie said. "Gotta be the voodoo boys."

The wind had blown the first letters to shreds, but there was more. . . . = A __ __ S. . .

"Three A Three Vee Blank Zero Back-slash Equals A Blank Blank S," the Aussie repeated slowly. "What in bloody hell are they getting at?"

"Maybe it's their evacuation signal," said the big man.

"You wish," the Aussie said.

The smaller Japanese began laughing. "No verticals in the letters," he announced triumphantly. "Bad programming. Grenada was never any good with drones."

"No verticals?" the Aussie said, staring upward. "Oh. I get it. 'BABYLON FALLS,' eh? Cheeky bastards."

"I guess they never really thought this would happen," the small man said. "Or they'd have done a better job announcing it."

"Still, you gotta give 'em credit," the Aussie said. "Invisible finger, writing in blood on the sky . . . probably would have scared the living crap out of people, if they hadn't fucked it up." He chuckled. "Murphy's Law, huh? Now it's just more weirdness."

Laura left them on their luggage trolley. Another chopper had appeared, coming in—a small one. She decided she would take it if she could—the talk had unsettled her.

As she neared the pad she heard low, piteous sobbing. Not demonstrative—just uncontrollable moans and snivels.

The sobbing man was crouched under the rounded bulk of a rooftop storage tank. He was scanning the sky again and again, as if in terror of another message.

He was a sharpie—like the villains on Chinese television. Thirtyish bedroom-eyed guys who were all laser-cut hairdos and jade cig holders. Only now he was squatting on his heels, under the cool white bulk of the tank, his shoulders wrapped in a black felt blanket clutched two-handed across his chest. He was twitchy as a basket of crabs.

As she watched him he somehow got a grip on himself, wiped his eyes. He looked like he'd once been important. Years of tailored suits and handball and complaisant massage girls. But now he looked like some kind of rat-eating terrier from a sawdust pit.

One of those Grenadian pellets was in him somewhere, oozing its milligrams of liquid fear. He knew it, anyone who saw him knew it: news about the pellets had been all over Government TV. But he hadn't had time to have it located and dug out of him.

The others were avoiding him. He was bad luck.

A twin-rotored Coast Guard chopper settled to the pad. Its wind gust scoured the building and Laura tightened the sari over her head. Bad Luck jumped to his feet and made a run for it; he was there at the door, panting, before anyone else. When it shunted open he scrambled aboard.

Laura followed him and buckled into one of the hard plastic benches at the back. A dozen more refugees crowded on, avoiding Bad Luck.

A tight-faced little Coast Guard sergeant in camo flight suit and helmet looked in on them. "Hey, missy," yelled the fat guy ahead of Laura. "When we getting salted almonds?" The other refugees chuckled dismally.

Power went into the rotors and the world fell away under them.

They flew southwest, through the brutal, thrusting sky-scrapers of Queenstown. Then over a cluster of offshore islands with names like the bonging of gamelans: Samulun, Merlimau, Seraya. Clumps of clotted tropical green cut with towering beachfront hotels. White, sandy shorelines cinched in by elaborate dams and jetties.

Good-bye, Singapore.

They changed course over the monsoon-ruffled waters of the Malacca Straits. It was loud inside the cabin. The passengers made a little hoarse, guarded conversation, but no one approached her. Laura leaned her head against the bare plastic by the little fist-sized porthole and fell into a stunned half-doze.

She came to as the chopper pulled up, yawing dizzily.

They were hovering over a cargo ship. Ships had become familiar to her at the loading docks: this was a tramp clipper, with the strange rotating wind columns that had been a big hit back in the 'teens. Crewpeople—or rather, more refugees—lurked on the deck, in a variety of rumpled skivvies.

The little sergeant came back again. She had a jelly-gun slung over her shoulder. "This is it," she shouted.

"There's no landing pad!" pointed out the fat guy.

"You jump." She slung open the cargo door. Wind gusted through. They were hovering five feet over the deck. The sergeant slapped another woman on the shoulder. "You first. Go!"

Somehow they all left. Thumping, falling, sprawling onto the gently rolling deck. Those onboard helped a little, clumsily trying to catch them.

The last one out was Bad Luck. He tumbled out as if kicked. Then the chopper peeled away, showing them an underbelly lumpy with flotation pads. "Where are we?" Bad Luck demanded, rubbing a bruised kneecap.

A mossy-toothed Chinese technician in a songkak hat answered him. "This is the *Ali Khamenei*. Bound for Abadan."

"Abadan!" Bad Luck screeched. "No! Not the fucking Iranians!" People stared at him—recognizing his affliction, some began to edge away.

"Islamic Republic," the technician corrected.

"I knew it!" Bad Luck said. "They gave us to the damn Koran thumpers! They'll chop our hands off! I'll never punch deck again!"

"Calming down," advised the tech, giving Bad Luck a sidelong look.

"They sold us! They dumped us on this robot ship to starve to death!"

"Not to worry," said a hefty European woman, sensibly dressed for catastrophe in a sturdy denim work shirt and corduroy jeans. "We've examined the cargo—there's plenty of Soy Moo and Weetabix." She smirked, raising one plucked eyebrow. "And we met the ship's captain—poor little bloke! He's got a retrovirus—no immune system left."

Bad Luck went even paler. "No! The captain has plague?"

"Who else would take such a rotten job, working all alone on this barge?" the woman said. "He's hiding now in the wheelhouse. Afraid of catching an infection from us. He's a lot more afraid of us than we are of him." She looked at Laura curiously. "Do I know you?"

Laura looked down at the deck and muttered something about being in data processing. "Is there a phone here, la?"

"You'll have to stand in line, dearie. Everybody wants on the Net. . . . You kept money outside Singapore, yes? Very smart."

"Singapore robbed us," Bad Luck grumbled.

"At least they got us out," said the European woman practically. "It's better than waiting for those voodoo cannibals to poison us. . . . Or the globalist law courts. . . . The Islamics aren't so bad."

Bad Luck stared at her. "They *murder* technicians! Anti-Western purges!"

"That was years ago—anyway, maybe that's why they want us now! Stop fretting, eh! People like us, we can always find a place." She glanced at Laura. "You play bridge, dearie?"

Laura shook her head.

"Cribbage? Pinochle?"

"Sorry." Laura adjusted her hood.

"You getting used to the *chador* already?" The woman traipsed off, defeated.

Laura walked unobtrusively toward the bow, avoiding scattered groups of dazed, shiftless refugees. No one tried to bother her.

Around the *Ali Khamenei* the gray waters of the straits were full of shipping—reefers, dry-bulk carriers, pallet ships. Korean, Chinese, Maphilindonesian, some with no flag at all, simply corporate logos.

There was real majesty in the sight. Distance-tinged blue ships, gray sea, the distant green-humped rise of Sumatra. These straits, between the bulk of Asia and the offshore sprawl of Sumatra and Java and Borneo, had been one of the world's great routes since the dawn of civilization. The location had made Singapore; and lifting the embargoes on the island would be like unclogging a global artery.

She had been part of this, she thought. And it was no small thing. Now that she was standing alone at the bow's railing, with the primordial surging of the deck beneath her feet, she could feel what she'd done. A little moment of numinous prompting, a mystic satisfaction. She had been doing the work of the world—she could sense the subtle flow of its Taoist tides, buoying her up, carrying her.

Standing there, shedding tension, breathing the damp monsoon air under endless gray skies, she could no longer believe in her personal danger. She was bulletproof again.

The pirates were the ones with problems, now. The Bank's brass were all over the deck, in little conspiratorial groups, muttering and looking over their shoulders. There was a surprising number of brass on this ship—the first ones aboard, apparently. She could tell they were bosses, because they were well dressed, and snotty looking. And old.

They had that tight-stretched, spotty vampire look that came from years of Singapore's half-baked longevity treatments. Blood filtering, hormone therapy, vitamin-E, electric acupuncture, God knew what kind of insane black-market bullshit. Maybe they *had* stretched a few extra years out of their expensive meddling, but now they were going to have to go off their treatments cold-turkey. And she didn't imagine it would be easy.

At dusk, a large civilian chopper arrived with a final load of refugees. Laura stood by one of the tall, gently hissing wind columns as the refugees decamped. More top brass.

One of them was Mr. Shaw.

Laura flinched away in shock, and walked slowly toward the bow, not looking back. There must have been some kind of special arrangement, she thought—this Abadan business. Probably Shaw and his people had set it up long ago. Singapore might be finished, but the top data pirates had their own survival instincts. No cheap-shot Naurus and Kiribatis for them—that was for suckers. They were headed where the oil money still ran fast and deep. The Islamic Republic was no friend of Vienna's.

She doubted that they'd make it there scot-free, though. Singapore might try to ditch the Bank gangsters and the evidence, but too many people must know. There'd be a hot trail to a ship with this many big operators on it. The video press were already swarming into Singapore under the shadow of the Red Cross—eager pioneers of another gunless global army, packing mikes and minicams. Once the ship was out in international waters, Laura was half convinced that reporters would show up.

Should be interesting. The pirates wouldn't like it much— their skin blistered under publicity. But at least they'd escaped the Grenadians.

There seemed to be an unspoken conviction among the Singaporeans that the Grenadians had finished. That with the Bank scattered, and the Government in ruin, there was simply no point left in their terror campaign.

Maybe they were right. Maybe successful terrorism had always worked like this—provoking a regime till it crumbled under the weight of its own repression. "Babylon Falls" —they'd bragged about it. Maybe Sticky and his friends would now slip out of Singapore in the confusion of the revolt.

If there was any sanity left in them, they'd be glad to run, puffed and proud, triumphant. Probably amazed to be alive. They could swagger back to their Caribbean shadows as true voodoo legends, new-millennium spooks nonpareil. Why not live? Why not enjoy it?

She wanted to believe that they'd do it. She wanted it to be over—she couldn't bear to think back to Sticky's feverish menu of technical atrocities.

A shudder struck her where she stood. A rocketing wave of intense, unfocused, ontological dread. For a moment she wondered if she'd been pellet-shot. Maybe Sticky had dosed her while she was unconscious and the fear drug was just now coming on. . . . God, what an awful suspicion.

She remembered suddenly the Vienna agent she'd met in Galveston, the polite, handsome Russian who had talked about the "evil pressure in a bullet."

Now, for the first time, she was grasping what the man had meant. The pressure of *raw possibility*. If something was *possible*—didn't that mean that somewhere, somehow, someone *had to do it?* The voodoo urge to truck with demons. The imp of the perverse. Deep in the human spirit, the carnivorous shadow of science.

It was a dynamic, like gravity. Some legacy of evolution, deep in human nerves, invisible and potent, like software.

She turned around. No sign of Shaw. A few yards behind her, Bad Luck was retching, loudly, over the guard rail. He looked up, wiping his mouth on his sleeve.

She could have been him. Laura forced herself to smile at him.

He gave her a look of tremulous gratitude and came to join her. She almost fled at once, but he held up a hand. "It's okay," he said. "I know I'm dosed. It comes in waves. I'm better now."

"You're very brave," Laura said. "I'm sorry for you, sir."

Bad Luck stared at her. "That's nice. You're nice. You don't treat me like a leper." He paused, hot little rat eyes studying her. "You're not one of us, are you? You're not with the Bank."

"What makes you say that?" Laura said.

"You're somebody's girl friend, is it?" He grinned in a cadaverous parody of flirtation. "Lot of bosses on this ship. Top brass goes for those hot Eurasian girls."

"We're getting married, la," Laura said, "so you can forget all about it, fellow."

He dug into his jacket. "Want a cigarette?"

"Maybe you'd better save them," Laura said, accepting one.

"No, no. No problem. I can get anything! Cigarettes, blood components. Megavitamins, embryos. . . . My name's Desmond, miss. Desmond Yaobang."

"Hi," Laura said. She accepted a light. Her mouth immediately filled with choking poisoned soot.

She couldn't understand why she was doing this.

Except that it was better than doing nothing. Except that she felt sorry for him. And maybe the presence of Desmond Yaobang would keep everyone else at a distance.

"What do you think they'll do to us, in Abadan? Do *with* us, I mean." Yaobang's head just topped her shoulder. There was nothing obviously repulsive about him, but the chemical fear had etched itself into the set of his eyes, the lines of his face. It had soaked him through with an aura of creepiness.

She felt the strong, irrational urge to kick him. The way a flock of crows will peck an injured one to death.

"I dunno," Laura drawled, contempt making her careless. She looked at her sandaled feet, avoiding his eyes. "Maybe they'll give me some decent shoes. . . . I'll be okay if I can make a few phone calls."

"Phone calls," Yaobang parroted nervously, "capital idea. Yes, get Desmond to a phone and he can get you anything. Shoes. Surely. You want to try it?"

"Mmm. Not just yet. Too crowded."

"Tonight then. Fine, miss. Splendid. I won't be sleeping anyway."

She turned away from him and put her back to the rail. The sun was setting between two of the whirling wind columns. Vast underlit cloud banks of mellow Renaissance gold. Yaobang turned and looked as well, biting his lip, mercifully silent. Along with the filthy brain buzz of the cigarette, it gave Laura an expansive feeling of sublimity. Beautiful, but it wouldn't last long—the sun sank fast in the tropics.

Yaobang straightened, pointed. "What is that?"

Laura looked. His paranoia-sharpened senses had caught something—a distant, airborne glint.

Yaobang squinted. "Some little kind of chopper, maybe?"

"It's too small!" Laura said. "It's a drone!" Light had winked briefly from its blades and now she'd lost it against the clouds.

"A drone?" he said, alarmed by her tone of voice. "Is it voodoo? Can it hurt us?"

"Shut up!" Laura shoved away from the rail. "I'm gonna climb up to the crow's nest—I want a better look." She hurried across the deck, her sandals flopping.

The ship's foremast had a radar horn and video for the guidance computer. But there was access for repair and human backup: a crow's nest, three stories above the deck. Laura grabbed the cool iron rungs, then stopped in frustration. The damned sari—it would tangle her feet. She turned and beckoned to Yaobang.

There was a shout from above. "Hey!"

A man in a popsicle-red rain slicker was leaning over the crow's-nest railing. "What are you doing?"

"Are you crew?" Laura shouted, hesitating.

"No, are you?"

She shook her head. "I thought I saw something"—she pointed—"over there!"

"What did you see?"

"I think it was a Canadair CL-227!"

The man's shoes clattered as he came down quickly to the deck. "What's a canadare?" Yaobang demanded plaintively, hopping from foot to foot. He noticed a pair of Zeiss binoculars around the other's neck. "Where'd you get those?"

"Deck room," said Red Raincoat, meaninglessly.

"I know you, right? Henderson? I'm Desmond Yaobang. Countertrade section."

"Hennessey," Red Raincoat said.

"Hennessey, yes . . ."

"Give me those," Laura demanded. She grabbed the binoculars. Under the flimsy poncho, Hennessey's chest was padded and huge. He was wearing something. Bulletproof vest?

A life jacket.

Laura tore her sunglasses off, felt hastily for a pocket—none, in a sari—and propped them on her head. She focused the binoculars.

She found the thing almost at once. There it was, hovering malignantly at the twilit skyline. It had been in her nightmares so many times that she couldn't believe she was seeing it.

It was the drone that had strafed her Lodge. Not the identical one, because this one was military green, but the same model—double rotors, dumbbell shape. Even the stupid landing gear.

"Let me see!" Yaobang demanded frantically. To shut him up, Laura passed him the binoculars.

"Hey," Hennessey protested mildly. "Those are mine." He was a thirtyish Anglo with prominent cheekbones and a small, neatly trimmed mustache. He had no accent—straight Mid-Atlantic Net talk. Below the baggy plastic poncho there was something lithe and weaselish about him.

He smiled at her, tightly, looking into her eyes. "You American? USA?"

Laura felt for her sunglasses. They'd pushed the sari back, showing her blond hair.

"I see it!" Yaobang burst out excitedly. "A flying ground nut!"

Hennessey's eyes widened. He'd recognized her. He was thinking fast. She could see him shift forward onto the balls of his feet.

"Maybe it's Grenadian!" Yaobang said. "Better warn everyone! I'll watch the thing—missy, you go running!"

"No, don't do that," Hennessey told her. He reached under his poncho and tugged out a piece of machinery. It was small and skeletal and looked like a cross between a vice-grip wrench and a putty applicator. He stepped near Yaobang, holding the device with both hands.

"Oh, God," Yaobang said blindly. Another wave of it was hitting him—he was trembling so hard he could barely hold up the binoculars. "I'm frightened," he sniveled. A cracked, reflexive, little-boy voice. "I can see it coming. . . . I'm afraid!"

Hennessey pointed the machine at Yaobang's ribs and pulled its trigger, twice. There were two discreet little coughs, barely audible, but the thing jumped viciously in Hennessey's hands. Yaobang convulsed with impact, arms flying, chest buckling as if hit with an axe. He fell over his own feet and hit the deck with a clatter of binoculars.

Laura stared at him in stunned horror. Hennessey had just blown two great smoking holes in Yaobang's jacket. Yaobang lay unmoving, face livid and black. "You killed him!"

"No. No problem. Special narcotic dye," Hennessey blurted.

She looked again. Just for a second. Yaobang's mouth was clogged with blood. She stared at Hennessey and began backing away.

With a sudden smooth, reflexive motion Hennessey centered the gun on her chest. She saw the cavernous barrel of it and knew suddenly that she was looking at death. "Laura Webster!" Hennessey said. "Don't run, don't make me shoot!"

Laura froze.

"Police officer," Hennessey said. He glanced nervously off the port bow. "Vienna Convention, Special Operations Task Force. Just obey orders and everything will be fine."

"That's a lie!" Laura shouted. "There's no such thing!"

He wasn't looking at her. He kept looking out to sea. She followed his gaze.

Something was coming toward the ship. It was rushing over the waves, with astonishing, magic swiftness. A long white stick, like a wand, with sharp square wings. Behind it a slim straight billow of contrail air.

It rushed toward the bridge, at the stern, a needle on a thread of steam. Into it. Through it.

Raw fire bloomed, taller than houses. A wall of heat and sound surged up the deck and knocked her from her feet. She was down, bruised, flash-blinded. The bow of the ship bucked under her like a huge steel animal.

Roaring seconds. Pieces of plastic and steel were pattering onto the deck. The bridge superstructure—the radar mast, the phone antennas—was one vast, ugly conflagration. It was like someone had built a volcano in it—thermite heat and white-hot twisting spars of metal and lava globs of molten ceramic and plastic. Like a firecracker in a white wedding cake.

Below them, the ship was still pitching. Hennessey had lurched to his feet and made a run for the railing. For a moment she thought he was going to jump. Then he was back with a life preserver—a big ceremonial flotation ring marked in Parsi script. He stumbled and rolled and got back to her. There was no sign of his gun now—he'd folded it again, tucked it away.

"Get this on!" he shouted in her face.

Laura grabbed it reflexively. "The lifeboat!" she shouted back.

He shook his head. "No! No good! Booby-trapped!"

"You bastard!"

He ignored her. "When she goes down, you have to swim hard, Laura! Hard, away from the undertow!"

"No!" She jumped to her feet, dancing away from his lunging attempt to tackle her. The back of the ship was vomiting smoke now, huge black explosive volumes of it. People were scrambling across the deck.

She turned back to Hennessey. He was down and doubled over, hands knotted behind his neck, bent legs crossed at the ankles. She gaped at him, then looked to sea again.

Another missile. It slid just above the waves, its jet flare lighting the rippled water with flashbulb briefness. It hit.

A catastrophic explosion belowdecks. Hatch covers leapt free from their hinges and tumbled skyward like flaming dominoes. Up-leaping geysers of fire. The ship lurched like a gut-shot elephant.

The deck tilted, slowly, inexorably, gravity clutching at them like the end of the world. Steam rose with a stink of scalded seawater. She fell to her knees and slid.

Hennessey had crawled to the bow rail. He had an elbow hooked around it and was talking into something—a military field telephone. He paused and yanked its long antenna out and resumed shouting. Gleefully. He caught her eye and waved and gestured at her. Jump! Swim!

She lurched to her feet again, lusting blindly to get at him and kill him. Strangle him, claw his eyes out. The deck dropped under her like a broken elevator and she fell again, bruising her knees. She almost lost the flotation ring.

Her shins were wet. She turned. The sea was coming up over the starboard bow. Gray ugly waves thick with blasted chunks of flotsam. The ship was eviscerated, its guts spewing out.

Fear overwhelmed her. A panic strength to live. She ripped and kicked her way out of the enveloping sari. Her sandals were long gone. She pulled the ring over her head and shoulders. Then she scrambled to the bow rail, clambered over it, and jumped.

The water rushed over her, warm and dank. Twilight was leaching from the sky, but the ship's blaze lit the straits like a battlefield.

Another minor explosion, and a flare of light by the ship's single lifeboat. He'd killed them. Good God, they were going to *kill them all!* How many people—a hundred, a hundred and fifty? They'd been herded into a cattle car and taken out to sea and butchered! Burned and drowned, like vermin!

A drone hummed angrily just over her head. She felt the wind of it on her sodden hair.

She got the ring wedged under her armpits and started swimming hard.

The sea seemed to be boiling. She thought of sharks.

Suddenly the opaque depths beneath her naked legs were full of lurking presences. She swam hard, until the panic strength faded into chilly shock. She turned and looked.

It was going. Stern last, rising above the sea in the last hissing remnants of flame, like a distant candlelit tombstone. She watched it for long, thudding heartbeat seconds. Then it was gone, sinking into nothingness, blackness, and ooze.

The night was overcast. Darkness came on like a shroud. The rush of afterwash hit her and bobbed her like a buoy.

Another hum overhead. Then, in the distance, in the darkness, the chatter of machine-gun fire.

They were killing the survivors in the water. Shooting them from drones, out of darkness, with infrareds. She began swimming again, desperately, away.

She couldn't die out here. No, not blown to shreds out here, killed like a statistic. . . . David, the baby . . .

An inflatable boat surged by, dark man-shapes and the quiet mutter of an engine. A slap in the water—someone had tossed her a line. She heard Hennessey's voice. "Grab it. Hurry up!"

She did it. It was that, or die here. They tugged her in and hauled her up, over the inflatable's hull. Hennessey grinned at her in his drenched clothes. He had companions: four sailors in white round hats, neat silky uniforms, dark with a gleam of gold.

She sprawled in the rippling bottom of the boat, against a hull black and slick as a gut, in her sari blouse and underwear. One of the sailors tossed the flotation ring overboard. They picked up speed, heading away, up the straits.

The closest sailor leaned toward her, an Anglo about forty. His face looked as white as a sliced apple. "Cigarette, lady?"

She stared at him. He leaned back, shrugging.

She coughed on seawater, then gathered her legs in, trembling, wretched. A long time passed. Then her brain began to work again.

The ship had never had a chance. Not even to scream out an SOS. The first missile had wiped out the bridge—radio, radar, and all. The killers had cut their throat first thing.

But to kill a hundred people in the middle of the Malacca Straits! To commit an atrocity like that—surely other ships must have seen the explosion, the smoke. To have done such a thing, so viciously, so blatantly . . .

Her voice, when she finally got it out, was cracked and weak. "Hennessey . . . ?"

"Henderson," he told her. He tugged his drenched red rain slicker over his head. Beneath it was a bright orange life jacket. Under that a sleeveless utility vest, bulges and little metal zips and Velcro flaps. "Here, put this slicker on."

He shoved it at her. She held it numbly.

Henderson chuckled. "Put it on! You want to meet a hundred red-blooded sailors in wet underwear?"

The words didn't quite register, but she started on it anyway. They were speeding in darkness, the boat bouncing, the wind tearing and flapping at the raincoat. She struggled with it for what seemed an endless time. It clung to her bare wet skin like a bloody hide.

"Looks like you need a hand," Henderson said. He crawled forward and helped her into it. "There. That's better."

"You killed them all," Laura croaked.

Henderson aimed amused glances at the sailors. "None of that, now," he said loudly. "Besides, I had a little help from the attack ship!" He laughed.

Sailor number two cut back the engine. They were coasting forward in darkness. "Boat," he said. "A sub is a 'boat.' Sir."

In the darkness, she heard water cascading and the gurgle of surf. She could barely see it in the dimness, a vague blue-black sheen. But she could smell it and feel it, almost taste it on her skin.

It was huge. It was close. A vast black rectangle of painted steel. A conning tower.

A monstrous submarine.

9

*I*T was huge and alive, ticking over like some transatlantic jet, drizzling seawater with sharp pneumatic huffing and a deep shuddering hum. Laura heard drones hissing past her in the darkness, taxiing in to land on the hull. Evil, waspish sounds. She couldn't see them, but she knew the machines could see her, lit by her own body heat.

The inflatable collided gently with the sub, a rubbery jolt.

The sailors climbed a detachable rope ladder up the dark curving hull. Henderson waited as they left. Then he smeared wet hair from his eyes and grabbed her arm.

"Don't do stupid shit," he told her. "Don't yell, don't act up, don't be a bitch. I saved your life. So don't embarrass me. Because you'll die."

He sent her up the ladder ahead of him. The rungs hurt her hands, and the slick steel hull was deep-water-cold under her bare feet. The flattened hull stretched out endlessly into washing darkness. Behind her, the conning tower loomed thirty feet high. Long spines of black-and-white antennas sprouted from its peak.

A dozen more sailors clustered on the hull, in elegant bell-bottom trousers and long-sleeved blouses with gold-braided cuffs. They tended to the drones, manhandling them down a series of yawning hatches. They moved with a strange tippy-toeing, hunch-shouldered look. As if they found the empty night sky oppressive.

The inflatable's crew expertly hauled it up after them, flinging rope hand over hand. They deflated it, trampling out air in a demented sombrero dance, then stuffed the wet rubber mass into a seabag.

It was all over in a few moments. They were jumping back

into their vast steel warren, like rats. Henderson hustled Laura over a hatch coaming onto a recessed floor. It sank beneath their feet. The hatch slammed over her head with an ear-popping huff and a squeal of hydraulics.

They emerged from the elevator shaft into a vast cylindrical warehouse lit with sullen yellow bulbs. It had two decks: a lower floor, beneath her bare feet, of solid iron, and an upper one of perforated grating. It was cavernous, two hundred feet long; every ten feet it was cut, left and right, by massive bulging elevator shafts. Shafts nine feet across, steel silos, their bases stuck with plugs and power cables. Like bio-tech tanks, she thought, big fermenters.

Two dozen sailors padded silently in foam-soled deck shoes on the narrow walkways between the silos. They were working on the drones in hushed concentration. An incense stink of hot aircraft oil and spent ammunition. Some scrambled vibe of war and industry and church.

The compartment was painted in sky blue, the tubes in spacy midnight indigo. Henderson headed aft. As he hauled her along, Laura touched the cold latex surface of a tube, wonderingly. Someone had painstakingly stenciled it with dizzy five-pointed stars, comets with whizzing comic-book tails, little yellow ringed Saturns. Like surfboard art. Dreamy and cheap.

Some silos had been welder-cut and hung with arcane repair tools—they were retrofitted for drone launches. The others were older, they looked intact. Still serving their original function, whatever that was.

Henderson spun the manual wheel in the center of a watertight door. It opened with a thermos-bottle thump and they ducked through. Into a coffinlike chamber plated with egg-carton antisound padding.

Laura felt the world tilt subtly beneath her feet. A river rush of ballast tanks and the distant whir of motors. The sub was diving. Then a startling junkyard chorus of pops, harsh creaks, glass-bottle clinking, as pressure began to bite into the hull.

Through the chamber into another room flooded with clean white light. Supersharp fluorescents overhead, that strange laserish light of three-peak spectrum radiance, casting everything into edgy superrealism. Some kind of control room, with a Christmas-tree profusion of machinery. Vast tilted consoles loomed, with banks of switches, flickering readouts, needle-twitching glassy dials. Sailors with short, neat haircuts sat before them in sumptuous padded swivel chairs.

The room was full of crewmen—she kept noticing more and more of them, their heads peeking out through dense clusters of piping and monitors. The room was jammed floor to ceiling with equipment and she couldn't find the walls. There were men in it elbow to elbow, crammed into arcane little ergonomic nooks. People sockets.

Acceleration hit them; Laura staggered a little. Somewhere, a faint high-pitched whine and a liquid trembling as the great steel mass picked up speed.

Just before her was a sunken area about the size of a bathtub. A man sat in it, wearing bulging padded headphones and clutching a knobbed steering wheel. He was like a child's doll surrounded by pricey stereo equipment. Just above his head was a gray gasketed lump with the stenciled legend ANTI-COLLISION LIGHT—SWITCH TO FLASH. He was staring fixedly at half a dozen round glass gauges.

This was the pilot, Laura thought. No way to look outside a submarine. Just dials.

Footsteps on a curved stairway at the back of the room—someone coming down from the upper deck. "Hesseltine?"

"Yo!" said Henderson cheerfully. He tugged Laura along by the wrist, and she slammed her elbow jarringly into a vertical column. "Come on," he insisted, dragging her.

They threaded the maze, to meet their interrogator. The new man was portly, with black curled hair, pouting lips, his eyes heavy-lidded and solemn. He wore shoulder tabs, elaborate sleeve insignia, and a round black-brimmed sailor's cap with gold lettering. REPUBLIQUE DE MALI. He shook Henderson/Hesseltine's hand. Maddeningly, the two of them began speaking fluent French.

They climbed the spiral stairs, walked down a long dim stifling corridor. Hesseltine's shoes squelched loudly. They chattered in French, with enthusiasm.

The officer showed them into a set of narrow shower stalls. "Great," said Hesseltine, stepping in and pulling Laura after him. For the first time, he let go of her wrist. "You up to taking your own shower, girl? Or do I have to help?"

Laura stared at him mutely.

"Relax," Hesseltine said. He zipped out of his utility vest. "You're with the good guys now. They're gonna bring us something new to wear. Later we'll eat." He smiled at her, saw it wasn't working, and glowered. "Look. What were you doing on that ship? You didn't turn data banker, did you? Some kind of double-agent scam?"

"No, of course not!"

"You got some special reason to regret those criminals?"

The moral vacuity in it stunned her. They were human beings. "No . . ." she blurted, almost involuntarily.

Hesseltine pulled off his shirt, revealing a narrow suntanned chest densely packed with muscle.

She stole a sidelong glance at his utility vest. She knew he had a gun in it somewhere.

He caught her looking and his face hardened. "Look. We'll make this simple. Get in the shower stall and don't come out till I say. Or else."

She got into the shower and shut its door and turned it on. She stayed in it for ten minutes, while it squeezed out maybe a quart of buzzing ultrasonic mist. She rinsed salt from what was left of her clothes and ran some thin acrid soap through her hair.

"Okay," Hesseltine shouted at her. She stepped out, wearing the raincoat again. Hesseltine was neatly groomed. He wore a midnight-blue naval uniform and was lacing his deck shoes. Someone had laid out a gray terry-cloth sweatsuit for her: drawstring pants, a hooded pullover.

She stepped into the pants, turned her back on him, threw off the raincoat, and tunneled quickly into the pullover. She turned back, saw that he had been watching her in the mirror. Not with lust or even appreciation—there was a chill, vacant look on his face, like an evil child methodically killing a bug.

As she turned back, the look vanished like a card trick.

He'd never sneaked a glimpse at all. Hesseltine was a gentleman. This was an embarrassing but necessary situation that the two of them were working through like adults. Somehow Hesseltine was managing to say all this to her, while bent over and tying his shoes. The lie was radiating out of him. Out of his pores, like sweat.

A sailor waited for them outside, a wiry little veteran with a gray mustache and faraway eyes. He led them aft to a tiny cabin, where the hull formed a rounded, sloping roof. The place was about the size of a garden tool shed. Four deathly pale sailors, with their sleeves rolled up and collars open, were sitting at a tiny café table, silently playing a checker game.

The French-speaking officer was there. "Sit down," he said in English. Laura sat on a cramped wall bench, close enough to one of the four sailors that she smelled his floral deodorant.

Across the cabin, stuck to the curved ceiling, were idealized portrait posters of men in elaborate uniforms. She had a quick look at two of the names: DE GAULLE, JARUZELSKI. Meaningless.

"My name is Baptiste," said the sailor. "Political Officer aboard this vessel. We are to have a discussion." Pause, for two beats. "Would you like some tea?"

"Yes," Laura said. The mist-shower hadn't offered enough for drinking. Her throat felt leathery with seawater and shock. She felt a sudden trembling shoot through her.

She didn't delude herself that this was a situation she could handle. She was in the hands of murderers. It surprised her that they would pretend to consult her about her own fate.

They must want something from her, though. Hesseltine's lean, weasely face had a look on it like something she would have scraped from a boot. She wondered how badly she wanted to live. What she was willing to do for it.

Hesseltine laughed at her. "Don't look that way, uh, Laura. Stop worrying. You're *safe* now." Baptiste shot him a cynical look from beneath heavy eyelids. A sudden sharp cascade of metallic pressure pops rang from the wall. Laura started like an antelope. One of the four sailors nearby languidly moved a checker piece with one forefinger.

She stared at Hesseltine, then took a cup from Baptiste and drank. It was tepid and sweet. Were they poisoning her? It didn't matter. She could die at their whim.

"My name is Laura Day Webster," she told them. "I'm

an associate of Rizome Industries Group. I live in Galveston, Texas." It all sounded so pathetically brittle and faraway.

"You're shivering," Baptiste observed. He leaned backward and turned up a thermostat on the bulkhead. Even here, in some sort of rec room, the bulkhead was grotesquely cluttered: a speaker grille, an air ionizer, an eight-socketed surge-protected power plug, a wall clock reading 12:17 Greenwich Mean Time.

"Welcome aboard the SSBN *Thermopylae*," Baptiste said. Laura said nothing.

"Cat got your tongue?" Hesseltine said. Baptiste laughed.

"Come on," Hesseltine said. "You were chattering away like a magpie when you thought I was a goddamn data pirate."

"We are not pirates, Mrs. Webster," Baptiste soothed. "We are the world police."

"You're not Vienna," Laura said.

"He means the *real* police," Hesseltine said impatiently. "Not that crowd of lead-assed bureaucrats."

Laura rubbed one bloodshot eye. "If you're police, then am I under arrest?"

Hesseltine and Baptiste shared a manly chuckle over her naivete. "We are not bourgeois legalists," Baptiste said. "We do not issue arrests."

"*Cardiac* arrests," Hesseltine said, tapping his teeth with his thumbnail. He truly believed he was being funny. Baptiste stared at him, puzzled, missing the English idiom.

"I saw you on Singapore TV," Hesseltine told her suddenly. "You said you opposed the data havens, wanted them shut down. But you sure went about it in a screwy way. The haven bankers—my former coworkers, you know—laughed their asses off when they saw you handing that democratic guff to Parliament."

He poured himself tea. "Of course, they're mostly refugees now, and a pretty good number of the bastards are on the bottom of the sea. No thanks to you, though—you were trying to kiss them into submission. And you, a rootin-tootin' cowboy Texan, too. It's a good thing they didn't try that at the Alamo."

Another sailor made a move in the checker game, and the third one swore in response. Laura flinched.

"Pay them no mind," Baptiste told her quickly. "They're off duty."

"What?" Laura said blankly.

"*Off duty,*" he said impatiently, as if it embarrassed him. "They are Blue Crew. *We* are Red Crew."

"Oh . . . what's that they're playing?"

He shrugged. "Uckers."

"Uckers? What's that?"

"It's a kind of ludo."

Hesseltine assembled, aimed, and fired a grin at her. "Sub crews," he said. "A very special breed. Highly trained. A disciplined elite."

The four Blue Crewmen hunched closer over their board. They refused to look at him.

"It's an odd situation," said Baptiste. He was talking about her, not himself. "We don't quite know what to do with you. You see, we exist to protect people like you."

"You do?"

"We are the cutting edge of the emergent global order."

"Why did you bring me here?" Laura said. "You could have shot me. Or left me to drown."

"Oh, come on," said Hesseltine.

"He's one of our finest operatives," explained Baptiste. "A real artist."

"Thanks."

"Of course he would rescue a pretty woman at the end of his assignment—he couldn't resist a final dramatic grace note!"

"Just the kind of guy I am," Hesseltine admitted.

"That's it?" Laura said quietly. "You saved me just on a whim? After killing all those people?"

Hesseltine stared at her. "You're gonna piss me off in a minute. . . . Don't you think they'd have killed *me* if they knew what I was? That wasn't just your mickey-mouse industrial espionage, y'know. I spent months and months in a deadly deep-cover operation for the highest geopolitical stakes! Those Yung Soo Chim guys had background checks like nobody's business, and they watched my ass like a hawk."

He leaned back. "But will I get credit? Hell, no, I won't." He stared at his cup. "I mean, that's part of the whole undercover biz, no credit. . . ."

"It was a very slick operation," said Baptiste. "Compare it to Grenada. Our attack on the Singapore criminals was surgical, almost bloodless."

Laura realized something. "You want me to be grateful."

"Well, yeah," said Hesseltine, looking up. "A little of that wouldn't be too out of line, after all the effort we put into it."

He smiled at Baptiste. "Look at that face! You should've heard her in Parliament, going on and on about Grenada. The carpet bombing took out this big mansion the Rastas gave her. It really pissed her off."

It was as if he'd stabbed her. "You killed Winston Stubbs in my house! While I was standing next to him. With my baby in my arms."

"Oh," Baptiste said, relaxing ostentatiously. "The Stubbs killing. That wasn't us. That was one of Singapore's."

"I don't believe it," Laura said, sagging back. "We got a FACT communiqué taking credit!"

"A set of initials means very little," said Baptiste. "FACT was an old front-group. Nothing compared to our modern operations. . . . In truth, it was Singapore's Merlion-Commandos. I don't think the Singapore civilian government ever knew of their actions."

"Lots of ex-paras, Berets, Spetsnaz, that sort of thing," Hesseltine said. "They tend to run a little wild. I mean, face it—these are guys who gave their lives to the art of warfare. Then all of a sudden, you know, Abolition, Vienna Convention. One day they're the shield of their nation, next day they're bums, got their walking papers, that's about it."

"Men who once commanded armies, and billions in government funds," Baptiste recited mournfully. "Now, nonpersons. Spurned. Purged. Even vilified."

"By lawyers!" said Hesseltine, becoming animated. "And chickenshit peaceniks! Who would have thought it, you know? But when it came, it was so sudden. . . ."

"Armies belong to nation-states," said Baptiste. "It is hard to establish true military loyalty to a more modern,

global institution. . . . But now that we own our own country—
the Republic of Mali—recruiting has picked up remarkably."

"And it helps, too, that we happen to be the global good
guys," Hesseltine said airily. "Any dumbass merc will fight
for pay for Grenada or Singapore, or some jungle-jabber
African regime. But *we* get committed personnel who truly
recognize the global threat and are prepared to take action.
For justice." He leaned back, crossing his arms.

She knew she could not take much more of this. She was
holding herself together somehow, but it was a waking nightmare. She would have understood it if they'd been heel-
clicking Nazi executioners . . . but to meet with this smarmy
little Frenchman and this empty-eyed good-old-boy psychotic.
. . . The utter banality, the *soullessness* of it . . .

She could feel the iron walls closing in on her. In a minute
she was going to scream.

"You look a little pale," Hesseltine remarked. "We'll get
some chow into you, that'll perk you up. There's always
great chow on a sub. It's a navy tradition." He stood up.
"Where's the head?"

Baptiste gave him directions. He watched Hesseltine go,
admiringly. "More tea, Mrs. Webster?"

"Yes-thank-you . . ."

"I don't think you recognize the genuine *quality* of Mr.
Hesseltine," Baptiste chided, pouring. "Pollard, Reilly, Sorge
. . . he could match with history's finest! A natural operative!
A romantic figure, really—born out of his own true time. . . .
Someday your grandchildren will talk about that man."

Laura's brain went into automatic pilot. She slipped into
babbling surrealism. "This is quite a ship you have here.
Boat, I mean."

"Yes. It's a nuclear-powered American Trident, which
cost over five hundred million of your country's dollars."

She nodded stupidly: right, yes, uh-huh. "So, this is an old
Cold War sub?"

"A ballistic missile sub, exactly."

"What's that mean?"

"It's a launch platform."

"What? I don't understand."

He smiled at her. "I think 'nuclear deterrent' is the concept you're searching for, Mrs. Webster."

" 'Deterrent.' Deterring what?"

"Vienna, of course. I should think that would be obvious."

Laura sipped her tea. Five hundred million dollars. Nuclear powered. Ballistic missiles. It was as if he'd told her that they were reanimating corpses on board. It was far too horrible, way off the scale of reason and credibility.

There was no proof. He hadn't shown her anything. They were bullshitting her. Magic tricks. They were liars. She didn't believe it.

"You don't seem disturbed," Baptiste said approvingly. "You're not superstitious about wicked nuclear power?"

She shook her head, not trusting herself to speak aloud.

"Once there were dozens of nuclear submarines," said Baptiste. "France had them. Britain, U.S., Russia. Training, techniques, traditions, all well established. You're in no danger—these men are thoroughly trained from the original coursework and documents. Plus, many modern improvements!"

"No danger."

"No."

"Then what are you going to do with me?"

He shook his head, ruefully. Bells rang. It was time to eat.

Baptiste found Hesseltine and took them both to the offi- cers' mess. It was a nasty little place, next to the clattering, hissing racket of the galley. They sat at a solidly anchored square table on metal chairs covered in green-and-yellow vinyl. Three officers were already there, being served by a cook in an apron and crisp paper hat.

Baptiste introduced the officers as the captain-lieutenant, captain second rank, and the senior executive officer, who was actually the junior of the bunch. He gave no names and they didn't seem to miss them. Two were Europeans, Ger- mans maybe, and the third looked Russian. They all spoke Net English.

It was clear from the beginning that this was Hesseltine's show. Laura was some kind of battle trophy Hesseltine had won, blond cheesecake for the camera to dwell on during slow moments in his cinema biography. She didn't have to say anything—they didn't expect it from her. The crewmen gave her strange, muddied looks compounded of regret, speculation, and some kind of truly twisted superstitious dread. They dug into their meals: foil-covered microwave trays marked "Aero Cubana: Clase Primera." Laura picked at her tray. Aero Cubana. She'd flown on Aero Cubana, with David at her side and the baby in her lap. David and Loretta. Oh, God . . .

The officers were edgy at first, disturbed and excited by strangers. Hesseltine oozed charm, giving them a thrilling eyewitness account of their attack on the *Ali Khamenei*. His vocabulary was bizarre: it was all "strikes" and "impacts" and "targeting," no mention at all of burned and lacerated human beings. Finally, his enthusiasm broke the ice, and the officers began talking more freely, in a leaden jargon consisting almost entirely of acronyms.

It had been an exhilarating day for these officers of the Red Crew. After weeks, possibly months of what could only have been inhuman suffocating tedium, they had successfully stalked and destroyed a "terrie hard target." They were going to get some kind of reward for it, apparently—it had something to do with "Hollywood baths," whatever that meant. The Yellow Crew, now on duty, would now spend their own six-hour shift in a boring escape run across the bottom of the Indian Ocean. As for the Blue Crew, they had missed their chance at action and were bitterly sulking.

She wondered what they were trying to escape *from*. The missiles—"Exocets," they called them—had flown for miles before hitting. They could have been launched from almost any large surface ship in the straits, or even from Sumatra. No one had seen the sub.

And how would anyone suspect its existence? A submarine was a monster from a lost era. It was *useless*, designed only for killing—there was no such thing as a "cargo sub" or a "Coast Guard sub" or a "search-and-rescue sub."

Sure, there were little deep-sea research vessels, bathyscaphes or whatever the word was—just like there were still a few manned spacecraft, both equally obscure and quaint and funny-looking. But this thing was *huge*. And the truth, or a dread strong enough to pass for one, was beginning to seep in.

It reminded her of something she'd heard when she was

eleven or so. One of those horror folk tales that kids told each other. About the boy who accidentally swallowed a needle. . . . Only to have it show up, years or decades later, rusty but still whole, in his ankle or kneecap or elbow . . . silent steel entity sliding unknown and unknowable through his living breathing body . . . while he grew up and married and held down some unremarkable service job . . . till he goes to the doctor one day and says: Doc, I'm getting old, may be rheumatism but I have this strange stabbing pain in my leg. . . . Well, says kindly Doc, put 'er here under the scanner and we'll have a look. . . . My word, Mr. World-Everyman, you seem to have a vicious septic needle hiding under your kneecap. . . . Oh yeah, gosh Doc, I kinda forgot about it but as a young boy I used to play with needles habitually, in fact most of my allowance went toward buying extremely sharp and deadly needles which I scattered lavishly in every direction, but when I grew up and got a little wiser I was sure that I'd picked up *every last one*. . . .

"You okay?" Hesseltine said.

"Excuse me?" Laura said.

"We're talking about you, Laura. About whether to put you straight in a tank, or let you hang out a while."

"I don't understand," she said numbly. "You have tanks? I thought you were navy people."

The officers laughed, false yo-ho-ho club-room laughter. The Russian-looking one said something about how the world's women hadn't gotten any smarter. Hesseltine smiled at her as if it were the first thing she'd done right.

"Hell," he said, "we'll show 'em to you. That all right, Baptiste?"

"Why not?"

Hesseltine shook hands all around and made a studied exit. He and Baptiste and Laura emerged into a dining hall where thirty neatly groomed Red Crewmen were eating, jammed elbow to elbow around collapsible tables. As Hesseltine entered, they set down their forks with a clatter and applauded politely.

Hesseltine offered her his elbow. Frightened by their flat, fishlike eyes, she took his arm. He paraded her down the narrow aisle between rows of tables. The men were all close enough to grab at her, to wink or grin or hoot, but none of them did, or even looked like they wanted to. It smelled of them: their soap and shampoo, their beef stroganoff and green beans. In the corner a wide-screen TV was showing an illegal kick-boxing match, two wiry Thais silently beating each other bloody.

They were out. Laura shivered helplessly and let go of his arm, her skin crawling. "What's wrong with them?" she hissed at him. "They're so quiet and numb. . . ."

"What's wrong with *you?*" he riposted. "A long face like that . . . you're making everyone nervous."

They took her back to the first room she'd seen, with the elevators. They emerged on the upper deck of grating. Below them, Yellow Crewmen were at work on the drones, examining stripped-down bits of machinery on cramped little blankets of tarpaulin.

Baptiste and Hesseltine stopped by one of the elaborately painted silos. The crude stars and whizzing comets . . . she saw that it had a black silhouette, the nude outline of a stylized buxom babe. Long leg kicked out, hair flung back, a stripper's pose. And lettering: TANYA. "What's this?" Laura said.

"That's the tank's name," Baptiste said. A little apologetic, like a gentleman forced to bring up an off-color subject. "The men did it . . . high spirits . . . you know how it is."

High spirits. She couldn't imagine anything less likely from the men she'd seen aboard. "What is this thing?"

Hesseltine spoke up. "Well, one climbs inside there, of course, and . . ." He paused. "You're not lesbian, are you?"

"What? No . . ."

"Too bad, I guess. . . . If you're not gay, the *special features* aren't going to do much for you. . . . But even without the simulations, they says it's very relaxing."

Laura backed a step away. "Are . . . are they all like this?"

"No," said Baptiste. "Some are drone ports, and the others launch warheads. But five of them are our recreation tanks—'Hollywood baths,' the men call them."

"And you want *me* to go inside there?"

"If you like," said Baptiste reluctantly. "We won't acti-vate the machinery—nothing will *touch* you—you simply float within it, breathing, dreaming, in nice heated seawater."

"Keep you out of trouble a few days," Hesseltine said.

"Days?"

"They're very advanced and well designed," Baptiste said, annoyed. "This isn't something we *invented,* you know."

"A few days is nothing!" Hesseltine said. "Now if they leave you in a few *weeks,* you might start seeing your Opti-mal Persona and all kinds of twisted shit. . . . But in the meantime you're perfectly safe and happy. And we know where you are. Sound good?"

Laura shook her head, minutely. "If you could just find me a bunk . . . a little corner somewhere. . . . I really don't mind."

"Not much privacy," Baptiste warned. "Crowded condi-tions." He seemed relieved, though. Glad that she wouldn't be taking up valuable tank room.

Hesseltine frowned. "Well, I don't want to hear you bitch-ing later."

"No, no."

Hesseltine looked restless. He glanced at his waterproof watchphone. "I really need to uplink with HQ and debrief."

"Please go ahead," Laura said. "You've done more than enough. I'm sure I'll be fine, really."

"Wow," said Hesseltine. "That almost sounds like a thank you."

They found room for her in a laundry space. It was a chill, steamy warren, stinking of detergent and crammed with sharp-edged machinery. A bare little single bunk slid out over chromed storage rails. Towels hung from a forest of gray, stenciled pipes overhead: there were a couple of steam presses inside, old laundry mangles.

And carton after strapped carton of old Hollywood movie films, the thick mechanical kind that ran through projectors. They were neatly labeled with hand-printed tape: MONROE #1, MONROE #2, GRABLE, HAYWORTH, CICCONE. There was a closed-circuit phone on the wall, an old-fashioned sound-only hand-set with a long, curly cord. The sight of it made her think of the Net. Then, of David. Her family, her people.

She had vanished from their world. Did they think she was dead? They were still looking for her, she was sure. But they would look in Singapore's jails, and hospitals, and, finally, the morgues. But not here. Never.

A Red Crewman made up her bunk with clean, sheet-whipping efficiency.

He produced a nasty-looking pair of chromed tin snips. "Let's see them hands," he said. The two remaining bracelets of plastic handcuff still looped Laura's wrists. He pinched and worried at them till they came loose, reluctantly. "Musta been a mighty sharp knife that cut those," he said.

"Thanks."

"Don't thank me. It was your pal Mr. Hesseltine's idea."

Laura rubbed her skinned wrists. "What's your name, sir?"

" 'Jim' will do. I hear you're from Texas."

"Yeah. Galveston."

"Me too, but down the coast. Corpus Christi."

"Jesus, we're practically neighbors."

"Yeah, I reckon so." Jim looked about thirty-five, maybe forty. He was broad-faced and chunky, with reddish, thinning hair. His skin was the color of cheap printout, so pale she could see bluish veins in his neck.

"Can I ask?" she said. "What are you doing here?"

"Protectin' people," Jim said nobly. "Protecting you right now, in case you decide to do something stupid. Mr. Hesseltine says you're a funny little duck. Some kind of political."

"Oh," she said. "I meant, how did you get here?"

"Since you ask, I'll tell you," Jim said. He popped down a steel-wired bunk from a space high on the wall and hoisted himself in. He sat above her, legs dangling, neck bent to avoid the ceiling. "Once upon a time, I was a professional fisherman. A shrimper. My dad was, too. And his dad before him. . . . But they put us in a squeeze we couldn't get out of. Texas Fish & Game police, a million environment laws. Not that I'm speakin' against those laws. But American law didn't stop the Nicaraguans and Mexicans. They cheated. Cleaned out the best grounds, took everything, then undersold us in our own markets. We lost our boat! Lost everything. Went on the Welfare, had nothin'."

"I'm sorry," Laura said.

"Not half as sorry as us. . . . Well, me and some friends in the same jam, we tried to organize, protect our lives and families. . . . But the Texas Rangers—some goddamn informer is what it was—caught me with a gun. And you know a man can't own a handgun in the States these days, not even to protect his own home! So it looked pretty bad for me. . . . Then I heard from some pals in my, uhm, organization . . . about recruitment overseas. Groups to protect you, hide you out, teach you how to fight.

"So, that's how I ended up in Africa."

"Africa," Laura repeated. The very sound of it scared her.

"It's bad there," he said. "Plagues, and dustbowls, and wars. Africa's full of men like me. Private armies. Palace guards. Mercenaries, advisers, commandos, pilots. . . . But you know what we lacked? Leadership."

"Leadership."

"Exactly."

"How long have you been inside this submarine?"

"We like it here," Jim said.

"You never go out, do you? Never surface or go on, whatever you call it—shore leave?"

"You don't miss it," he said. "Not with what we have. We're kings down here. Invisible kings. Kings of the whole damn world." He laughed quietly, pulled up his feet, a little balding man in deck shoes. "You look pretty tired, eh."

"I . . ." There was no point. "Yeah. I am."

"You go ahead and get yourself some sleep. I'll just sit here and watch over you."

He didn't say anything more.

Hesseltine was being sympathetic. "A little tedious."

"No, no, really," Laura said. She slid away from him, rumpling the sheets of her bunk. "I'm fine, don't mind me."

"Don't worry!" he told her. "Good news! I straightened it all out with HQ, while you were sleeping. Turns out you're in their files—they know who you are! They actually *commended* me for picking you up."

"HQ?" she said.

"Bamako. Mali."

"Ah."

"I knew it was a good idea," he said. "I mean, an operative like me learns to go by his gut instincts. Seems you're a pretty important gal, in your own little way." He beamed, then shrugged apologetically. "Meanwhile, though, you're stuck in this laundry."

"It s okay," she said. "Really." He stared at her. They were alone in the tiny cabin. An awful silence. "I could wash some clothes if you want."

Hesseltine laughed. "That's cute, Laura. That's funny. No, I thought, as long as you're stuck here, maybe some video games."

"What're those?"

"Computer games, you know."

"Oh!" She sat up. To get away, partially, for a while, from these walls, from him. Into a screen. Wonderful. "You have a Worldrun simulation? Or maybe Amazon Basin?"

"No, these are early games from the seventies, eighties. . . . Games played by the original sub crews, to pass time. Not much graphics or memory of course, but they're interesting. Clever."

"Sure," Laura said. "I can try it."

"Or maybe you'd rather read? Gotta big library onboard. You'd be surprised what these guys are into. Plato, Nietzsche, all the greats. And a lot of specialty stuff."

"Specialty . . ."

"That's right."

"Do you have *The Lawrence Doctrine and Postindustrial Insurgency* by Jonathan Gresham?"

Hesseltine's eyes widened. "You're putting me on. Where the hell did you hear about that?"

"Sticky Thompson showed it to me." She paused. She had impressed him. She was glad she'd said it. It was stupid and reckless to say it, to brag at Hesseltine, but she was glad she'd stung him somehow, put him off-balance. She brushed hair from her eyes and sat up. "Do you have a copy? I didn't read as much as I'd have liked."

"Who's this Thompson?"

"He's Grenadian. The son of Winston Stubbs."

Hesseltine smiled mockingly, back on his feet again. "You can't mean Nesta Stubbs."

Laura blinked, surprised. "Is Sticky's real name Nesta Stubbs?"

"No, it can't be. Nesta Stubbs is a psycho. A drug-crazed killer! A guy like that is voodoo, he could eat a dozen of you for breakfast."

"Why can't I know him?" Laura said. "I know *you,* don't I?"

"Hey!" Hesseltine said. "I'm no terrie—I'm on *your* side."

"If Sticky—Nesta—knew what you'd done to his people, he'd be a lot more scared of you than you are of him."

"Really!" mused Hesseltine. He thought it over, then looked pleased. "I guess he would! And he'd be damned right, too, wouldn't he?"

"He'd come after you, somehow, though. If he knew."

"Whoa," Hesseltine said. "I can tell you'd be all broken up about it, too. . . . Well, no problem. We kicked their ass once, and a couple months from now there won't *be* a Grenada. . . . Look, nobody with your attitude needs to be reading a crazy fucker like Gresham. I'll have 'em bring you the computer instead."

"Okay."

"You won't see me again, Laura. They're flying me out on the next Yellow shift."

It was the way it had always been with Hesseltine. She had no idea what to say to him, but had to say something. "They sure keep you busy, don't they."

"Don't I know it. . . . There's still Luxembourg, you know. The EFT Commerzbank. They think they're safe, since they're embedded in the middle of Europe. But their banking centers are in Cyprus, and Cyprus is a groovy little island. You can think of me there, when they start poppin' caps."

"I certainly will." He was lying. He wasn't going anywhere near Cyprus. He might not even be leaving the boat. He was probably going into a tank, she thought, to be rubbed down by wet rubber Hollywood dolls while floating in limbo. . . . But he must have some reason to want her to think about Cyprus. And that might mean that someday they would let her go. Or at least that Hesseltine thought they might.

* * *

But she didn't see Hesseltine again.

Time passed. The sub ran on an eighteen-hour cycle: six hours on duty, twelve hours off. Sleep fractured between shifts so that day and night—as in all ocean depths—became meaningless. On each shift a crewman would bring her a meal and escort her to the head. They were careful not to touch her.

They always took her to the same toilet. It was always freshly sterilized. No contact with bodily fluids, she thought.

They were treating her as if she were a retrovirus case. Maybe they thought she was. In the old days, sailors used to rush onshore, drink everything in sight, and fuck anything in skirts. But then harbor hookers all over the world began dying of retrovirus.

But the world had the virus pretty much whipped now. Contained anyway. Under control.

Except in Africa.

Could it be that the *crew* had retrovirus?

The video-game machine had about as much smarts as a kid's watchphone. The games plugged into the deck, little spring-loaded cassettes, worn by endless play. The graphics were crude, big stairstep pixels, and you could see the screens refreshing themselves, jerky and Victorian.

She didn't mind the crudity—but the themes were amazing. One game was called "Missile Command." The player controlled little lumps on the screen meant to represent cities. The computer attacked them with nuclear weaponry: bombs, jets, ballistic missiles.

The machine always won—annihilating all life in a big flashy display. *Children* had once played this game. It was utterly morbid.

Then there was one called "Space Invaders." The invading creatures were little pixeled crabs and devil dogs, UFO things from another planet. Dehumanized figures, marching down the screen in lockstep. They always won. You could slaughter them by the hundreds, even win new little forts to fire things— lasers? bombs?—but you always died in the end. The *computer* always won. It made so little sense—letting the computer win every time, as if circuitry could enjoy winning. And every effort, no matter how heroic, ended in Armageddon. It was all so eldritch, so twentieth century.

There was a third game that involved a kind of round yellow consumer—the object was to eat everything in sight, including, sometimes, the little blue pursuing enemies.

She played this game, mostly, as the level of violence was less offensive. It wasn't that she liked them much, but as the shifts passed, empty hours spinning over and over, she discovered their compulsive, obsessive quality . . . the careless insistence on breaking all sane bounds that was the mark of the premillennium. She played them until her hands blistered.

Rub-a-dub-dub, three men in a tub: the butcher, the butcher, and the butcher. . . . Three sailors manned the inflatable, under a hot towering sun and a cloudless, infinite sky, on an endless flat, gentle swell of blue-green ocean. The four of them were the only people who had ever existed. And the little rubber blob of boat was the only land.

They sat hunched together, wearing shiny drawstring hooded overgarments of thin reflective foil. The foil glittered painfully in the pitiless tropic glare.

Laura pulled her hood off. She flicked at greasy strands of hair. Her hair had grown longer. Since entering the sub she had never truly managed to get it clean.

"Put your hood up," warned sailor #1.

Laura shook her head dizzily. "I want to feel the open sky."

"It's not good for you," said #1, adjusting his sleeves. "With that ozone layer gone, you're asking for skin cancer in sunlight like this."

Laura was cautious. "They say that ozone problem was mostly scare talk."

"Oh, sure," sneered #1. "If you take your government's word for it." The other two sailors chuckled darkly, brief laughter evaporating into utter oceanic stillness.

"Where are we?" Laura said.

Sailor #1 looked over the side of the boat. He dipped his pale fingers into seawater and watched it drip, murmuring. "Coelacanth country . . ."

"What time is it?" Laura said.

"Two hours to end of Yellow shift."

"What *day*, though?"

"I'm gonna be glad to see you go," said sailor #2 suddenly. "You make me itch."

Laura said nothing. A dreadful silence descended again. They were flotsam, chromed tinfoil dummies in their matte-black floating blob. She wondered how deep the ocean was beneath the film of hull.

"You always liked the Red Shift better," said sailor #3 with sudden shocking venom. "You smiled at Red Crewmen over fifteen times. You hardly ever smiled at anyone from Yellow Crew."

"I had no idea," Laura said. "I'm really sorry."

"Oh, yeah. Sure you are. Now."

"Here comes the plane," commented sailor #1.

Laura looked up, shading her eyes. The empty sky was full of little vision blurs, strange little artifacts of sight, trailing along with the movements of her eyeball. She wasn't sure what they were called or what made them, but it had something to do with brightness levels. Then she saw something opening in the sky, something shredding and popping and, finally, unfolding stiffly like an origami swan. Huge parafoil wings of bright life-jacket orange. It was gliding in.

Sailor #2 examined his military phone, checking for the homing signal. Sailor #3 attached a long flabby bag to a tank of hydrogen and began inflating it with a loud flatulent hissing.

Then another cargo drop, and another. Sailor #2 whooped happily. Cargo dumpsters crossed the empty sky, bus-sized brown lozenges with broad, unfolding wings of riffling dayglo-orange plastic. They reminded Laura of June bugs, fat-bellied flying beetles from Texas summer nights. They came down in broad, wheeling descent.

Their curved hulls splashed and settled with surprising, ponderous grace. Curling bow waves. Wings refolding with loud pops and creaks.

Now she could see the plane that had dumped them, a broad-winged ceramic air-bus, sky-blue beneath, its upper surfaces cut with dun-and-yellow desert camouflage. Sailor #1 switched on the inflatable's engine, and the boat mumbled its way toward the nearest cargo drop. The drop was bigger than the boat, a bulging floating cylinder, its bow and sides studded with sturdy tow rings.

Sailors #2 and #3 were fighting with the weather balloon. They let it go, and it rushed suddenly upward, uncoiling length after length of thin cable with a savage hiss.

"Okay," said #1. He hooked the end of the cable to a series of clips on the back of Laura's life jacket. "You want to hold your knees up and in, with your arms," he told her. "Also keep your head well down and your jaw clenched. You don't want your neck to whiplash, see, or your teeth to clack. When you feel the aircraft snag this cable, you're gonna go up in a real hurry. So just uncoil, let your legs go. Like a parachute drop."

"I didn't know it would be like this!" Laura said anxiously. "Parachuting! I don't know how to do that!"

"Yeah," said #2 impatiently, "but you've *seen it,* on *television.*"

"A skyhook is just the same as a para-drop, only in reverse," said sailor #1 helpfully. He steered them to the bow of the first cargo bulk. "What do you suppose this one is?"

"New missile consignment," said #2.

"No, man, it's the new chow. Refrigerator drop."

"No way. That one's the fridge, over there." He turned to Laura. "Didn't you hear a word I said? Grab your legs!"

"I—" It hit her like a car wreck. A sudden terrific jerk, as if the skyhook wanted to yank the bones from her flesh. She soared upward as if fired by a cannon, arms and knee joints wrenched and burning.

Her vision went black, the blood of acceleration draining to her feet. She was helpless, close to fainting, wind tearing furiously at her clothes. She began to twist, blue world flopping and spinning around her like an unlimited carousel. Suspended in space, she felt a sudden roaring sense of mystic ecstasy. Sublime terror, helpless awe: Sinbad yanked up by the roc of Madagascar. East of Africa. Below her, blue bed sheet of turning sea: toy boats, toy minds . . .

A shadow fell across her. Mighty buzz of propellers, the whine of a whirling pulley. Then she was up and inside it, in the belly of the plane. Underlit splash of daylight: stenciled boxes, crates, a spiderwebbing of steel bracing cord. An interior crane arm plucked at her cable, swung her neatly across from the cargo bay, and plunked her onto the deck. She lay there bruised and gasping.

Then the bay doors banged shut and pitch darkness fell.

She felt speed hit the plane. Now that it had her, it was climbing, putting its nose up and pouring energy into continental flight.

She was in a flying black cavern smelling of plastic and oiled tarpaulin and the sharp primal aroma of African dust. It was dark as the inside of a thermos.

She yelled. "Lights, come on!" Nothing. She heard her words echo.

She was alone. This plane had no crew. It was a giant drone, a robot.

She managed to fumble blindly out of the life jacket. She tried variants of the lighting command. She asked for general systems help, in English and Japanese. Nothing. She was cargo—no one listened to cargo.

It began to grow cold. And the air grew thin.

She was freezing. After days in the unchanging air of the sub the cold bit her like electricity. She huddled in her tinfoil survival gear. She pulled the drawstring sleeves and trouser cuffs over her hands and feet. She put her foiled hands before her face: too dark to see them, even an inch away. She covered her face with her hands and breathed into them. Icy puffs of thin Himalayan air. She curled into a ball, shivering.

Isolation and blackness and the distant trembling hum of motors.

Landing woke her. The butterfly touchdown of cybernetic precision. Then, half an hour of timeless anxiety as heat crept into the cabin and dread crept into her. Had they forgotten about her? Was she misplaced now? A computer screwup in some F.A.C.T. datafile? An annoying detail that would be shot and buried . . .

Creak of bay doors. White-hot light poured in. A rush, a stink of dust and fuel.

The rumble and squeak of boarding stairs. Clomp of booted

feet. A man looked in, a sunburned blond European in a khaki uniform. His shirt was blackened with sweat down both sides. He spotted her where she crouched beside a tarpaulined mass of cargo.

"Come on," he told her. He waved at her with one arm. There was a little snout of metal in his clenched fist, part of a flexible snaky thing strapped to his forearm. It had a barrel. It was a submachine gun.

"Come on," he repeated.

Laura stood up. "Who are you? Where is this?"

"No questions." He shook his head, bored. "Now."

He marched her down into superheated, desiccating air. She was in a desert airport. Dust-heavy, heat-shimmered runways, low whitewashed blockhouse with a faded wind sock, a tricolor flag hanging limply: red, gold, and green. Huge white aircraft hangar in the distance, pale and barnlike, a distant angry whine of jets.

There was a van waiting, a paddy wagon, painted white like a bakery truck. Thick lugged tires, wire-reinforced windows, heavy iron bumpers.

Two black policemen opened the back of the van. They wore khaki shorts, ribbed knee-high socks, dark glasses, billy clubs, holstered pistols with rows of lead-tipped bullets. The two cops were sweating and expressionless, faces blank, radiating careless menace, calloused hands on their clubs.

She climbed into the van. Doors slammed and locked. She was alone and afraid. The rooftop metal was too hot to touch and the rubber-covered floor stank of blood and fear-sweat and a nauseating reek of dried urine.

People had died in here. Laura knew it suddenly, she could feel the presence of their dying like a weight on her heart. Death, beaten and bleeding, here on these filthy rubber mats.

The engine started and the wagon lurched into movement, and she fell.

After a while, she mustered courage and looked out the wire-netted window.

Flaming heat, flashbulb glare of sun, and dust. Round adobe huts—not even real adobe, just dried red mud—with ramshackle verandahs of plastic and tin. Filthy stretched rags throwing patches of shade. Trickles of smoke. The little domed huts were crowded thick as acne, an almighty slum stretching up slopes, down slopes, through gullies and trash heaps, as far as she could see. In the remote distance, a row of smokestacks gushed raw filth into the cloudless sky. A smelter? A refinery?

She could see people. None of them moved: they crouched stunned, torpid as lizards, in the shade of doorways and tent flaps. She could sense enormous invisible crowds of them, waiting in hot shadows for evening, for whatever passed for coolness in this godforsaken place. There were patches of raw night soil in certain crooked alleys, hard yellow sunbaked human shit, with vast explosive hordes of African flies. The flies were fierce and filthy and as big as beetles.

No paving. No ditches, no plumbing, no power. She saw a few klaxon speakers mounted on poles in the midst of the thickest slums. One rose over a fetid coffeehouse, a cobbled superhovel of plastic and crating. There were men in front of it, dozens of them, squatting on their haunches in the shade and drinking from ancient glass pop bottles and playing pebble games in the pitted dirt. Over their heads, the klaxon emitted a steady squawking rant in a language she couldn't recognize.

The men looked up as the van went past, guardedly, motionless. Their clothes were caked with filth. And they were *American* clothes: ragged souvenir T-shirts and checkered polyester pants and thick-heeled vinyl dance shoes decades out of fashion and laced with bits of wire. They wore long turbans of bright quilted rag.

The van drove on, crunching through potholes, kicking up a miasma of dust. Her bladder was bursting. She relieved herself in a corner of the truck, the one that smelled worst.

The slums failed to end. They became, if anything, thicker and more ominous. She entered an area where the men were scarred and openly carried long knives on their belts, and had shaved heads and tattoos. A group of women in greasy burlap were wailing, without much enthusiasm, over a dead boy stretched out in the doorway of his hovel.

She spotted familiar bits and pieces of the outside world, her world, which had lost a grip on reality and swirled here into hell. Burlap bags, with fading blue stencil: hands in a friendly clasp and the legend in French and English: 100% TRITICALE FLOUR, A GIFT TO THE PEOPLE OF MALI FROM THE PEOPLE OF CANADA. A teenage boy wearing a Euro–Disney World T-shirt, with the slogan "Visit the Future!" Oil barrels, blackened with trash soot over curlicued Arabic. Pieces of a Korean pickup, plastic truck doors and windows painstakingly cemented into a wall of red mud.

Then a foul, smoke-stained lodge or church, its long, rambling walls carefully outlined in a terrifying iconography of grinning, horn-headed saints. Its sloped mud roof glittered with the round, stained-glass disks of broken bottles.

The van drove for hours. She was in the middle of a major city, a metropolis. There were hundreds of thousands living here. The entire country, Mali, a huge place, bigger than Texas—this was all that was left of it, this endless rat warren. All other choices had been stolen by the African disaster. The drought survivors crowded into gigantic urban camps, like this one. She was in Bamako, capital of Mali.

The capital of the F.A.C.T. They were the *secret police* here, the people who ran the place. They were running a nation ruined beyond hope, a series of monstrous camps.

In a sudden repellent flash of insight Laura understood how FACT had casually carried out massacres. There was a sump of misery in this camp city big enough to choke the world. She had always known it was bad in Africa, but she'd never known that life here meant so utterly little. She realized with a rush of fatalistic terror that her own life was simply too small to matter anymore. She was in hell now and they did things differently here.

At last they rolled past a barbed-wire fence, into a cleared area, dust and tarmac and skeletal watchtowers. Ahead—Laura's heart leapt—the familiar, friendly look of brown walls of concretized sand. They were approaching a fat domed building, much like her own Rizome Lodge in Galveston. It was much bigger, though. Efficiently built. Progressive and modern, the same techniques David had chosen.

Thinking of David was something so amazingly painful that she shut it off at once.

Then they rolled into the building, through its double walls of solid sand four feet thick, under cruel portcullises of welded iron.

The van stopped. A wait.

The European flung open the doors. "Out."

She stepped out into dazzling heat. She was in a bare arena, round baked-earth exercise yard surrounded by a two-story ring of brown fortress walls. The European led her to an iron hatchway, an armored door leading into the prison. Two guards loomed behind her. They went inside, into a hall lit by cheap sunlight pipes bracketed to the ceiling. "Showers," the European said.

The word had an evil ring. Laura stopped in place. "I don't want to go to the showers."

"There's a toilet, too," the European offered.

She shook her head. The European looked over her shoulder and nodded fractionally.

A club hit her from behind, at the juncture of her neck and shoulder. It was as if she'd been struck by lightning. Her entire right side went numb and she fell to her knees.

Then the shock faded and pain began to seep in. True pain, not the pastel thing she'd called "pain" in the past, but a sensation truly profound, biological. She couldn't believe that that was all, that she'd simply been hit with a stick. She could already feel it, changing her life.

"Get up," he said, in the same tired voice. She got up. They took her to the showers.

There was a prison matron there. They stripped her, and the woman did a body-cavity search, the men examining Laura's nakedness with distant professional interest. She was pushed into the shower and handed a cake of raw lye that stank of insecticide. The water was hard and briny and wouldn't lather. It shut off before she had rinsed.

She got out. Her clothes and shoes had been stolen. The prison matron jabbed her in the buttock with five cc's of yellow fluid. She felt it sink in and sting.

The European and his two goons left, and two female goons showed up. Laura was given trousers and shirt of striped black-and-white canvas, creased and rough. She put them on, trembling. Either the injection was beginning to take effect or else she was scaring herself into the belief that it was. She felt lightheaded and sick and not far from genuine craziness.

She kept thinking that there was going to come a time when she could take a stand and demand that they kill her with her dignity intact. But they didn't seem anxious to kill her, and she didn't feel anxious to die, and she was beginning to realize that a human being could be beaten into almost anything. She didn't want to be hit again, not till she had a better grip on herself.

The matron said something in Creole French and indicated the toilet. Laura shook her head. The matron looked at her as if she were an idiot, and shrugged, and made a note on her clipboard.

Then two female goons cuffed her hands behind her back. One of them pulled a billy club, wrapped it cleverly through the metal chain of the old-fashioned handcuffs, and levered Laura's arms up in their sockets until she was forced to double over. They then marched her out, steering her like a grocery cart, down the hall, and up narrow stairs barred at top and bottom. Then, on the upper floor, past a long series of iron doors equipped with sliding peepholes.

They stopped at cell #31, then waited there until a turnkey showed up. It took about five minutes, and they passed the time chewing gum and wisecracking about Laura in some Malian dialect.

The turnkey finally flung the door open and they threw her in. The door slammed. "Hey!" Laura shouted. "I'm handcuffed! You forgot your handcuffs!" The peephole opened and she saw a human eye and part of the bridge of a nose. It shut again.

She was in a cell. In a prison. In a fascist state. In Africa.

She began to wonder if there were worse places in the world. Could anything be worse? Yes, she thought, she could be sick.

She began to feel feverish.

An hour is:

A minute and a minute and a minute and a minute and a minute.

And a minute, and a minute, and a minute and a minute
and a minute.

Then another, and another minute, and another, and yet
another, and another.

And a minute, then two more minutes. Then, two more
minutes.

Then, two minutes. Then, two minutes. Then a minute.

Then a similar minute. Then two more. And two more
again.

That's thirty minutes so far.

So do them all over again.

Laura's cell was slightly less than four paces long and
slightly more than three paces across. It was about the size of
the bathroom in the place-where-she'd-used-to-live, the place
she didn't allow herself to think about. Much of this space
was taken up by her bunk. It had four legs of tubular steel,
and a support frame of flattened iron struts. Atop the frame
was a mattress of striped cotton ticking, stuffed with straw.
The mattress smelled, faintly and not completely unpleas-
antly, of a stranger's long sickness. One end was lightly
spattered with faded bloodstains.

There was a window hole in the wall of the cell. It was a
good-sized hole, almost six inches around, the size of a
drainpipe. It was approximately four feet long, bored through
the massive concretized sand, and it had a crisscrossed grill of
thin metal at the far end. By standing directly before the hole
Laura could see a simmering patch of yellowish desert sky.
Faint gusts of heated air sometimes rippled down the tube.

The cell had no plumbing. But she learned the routine
quickly, from hearing other prisoners. You banged the door
and yelled, in Malian Creole French, if you knew it. After a
certain period, depending on whim, one of the guards would
show and take you to the latrine: a cell much like the others,
but with a hole in the floor.

She heard the screaming for the first time on her sixth day.
It seemed to be oozing up from the thick floor beneath her
feet. She had never heard such inhuman screaming, not even
during the riot in Singapore. There was a primal quality to it

that could pass through solid barriers: concrete, metal, bone, the human skull. Compared to this howling the screams of mob panic were only a kind of gaiety.

She could not make out any words, but she could hear that there were pauses, and occasionally she thought she could hear a low electrical buzzing.

They would unlock her handcuffs for meals and for the latrine. They would then seal them up again, tightly, carefully, high on her wrists, so she couldn't wriggle through the circle of her own arms and get her hands in front of her. As if it mattered, as if she might break free with a single bound and tear her steel door from its hinges with her fingernails.

After a week her shoulders were in a constant state of low-level pain, and she had worn raw patches on her chin and cheek from sleeping on her stomach. She did not complain, however. She had briefly spotted one of her fellow prisoners, an Asian man, Japanese she thought. He was handcuffed, his legs were fettered, and he wore a blindfold.

During the second week, they began handcuffing her hands from the front. This made an amazing difference. She felt with giddy irrationality that she had truly accomplished something, that some kind of minor but definite message had been sent her from the prison administration.

Surely, she thought, as she lay waiting for sleep, her mind gently and luxuriously disintegrating, some mark had been made, maybe only a check on a clipboard, but some kind of institutional formality had taken place. She existed.

In the morning she convinced herself that it could not possibly mean anything. She began doing pushups.

She kept track of days by scratching the grainy wall under her bunk with the edge of her handcuffs. On her twenty-first day she was taken out, given another shower and another body search, and taken to meet the Inspector of Prisons.

The Inspector of Prisons was a large smiling sunburned white American. He wore a long silk djellaba, blue suit pants, and elaborate leather sandals. He met her in an air-conditioned office downstairs, with metal chairs and a large steel desk topped with lacquered plywood. There were gold-framed portraits on the walls, men in uniform: GALTIERI, NORTH, MACARTHUR.

A goon sat Laura down in a metal folding chair in front of the desk. After sweltering days in her cell, the air conditioning felt arctic, and she shivered.

The goon unlatched her handcuffs. The skin below them was calloused, the left wrist had an oozing scab.

"Good afternoon, Mrs. Webster," said the Inspector.

"Hello," Laura said. Her voice was rusty.

"Have some coffee. It's very good. Kenyan." The Inspector slid a cup and saucer across the desk. "They had good rains this year."

Laura nodded dumbly. She picked up the coffee and sipped it. She had been eating prison fare for weeks: scop, with the occasional bowl of porridge. And drinking the harsh metallic water, two liters every day, salted, to prevent heatstroke. The hot coffee hit her mouth with an astonishing gush of richness, like Belgian chocolate. Her head swam.

"I'm the Inspector of Prisons," said the Inspector of Prisons. "On my usual tour of duty here, you see."

"What is this place?"

The Inspector smiled. "This is the Moussa Traore Penal Reform Institute, in Bamako."

"What day is this?"

"It's . . ." He checked his watchphone. "December 6, 2023. Wednesday."

"Do my people know I'm still alive?"

"I see you're getting right to the crux of matters," said the Inspector languidly. "As a matter of fact, Mrs. Webster, no. They don't know. You see, you represent a serious breach of security. It's causing us a bit of a headache."

"A bit of a headache."

"Yes. . . . You see, thanks to the peculiar circumstances in which we saved your life, you've learned that we possess the Bomb."

"What? I don't understand."

He frowned slightly. "The *Bomb,* the atomic bomb."

"That's it?" Laura said. "You're keeping me here because of an atomic bomb?"

The frown deepened. "What's the point of this? You've been on the *Thermopylae*. Our ship."

"You mean the *boat*, the submarine?"

He stared at her. "Should I speak more clearly?"

"I'm a little confused," Laura said giddily. "I just spent three weeks in solitary." She put her cup onto the desk, carefully, hand shaking.

She paused, trying to sort her thoughts. "I don't believe you," she told him at last. "I saw a submarine, but I don't know that it's a genuine nuclear missile submarine. I have only your word for that, and the word of the crew onboard. The more I think about it the harder it is to believe. None of the old nuclear governments were stupid enough to lose an entire submarine. Especially with nuclear missiles onboard."

"You certainly have a touching faith in governments," said the Inspector. "If we have the launch platform, it scarcely matters where or how we got the warheads, does it? The point is that the Vienna Convention *does* believe in our deterrent, and our arrangement with them requires that we keep our deterrent secret. But you know the secret, you see."

"I don't believe that the Vienna Convention would make a deal with nuclear terrorists."

"Possibly not," said the Inspector, "but we are *counter*-terrorists. Vienna knows very well that we are doing their own work for them. But imagine the unhappy reaction if the news spread that our Republic of Mali had become a nuclear superpower."

"What reaction," Laura said dully.

"Well," he said, "the great unwashed, the global mob, would panic. Someone would do something rash and we would be forced to use our deterrent, unnecessarily."

"You mean explode an atomic bomb somewhere."

"We'd have no choice. Though it's not a course we would relish."

"Okay, suppose I believe you," Laura said. The coffee was hitting her now, nerving her up like fine champagne. "How can you sit there and tell me that you would explode an atomic bomb? Can't you see that that's all out of proportion to whatever you want to accomplish?"

The Inspector shook his head slowly. "Do you know how

many people have died in Africa in the last twenty years? Something over eighty millions. It staggers the mind, doesn't it: eighty millions. And the hell of it is that even *that* has barely got a handle on it: the situation is getting *worse*. Africa is sick, she needs major surgery. The side shows we've run in Singapore and Grenada are like *public relations events* compared to what's necessary here. But without a deterrent, we won't be left alone to accomplish what's necessary."

"You mean genocide."

He shook his head ruefully, as if he'd heard it all before and expected better from her. "We want to save the African from himself. We can give these people the order they need to survive. What does Vienna offer? Nothing. Because Africa's regimes are sovereign national governments, most of them Vienna signatories! Sometimes Vienna dabbles in subverting a particularly loathsome regime—but Vienna gives no permanent solution. The outside world has written Africa off."

"We still send aid, don't we?"

"That only adds to the misery. It props up corruption."

Laura rubbed her sweating forehead. "I don't understand."

"It's simple. We must succeed where Vienna has failed. Vienna did nothing about the terrorist data havens, nothing about Africa. Vienna is weak and divided. There's a new global order coming, and it's not based in obsolete national governments. It's based in modern groups like your Rizome and my Free Army."

"No one voted for you," Laura said. "You have no authority. You're vigilantes!"

"You're a vigilante yourself," the Inspector of Prisons said calmly. "A vigilante diplomat. Interfering with governments for the sake of your multinational. We have everything in common, you see."

"No!"

"We couldn't *exist* if it weren't for people like you, Mrs. Webster. You financed us. You created us. We serve your needs." He drew a breath and smiled. "We are your sword and shield."

Laura sank back into the chair. "If we're on the same side, then why am I in your jail?"

He leaned forward, steepling his fingers. "I *did* tell you, Mrs. Webster—it's for reasons of atomic security! On the other hand, we see no reason why you shouldn't contact your coworkers and loved ones. Let them know you're alive and safe and well. It would mean a great deal to them, I'm sure. You could make a statement."

Laura spoke numbly. She'd known something like this was coming. "What kind of statement?"

"A prepared statement, of course. We can't have you babbling our atom secrets over a live phone link to Atlanta. But you could make a videotape. Which we would release for you."

Her stomach roiled. "I'd have to see the statement first. And read it. And think about it."

"You do that. Think about it." He touched his watchphone, spoke in French. "You'll let us know your decision."

Another goon arrived. He took her to a different cell. They left the handcuffs off.

Laura's new cell was the same length as the first, but it had two bunks and was a stride and a half wider. She was no longer forced to wear handcuffs. She was given her own chamber pot and a larger jug of water. There was more scop, and the porridge was of better quality and sometimes had soybean bacon bits.

They gave her a deck of cards, and a paperback Bible that had been distributed by the Jehovah's Witness Mission of Bamako in 1992. She asked for a pencil to make notes on her statement. She was given a child's typer with a little flip-up display screen. It typed very nicely but had no printout and couldn't be used to scribble secret messages.

The screaming was louder under her new cell. Several different voices and, she thought, different languages too. The screaming would go on, raggedly, for about an hour. Then there would be a coffee break for the torturers. Then they would set back to work. She believed that there were several different torturers. Their habits differed. One of them liked to play moody French café ballads during his break.

One night she was woken by a muffled volley of machine-gun fire. It was followed by five sharp coup-de-grâce shots.

They had killed people, but not the people being tortured—two of them were back next night.

It took them two weeks to bring her statement. It was worse than she had imagined. They wanted her to tell Rizome and the world that she had been kidnapped in Singapore by the Grenadians and was being held in the underground tunnel complex at Fedon's Camp. It was a ridiculous draft; she didn't think that the person who had written it fully understood English. Parts of it reminded her of the FACT communiqué issued after the assassination of Winston Stubbs.

She no longer doubted that FACT had killed Stubbs and shot up her house. It was obvious. The remote-control killing smelled of them. It couldn't have been Singapore, poor brilliant, struggling Singapore. Singapore's military, soldiers like Hotchkiss, would have killed Stubbs face-to-face and never bragged about it afterward.

They must have launched the drone from a surface ship somewhere. It couldn't have come from their nuclear submarine—unless they had more than one, a horrible thought. The sub couldn't have traveled fast enough to attack Galveston, Grenada, and Singapore during the time of her adventure. (She was already thinking of it as her adventure—something over, something in her past, something pre-captivity.) But America was an open country and a lot of the F.A.C.T. were Americans. They bragged openly that they could go anywhere, and she believed them.

She believed now they had someone—a plant, a spy, one of their Henderson/Hesseltines—in Rizome itself. It would be so easy for them, not like Singapore. All he would have to do was show up and work hard and smile.

She refused to read the prepared statement. The Inspector of Prisons looked at her with distaste. "You really think this defiance is accomplishing something, don't you?"

"This statement is disinformation. It's black propaganda, a provocation, meant to get people killed. I won't help you kill people."

"Too bad. I'd hoped you could send your loved ones a New Year's greeting."

"I've written my own statement," Laura offered. "It doesn't

say anything about you, or Mali, or the F.A.C.T., or your bombs. It just says I'm alive and it has a few words my husband will recognize so that he'll know it's really me."

The Inspector laughed. "What kind of fools do you take us for, Mrs. Webster? You think we'd let you spout secret messages, something you'd cooked up in your cell after weeks of your . . . oh . . . feminine ingenuity?"

He tossed the statement into a bottom drawer of his desk. "Look, I didn't write the thing. I didn't make the decision. Personally, I don't think it's all that great a statement. Knowing Vienna, it's more likely to make them tiptoe their way into that termite castle under Fedon's Camp, instead of shelling it into oblivion, like they should have done way back in '19." He shrugged. "But if you want to ruin your life, be declared legally dead, be forgotten, then go right ahead."

"I'm your prisoner! Don't pretend it's my decision."

"Don't be silly. If it meant anything serious, I could make you do it."

Laura was silent.

"You think you're strong, don't you?" The Inspector shook his head. "You think that, if we tortured you, it would be some kind of romantic moral validation. Torture's not romantic, Mrs. Webster. It's a thing, a process: torture is torture, that's all. It doesn't make you any nobler. It only breaks you. Like the way an engine wears out if you drive it too fast, too hard, too long. You never really heal, you never really get over it. Any more than you get over growing old."

"I don't want to be hurt. Don't pretend I do."

"Are you going to read the stupid thing? It's not that important. *You're* not that important."

"You killed a man in my house," Laura said. "You killed people around me. You kill people in this prison every day. I know I'm no better than them. I don't believe you'll ever let me go, if you can help it. So why don't you *kill me too?*"

He shook his head and sighed. "*Of course* we'll let you go. We have no reason to keep you here, once your security threat is over. We won't stay covert forever. Someday, very soon, we'll simply rule. Someday Laura Webster will be an upstanding citizen in a grand new global society."

A long moment passed. His lie had slid past her comprehension, like something at the other end of a telescope. At last she spoke, very quietly. "If it matters at all, then listen to me. I'm going to go insane, alone in that cell. I'd rather be dead than insane."

"So now it's suicide?" He was avuncular, soothing, skeptical. "Of course you've been *thinking* of suicide. Everyone does. Very few ever really do it. Even men and women doing hard labor in death camps find reason to go on living. They never bite their own tongues out, or open their veins with their fingernails, or run headlong into the wall, or any of those childish jailbirds' fantasies." His voice rose. "Mrs. Webster, you're in the *upper level* here. You're in *special custody*. Believe me, this city's slums are full of men and women, and even *children*, who'd cheerfully *kill* to have it as easy as you do."

"Then why don't you let them kill me?"

His eyes clouded. "I really wish you wouldn't be like this."

He sighed and spoke into his watchphone. After a while the goons came and took her away.

She went on hunger strike. They let her do it for three days. Then they sent her a cellmate.

Her new cellmate was a black woman who spoke no English. She was short and had a broad, cheerful face and two missing front teeth. Her name was something like Hofuette, or Jofuette. Jofuette would only smile and shrug at Laura's English: she had no gift for languages and couldn't remember a foreign word two days running. She was illiterate.

Laura had poor luck with Jofuette's language. It was called something like Bambara. It was full of aspirations and clicks and odd tonalities. She learned the words for *bed* and *eat* and *sleep* and *cards*. She taught Jofuette how to play Hearts. It took days but they had a lot of time.

Jofuette came from downstairs, the lower level, where the screaming came from. She hadn't been tortured; or, at least, no marks showed. Jofuette had seen people shot, however. They shot them out in the exercise yard, with machine guns. They would often shoot a single man with five or six machine guns; their ammunition was old, with a lot of duds that tended to choke up the guns. They had a worldful of ammunition, though. All the ammunition of fifty years of the Cold War had ended up here in African war zones. Along with the rest of the junk.

She didn't see the Inspector of Prisons again. He wasn't the guy who ran the place. Jofuette knew the warden. She could imitate the way he walked; it was quite funny.

Laura was pretty sure that Jofuette was some kind of trusty, maybe even a stool pigeon. It didn't bother her much. Jofuette didn't speak English and Laura had no secrets anyway. But Jofuette, unlike Laura, was allowed to go out into the exercise yard and mingle with the prisoners. She could get hold of little things: harsh, nasty cigarettes, a box of sugared vitamin pills, a needle and thread. She was good to have around, wonderful, better than anyone.

Laura learned about prison. The tricks of doing time. Memory was the enemy. Any connection with the outside world would be, she knew, too painful to survive. She just did her time. She invented antimemory devices, passivity devices. When it was time for a cry she would have a cry. She didn't think about what might happen to her, to David and the baby, to Galveston, to Rizome, to the world. She thought about professional activities, mostly. Writing public relations statements. Testifying to public bodies about Malian terrorism. Writing campaign documents for imaginary Rizome Committee candidates.

She spent several weeks writing a long imaginary sales brochure called *Loretta's Hands and Feet*. She memorized it and would spin it off sentence by sentence, silently, inside her head, slowly, one second per word, until she reached the end. Then she would add on a new sentence, and then start over.

The imaginary brochure was not about the baby herself, that would have been too painful. It was simply about the baby's hands and feet. She described the shape and texture of the hands and feet, their smell, their grasp, their potential usefulness if mass-produced. She designed boxes for the hands and feet, and old-fashioned marketing slogans, and ad jingles.

She organized a mental dress store. She had never been

much of a fashion maven, at least not since junior high school days, and her discovery of boys. But this was a top-of-the-line fashion outlet, a trend-setting emporium catering to the wealthy Atlanta crowd. There were galaxies of hats, marching armies of hosiery and shoes, whirlwinds of billowing skirts, vast technicolor brothels of sexy lingerie.

She had decided on ten years. She was going to be in this jail for ten years. It was long enough to destroy hope, and hope was identical with anguish.

A month, and a month, and a month, and a month.
And another month, and another and another and another.
And then three, and then one more.

A year.

She had been in prison for a year. A year was not a particularly long time. She was thirty-three years old. She had spent far more time outside captivity than in, thirty-two times as much. People had done far more time in prison than this. Gandhi had spent years in prison.

They were treating her better now. Jofuette had made some kind of arrangement with one of the female goons. When the goon was on duty she let Laura run in the exercise yard, at night, when no other prisoners were present.

Once a week they brought an ancient video recorder into the cell. It had a black-and-white TV manufactured in Algeria. There were tapes, too. Most of them were old-fashioned American football games. The old full-contact version of football had been banned for years now. The game was spectacularly brutal: huge lumbering gladiators in helmets and armor. Every fourth play seemed to leave one of them sprawling and wounded. Sometimes Laura would simply close her eyes and listen to the wonderful flow of English. Jofuette liked the games.

Then there were movies. *The Sands of Iwo Jima. The Green Berets.* Fantastic, hallucinatory violence. Enemies would be shot and fall down neatly, like paper cutouts. Sometimes the good guys were shot, in the shoulder or arm usually. They would just grimace a bit, maybe bind it up.

One week a film arrived called *The Road to Morocco*. It was set in the African desert and had Bing Cosby and Bob Hope. Laura had vague memories of Bob Hope, she thought she must have seen him when she was very young and he was very old. He was young in the film, and quite funny, in a quaint premillennial way. It hurt terribly to watch him, like having a bandage ripped away, touching deep parts of her that she had managed to numb. She had to stop the tape several times to mop at tears. Finally she snatched the tape out and jammed it back in the box.

Jofuette shook her head, said something in Bambara, and plugged the tape back in. As she did so a folded slip of tissue, cigarette paper, fell from a crevice in the box's cardboard side. Laura picked it up.

She unfolded it as Jofuette watched the TV, riveted. It was covered with smudgy, minuscule writing. Not ink. Blood, maybe. A list.

> Abel Lacoste—Euro. Cons. Service
> Steven Lawrence—Oxfam America
> Marianne Meredith—ITN Channel Four
> Valeri Chkalov—Vienna
> Georgi Valdukov—Vienna
> Sergei Ilyushin—Vienna
> Kazuo(?) Watanabe—Mitsubishi
> (?)Riza-Rikabi—EFT Commerzbank
> Laura Webster—Rizome IG
> Katje Selous—A.C.A. Corps
> and four others

10

THE second year went faster than the first. She was used to it. It had become her life. She no longer thirsted for the things she had lost—she could no longer name them to herself, without an effort. She was past thirst: she was mummified. Monastic, sealed.

But she could sense the pace picking up, spiderweb tremors of movement in the distant world outside.

There were shootings almost every night now. When they took her down for exercise in the yard, she could see bullet-pounded patches in the wall, cratered, just like the Lodge had been. Below the pockmarks the baked bare earth had turned foul, carpeted with swarming flies and the coppery reek of blood.

One day the desert sky outside the wall hole of her cell showed endless dark skeins of drifting smoke. Trucks squealed in and out of the prison for hours, and they shot people all night. Assembly style: shouts, orders, screams, pleading, fierce chatter of machine-gun fire. Quick finishing shots. Doors slamming, engines. Then more. Then more. Then more again.

Jofuette had been frightened for days. Finally the goons came for her, two women. They came smiling and talking her language, seeming to tell her that it was over, they were going to let her go. The bigger goon grinned suggestively and put her hands on her hips and did a bump-and-grind. A boyfriend, she was saying—or Jofuette's husband maybe. Or maybe she was suggesting a night on the town in glamorous downtown Bamako.

Jofuette smiled tremulously. One of the goons gave her a cigarette and lit it with a flourish.

Laura never saw her again.

When they brought in the video recorder for the usual weekly session Laura waited till they were gone. Then she picked up the machine with both hands and smashed it into the wall repeatedly. It came apart, a tangle of wiring and circuit cards. She was crushing them underfoot when the door rattled and two of the male goons burst in.

They had drawn clubs. She threw herself at them with her fists clenched.

They knocked her to the ground immediately, with contemptuous ease.

Then they picked her up and began beating her. With thoroughness, methodically. They hit her on the neck, on the kidneys. They threw her onto the bunk and hit her across the spine. Lightning flared inside her, great electrocuting swathes, white-hot, bloody-red. They were hitting her with axes, chopping her body apart. She was being butchered with sticks.

Roaring filled her head. The world faded.

A woman sat across the cell, sitting in Jofuette's bunk. A blond woman in a blue dress. How old—forty, fifty? Sad, composed face, laugh lines, yellow-green eyes. Coyote eyes.

Mother . . . ?

The woman looked at her: remembrance, pity, strength. It was restful to look at the woman. Restful as dreaming: *she's wearing my favorite shade of blue*.

But who is it . . .?

Laura recognized her self. *Of course*. Rush of relief and joy. *That's who it is. It's me.*

Her Persona rose from the bunk. She crossed the cell, drifting, graceful, soundless. Radiant. She knelt silently by Laura's side and looked into her face: her own face. Older, stronger, wiser.

Here I am.

"I'm dying."

No, you'll live. You'll be as I am.

The hand stopped an inch from her face, caressed the air. She could feel its warmth—she could see herelf, face-down on the bunk, beaten, paralyzed. Sad Laura. She could feel the warm torrent of healing and sympathy rush in from outside, Olympian, soaring. Poor beaten body, our Laura, but she won't die. She lives. I lived.

Now, sleep.

She was sick for a month. Her urine was tinged with blood: kidney damage. And she had huge aching patches of bruises on her back, her arms, her legs. Deep bruises, into the muscle, bumps swollen on the bone: hematomas, they were called in first-aid. She was sick and creaky, barely able to eat. Sleep was a struggle for position, for the least amount of pain.

They had taken away the wreckage of the video machine. She was pretty sure that someone had shot her up with something, too: there seemed to be an injection bruise just above her wrist, one of the few spots the goons had missed. A woman, she thought: she had seen a woman medic, maybe even spoken to her semiconscious, and that was it: an Optimal Persona experience.

She had been beaten up by fascist goons. And she had seen her Optimal Persona. She wasn't sure which was the most important but she knew that they were both turning points.

It was probably a medic that she'd seen. She'd just slotted it in, dreamed of seeing herself. That was probably all that an Optimal Persona ever was, for anybody: stress and illusion and some deep psychic need. But none of that mattered.

She had had a vision. It didn't matter where it came from. She clung to it and she was glad they were leaving her in solitary because she could chuckle over it aloud and hug it to herself. And cherish it.

Hatred. She'd never really hated them before, not like she did now. She'd always been too small and too scared and too hopeful of figuring some angle, as if they were people like herself and could be dealt with like people. That's what they'd pretended, but now she knew their pretense was another of their lies. She would never, ever join them, or belong to them, or see the world through their eyes. She was their enemy till death. That was a peaceful thought.

She knew she would survive. Someday she would dance on

their graves. It made no sense, not rationally. It was faith. They had blundered and given her faith.

She was woken by a roar. It sounded like a giant water faucet, rush of water and the high-pitched scream of a vibrating pipe. Coming nearer. Louder. *Wa-woosh.*

Then: monster drumbeats. Boom. Boom. Boom-wham-bam, firecracker sounds. Her cell wall flashed as hot light flickered through the window hole. Then another flash. Then a sudden thunderous explosion, very near. Earthquake. The walls shook. Hot red light—the horizon was on fire.

The goons ran up and down the hall, shouting at each other. They were afraid, and Laura heard the fear in their voices with a wild leap of animal joy. Outside, the feeble crackle of small-arms fire. Then, distantly, belatedly, the banshee wail of sirens.

A burst of pounding from inside the prison. Someone on level two was beating on his door, not the bathroom pounding, but sheer ferocious battering. Muffled shouts. The upper-level prisoners were yelling from their cells. She couldn't make out the words. But she knew the tone. Rage and glee.

She swung out her legs and sat up in the bunk. In the distance, belatedly, she heard antiaircraft guns. Crump, whump, crump, spider webs of flak searing the sky.

Someone was bombing Bamako.

"Yeah!" Laura screamed. She jumped from bed and rushed to the door and kicked it for all she was worth.

Next night they came in strafing. That sudden *wa-whoosh* again, treetop-level fighter jets in close formation. She could hear their aircraft cannon cutting loose, a weird convulsive belching, thup-thup-thup-thup, the sound of it dopplering off as the jets peeled away over the city. Then the sound of bombs, or missiles maybe: whump, crump, sky flashbulb-white as explosions hit.

Then the belated antiaircraft. There was more of it this time, better organized. Batteries of cannon, and even the hollow roar of what must be rockets, surface-to-air missiles.

But the jets were already gone. Mali's radar must be down, she concluded smugly. Otherwise they would surely fire at the jets as they were coming in, not too late, after they'd already blasted the living bejeezus out of something or somebody. The attackers had probably knocked out the radar first thing.

She had never heard anything that sounded so sublime. The sky was full of hell, the rage of angels. She didn't even care if they hit the prison. All the better.

Outside the guards were firing machine guns: staccato bursts into the black sky. Bullets would rain down somewhere on a slum. Fools. They were fools. Amateurs.

They came for her in the morning. Two goons. They were sweating, which was nothing new, everyone sweated in the prison, but they were twitchy and wired, their eyes wide, and they stank of fear.

"How's the war going?" Laura said.

"No war," said goon #1, a middle-aged male thug she'd seen many times. He wasn't one of the ones who had hit her. "Practice."

"Air-raid practice? In the middle of the night? In downtown Bamako?"

"Yes. Our army. Practice. Do not worry."

"You think I believe that bullshit?"

"No talking!" They clamped her into handcuffs, hard. They hurt. She laughed at them, inside.

They marched her downstairs, and into the courtyard. Then they prodded her into the back of a truck. Not a secret-police paddy wagon but a canvas-topped military truck daubed in dun-and-yellow desert camouflage. It had wooden benches inside for troops, and jerry cans of water and gasohol.

They shackled her legs to one of the support bars beneath the wooden bench. She sat there exulting. She didn't know where she was going, but it was going to be different now.

She sat sweating in the heat for ten minutes. Then they brought in another woman. White, blond. They shackled her to the opposite bench, and jumped out, and slammed the tailgate.

The engine started up with a roar. They jolted into movement. Laura examined the stranger. She was blond and thin and bony and wearing striped canvas prison garb. She looked about thirty. She looked very familiar. Laura realized that she and the stranger looked enough alike to be sisters. They looked at each other and grinned shyly.

The truck cleared the gates.

"Laura Webster!" Laura said.

"Katje Selous." The stranger leaned forward, extending both cuffed hands. They grabbed at each other's wrists and shook hard, clumsily, smiling.

"Katje Selous, A.C.A. Corps!" Laura said triumphantly.

"What?"

"I don't know what it means. . . . But I saw it on a list of prisoners."

"Ah!" Selous said. "Azanian Civil Action Corps. Yes, I'm a doctor. Relief camp."

Laura blinked. "You're from South Africa?"

"We call it Azania now. And you, you're American?"

"Rizome Industries Group."

"Rizome." Selous wiped sweat from her forehead, a jail-bird's pallor. "I can't tell them apart, the multinationals. . . ." She brightened. "Do you make suntan oil? That oil that makes you turn black?"

"Huh? No!" Laura paused, thinking about it. "I dunno. Maybe we do, nowadays. I've been out of touch."

"I think you do make it." Selous looked solemn. "It's very important and wonderful."

"My husband used that stuff," Laura said. "He might have given Rizome the idea. He's very bright, my husband. David's his name." Speaking of David made a whole buried section of her soul rise suddenly from the tomb. Here she was, chained in the back of a truck headed for God knew where, but with a few revivifying words she was part of the world again. The big sane world of husbands and children and work. Tears gushed suddenly down her face. She smiled at Selous and shrugged apologetically and looked at the floor.

"They kept you in solitary, eh," Selous said gently.

"We have a baby, too," Laura babbled. "Her name's Loretta."

"They had you longer than me," Selous said. "It's been almost a year since they took me from camp."

Laura shook her head, hard. "Did, uh . . ." She cleared her throat. "Do you know what's going on?"

Selous nodded. "I know a little. What I heard from the other hostages. The last two nights—those were Azanian air raids. My people. Our commandos, too, maybe. I think they hit some fuel dumps—the sky burned all night!"

"Azanian," Laura said aloud. So that was it. What she'd just lived through. An armed clash between Mali and Azania. It seemed obscure and improbable. Not that an African war was unlikely, they happened all the time. Back pages in newspapers, a few seconds on cable news. But that they were for real, they took place in a real world of dust and heat and flying metal.

The South Africans weren't in the news much. They weren't very fashionable. "Your people must have flown a long way."

"We have aircraft carriers," Selous said proudly. "We never signed your Vienna Convention."

"Oh. Uh-huh." Laura nodded blankly.

Selous looked at her clinically, a doctor hunting for signs of damage. "Were you tortured?"

"What? No." Laura paused. "About three months ago they beat me up. After I wrecked a machine." She felt embarrassed even to have mentioned it. It seemed so inadequate. "Not like those poor people downstairs."

"Mmmm . . . yes, they've suffered." It was a statement of fact. Curiously detached, a judgment by someone who'd seen a lot of it. Selous glanced out the back of the truck. They were in the middle of Bamako now, endless nightmare landscape of foul shacks and huts. Wisps of evil yellowish smoke rose from a distant refinery.

"Were *you* tortured, Dr. Selous?"

"Yes. A little. At first." Selous paused. "Were you assaulted? Raped?"

"No." Laura shook her head. "They never even seemed to think of it. I don't know why. . . ."

Selous leaned back, nodding. "It's their policy. It must be true, I think. That the leader of FACT is a woman."

Laura felt stunned. "A woman."

Selous smiled sourly. "Yes . . . we of the weaker sex do tend to get around these days."

"What kind of woman would . . ."

"Rumor says she's a right-wing American billionaire. Or a British aristocrat. Maybe both, eh—why not?" Selous tried to spread her hands skeptically; her cuffs rattled. "For years FACT was nothing much . . . mercenaries. Then quite suddenly . . . very organized. A new leader, someone smart and determined—with a vision. One of us modern girls." She chuckled lightly.

There didn't seem to be more to say on that topic. It was probably a lie anyway. "Where do you think they're taking us?"

"North, into the desert—I know that much." Selous thought it over. "Why did they keep you locked away from the rest of us? We never saw you. We used to see your maid, that's all."

"My what?"

"Your cellmate, the little Bambara informer from downstairs." Selous shrugged. "Sorry. You know how it is in a cell block. People get crazy. We used to call you the Princess. Rapunzel, eh."

"People get crazy," Laura said. "I thought I saw my Optimal Persona. But it was *you,* wasn't it, doctor. You and I look a lot alike. You came in and treated me after I was beaten, didn't you."

Selous blinked doubtfully. " 'Optimal Persona.' That's very American. . . . Are you from California?"

"Texas."

"It certainly wasn't me, Laura. . . . I've never seen you before in my life."

Long, strange pause.

"You really think we look alike?"

"Sure," Laura said.

"But I'm a Boer, an Afrikaaner. And you have that hybrid American look."

They had reached an impasse. The conversation hung there as heat and dust boiled over the empty end of the truck. She was dealing with an alien. They had missed a connection somehow. Laura felt thirsty already and they were not even out of the city.

She struggled to pick up the thread.

"They kept me in solitary because they said I had atomic secrets."

Selous sat upright, startled. "Have you seen a Bomb?"

"What?"

"There are rumors of a test site in the Malian desert. Where the F.A.C.T. tried to build a Bomb."

"First I've ever heard of that," Laura said. "I saw their submarine, though. They said it had atomic warheads on-board. The sub did have some missiles. I know that much, because they hit and sank a ship I was on."

"Exocets?" Selous said gravely.

"Yes, that's right, exactly."

"But there could have been other missiles with a longer range, eh? Long enough to hit Pretoria?"

"I guess so. But it doesn't prove they were nuclear bombs."

"But if they take us to this test site, and we find a huge crater of sand melted into glass, that would prove something, wouldn't it?"

Laura said nothing.

"It ties in with something the warden told me once," Selous said. "That they didn't really need me as a hostage—that our cities were hostage if we only knew."

"God, why do people talk like that?" Laura said. "Grenada, Singapore . . ." It made her feel very tired.

"You know what I think, Laura? I think they are taking us to their test site. To make a statement, yes? Me, because I am Azanian, and we Azanians are the people they need to impress at the moment. You, because you have witnessed their weapon ship. Their delivery system."

"Could be, I guess." Laura thought it over. "What then? Do they free us?"

Selous's greenish eyes went remote and distant. "I'm a hostage. They will not let Azania attack them without a price."

Laura could not accept it. "That's not much of a price, is it? Killing two helpless prisoners?"

"They'll probably kill us on camera. And send the tape to Azanian Army Intelligence," Selous said.

"But you Azanians would tell everyone, anyway, wouldn't you?"

"We've been telling people about FACT from the beginning," Selous scoffed. "No one would trust us if we said Mali had the bomb. No one believes what we say. They only sneer at us and call us an 'aggressive imperialist state.'"

"Oh," Laura hedged.

"We *are* an empire," Selous said firmly. "President Umtali is a great warrior. All Zulus are great warriors."

Laura nodded. "Yeah, we Americans, uh, we had a black president ourselves."

"Oh, that fellow of yours didn't amount to anything," Selous said. "You Yankees don't even *have* a real government—just capitalist cartels, eh. But President Umtali fought in our civil war. He brought order, where there was savagery. A brilliant general. A true statesman."

"Glad to hear it's working out," Laura said.

"Azanian black people are the finest black people in the world!"

They sat there sweating. Laura could not let it pass. "Look, I'm no big Yankee nationalist, but what about . . . you know . . . jazz, blues, Martin Luther King?"

Selous shifted on her bench. "Martin King. He had a dinner party, compared to our Nelson Mandela."

"Yeah but . . .''

"Your Yankee black people aren't even real black people, are they? They're all Coloureds, actually. They look like Europeans."

"Wait a minute . . ."

"You've never seen *my* black people, but I've certainly seen yours. Your American blacks crowd all our best restaurants and gamble their global hard currency in Sun City and so on. . . . They're rich, and soft."

"Yeah, I come from a tourist town, myself."

"We have a wartime economy, we need the exchange money. . . . Fighting the chaos . . . the endless nightmare that is Africa. . . . We Africans know what it means to sacrifice." She paused. "It seems harsh, eh? I'm sorry. But you outsiders don't understand."

Laura looked out the back of the truck. "That's true."

"It seems to be the duty of my generation to pay for history's mistakes."

"You're really convinced they'll kill us, aren't you?"

She looked remote. "I'm sorry you should be involved."

"They killed a man in my house," Laura said. "That's where it all started for me. I know it doesn't seem like much, one death compared to what's happened in Africa. But I couldn't let it pass. I couldn't shrug off my responsibility for what happened on my own home ground. Believe me, I've had a long time to think about it. And I still think I was right, even if it costs me everything."

Selous smiled.

They had picked up a convoy. Two armored half-tracks had swung into action behind them, jouncing over the rutted road, the long, ridged wands of machine guns swaying in the turrets.

"They think they have an answer," Selous said, looking at the half-tracks. "It was worse in Mali before they came."

"I can't imagine anything worse."

"It's not something you can *imagine*—you have to see it."

"Do *you* have an answer?"

"We hold on and wait for a miracle—save whoever we can. . . . We were getting somewhere in the camp, I think, before the F.A.C.T. seized it. They captured me, but the rest of our Corps escaped. We're used to raids—the desert is full of scorpions."

"Were you stationed in Mali?"

"Niger actually, but that's a formality only. No central authority. It's tribal warlords mostly, in the outback. Fulani Tribal Front, the Sonrai Fraternal Forces, all kinds of bandit armies, thieves, militias. The desert crawls with them. And FACT's machineries, too."

"What do you mean?"

"That's how they prefer to work. By remote control. When they locate the bandits, they attack them with robot planes. They pounce on them in the desert. Like steel hyenas killing rats."

"Jesus."

"They're specialists, technicians. They learned things, in Lebanon, Afghanistan, Namibia. How to fight Third Worlders without letting them touch you. They don't even look at them, except through computer screens."

Laura felt a thrill of recognition. "That's them all right. . . . I saw all that happen in Grenada."

Selous nodded. "The president of Mali thought they did fine work. He made them his palace guard. He's a puppet now. I think they keep him drugged."

"I've seen the guy who runs Grenada—I bet this Mali president doesn't even *exist*. He's probably nothing but an image on a screen and some prerecorded speeches."

"Can they *do* that?" Selous said.

"Grenada can—I saw their prime minister disappear into thin air."

Selous thought it over. Laura could see it working in her face—wondering if Laura was insane, or she herself was insane, or whether the bright television world was brewing something dark and awful in its deepest voodoo corners. "It's as if they're magicians," she said at last. "And we're just people."

"Yeah," Laura said. She lifted two fingers. "But we have solidarity, and they're busy killing each other."

Selous laughed.

"We're going to win, too."

They began talking about the others. Laura had long since memorized the list. Marianne Meredith, the television correspondent, had been the ringleader. It was she who had invented—or already knew, maybe—the best methods of smuggling messages. Lacoste, the French diplomat, was their interpreter—his parents had been African emigrés, and he knew two of Mali's tribal languages.

They had tortured the three agents of Vienna. One of them had turned, the other two had been released or, probably, shot.

Steven Lawrence had been taken from an Oxfam camp. The camps were often raided—they were dumping grounds for scop, the primary source of food for millions of Saharans. The black market for single-cell protein was the major economy of the region—the "government" of Mauritania, for instance, was little more than a scop cartel. Foreign handouts, a few potash mines, and an army—that was Mauritania.

Chad was a malignant welfare bureaucracy, a tiny fraction of aristocrats whose thugs periodically emptied automatic weapons into starving crowds. The Sudan was run by a radical Muslim lunatic who consulted dervishes while factories washed away and airports cracked and burst. Algeria and Libya were one-party states, more or less organized in the coastal provinces but roiling tribalist anarchy in their Saharan outback. Ethiopia's government was preserved by Vienna's fiat; it was as frail as a pressed bouquet, and under siege by a dozen rural "action fronts."

All of them drawing venom from the lethal inheritance of the last century, a staggering tonnage of outdated armaments, passed from government to government at knock-down prices. From America to Pakistan to mujahideen to a Somalian splinter group with nothing to recommend it but a holy desperation for martyrdom. . . . From Russia to a cadre of bug-eyed Marxist strongmen shooting anything that even looked like a bourgeois intellectual. . . . Billions in aid had been poured into the sub-Sahara, permanently warping governments into bizarre funnels of debt and greed, and as the situation worsened more and more arms were necessary for "order" and "stability" and "national security," the outside world heaved a cynical sigh of relief as its lethal junk was disposed of to people still desperate to kill each other. . . .

At noon the convoy stopped. A soldier gave them water and gruel. They were in the Sahara now—they'd been driving all day. The driver unchained their legs. There was no place to run, not now.

Laura jumped out under the hammer blow of sun. A haze of heat distorted the horizons, marooning the convoy in a shimmering plaza of cracked red rock. The convoy had three trucks: the first carried soldiers, the second radio equipment, the third was theirs. And the two armored half-tracks in the rear. No one came out of the half-tracks or offered any food to their crews. Laura began to suspect that they had no crews. They were robots, big carnivorous versions of a common taxi-bus.

The desert shimmer was seductive. She felt a hypnotic urge to run out into it, into the silver horizon. As if she would dissolve painlessly into the infinite landscape, vanish like dry ice and leave only pure thought and a voice from the whirlwind.

Too long inside a cell. The horizon was strange, it was

pulling at her, as if it were trying to tug her soul out through the pupils of her eyes. Her head filled with strange pounding pulses of incipient heatstroke. She relieved herself quickly and climbed back into the canvas shade of the truck.

They drove all afternoon, all evening. There was no sand, it was various kinds of bedrock, blasted and Martian-looking. Miles of heat-baked flints for hours and hours, then sandstone ridges in a million shades of dun and beige, each more tedious than the last. They passed another military convoy in the afternoon, and once a distant airplane flew across the southern horizon.

At night they left the road, drew the trucks in a circle. The soldiers set metal stakes, pitons, into the rock all around the camp. Monitors, Laura thought. They ate again and the sun fell, an eerie desert sunset that lit the horizon with roseate fire. The soldiers gave them each a cotton army blanket and they slept in the truck, on the benches, one foot cuffed to prevent them from sneaking up on a soldier in the dark and tearing him apart with their fingernails.

The heat fled out of the rocks as soon as the sun was gone. It was bitterly cold all night, dry and arctic. In the first light of morning she could hear rocks cracking like gunshots as the sunlight hit.

The soldiers gassed up the trucks from jerry cans of fuel, which was too bad, because it occurred to her for the first time that a jerry can of fuel might be poured over the trucks and set alight, if she could get loose, and if she was strong enough to carry one, and if she had a match.

They had more gruel, with lentils in it this time. Then they were off again, the usual thirty miles an hour, jouncing hard, bruised and sucking dust from the two trucks ahead.

They had told each other everything by now. How Katje had grown up in a reeducation camp, because her parents were *verkrampte,* reactionaries, rather than *verligte,* liberals. It was not bad as such camps went, she said. The Boers were used to camps. The British had invented them during the Boer War, and in fact the very term "concentration camp" was invented by the British as a term for the place where they concentrated kidnapped Boer civilians. Katje's father had actually kept up his banking job in the city while rival black factions were busy "necklacing" one another, cramming tires full of petrol over the heads of victims and publicly roasting them alive. . . .

Azania had always been a series of camps, of migrant laborers crammed into barracks, or black townships kept in isolation by cops with rhino-hide whips and passcards, or intellectuals kept for years under "the ban," in which they were forbidden by law to join any group of human beings numbering more than three, and thus forming a kind of independent tribal homeland consisting of one person in a legal bell jar. . . .

Laura heard her say all this, this blond woman who looked so much like herself, and in return she could only say . . . well . . . sure, I have problems too . . . for instance my mother and I don't get along all that well. I know it doesn't sound like much but I guess if you'd been me you'd think more of it. . . .

The trucks slowed. They were winding downhill.

"I think we're getting somewhere," Laura said, stirring.

"Let me look," Katje said casually, and got up and shuffled to the back of the truck and peered outside around the back of the canvas, bracing herself. "I was right," she said. "I see some concrete bunkers. There are jeeps and . . . oh, dear, it's a crater, Laura, a crater as big as a valley."

Then the half-track behind them blew up. It simply flew to pieces like a china figurine, instantly, gracefully. Katje looked at it with an expression of childish delight and Laura suddenly found herself down on the floor of the truck, where she'd flung herself, some reflex hitting her faster than she could think. Roaring filled the air and the maddened stammer of automatic weapons, bullets piercing the canvas in a smooth line of stitching that left glowing holes of daylight and crossed the figure of Katje where she stood. Katje jumped just a bit as the line of stitching crossed her and turned and looked at Laura with an expression of puzzlement and fell to her knees.

And the second half-track tumbled hard as something hit it in the forward axle and it went over smoldering, and the air was full of the whine of bullets. Laura slithered to where Katje crouched on her knees. Katje put both hands to her stomach and brought them away caked with blood, and she looked at Laura with the first sign of understanding, and lay down on the floor of the truck, clumsily, carefully.

They were killing the soldiers in the front truck. She could hear them, dying. They didn't seem to be shooting back, it was all happening instantly, with lethal quickness, in seconds. She heard machine-gun fire raking the cab of her own truck, glass flying, the elegant ticking of supersonic metal piercing metal. More bullets came and ripped the wooden floor of the truck and bits of splinter flung themselves gaily into the air like deadly confetti. And again it came across, the old sword-through-a-barrel trick, thumb-sized rounds punching through the walls below the canvas mounting with joyful shouts of impact.

Silence.

More shots, close, point-blank. Mercy shots.

A dark hand clutching a gun came over the back of the truck. A figure in dust-caked goggles with its face wrapped in a dark blue veil. The apparition looked at the two of them and murmured something unintelligible. A man's voice. The veiled man vaulted over the back of the truck, landed in a crouch and pointed the gun at Laura. Laura lay frozen, feeling invisible, gaseous, nothing there but the whites of eyes.

The veiled man shouted and waved one arm outside the truck. He wore a blue cloak and woolen robes and his chest was clustered with blackened leather bags hung on thongs. He had a bandolier of cartridges and a curved dagger almost the size of a machete and thick, filthy sandals over bare, calloused feet. He stank like a wild animal, the radiant musk of days of desert survival and sweat.

Moments passed. Katje made a noise deep in her throat. Her legs jerked twice and her lids closed, showing rims of white. Shock.

Another veiled man appeared at the back of the truck. His eyes were hidden in tinted goggles and he was carrying a shoulder-launched rocket. He aimed it into the truck. Laura looked at it, saw the sheen of a lens, and realized for the first time that it was a video camera.

"Hey," she said. She sat up and showed the camera her bound hands.

The first marauder looked up at the second and said something, a long fluid rush of polysyllables. The second nodded and lowered his camera.

"Can you walk?" he said.

"Yes, but my friend's hurt."

"Come on out then." He yanked down the back of the truck, one-handed. It screeched—bullets had bent it out of shape. Laura crawled out quickly.

The cameraman looked at Katje. "She's bad. We'll have to leave her."

"She's a hostage. Azanian. She's important."

"The Malians will stitch her up, then."

"No, they won't, they'll kill her! You can't let her die here! She's a doctor, she works in the camps!"

The first marauder returned at a trot, bearing the belt of the dead driver, with rows of bullets and a ring of keys. He studied Laura's handcuffs alertly, picked the correct key at once, and clicked them loose. He gave her the cuffs and keys with a little half-bow and an elegant hand to his heart.

Other desert raiders—about two dozen—were looting the broken trucks. They were riding thin, skeletal dune buggies the size of jeeps, all tubes, spokes, and wire. The cars bounded along, agilely, quiet as bicycles, with a wiry scrunching of metal-mesh wheels and faint creak of springs. Their drivers were wrapped in cloaks and veils. They looked puffy, huge, and ghostlike. They steered from saddles over heaps of cargo lashed down under canvas.

"We don't have time." The big raider with the camera waved at the others and shouted in their language. They whooped in return and the men on foot began mounting up and stowing loot: ammo, guns, jerry cans.

"I want her to live!" Laura shouted.

He stared down at her. The tall marauder in his goggles, his masked and turbanned face, body cinched with belts and weaponry. Laura met his eyes without flinching.

"Okay," he told her. "It's your decision." She felt the weight of his words. He was telling her she was free again. Out of prison, in the world of decisions and consequences. A fierce sense of elation seized her.

"Take my camera. Don't touch its triggers." The stranger

took Katje in his arms and carried her to his own buggy, parked five yards from the truck.

Laura followed him, lugging the camera. The bulldozed roadbed scorched her bare feet and she hopped and lurched to the shade of the buggy. She looked down the slope.

The iron stump of a vaporized tower marked Ground Zero. The atomic crater was not as deep as she'd expected. It was shallow and broad, marked with eerie streaks, puddles of glassy slag broken like cracked mud. It looked mundane, wretched, forgotten, like an old toxic-waste excavation.

Jeeps were peeling away from the bunker, roaring upslope. They had soldiers in back, the test site's garrison, manning swivel-mounted machine guns.

From half a mile away they opened fire. Laura saw impact dust puffing twenty yards below them, and following that, languidly, the distant chatter of the shots.

The stranger was rearranging his cargo. Carefully, thoughtfully. He glanced briefly at the approaching enemy jeeps, the way a man would glance at a wristwatch. He turned to Laura. "You ride in back and hold her."

"All right."

"Okay, help me with her." They set Katje into the vacated cargo space, on her side. Katje's eyes were open again but they looked glassy, stunned.

Machine-gun fire clattered off the wreckage of one of the half-tracks.

The lead jeep suddenly lurched clumsily into the air. It came down hard, pancaking, men and wreckage flying. Then the sounds of the exploding land mine reached them. The two other jeeps pulled up short, fishtailing in the shoulder of the road. Laura climbed on, throwing her arm over Katje.

"Keep your head down." The stranger saddled up, threw the buggy into motion. They whirred away. Off the track, into wasteland.

In moments they were out of sight. It was low, rolling desert, studded with red, cracked rubble and heat-varnished boulders. The occasional waist-high thornbush, tinsel-thin wisps of dry grass. The afternoon heat was deadly, blasting up from the surface like X-rays.

A slug had hit Katje about two inches left of the navel and

exited her back, nicking the floating rib. In the fierce dry heat both wounds had clotted quickly, dark shiny wads of congealed blood on her back and stomach. She had a bad cut on her shin, splinter damage, Laura thought.

Laura herself was untouched. She had barked a knuckle a little, flopping down for cover in the back of the truck. That was all. She felt amazed at her luck—until she considered the luck of a woman who had been machine-gunned twice in her life without even joining a goddamned army.

They covered about three miles, careening and weaving. The marauder slowed. "They'll be after us," he shouted back at her. "Not the jeeps—aircraft. I've got to keep moving, and we'll spend some time in the sun. Get her under the tarp. And cover your head."

"With what?"

"Look in the kit bag there. No, not that one! Those are land mines."

Laura loosened the tarp and pulled a flap over Katje, then tugged the kit bag loose. Clothes—she found a grimy military shirt. She draped it over her head and neck like a burnoose, and turbanned it around her forehead with both sleeves.

With much jarring and fumbling she managed to get Katje's handcuffs off. Then she flung both sets of them off the back of the truck, flung away the keys. Evil things. Like metal parasites.

She climbed up onto the cargo heap, behind her rescuer. He passed her his goggles. "Try these." His eyes were bright blue.

She put them on. Their rubber rims touched her face, chilled with his sweat. The torturing glare faded at once. She was grateful. "You're American, aren't you?"

"Californian." He tugged his veil down, showing her his face. It was an elaborate tribal veil, yards of fabric, wrapping his face and skull in a tall, ridged turban, the ends of it draping his shoulders. Crude vegetable dye had stained his cheeks and mouth, streaking his creased Anglo face with indigo.

He had about two weeks of reddish beard stubble, shot with gray. He smiled briefly, showing a rack of impossibly white American teeth.

He looked like a TV journalist gone horribly and permanently wrong. She assumed at once that he was a mercenary, some kind of military adviser. "Who *are* you people?"

"We're the Inadin Cultural Revolution. You?"

"Rizome Industries Group. Laura Webster."

"Yeah? You must have some story to tell, Laura Webster." He looked at her with sudden intense interest, like a sleepy cat spotting prey.

Without warning, she felt a sudden powerful flash of déjà vu. She remembered traveling out to an exotic game park as a child, with her grandmother. They'd pulled up in the car to watch a huge male lion gnawing a carcass at the side of the road. The memory struck her: those great white teeth, tawny fur, the muzzle flecked with blood up to the eyes. The lion had looked up calmly at her through the window glass, with a look just like the one the stranger was giving her now.

"What's an Inadin?" Laura said.

"You know the Tuaregs? A Saharan tribe? No, huh?" He pulled the brow of his turban lower, shading his bare eyes. "Well, no matter. They call themselves the 'Kel Tamashek.' 'Tuareg' is what the Arabs call them—it means 'the godforsaken.' " He was picking up speed again, weaving expertly around the worst of the boulders. The suspension soaked up shock—good design, she thought through reflex. The broad wire wheels barely left a track.

"I'm a journalist," he told her. "Freelance. I cover their activities."

"What's your name?"

"Gresham."

"*Jonathan* Gresham?"

Gresham looked at her for a long moment. Surprised, thinking it over. He was judging her again. He always seemed to be judging her. "So much for deep cover," he said at last. "What's the deal? Am I famous now?"

"You're Colonel Jonathan Gresham, author of *The Lawrence Doctrine and Postindustrial Insurgency*?"

Gresham looked embarrassed. "Look, I was all wrong in that book. I didn't know anything back then, it's theory, half-ass bullshit mostly. You didn't *read* it, did you?"

"No, but I know people who really thought the world of that book."

"Amateurs."

She looked at Gresham. He looked like he'd been born in limbo and raised on the floor of hell. "Yeah, I guess so."

Gresham mulled it over. "You heard about me from your jailers, huh? I *know* they've read my stuff. Vienna read it too—didn't seem to do them much good, though."

"It must mean something! Your bunch of guys on little bicycles just wiped out a whole convoy!"

Gresham winced a little, like an avant-garde artist praised by a philistine. "If I'd had better intelligence. . . . Sorry about your friend. Fortunes of war, Laura."

"It could have just as easily been me."

"Yeah, you learn that after a while."

"Do you think she'll make it?"

"No, I don't. If one of us took a wound that bad, we'd have just put a bullet in him." He glanced at Laura. "I could do it," he said. He was being genuinely generous, she could see that.

"She doesn't need more bullets, she needs surgery. Is there a doctor we can reach?"

He shook his head. "There's an Azanian relief camp, three days from here. But we're not going there—we need to regroup at our local supply dump. We have our own survival to look after—we can't make chivalrous gestures."

Laura reached forward and grabbed the thick robe at Gresham's shoulder. "She's a dying woman!"

"You're in Africa now. Dying women aren't rare here."

Laura took a deep breath.

She had reached bedrock.

She tried hard to think. She looked around herself, trying to clear her head. Her mind was all rags and tatters. The desert around her seemed to be evaporating her. All the complexities were going—it was stark and simple and elemental. "I want you to save her life, Jonathan Gresham."

"It's bad tactics," Gresham said. He kept his eyes from her, watching the road. "They don't know she's mortally wounded. If she's an important hostage, they'll expect us to head for that camp. And we haven't lived this long by doing what FACT expects."

She backed away from him. Switched gears. "If they touch that camp the Azanian Air Force will stomp all over what's left of their capital."

He looked at her as if she'd gone mad.

"It's true. Four days ago the Azanians hit Bamako, hard. Fuel dumps, commandos, everything. From their aircraft carrier."

"Well, I'll be damned." Gresham grinned suddenly. No reassurance there—it was feral. "Tell me more, Laura Webster."

"That's why they were taking us to the atom-bomb test site. To make a propaganda statement, frighten the Azanians. I've seen their nuclear submarine. I even lived aboard it. For weeks."

"Jesus Christ," Gresham said. "You saw all that? An eyewitness?"

"Yes. I did."

He believed her. She could see it was hard for him, that it was news that was changing the basic assumptions of his life. Or at least the basic assumptions of his war, if there was any difference between his living and his warring. But he recognized that she was telling him the truth. It was coming across between them, something basic and human.

"We gotta do an interview," he muttered.

An interview. He had a camera, didn't he? She felt confused, relieved, obscurely ashamed. She looked back for that moral bedrock. It was still there. "Save my friend's life."

"We can try it." He stood up in the saddle and yanked something from his belt—a white folding fan. He flicked it open and held it over his head, waved it, sharp semaphore motions. For the first time Laura realized that there was another Tuareg in sight—a buglike profile, almost lost in heat haze, a mile to the north. A dotlike answering flicker.

Katje groaned in the back, a raw animal sound. "Don't let her drink too much," Gresham warned. "Mop her down instead."

Laura moved into the back.

Katje was awake, conscious. There was something vast and elemental, terrifying, about her ordeal. There was so little that talking or thinking could do about it—no way to debate with death. Her face was like a skull and she was fighting alone.

As hours passed Laura did what she could. A word or two with Gresham and she found what little he had that could help. Padding for Katje's head and shoulders. Leather bags of water that tasted flat and distilled. Some skin grease that smelled like animal fat. Black smudge on cheekbones to cut the glare.

The exit wound in the back was worst. It was ragged and Laura feared it would soon turn septic. The scab broke open twice during the worst jolts and a little rill of blood ran across Katje's spine.

They stopped once when they hit a boulder and the right front wheel began complaining. Then again when Gresham spotted what he thought were patrol planes—it was a pair of vultures.

As the sun set Katje began muttering aloud. Bits and pieces of a life. Her brother the lawyer. Mother's letters on flowered stationery. Tea parties. Charm school. Her mind groped in delirium for some vision, miles and years away. A tiny center of human order in a circle of desolate horizon.

Gresham drove until well after twilight. He seemed to know the country. She never saw him look at a map.

Finally he stopped in the channeled depth of an arroyo—a "wadi," he called it. The sandy depths of the dry river were crowded with waist-high bushes that stank of creosote and were full of tiny irritating burrs.

Gresham dismounted, shouldering a duffel bag. He pulled his curved machete and began chopping bushes. "The planes are worst after dark," he said. "They use infrareds. If they hit us at all, they'll probably take out the scoot." He began placing bushes over the buggy, camouflaging it. "So we'll sleep away from it. With the baggage."

"All right." Laura crawled from the back of the buggy, battered, filthy, bone-weary. "What can I do to help?"

"You can dress yourself for the desert. Try the knapsack."

She took the knapsack around the far side of the truck and fumbled it open. Shirts. Spare sandals. A long, coarse tunic of washed-out blue, wrinkled and wadded and stained. She shrugged out of her prison blouse.

God, she was so thin. She could see every rib. Thin and old and exhausted, like something that ought to be killed. She tunneled into the tunic—its shoulder seams came halfway down her biceps and the sleeves hung to her knuckles. It was thick though, and beaten soft with long wear. It reeked of Gresham, as if he had embraced her.

Strange thought, dizzying. She was embarrassed. She was a spectacle, pathetic. Gresham couldn't want a madwoman. . . .

The ground rose up and struck her. She lay in a heap of her own arms and legs, wondering. A muddle of time passed, vague pain and rushing waves of dizziness.

Gresham was gripping her arms.

She looked at him blankly. He gave her water. The water revived her enough to feel her own distress. "You passed out," he said. She nodded, understanding for the first time. Gresham picked her up. He carried her like a bundle of balloons; she felt light, hollow, bird-boned.

There was a lean-to pegged to the wall of the arroyo. A windbreak with a short arching tent roof of desert camo-cloth. Under the roof a dark figure crouched over the white-striped prison form of Katje—another of the Tuareg raiders, a long sniper's rifle strapped to his back. Gresham set Laura down, exchanged words with the Tuareg, who nodded somberly. Laura crawled into the tent, felt rough wool beneath her fingers—a carpet.

She curled up on it. The Tuareg was humming tonelessly to himself, under a ramp of blazing stars.

She was woken by the steaming smell of tea. It was barely dawn, a red auroral brightening in the east. Someone had thrown a warm rug over her during the night. She had a pillow too, a burlap bag stenciled in weird angular script. She sat up, aching.

The Tuareg handed her a cup, gently, courteously, as if it were something precious. The hot tea was dark brown and frothy and sweet, with a sharp minty reek. Laura sipped it. It had been boiled, not brewed, and it hit her like a hard narcotic, astringent and strong. It was foul, but she could feel it toughening her throat like tanned leather, bracing her for another day's survival.

The Tuareg half turned away, shyly, and discreetly lifted his veil. He slurped noisily, appreciatively. Then he opened a drawstring bag and offered it to her. Little brown pellets of something—like peanuts. Some kind of dried scop. It tasted like sugared sawdust. Breakfast. She ate two handfuls.

Gresham emerged from the lightening gloom, an enormous figure wrapped to the eyes, yet another bag slung over his shoulder. He was tossing handfuls of something over the dirt, with swift, ritual gestures. Tracer dust, maybe? She had no idea.

"She made it through the night," Gresham told her, dusting his hands. "Even spoke a little this morning. Stubborn, those Boers."

Laura stood up, painfully. She felt ashamed, "I'm not much use, am I?"

"It's not your world, is it." Gresham helped the Tuareg unpeg and fold the tent. "Not much pursuit, this time. . . . We planted some heat flares, maybe that sidetracked the planes. Or they may think we were Azanian commandos. . . . I hope so. We might provoke something interesting."

His relish terrified her. "But if FACT has the Bomb. . . . You can't provoke people who can destroy whole cities!"

He was unimpressed. "The world's full of cities." Gresham glanced at a wristwatch on a braided leather bracelet. "Got a long day ahead, let's move."

He'd repacked the buggy—shifted some of his cargo to another truck. Katje lay in a nest of carpet, shaded by the tarp, her eyes open.

"Good morning," she whispered.

Laura sat beside her, bracing her back and legs. Gresham kicked the buggy into motion. It whined reluctantly as it picked up speed—battery draining, she thought.

She took Katje's wrist. Light, fluttery pulse. "We're gonna get you back to your own people, Katje."

Katje blinked, her lids veiny and pale. She forced the words. "He is a savage, an anarchist. . . ."

"Try to rest. You and I, we're gonna live through this.

Live to tell about it.'' The sun peered over the horizon, a vivid yellow blister of heat.

Time passed, and the heat mounted sullenly as the miles passed. They were leaving the deep Sahara and crossing country with something more akin to soil. This had been grazing land once—they passed the mummies of dead cattle, ancient bone stick-puppets in cracked rags of leather.

She had never realized the scale of the African disaster. It was continental, planetary. They had traveled hundreds of miles without glimpsing another human being, without seeing anything but a few wheeling birds and the tracks of lizards. She'd thought Gresham was being cavalier, deliberately brutal, but she understood now how truly little he must care for FACT and its weaponry. They lived here, it was their home. Atomic bombardment could scarcely have made it worse. It would only make more of it.

At midafternoon a FACT pursuit plane found one of the Tuareg buggies and torched it. Laura never even saw the plane, no sign of the deadly encounter except a distant column of smoke. They stopped and sought cover for half an hour, until the drone had exhausted its fuel or ammo.

Flies found them immediately as they waited. Huge, bold Saharan flies that settled on Katje's blood-stained clothes like magnets. They had to be knocked loose, slapped away, before they would leave. Even then they moved only in short buzzing arcs and lit again. Laura fought them grimly, wincing as they landed on her goggles, tried to sip moisture from her nose and lips.

At last the scattered caravan passed signals by their semaphore. The driver had survived unwounded; a companion had picked him up and packed out the usable wreckage.

"Well, that's torn it," Gresham told her as they drove on. From somewhere he had dug up a battered pair of mirrored sunglasses. "They know where we're heading now, if they didn't before. If we had any sense we'd lie low, rest up, work on the vehicles."

"But she'll die."

"The odds say she won't even make it through the night."

"If she can make it, then we can, too."

"Not a bad bet," he said.

They stopped after dusk in a dead farming village of roof-less, wind-carved adobe walls. There were thornbushes in the ruins of a corral and a long, creeping gully had split the village threshing ground. The soil in the rudimentary irrigation ditches was so heavily salinized that it gleamed with a salted crust. The deep stone well was dry. People had lived here once—generation after generation, a thousand tribal years.

They left the buggy hidden in one of the ruined houses and set up camp in the depths of a gully, under the stars. Laura had more strength this time—she was no longer giddy and beaten. The desert had sand-blasted her down to some reflexive layer of vitality. She had given up worrying. It was an animal's asceticism.

Gresham set up the tent and heated a bowl of soup with an electric coil. Then he vanished, off on foot to check on some outflung post of his caravan. Laura sipped the oily protein broth gratefully. The smell of it woke Katje where she lay.

"Hungry," she whispered.

"No, you shouldn't eat."

"Please, I must. I must, just a little. I don't want to die hungry."

Laura thought it over. Soup. It wasn't much worse than water, surely.

"You've been eating," Katje accused her, her eyes glazed and ghostly. "You had so much. And I had nothing."

"All right, but not too much."

"You can spare it."

"I'm trying to think of what's best for you. . . ." No answer, just pain-brimming eyes full of suspicion and feverish hope. Laura tilted the bowl and Katje gulped desperately.

"God, that's so much better." She smiled, an act of heart-breaking courage. "I feel better. . . . Thank you so much." She curled away, breathing harshly.

Laura leaned back in her sweat-stiff djellaba and dozed off. She woke when she sensed Gresham climbing into the lean-to. It was bitterly cold again, that lunar Saharan cold, and she could feel heat radiating off the bulk of him, large and male and carnivorous. She sat up and helped him kick his way under the carpet.

"We made good time today," he murmured. The soft

voice of the desert, a bare disturbance of the silence. "If she lives, we can make it to her camp by midmorning. I hope the place isn't full of Azanian commandos. The long arm of imperialist law and order."

" 'Imperialist.' That word doesn't mean anything to me."

"You gotta hand it to 'em," Gresham said. He was looking down at Katje, who lay heavily, unconscious. "Once it looked like their little anthill was sure to go, but they pulled through somehow. . . . The rest of Africa has fallen apart, and every year they move a little farther north, them and their fucking cops and rule books."

"They're better than FACT! At least they help."

"Hell, Laura, half of FACT are white fascists who split when South Africa went one-man, one-vote. There's not a dime's worth of difference. . . . Your doctor friend may have a carrot instead of a stick, but the carrot's just the stick by other means."

"I don't understand." It seemed so unfair. "What do you want?"

"I want freedom." He fumbled in his duffel bag. "There's more to us than you'd think, Laura, seeing us on the run like this. The Inadin Cultural Revolution—it's not just another bullshit cover name, they *are* cultural, they're fighting for it, dying for it. . . . Not that what we have is pure and noble, but the lines crossed here. The line of population and the line of resources. They crossed in Africa at a place called disaster. And after that everything's more or less a muddle. And more or less a crime."

Déjà vu swept over her. She laughed quietly. "I've heard this before. In Grenada and Singapore, in the havens. You're an islander too. A nomad island in a desert sea." She paused. "I'm your enemy, Gresham."

"I know that," he told her. "I'm just pretending otherwise."

"I belong out there, if I ever get back."

"Corporate girl."

"They're my people. I have a husband and child I haven't seen in two years."

The news didn't seem to surprise him. "You've been in the War," he said. "You can go back to the place you called home, but it's never the same."

It was true. "I know it. I can feel it inside me. The burden of what I've seen."

He took her hand. "I want to hear all of it. All about you, Laura, everything you know. I *am* a journalist. I work under other names. Sacramento Internet, City of Berkeley Municipal Video Cooperative, about a dozen others, off and on. I've got my backers. . . . And I've got video makeup in one of the bags."

He was very serious. She began laughing. It turned her bones to water. She fell against him in the dark. His arms surrounded her. Suddenly they were kissing, his beard raking her face. Her lips and chin were sunburned and she could feel the bristles piercing through a greasy lacquer of oil and sweat. Her heart began hammering wildly, a manic exaltation as if she'd been flung off a cliff. He was pinning her down. It was coming quick and she was ready for it—nothing mattered.

Katje groaned aloud at their feet, a creaking, unconscious sound. Gresham stopped, then rolled off her. "Oh, man," he said. "Sorry."

"Okay," Laura gasped.

"Too weird," he said reluctantly. He sat up, pulling his robed arm from under her head. "She's down there dying in that fucking Dachau getup . . . and I left my condoms in the scoot."

"I guess we need those."

"Hell, yes, we do, this is Africa. Either one of us could have the virus and not know for years." He was blunt about it, not embarrassed. Strong.

She sat up. The air crackled with their intimacy. She took his hand, caressed it. It didn't hurt to do it. It was better now between them, the tension gone. She felt open to him and glad to be open. The best of human feelings.

"It's okay," she said. "Put your arm around me. Hold me. It's good."

"Yeah." Long silence. "You wanna eat?"

Her stomach lurched. "Scop, God, I'm sick of it."

"I've got some California abalone and a couple of tins of smoked oysters I've been saving for a special occasion."

Her mouth flooded with hunger. "Smoked oysters. No. Really?"

He patted his duffel bag. "Right here. In my bail-out bag. Wouldn't want to lose 'em, even if they torched the scoot. Hold on, I'll light a candle." He pulled the zip. Light flared.

Her eyes shrank. "Will the planes see that?"

The candle caught, backlighting his head. Snarl of reddish-brown hair. "If they do, let's die eating oysters." He pulled three tins from the bottom of the bag. Their bright American paper gleamed. Treasure marvels from the empire of consumerism.

He opened one tin with his knife. They ate with their fingers, nomad style. The rich flavor hit Laura's shriveled taste buds like an avalanche. The aroma flooded her whole head; she felt dizzy with pleasure. Her face felt hot and there was a faint ringing in her ears. "In America, you can have these every day," she said. She had to say it aloud, just to test the miracle of it.

"They're better when you can't have them," he said. "It's a hell of a thing, isn't it? Perverse. Like hitting your head with a hammer 'cause it feels so good when you stop." He drank the juice out of the can. "Some people are wired that way."

"Is that why you came to the desert, Gresham?"

"Maybe," he said. "The desert's pure. The dunes—all lines and form. Like good computer graphics." He set the can aside. "But that's not all of it. This place is the core of disaster. Disaster is where I live."

"But you're an American," she said, looking down at Katje. "You chose to come here."

He thought about it. She could feel him working up to something. Some deliberate confession.

"When I was a kid in grade school," he said, "some network guys with cameras showed up in my classroom one day. They wanted to know what we thought about the future. They did some interviews. Half of us said they'd be doctors, or astronauts, and all that crap. And the other half just said they figured they'd fry at Ground Zero." He smiled distantly. "I was one of those kids. A disaster freak. Y'know, you get used to it after a while. You get to where you feel uneasy when things start looking up." He met her eyes. "You're not like that, though."

"No," she said. "Born too late, I guess. I was sure I could make things better."

"Yeah," he said. "That's my excuse, too."

Katje stirred, listlessly.

"You want some abalone?"

Laura shook her head. "Thanks, but I can't. I can't enjoy it, not now, not in front of her." The rich food was flooding her system with a rush of drowsiness. She leaned her head on his shoulder. "Is she going to die?"

No answer.

"If she dies, and you don't go to the camp, what'll you do with me?"

Long silence. "I'll take you to my harem where I'll cover your body with silver and emeralds."

"Good God." She stared at him. "What a wonderful lie."

"No, I won't. I'll find some way to get you back to your Net."

"After the interview?"

He closed his eyes. "I'm not sure that's a good idea after all. You might have a future in the outside world, if you kept your mouth shut, about FACT and the Bomb and Vienna. But if you try to tell what you know . . . it's a long shot."

"I don't care," she said. "It's the truth and the world has to know it. I've got to tell it, Gresham. Everything."

"It's not smart," he said. "They'll put you away, they won't listen."

"I'll *make* them listen, I can do it."

"No, you can't. You'll end up a nonperson, like me. Censored, forgotten. I know, I've tried. You're not big enough to change the Net."

"Nobody's big enough. But it's got to change."

He blew out the light.

Katje woke them before dawn. She had vomited and was coughing. Gresham lit the candle, quickly, and Laura knelt over her.

Katje was bloated, and radiant with fever. The scab had broken on her stomach and she was bleeding again. The wound smelled bad, a death smell, shit and infection. Gresham held the candle over her. "Peritonitis, I think."

Laura felt a rush of despair. "I shouldn't have fed her."

"You *fed* her?"

"She begged me to! I had to! It was a mercy. . . ."

"Laura, you can't feed someone who's been gut-shot."

"Goddamn it! There isn't any right thing to do with someone like this. . . ." She brushed away tears: rage. "Goddamn it, she's going to die, after everything!"

"She's not dead yet. We don't have that far now. Let's go."

They loaded her into the truck, stumbling in darkness. Amazingly, Katje began to speak. Mumbles, in English and Afrikaans. Prayers. She wouldn't die and now she was calling on God. To whatever mad God ran Africa, as if He were watching and condoning all this.

The camp was a square mile of white concrete blockhouses, surrounded by tall chain-link fence. They rolled up a roadway lined by fences on either side that led to the center of the place.

Children had rushed the fence. Hundreds of them, faces rushing past. Laura could not look at them. She stared at a single face among the crowd. A black teenaged girl in a bright red polyester pinafore from some charity bale of American clothing. A dozen cheap plastic digital watches hung like bangles on her rail-thin forearms.

She had caught Laura's eye. It galvanized her. She thrust her arms through the chain-link and begged enthusiastically. *"Mam'selle, mam'selle! Le thé de Chine, mam'selle! La canne à sucre!"* Gresham drove on grimly. The girl screamed louder, shaking the fence with her thin arms, but her voice was drowned in the shouting of others. Laura almost turned to look back, but stopped at the last moment, humiliated.

There were gates ahead. A striped military parachute had been spread for shade. Black soldiers in speckled desert fatigues, with broad-brimmed ranger's hats pinned up on one side with a regimental badge. Commandos, she thought, Azanian troops. Beyond the closed gates was a smaller camp within a camp, with taller buildings, Quonset huts, a helicopter pad. An administrative center.

Gresham slowed. "I'm not going into this fucking place."

"It's all right, I'll handle it."

One of the guards blew a whistle and held up his hand. They looked curious about the lone buggy, not particularly concerned. They looked well fed. City soldiers. Amateurs.

Laura jumped down, flopping in Gresham's spare sandals. "Medic!" she screamed. "I've got a wounded Azanian, she's camp personnel! Get a stretcher!"

They rushed forward to look. Gresham sat in his saddle, looming above them aloofly, in his flowing robes, his head wrapped in the veil and turban. A soldier with stripes approached her. "Who the fuck are you?" he said.

"I'm the one who brought her in. Hurry it up, she's dying! Him, he's an American journalist and he's wired for sound, so watch that language, Corporal."

The soldier stared down at her. Her stained tunic, a dirty shirt turbanned around her head, eyes undersmudged with black grease.

"Lieutenant," he said, hurt. "My rank is lieutenant, miss."

She talked with the Azanian administrators in one of their long Quonset huts. Wall shelves bulged with canned goods, medical equipment, spare parts packed in grease. Heavy insulation on the rounded walls and ceiling cut the roar of their air conditioners.

A camp trusty in a white jacket, his cheeks ridged with tribal scars, circled among them with iced bottles of Fanta orange pop.

She'd given them only the sketchiest version of events, but the Azanians were jumpy and confused, and didn't seem to expect much from a desert apparition like herself. The camp's director was a portly pipe-smoking black Azanian named Edmund Mbaqane. Mbaqane was bravely attempting to look bureaucratically unflappable and very much on top of things. "We're so very grateful, Mrs. Webster . . . forgive me if I seemed abrupt at first. To hear yet another story of this genocidal Bamako regime—it does make one's blood boil."

Mbaqane hadn't boiled very vigorously—none of them had. They were civilians thousands of miles from home, and they were exposed, and they were twitchy. They were glad they had their hostage back—one of their own crew—but she

hadn't come through government channels and they clearly
wondered what it meant.

The Azanian Civil Action Corps seemed to have been
assembled for multiracial political correctness. There were a
pair of black ("Coloured") orderlies. Briefly, earlier, Laura
had met a little slump-shouldered woman in braids and sneak-
ers, Dr. Chandrasekhar—but she was now in the clinic, tending to Katje. Laura surmised that little Dr. Chandrasekhar
was the life and soul of the place—she was the one who
talked fastest and looked most exhausted.

There was also an Afrikaaner named Barnaard, who seemed
to be some kind of diplomat or liaison. His hair was brown,
but his skin was a glossy, artificial black. Barnaard seemed to
have a better grasp of the political situation than the others,
which was probably why his breath smelled of whiskey and he
stayed close to the paratroop captain. The captain was a Zulu,
a bluff, ugly customer who looked like he'd be pretty good in
a bar fight.

They were all scared to death. Which was why they kept
reassuring her. "You may rest easy, Mrs. Webster," the
director told her. "The Bamako regime will not be trying any
more adventures! They won't be buzzing this camp again.
Not while the Azanian aircraft carrier *Oom Paul* is patrolling
the Gulf of Guinea."

"She's a good ship," said the paratroop captain.

Barnaard nodded and lit a cigarette. He was smoking Chinese "Panda Brand" unfiltereds. "After yesterday's incident,
Niger protested the violation of her airspace in the strongest
possible terms. And Niger is a Vienna signatory. We expect
Viennese personnel here, in this very camp, by tomorrow
morning. Whatever their quarrel with us, I don't believe
Bamako would care to offend the Viennese."

Laura wondered if Barnaard believed what he'd said. The
isolationist Azanians seemed to have far more faith in Vienna
than people who were more in the swing of things. "You
have any of that suntan oil?" Laura asked him.

He looked a bit offended. "Sorry."

"I wanted to see the label. . . . You know who makes it?"

He brightened. "Surely. A Brazilian concern. Unitika-
something."

"Rizome-Unitika."

"Oh, so, they're one of yours, are they?" Barnaard nodded at her, as if it explained a lot. "Well, I have nothing against multinationals! Any time you fellows would like to begin your investments again—under proper supervision, of course . . ."

A printer began chattering. News from home. The others drifted over. Director Mbaqane moved closer to Laura. "I'm not sure I understand the role of this American journalist you mentioned."

"He was with the Tuaregs."

The director tried not to look confused. "Yes, we do have some so-called Tuaregs here, or rather, Kel Tamashek. . . . I take it that he wants to assure himself that they are being treated in a fair and equal manner?"

"It's more of a cultural interest," Laura said. "He did mention something about wanting to talk to them."

"Cultural? They're coming along very nicely. . . . Perhaps I could send out a deputation of tribal elders—put his mind to rest. We gladly shelter any ethnic group in need—Bambara, Marka, Songhai. . . . We have quite a large contingent of Sarakolé, who are not even Nigeran nationals."

He seemed to expect an answer. Laura sipped her orange pop and nodded. Barnaard drifted back—he had quickly assessed the message as meaningless. "Oh, no. Not another journo, not now."

The director shut him up with a glance. "As you can see, Mrs. Webster, we're rather pressed at the moment . . . but if you *require* a tour, I'm sure that Mr. Barnaard would be more than happy to, ah, explain our policies to the international press."

"You're very thoughtful," Laura said. "Unfortunately I have to do an interview myself."

"Well, I can understand that—it must be quite a scoop. Hostages, freed from the notorious prisons of Bamako." He fiddled with his pipe avuncularly. "It'll certainly be the talk of Azania. One of our own, returned to us from bondage. Quite a boost for our morale—especially in the midst of this crisis." The director was talking over and through her for the benefit of his own people. It was working, too—he was cheering them up. She felt better about him.

He went on. "I know that you and Dr. Selous must be—are—very close. The sacred bond between those who have struggled together for freedom! But you needn't worry, Mrs. Webster. Our prayers are with Katje Selous! I am sure she will pull through!"

"I hope so. Take good care of her. She was brave."

"A national heroine! Of course we will. And if there's anything we can do for you . . ."

"I thought, maybe a shower."

Mbaqane laughed. "Good heavens. Of course, my dear. And clothing. . . . Sara is about your size. . . ."

"I'll keep this, uh, djellaba." She had puzzled him. "I'm going on camera with it, it's a better image."

"Oh, I see . . . yes."

Gresham was doing a stand-up at the edge of camp. Laura circled him, careful to stay out of camera range.

She was shocked by the beauty of his face. He had shaved and put on full video makeup: eyeliner, lip rouge, powder. His voice had changed: it was mellifluous, each word pronounced with an anchorman's precision.

". . . the image of a desolate wasteland. But the Sahel was once the home of black Africa's strongest, most prosperous states. The Songhai empire, the empires of Mali and Ghana, the holy city of Timbuktu with its scholars and libraries. To the Moslem world the Sahel was a byword for dazzling wealth, with gold, ivory, crops of all kinds. Huge caravans crossed the Sahara, fleets of treasure canoes traveled the Niger River . . ."

She walked past him. The rest of his caravan had arrived, and the Tuaregs had set up camp. Not the rags and lean-tos they'd skulked under while raiding, but six large, sturdy-looking shelters. They were prefabricated domes, covered in desert camo-fabric. Inside they were braced with mesh-linked metallic ribs.

From the backs of their skeletal desert cars, the hooded nomads were unrolling long linked tracks that looked like tank treads. In harsh afternoon sunlight the treads gleamed with black silicon. They were long racks of solar-power cells. They hooked the buggies' wheel hubs to long jumper cables from the power grid. They moved with fluid ease; it was as if they were watering camels. They chatted quietly in Tamashek.

While one group was recharging their buggies, the others rolled out mats in the shade of one of the domes. They began brewing tea with an electric heat coil. Laura joined them. They seemed mildly embarrassed by her presence, but accepted it as an interesting anomaly. One of them pulled a tube of protein from an ancient leather parcel and cracked it open over his knee. He offered her a wet handful, bowing. She scraped it from his long fingertips and ate it and thanked him.

Gresham arrived with his cameraman. He was wiping his powdered face with an oiled rag, fastidiously. "How'd it go in camp?"

"I wasn't sure they'd let me back out."

"They don't work that way," Gresham said. "It's the desert that locks people in there. . . ." He sat beside her. "Did you tell them about the Bomb?"

She shook her head. "I wanted to, but I just couldn't. They're so jumpy already, and there's commandos with guns. . . . But Katje will tell them, if she comes around. It's all so confused—*I'm* confused. I was afraid they'd panic and lock me away. And you, too."

The thought amused him. "What, come out and tangle with us? I don't think so." He patted the camera. "I had a talk with that para captain, when he came out to give us the once-over. . . . I know how he's thinking. Classic Afrikaaner tactics: he's got his covered wagons in a circle, every man to the ramparts, ready to repel the Zulus. Of course he's a Zulu himself, but he's read the rule books. . . . Got a camp full of childlike savage refugees to keep calm and pacified. . . . He's got us figured for friendlies, though. So far."

"Vienna's coming, too."

"Christ." Gresham thought about it. "A little Vienna, or a lot of Vienna?"

"They didn't say. I guess it depends on what Vienna wants. They gave me some song-and-dance about protests from the government of Niger."

"Well, Niger's no help, eighty-year-old Soviet tanks and an army that riots and burns down Niamey every other year. . . . If there's a lot of Vienna, it could be trouble. But they wouldn't send a lot of Vienna to a refugee camp. If Vienna were moving in force against Mali they'd just hit Bamako.''

"They wouldn't ever do that. They're too afraid of the Bomb.''

"I dunno. Spooks make lousy soldiers, but they took out Grenada six months ago, and that was a tough nut to crack.''

"They *did* that? Invaded Grenada?''

"Wiped 'em out in their hacker ratholes. . . . Stupid tactics though, frontal assault, clumsy. . . . They lost over twelve hundred men.'' He raised his brows at her shock. "You've *been* to Grenada, Laura—I thought you knew. FACT should have told you—it was such a triumph for their goddamn policy.''

"They never told me. Anything.''

"The cult of secrecy,'' he said. "They live by it.'' He paused, glancing toward the camp. "Oh, good. They've sent us out some of their tame Tamashek.''

Gresham withdrew within the dome, motioning Laura with him. Half a dozen camp inmates arrived outside, trudging reluctantly.

They were old men. They wore T-shirts and paper baseball hats and Chinese rubber sandals and ragged polyester pants.

The Inadin Tuaregs greeted them with languid, ritual politeness. Gresham translated for her. Sir is well? Yes, very well, and yourself? Myself and mine are very well, thank you. And sir's people, they are also well? Yes, very well. Thanks be to God, then. Yes, thanks be to God, sir.

One of the Inadin lifted the kettle high and began pouring tea with a long, ceremonial trickle. Everyone had tea. They then began boiling it again, pouring some coarse sugar over a kettle already half full of leaves. They spoke for some time about the tea, sitting politely, brushing without irritation at circling flies. The day's most virulent heat faded.

Gresham translated for her—strange bits of solemn platitude. They stayed in the back of the tent, out of the circle. Time passed slowly, but she was happy enough to sit beside him, letting her mind go desert blank.

Then one of the Inadin produced a flute. A second found

an intricate xylophone of wood and gourds, bound with leather. He tapped it experimentally, tightening a cord, while a third reached inside his robe. He tugged a leather thong—at the end was a pocket synthesizer.

The man with the flute opened his veil; his black face was stained blue with sweat-soaked indigo dye. He blew a quick trill on the flute, and they were off.

The rhythm built up, high resonant notes from the buzzing xylophone, the off-scale dipping warble of the flute, the eerie, strangely primeval bass of the synthesizer.

The others punctuated the music with claps and sudden piercing shrieks from behind their veils. Suddenly one began to sing in Tamashek. "He sings about his synthesizer," Gresham murmured.

"What does he say?"

I humbly adore the acts of the Most High,
Who has given to the synthesizer what is better than a soul.
So that, when it plays, the men are silent,
And their hands cover their veils to hide their emotions.
The troubles of life were pushing me into the tomb,
But thanks to the synthesizer,
God has given me back my life.

The music stopped. The camp refugees clapped a little, then stopped, confused. Gresham glanced at his watch, then rose to his feet, lugging his camera. "That's just a taste of it," he told Laura. "They'll be back for more, later—and bring their families I hope. . . ."

"Let's do the interview."

He hesitated. "You sure you're up for it?"

"Yeah."

She followed him to another tent. It was guarded by two of the Inadin Tuaregs and heaped with their baggage. There were carpets underfoot and a battery, a spare one from the buggies. Hooked to it, he had a keyboard and screen—a custom model with a console of hand-carved redwood.

Gresham sat cross-legged before it. "I hate this goddamned machine," he announced, and ran his hand lingeringly over its sleek lines. He hooked his videocam to one of the console's input ports.

"Gresham, where's your makeup case?"

He passed it to her. Laura opened the hand mirror. She was so gaunt and thin—a look like anorexia, rage turned helplessly in on itself.

The hell. She jabbed her fingertips in powder, smeared her hollow cheeks. Somebody was going to pay.

She began rouging her lips. "Gresham, we have to figure how to hustle those Azanians. They're old-fashioned, funny about information. They wouldn't let me near their damned telex, and they'll want to clear everything with Pretoria."

"We don't need them," he said.

"We do if we want to reach the Net! And they'll want to see the tape first—they'll learn everything."

He shook his head. "Laura, look around you."

She put down the mirror and humored him. They were in a dome. Fabric over metal ribs and chicken wire.

"You're sitting under a satellite dish," he told her.

She was stunned. "You access satellites?"

"How the hell else do you touch the Net from the middle of the Sahara? The coverage is spotty, but during the right tracking times you can make a pass."

"How can you *do* that? Where does the money come from?" An awful thought struck her. "Gresham, are you running a data haven?"

"No. I used to deal with them, though. All the time." He thought about it. "Maybe I should start my own haven now. The competition's down, and I could use the bread."

"Don't do it. Don't even think it."

"You must know that biz pretty well. You could be my adviser." The joke fell completely flat. He looked at her, meditatively. "You'd come right after me, wouldn't you. You and your little legions of straight-arrow corporate people."

She said nothing.

"Sorry," he said. "It hardly matters at the moment. . . . I wouldn't want to send this tape to a data haven anyway."

"What do you mean? Where *would* you send it?"

"To Vienna, of course. Let 'em see that I know—that I've got the goods on 'em. FACT has the Bomb, and they've blackmailed Vienna. So Vienna cut a deal with them—let 'em beat the crap out of the havens, while they covered up for nuclear terrorists. Vienna's failed, and I know they've failed. To shut me up, they might try to hunt me down and kill me, but I've gotten pretty good at avoiding that. With any luck they'd buy me off instead. Then leave me alone—the way they've left Mali alone.''

"That's not enough! Everyone must know. The whole world.''

Gresham shook his head. "I think we could hustle Vienna, if we play it right. They don't mind buying people when they have to. They'll pay for our silence. More than you might think.''

She held the mirror to her face. "I'm sorry, Gresham. I simply, truly don't care about Vienna or its money. That's not who I am. I care about the world I have to live in.''

"I don't live in your world,'' he told her. "Too bad if that makes me sound crass. But I can tell you this much—if you want to go back, and be-who-you-are, and live your cozy life in that whole world of yours, you'd better not try to kick its jams out. Maybe I could survive a stunt like that, ducking and dodging out here in the desert, but I don't think you could. The world doesn't give a shit how noble your motives are— it'll roll right over you. That's how it works.'' He was lecturing her. "You can hustle—cut a corner here, a corner there—but you can't tackle the world. . . .''

She examined her hair in the mirror. Wild prison hair. She'd washed it in the Azanian camp and the dry heat had fluffed it out. It stood up all over her head, like an explosion.

He kept after her. "It's no use even trying. The Net will never run this tape, Laura. News services never run tapes of terrorist hostages. Except for Vienna, who knows it's true, everyone will think it's wild bullshit. That you're speaking under duress, or that the whole thing is bogus.''

"You took tape of that nuclear test site, didn't you?'' she said. "You can tag it on to my statement. Let's see 'em refute that one!''

"I'll do that, certainly—but they could refute it anyway.''

"You've heard my story,'' she told him. "I made *you* believe it, didn't I? It happened, Gresham. It's the truth.''

"I know it is." He handed her a leather canteen.

"I can do it," she told him, feeling brittle. "Tackle the world. Not just some little corner of it, but the whole great grinding mass of it. I know I can do it. I'm good at it."

"Vienna will step on it."

"It's gonna step on Vienna." She squeezed a stream of canteen water into her mouth and shoved the makeup kit out of camera range. She set the canteen by her knee.

"It's too big for me to hold anymore," she said. "I've got to tell it. Now. That's all I know." At the sight of the camera, something was rising up within her, adrenaline-wild and strong. Electric. All that fear and weirdness and pain, packed down in an iron casing. "Put me on tape, Gresham. I'm ready. Go."

"You're on."

She looked into the world's glass eye. "My name is Laura Day Webster. I'm gonna start with what happened to me on the *Ali Khamenei* out of Singapore . . ."

She became pure glass, a conduit. No script, she was winging it, but it came out pure and strong. Like it would carry her forever. The truth, pouring through.

Gresham interrupted her with questions. He had a prepared list of them. Sharp, to the point. It was like he was stabbing her. It should have hurt, but it only broke open the flow. She reached some level that she'd never touched before. An ecstasy, pure fluid art. Possession.

She couldn't keep that edge. It was timeless while she had it, but then she could feel it go. She was hoarse and she began stumbling a little. Sliding off at the edges, passion slipping into babble.

"That's it," he said at last.

"Repeat the question?"

"I don't have any more. That's it. It's over." He shut off the camera.

"Oh." She wiped her palms on the carpet, absently. Drenched. "How long was it?"

"You talked for ninety minutes. I think I can edit it down to an hour."

Ninety minutes. It had felt like ten. "How was I?"

"Amazing." He was respectful. "That business when they buzzed the camp—that's the sort of thing nobody could fake."

She was puzzled. "What?"

"You know. When the jets came over just now." He stared at her. "Jets. The Malians just buzzed the camp."

"I didn't even hear it."

"Well, you looked up, Laura. And you waited. Then you went right on talking."

"The demon had me," she said. "I don't even know what the hell I said." She touched her cheek. It came away black with mascara. Of course—she'd been weeping. "I've run my makeup all over my goddamn face! And you let me."

"Cinema verité," he said. "It's real. Raw and real. Like a live grenade."

"Then throw it," she told him. Giddily. She let herself go and fell back where she sat. Her head hit a buried rock under the carpet, but the dull jolt of pain seemed a central part of the experience.

"I didn't know it would be like this," he said. There was real fear in his voice. It was as if, for the first time, he had realized he had something to lose. "It might just happen—it could get loose in the Net. People might really *believe* it." He shifted uneasily where he sat. "I've gotta figure the angles first. What if Vienna *falls?* That would be great, but they might just reform and come back with bigger teeth this time. In which case I've fucked myself and everything I've tried to create here. Crap like that can happen, when you throw live grenades."

"It *has* to get loose," she said passionately. "It *will* get loose, sometime. FACT knows, Vienna knows, maybe even governments. . . . A secret this huge is bound to come out, sooner or later. It's not just *our* doing. We just happen to be the people on the spot."

"I like that line of reasoning, Laura. It'll sound good if they catch us."

"That doesn't matter. Anyway, they can't *touch* us, if everybody learns the truth! Come on, Gresham! You've got goddamn satellites, think of a way to get through, damn it!"

He sighed. "I already have," he said. He got to his feet and walked past her, unrolling a spool of cable. After a moment she rose on one elbow and looked out the triangular pie slice of door, after him. It was late afternoon now, and the Tuaregs were throwing two of the domes onto their backs. Yawning teacup mouths open to the dry Saharan sky.

Gresham came back. He looked down at her as she sprawled on the carpet, breathing. "You okay?"

"I'm hollow. Eviscerated. Absolved."

"Yeah," he said. "You talked just like that, the whole time." He sat cross-legged before his console and typed away, carefully.

Minutes passed.

A woman's voice erupted from the console.

"Attention North Africa broadcast source, latitude eighteen degrees, ten minutes, fifteen seconds; longitude five degrees, ten minutes, eighteen seconds. You are broadcasting on a frequency reserved for the International Communications Convention for military use. You are advised to desist at once."

Gresham cleared his throat. "Is Vassily there?"

"Vassily?"

"Yeah. Da."

"Da, okay, looking good, hold on, please."

Moments later a man's voice came on. His English wasn't as good as the woman's. "Is Jonathan, right?"

"Yeah. How's it goin'?"

"Very well, Jonathan! You are receiving the tapes I sent?"

"Yes, Vassily, thank you, *spaseba,* you're very generous. As always. I have something very special for you this time."

The voice was cautious. "*Very* special, Jonathan?"

"Vassily, this is an item beyond price. Unobtainable elsewhere."

Unhappy silence. "I must ask, can it wait for our next pass over your area. We are having small docking problem here at the moment. Very small docking problem."

"I really think you'd better give this one your immediate attention, Vassily."

"Very well. I will key in scrambler." Moment's wait. "Ready for transmission."

Gresham tapped his console. High-pitched whir. He leaned back, turning to Laura. "This'll take a while. The scramblers are kind of clunky up on old Gorbachev Memorial."

"That was the Russian *space station?*"

"Yeah." Gresham rubbed his hands briskly. "Things are looking up."

"You just sent our tape to a *cosmonaut?*"

"Yeah." He tucked in his legs, resting his elbows on his knees. "I'll tell you what I think might happen. They're gonna look at it up there. They're gonna think it's craziness—at first. But they may believe it. And if they do, they won't be able to hold it back. Because the consequences are just too extreme.

"So—they'll pipe it down to Moscow, and that other place, Star City. And the ground teams will look it over, and the apparatchiks. And they'll copy it. Not because they think there *ought* to be a lot of copies, but because it needs study. And they're gonna start shipping it all around. To Vienna first, of course, because their people are all over Vienna. But to the rest of the Socialist bloc, too—just in case . . . ."

He yawned into his fist. "And then those guys on the station are going to realize they've got the publicity coup of a lifetime. And if anyone's willing to fool with it, they are. I've got a lot of contacts, here and there, but they're the craziest bastards I know! Five will get you ten, they start dumping it, direct broadcast. If they can get permission from Star City. Or maybe even without permission."

"I don't understand, Gresham. Direct broadcast? That just sounds lunatic."

"You don't know what it's like up there! Wait a minute, you *do* know—you've lived on a submarine. But see, they've been just burning, ever since little Singapore threw that guy up with the laser launch. Because they've been up there for *years,* hanging their ass on the edge of the infinite, and nobody paying attention. Didn't you hear how *pathetic* Vassily was? Like some ham-radio geezer locked in a basement."

"But they're cosmonauts! They're trained professionals, they do space science. Biology. Astronomy."

"Yeah. Lot of girls and glory in those two. Boy." Gresham shook his head. "I give it three days at the outside."

"Okay . . . what then? If it doesn't work."

"I call 'em again. Threaten to give it to somebody else. There are other contacts. . . . And we still have the original tape. We just keep trying, that's all. Till we get through. Or Vienna nails us. Or till FACT makes a demonstration on a city and makes the news obvious to everyone. Which is what we have to expect, isn't it?''

''My God! What we've just done could cause . . . *worldwide panic*. . . .''

He sneered. ''Yeah—I'm sure that's what Vienna has been telling itself while they sat on the truth. For years. And covered up, and protected the people who shot up your house.''

A bolt of rage short-circuited her fear. ''That's right!''

He grinned at her. ''It was one of the least of their crimes, actually. But I figured it'd bring you around.''

She thought aloud. ''Vienna let them do it. They knew who killed Stubbs and they came into my house and lied to me. Because they were afraid of something worse.''

''Worse? I'll say. Think of the political consequences. Vienna exists to keep order against terrorism, and they've been sucking up to terries for years. They're gonna pay. The hypocrites.''

''But Gresham, what if they start bombing people? Millions could die.''

''Millions? Depends on how many warheads they have. They're not a superpower. Five warheads? Ten? How many launch racks in that submarine?''

''But they could really do it! They could murder whole cities of innocent people while they're sleeping, peacefully. . . . For no sane reason! Just stupid fascist politics and power mongering—'' Her voice caught hoarsely.

''Laura—I'm older than you. I know that situation. I remember it vividly.'' He smiled. ''I'll tell you how it worked. We just waited and went on living, that's all. It didn't happen— maybe it'll never happen. In the meantime, what good is this doing you?'' He stood up. ''We're through here. Come with me, there are things I want you to see.''

She followed him unwillingly, feeling wretched, spooked. The way he talked about it so casually—*ten warheads*—but for him it *was* casual, wasn't it? He'd lived through a time where there were thousands of warheads, enough to exterminate *all human life*.

Responsible for mass death. It filled her with loathing. Her thoughts raced and suddenly she wanted to flee into the desert, vaporize. She never wanted to be near anyone who had ever touched such a thing, who was shadowed by that kind of horror.

And yet they were *everywhere*, weren't they? People who'd played politics with atomic weapons. Presidents, premiers, generals . . . little old men out in parks with grandkids and golf clubs. She had seen them, lived among them—

She was one of them.

Her mind went numb.

Gresham slowed, took her elbow. "Look."

It was evening now. A ragged crowd of about a hundred had gathered before one of the domes. The dome had been pulled in half, as a kind of crude amphitheater. The Inadin musicians were playing again, and one of them stood before the crowd, swaying, singing. His song had a wailing meter and many verses. The other Inadin swayed in time, sometimes giving a sharp cry of approval. The crowd looked on open-mouthed.

"What's he saying?"

Gresham began speaking again in his television voice. He was reciting poetry.

> *Listen, people of the Kel Tamashek,*
> *We are the Inadin, the blacksmiths.*
> *We have always wandered among the tribes and clans,*
> *We have always carried your messages.*
> *Our fathers' lives were better than ours,*
> *Our grandfathers' better still.*
> *Once our people traveled everywhere,*
> *Kano, Zanfara, Agadez.*
> *Now we live in the cities and are turned into numbers*
> *   and letters,*
> *Now we live in the camps and eat magic food from tubes.*

Gresham stopped. "Their word for magic is *tisma*. It means, 'the secret craft of blacksmiths.' "

"Go on," she said.

Our fathers had sweet milk and dates,
We have only nettles and thorns.
Why do we sufffer like this?
Is it the end of the world?
No, because we are not evil men,
No, because now we have tisma.
We are blacksmiths who have secret magic,
We are silversmiths who see the past and future.
In the past this was a rich and green land,
Now it is rock and dust.

Gresham paused, watching the Tuaregs. Two rose and began dancing, their outstretched arms curling and waving, their sandaled feet stamping in time. It was slow, waltzlike dancing, elegant, elegiac. The singer rose to his feet again. "Now comes the good part," Gresham said.

But where there is rock, there can be grass,
Where there is grass, the rain comes.
The roots of grass will hold the rain,
The leaves of grass will tame the sandstorm.
But we were the enemies of grass,
That is why we suffer.
What our cows did not eat, the sheep ate.
What the sheep refused, the goats consumed.
What the goats left behind, the camels devoured.
Now we must be the friends of grass,
We must apologize to it and treat it kindly.
Its enemies are our enemies.
We must kill the cow and the sheep,
We must butcher the goat and behead the camel.
For a thousand years we loved our herds,
For a thousand years we must praise the grass.
We will eat the tisma *food to live,*
We will buy Iron Camels from GoMotion
    Unlimited in Santa Clara California.

Gresham folded his arms. The singer continued. "There's a lot more," Gresham said, "but that's the gist of it."

The question was obvious. "Did you write it for them?"

"No," he said proudly. "It's an old song." He paused. "Retrofitted."

"Yeah."

"A few of this crowd may join us. A few of the few may stay. It's a hard life in the desert." He looked at her. "I'm gone in the morning."

"Tomorrow? That soon?"

"It has to be that way."

The cruelty of it hurt her badly. Not his cruelty but the pure cruelty of necessity. She knew immediately that she would never see him again. She felt lacerated, relieved, panicky.

"Well, you did it, didn't you?" she said hoarsely. "You rescued me and you saved my friend's life." She tried to embrace him.

He backed off. "No, not out here—not in front of them." He took her elbow. "Let's go inside."

He led her back into the dome. The guards were still there, patrolling. Against thieves, she thought. They were afraid of thieves and vandals from the camp. Beggars. It seemed so pathetic that she began weeping.

Gresham flicked on the screen of his computer. Amber light flooded the tent. He returned to the door of the dome, spoke to the guards. One of them said something to him in a sharp, high-pitched voice and began laughing. Gresham swung the door shut, sealed it with a clamp.

He saw her tears. "What's all this?"

"You, me. The world. Everything." She wiped her cheek on her sleeve. "Those camp people have nothing. Even though you're trying to help them, they'd steal all this *stuff* of yours, if they could."

"Ah," Gresham said, lightly. "That's what we high-falutin' cultural meddlers refer to as 'the vital level of corruption.' "

"You don't have to talk that way to me. Now that I can see what you're trying to do."

"Oh, Lord," Gresham said unhappily. He stalked across the dome in the mellow light of the monitor and gathered an armload of burlap bags. He lugged them next to his screen and terminal and spread them for pillows. "Come on, sit here with me."

She joined him. The pillows had a pleasant, resinous smell.

They were full of grass seed. She saw that some were already half empty. They'd been sowing the grass in the gullies as they ran from pursuit.

"Don't get to thinking I'm too much like you," he said. "Honest and sweet and wishing everybody the best. . . . I grant you good intentions, but intentions don't count for much. Corruption—that's what counts."

He meant it. They were sitting together inches apart, but something was eating at him so badly that he wouldn't look at her. "What you just said—it doesn't make any sense to me."

"I was in Miami once," he said. "A long time ago. The sky was pink! I stopped this rudie on the boardwalk, I said: looks like you got some bad particulate problems here. He told me the sky was full of Africa. And it was true! It was the harmattan, the sandstorms. Topsoil from the Sahara, blown right across the Atlantic. And I said to myself: there, that place, that's your home."

He looked at her, into her eyes. "You know when it really got bad here? When they tried to help. With medicine. And irrigation. They sank deep wells, with sweet, flowing water, and of course the nomads settled there. So instead of moving their herds on, leaving the pastures a chance to recover, they ate everything down to bare rock, for miles around every well. And the eight, nine children that African women have borne from time immemorial—they all *lived*. It wasn't that the world didn't care. They struggled heroically, for generations, selflessly and nobly. To achieve an atrocity."

"That's too complicated for me, Gresham. It's perverse!"

"You're grateful to me, because you think I saved you. The hell. We did our best to kill everyone in that convoy. We raked that truck with machine-gun fire, three times. I don't know how the hell you lived."

" 'Fortunes of war . . .' "

"I love war, Laura. I enjoy it, like the F.A.C.T. Them, they enjoy murdering rag-heads with robots. Me, I'm more visceral. Somewhere inside me, I wanted Armageddon, and this is as close as it ever got. Where the Earth is blasted and all the sickness comes to a head."

He leaned closer. "But that's not all of it. I'm not innocent enough to let chaos alone. I stink of the Net, Laura. Of power and planning and data, and the Western method, and the pure inability to let anything alone. Ever. Even if it destroys my own freedom. The Net lost Africa once, blew it so badly that it went bad and wild, but the Net will get it back, someday. Green and pleasant and controlled, and just like everywhere else.''

"So I win, and you lose—is that what you're telling me? That we're enemies? Maybe we are enemies, in some abstract way that's all in your head. But as people, we're friends, aren't we? And I'd never hurt you if I could help it.''

"You can't help it. You were hurting me even before I knew you existed.'' He leaned back. "Maybe my abstractions aren't your abstractions, so I'll give you some of your own. How do you think I *financed* all this? Grenada. They were my biggest backers. Winston Stubbs . . . now there was a man with vision. We didn't always see eye to eye, but we were allies. It hurt a lot to lose him.''

She was shocked. "I remember. . . . They said he gave money to terrorist groups.''

"I haven't been picky. I can't afford to be—this project of mine, it's all Net stuff, money, and money's corruption is in the very heart of it. The Tuaregs have nothing to sell, they're Saharan nomads, destitute. They don't have anything the Net wants—so I beg and scrape. A few rich Arabs, nostalgic for the desert while they tool around in their limousines. . . . Arms dealers, not many of those left. . . . I even took money from FACT, back in the old days, before the Countess went batshit.''

"Katje told me that! That it's a woman who runs FACT. The Countess! Is it true?''

He was surprised, sidetracked. "She doesn't 'run it,' exactly, and she's not really a countess, that's just her nom de guerre. . . . But, yeah, I knew her, in the old days. I knew her very well, when we were younger. As well as I know you.''

"You were *lovers*?''

He smiled. "Are we *lovers*, Laura?''

The silence stretched, a desert silence broken by the distant whooping of the Tuaregs. She looked into his eyes.

"I talk too much,'' he said sadly. "A theorist.''

She stood and pulled the tunic over her head, threw it to her feet. She sat beside him, naked, in the light of the screen.

He was silent. Clumsily, she pulled at his shirt, ran her hand over his chest. He opened his robe and put his weight on her.

He fumbled at her gently. For the first time, something vital, deep within her, realized that she was alive again. As if her soul had gone to sleep like a handcuffed arm, and now blood was returning. A torrent of sensation.

A moment passed with the muted crinkling of contraceptive plastic. Then he was on her, inside her. She wrapped her legs around him, her skin aflame. Flesh and muscle moving in darkness, the smell of sex. She closed her eyes, overwhelmed.

He stopped for a moment. She opened her eyes. He was looking at her, his face alight. Then he reached out with one arm and tapped the keyboard.

The machine scanned channels. Light flashed over them as it blasted one-second gouts of satellite video into the tent. Unable to stop herself, she turned her head to look.

Cityscape / cityscape / trees / a woman / brand names / Arabic script / image / image / image/

They were moving in time. They were moving in rhythm to the set, eyes lifted up, fixed on the screen.

Pleasure shot through her like channeled lightning. She cried out.

He gripped her hard and closed his eyes. He was going to finish soon. She did what she could to help him.

And it was over. He slid aside, touched the screen. The image froze on a weather station, ranks of silent numbers, cool computer-graphic blues of lows and highs.

"Thank you," he said. "You were good to me."

She was shaking in reaction. She found her robe and put it on, body-mind whirling in turmoil. As reality came seeping back, she felt a sudden giddy wash of joy, of pure release.

It was over, there was nothing to fear. They were people together, a man and woman. She felt a sudden rush of affection for him. She reached out. Surprised, he patted her hand. Then he rose and moved into the television dimness.

She heard him fumbling, opening a bag. He was back in a moment. Bright gleam of tin. "Abalone."

She sat up. Her stomach rumbled loudly. They laughed, comfortable in their embarrassment, the erotic squalor of intimacy. He pried open the can and they ate. "God, it's so good," she told him.

"I never eat anything grown in topsoil. Plants are full of deadly natural insecticides. People are nuts to eat that stuff."

"My husband used to say that all the time."

He looked up, slowly. "I'm gone tomorrow," he repeated. "Don't worry about anything."

"It's fine, I'll be all right." Meaningless words, but the concern was there—it was as if they had kissed. Night had fallen, it had grown cold. She shivered.

"I'll take you back to camp."

"I'll stay, if you want."

He stood up, helped to her feet. "No. It's warmer there."

Katje lay in a camp bed, white sheets, the floral smell of an air spray over the reek of disinfectant. There was not much machinery by modern standards, but it was a clinic and they had pulled her through.

"Where did you find such clothes?" she whispered.

Laura touched her blouse self-consciously. It was a red off-the-shoulder number, with a ruffled skirt. "One of the nurses—Sara . . . I can't pronounce her last name."

Katje seemed to think it was funny. It was the first time Laura had ever seen her smile. "Yes . . . there's such a girl in every camp. . . . You must be popular."

"They're good people, they've treated me very well."

"You didn't tell them . . . about the Bomb."

"No—I thought I'd leave that to you. I didn't think they'd believe me."

Katje let the lie float over her, not taken in, but letting it pass. Noblesse oblige, or maybe the anesthetic. "I told them . . . now I don't worry . . . let them worry."

"Good idea, save your strength."

"I won't do this anymore. . . . I'm going home. To be happy." She closed her eyes.

The door opened. The director, Mbaqane, barged through, followed by Barnaard the political man, and the paratroop captain.

And then the Vienna personnel. There were three of them. Two men in safari suits and speckled glasses, and a stylish, middle-aged Russian woman in a jacket, sleek khaki pants, and patent-leather boots.

They stopped by the bed. "So these are our heroes," the woman said brightly.

"Indeed, yes," said Mbaqane.

"My name is Tamara Frolova—this is Mr. Easton, and Mr. Neguib from our Cairo office."

"How do you do," Laura said reflexively. She almost rose to shake hands, then stopped herself. "This is Dr. Selous. . . . She's very tired, I'm afraid."

"And small wonder, yes? After such narrow escapes."

"Ms. Frolova has very good news for us," Mbaqane said. "A cease-fire is declared. The camp is out of danger! It seems the Malian regime is prepared to sue for peace!"

"Wow," Laura said. "Are they handing over the bombs?"

Unhappy silence.

"A natural question," said Frolova. "But there have been some errors. Honest mistakes." She shook her head. "There are no bombs, Mrs. Webster."

Laura jumped to her feet. "I expected that!"

"Please sit down, Mrs. Webster."

"Ms. Frolova—Tamara—let me speak to you as a person. I don't know what your bosses ordered you to say, but it's over now. You can't walk away from it anymore."

Frolova's face froze. "I know you have suffered an ordeal, Mrs. Webster. Laura. But one should not act irresponsibly. You must think first. Reckless allegations of such a kind— they are a clear public danger to the international order."

"They were taking me—both of us—to an *atomic test site!* For nuclear blackmail! To Azania, this time—God knows they already had you intimidated."

"The area you saw was not a test site."

"Stop being *stupid!* It doesn't even *need* Gresham's tape. You may have fast-talked these poor medicos, but the Azanian spooks aren't going to settle for words. They'll want to fly over the desert and look for the crater."

"I'm sure that could be arranged!" Frolova said. "After the current hostilities settle."

Laura laughed. "I knew you'd say that, too. That's an arrangement you'll never make, if you can help it. But the cover-up is still finished. You forget—we've *been there*. The air was full of dust. They can test our clothes, and they'll find radioactivity. Maybe not much, but enough for proof." She turned to Mbaqane. "Don't let them anywhere near those clothes. Because they'll grab the evidence, after they've grabbed us."

"We are not 'grabbing' anyone," Frolova said.

Mbaqane cleared his throat. "You did say you wanted them for debriefing. Interrogation."

"The clothes prove nothing! These women have been in the hands of a provocateur and terrorist! He has already committed a serious information crime, with the help of Mrs. Webster. And now that I hear her, I can see that it was not unwitting help." She turned to Laura. "Mrs. Webster, I must forbid you to speak any further! You are under arrest."

"Good heavens," Mbaqane said. "You can't mean that journalist fellow."

"This woman is his accomplice! Mr. Easton! Please draw your weapon."

Easton pulled a tangle-gun from his armpit.

Katje opened her eyes. "So much yelling . . . please don't shoot me, too."

Laura laughed recklessly. "That's funny . . . it's all ridiculous! Tamara, listen to what you're saying. Gresham saved us from the Malian death cells—so he could cover our clothes with sifted uranium. Can you expect anyone to believe that? What are you going to say after Mali nukes Pretoria? You should be ashamed."

Barnaard spoke to the Viennese. Wonderingly. "You *encouraged* us to attack Mali. You said we would have your support—secretly. You said—Vienna said—that we were Africa's great power, and we should restore order. . . . But you . . ." His voice trembled. "You knew they had the Bomb! You wanted to see if they would *use it* on us!"

"I resent that accusation in the gravest possible way! None of you are global diplomats, you are acting outside your experience—"

"How good do we have to be before we can judge you?" Laura said.

Easton aimed his gun. Mbaqane struck his wrist and the gun fell with a clatter. The two men stared at one another, amazed. Mbaqane found his voice: high-pitched, livid. "Captain! Arrest these miscreants at once!"

"Director Mbaqane," the captain rumbled. "You are a civilian. I take my orders from Pretoria."

"You cannot arrest us!" Frolova said. "You have no jurisdiction!"

The captain spoke again. "But I accept your *suggestion* with thanks. For an Azanian soldier, the course of honor is clear." He pulled his .45 sidearm and leveled it at Mr. Neguib's head. "Throw down your weapon."

Neguib pulled his tangle-gun carefully. "You are creating a serious international complication."

"Our diplomats will apologize if you force me to open fire."

Neguib dropped the gun.

"Leave this clinic. Keep your hands in plain sight. My soldiers will take you into custody."

He herded them slowly toward the door.

Barnaard could not resist a taunt. "Did you forget our country also has uranium?"

Frolova spun in her tracks. She flung her arm out, pointing at Laura. "You see? You see now? It's starting all over again!"

11

S HE lost the journalists at the Galveston airport. She was getting pretty good at it by now. They weren't as eager as they'd been at first and they knew they could pick her up again soon.

"Welcome to Fun City," the van told her. "Alfred A. Magruder, Mayor. Please announce your destination clearly into the microphone. *Anunce Usted—*"

"Rizome Lodge."

She turned on the radio, caught the last half of a new pop song. "Rubble Bounces in Bamako." Harsh, jittery, banging music. Strange how quickly that had come back into style. Weirdness, edginess, war nerves.

The city hadn't changed much. They didn't let it change much. Same grand old buildings, same palm trees, same crowds of Houstonians, thinned out by a December cold front.

The Church of Ishtar was advertising openly now. They were almost respectable, flourishing anyway, in a time of war and whores. Carlotta had been right about that. She thought about Carlotta, lost somewhere in her holy demimonde, smiling her sunny, drugged smile and batting her eyes at some client. Maybe their paths would cross again, somewhere somehow sometime, but Laura doubted it. The world was full of Carlottas, full of women whose lives were not their own. She didn't even know Carlotta's real name.

Storm surf was up, backwash from a tropical depression, broken up on the Texas coast in a ragged, cloudy array. Determined surfers were out in their transparent wetsuits. More than half the surfers had black skin.

She spotted the flagpole first. The Texas flag, the Rizome

emblem. The sight of it hit her very hard. Memory, wonder, sorrow. Bitterness.

The journos were waiting just outside the Rizome property line. They had cunningly managed to stick a bus in her way. Laura's van stopped short. The hat and sunglasses wouldn't help her now. She climbed out.

They surrounded her. Keeping ten feet away, like the privacy laws demanded. A very small blessing. "Mrs. Webster, Mrs. Webster!" Then one voice amid the chorus. "Ms. Day!"

Laura stopped short. "What."

Red-haired guy, freckles. Cocky expression. "Any word on your impending divorce action, Ms. Day?"

She looked them over. Eyes, cameras. "I know people who could eat the lot of you for breakfast."

"Thanks, thanks, that's *great*, Ms. Day . . ."

She crossed the beach. Up the old familiar stairs to the walkway. The stair rails had aged nicely, with the silken look of driftwood, and the striped awning was new. It looked like a good place, the Lodge, with its cheerful arches and sand-castle tower with the deep, round windows and the flags. Innocent fun, sunbathing and lemonade, a wonderful place for a kid.

She stepped into the bar, let the door shut itself behind her. Dim inside—the bar was full of strangers. Earth-cooled air, the smell of wine coolers and tortilla chips. Tables and wicker chairs. A man looked up at her—one of David's wrecking crew, she thought, not Rizome, but they'd always liked hanging out here—she had forgotten his name. He hesitated, recognizing her but not sure.

She ghosted past him. One of Mrs. Delrosario's girls passed her with a pitcher of beer. The girl stopped, turned on her heel. "Laura. It's you?"

"Hello, Inez."

They couldn't hug—Inez was carrying the beer. Laura kissed her cheek. "You're all grown up, Inez. . . . You can serve that stuff now?"

"I'm eighteen, I can serve it, I can't drink it."

"Well it won't be long now, will it?"

"I guess not. . . ." She was wearing an engagement ring. "My *abuela* will be glad to see you—I'm glad too."

Laura nodded toward the crowd from behind her sunglasses. "Don't tell them I'm here—everyone makes such a big deal of it."

"Okay, Laura." Inez was embarrassed. People got that way when you were a global celebrity. Tongue-tied and worshipful—this, from little Inez, who used to see her changing diapers and knocking around in her bathing suit. "I'll see you later huh?"

"Sure." Laura ducked behind the bar, went through the kitchen. No sign of Mrs. Delrosario, but the smell of her cooking was there, a rush of memory. She walked past copper-bottomed pans and griddles, into the dining room. Rizome guests talking politics—you could tell it by the strained looks on their faces, the aggression.

It wasn't just the fear. The world had changed. They had eaten up the Islands and it had settled in their belly like a drug. That Island strangeness was everywhere now, diluted, muted, and tingly. . . .

She couldn't face them, not yet. She went up the tower stairs—the door wouldn't open for her. She almost walked into it headlong. Codes must have changed—no, she was wearing a new watchphone, not programmed for the Lodge. She touched it. "David?"

"Laura," he said. "You at the airport?"

"No. I'm right here at the top of the stairs."

Silence. Through the door, across the few feet that still separated them, she could feel him, bracing himself. "Come on in. . . ."

"It's the door, I can't get it open."

"Oh! Yeah, okay, I can get it." It shunted. She put her sunglasses away.

She came up through the floor and threw the hat onto a table, into a round column of sunlight from a tower window. All the furniture was different. David rose from his favorite console—but no, it wasn't his, not anymore.

A Worldrun game was on. Africa was a mess. He came to greet her—a tall, gaunt black man, with short hair and reading glasses. They gripped each other's hands for a moment.

Then hugged hard, saying nothing. He'd lost weight—she could feel the bones in him.

She pulled back. "You look good."

"So do you." Lies. He took off the glasses and put them in his shirt pocket. "I don't really need these."

She wondered when she was going to cry. She could feel the need for it coming on. She sat down on a couch. He sat on a chair across the new coffee table.

"The place looks good, David. Really good."

"Webster and Webster, we build to last."

That did it. She began crying, hard. He fetched her some tissue and joined her on the couch and put his arm over her shoulders. She let him do it.

"The first weeks," he said, "about the first six months, I dreamed about this meeting. Laura, I couldn't believe you were dead. I thought, in jail somewhere. Singapore. She's a political, I told people, somebody's holding her, they'll let her go when things straighten out. Then they started talking about your being on the *Ali Khamenei*, and I knew that was it. That they'd finally gotten you, that they'd killed my wife. And I'd been half the world away. And hadn't helped." He put his thumbs into the corners of his eyes. "I'd wake up at night and think of you drowning."

"It wasn't your fault," she said. "It wasn't our fault, was it? What we had was good, it was really going to last, to last forever."

"I really loved you," he said. "When I lost you, it just destroyed me."

"I want you to know, David—I don't blame you for not waiting." Long silence. "I wouldn't have waited either, not if it was like that. What you and Emily did, it was right for you, both of you."

He stared at her, his eyes bloodshot. Her gesture, her forgiveness, had humiliated him. "There's just no end to what you're willing to sacrifice, is there?"

"Don't *blame* me!" she said. "I didn't sacrifice anything, I didn't want this to happen to us! It was stolen from us—they stole our life."

"We didn't have to do it. We chose to do it. We could have left the company, run off somewhere, just been happy."

He was shaking. "I would have been happy—I didn't need anything but you."

"We can't help it if we have to live in the world! We had bad luck. Bad luck happens. We stumbled over something buried, and it tore us up." No answer. "David, at least we're alive."

He gave a sharp bark of laughter. "Hell, you're more than *alive*, Laura. You're goddamn famous. The whole world knows. It's a fucking scandal, a soap opera. We don't 'live in the world'—the world lives in us now. We went out to fight for the Net and the Net just stretched us to pieces. Not our fault—oh hell no! All the fucking money and politics and multinationals just grabbed us and pulled us apart!"

He slammed his knee with his fist. "Even if Emily hadn't come in—and I don't love Emily, Laura, not like I loved you—how the hell could we have ever gone back to a real human life? Our little marriage, our little baby, our little house?"

He laughed, a high-pitched unhappy sound. "Back when I was a widower, there was a lot of rage and pain in that, but Rizome tried to take care of me, they thought it was . . . dramatic. I still hated their guts for what they led us into, but I thought, Loretta needs me, Emily cares, maybe I can make a go of it. Go on living."

He was as taut as strung wire. "But I'm just a little person, a private person. I'm not Hamlet, Prince of Denmark, I'm not God. I just wanted my wife and my baby and my work, and a few pals to drink beer with, and a nice place to live."

"Well they wouldn't let us have that. But at least we made them pay for what they did."

"*You* made them pay."

"I was fighting for us!"

"Yeah, and you won the battle—but for the Net, not for you and me." He knotted his hands. "I know it's a selfish thing. I feel ashamed sometimes, worthless. Those little bastards out in their submarine, they're still out there with their four precious home-made A-bombs, and if they fire one, it's gonna vaporize a million people just like us. They're evil, they have to be fought. So what do you and I matter, right?

But I can't see on that scale, I'm small, I can only see you and me."

She touched his hands. "David, we still have Loretta. We're not strangers. I was your wife, I'm the mother of your child. I didn't want to be what I've become now. If I'd had a choice I'd have chosen you."

He wiped his eyes. He was fighting the feelings back, becoming distant. Polite. "Well, we'll see each other sometimes, won't we? Holidays—that sort of thing. Even though I'm in Mexico now, and you're still in the company."

"I always liked Mexico."

"You can come down and see what we're working on. The Yucatan project . . . some of those guys from Grenada . . . their ideas weren't all bad."

"We'll be good friends. When the hurt passes. We don't hate each other—we didn't mean to hurt each other. It only hurts this bad because it was so good when we had it."

"It *was* good, wasn't it? Back when we had each other. When we were still the same size." He looked at her through his tear-streaked dark face. Suddenly she could see the David she had lost in there, somewhere. He was like a little boy.

They had a reception for her downstairs. It was like the other receptions in her honor, in Azania, in Atlanta, though the room was full of people she had loved. They had made her a cake. She cut it, and everyone sang. No journalists, thank God. A Rizome gathering.

She gave them a little speech that she'd written for them on the plane, coming in. About the Lodge—how the enemy had killed a guest, insulted their house and their company. About how they had fought back, not with machine guns, but with truth and solidarity. They had paid a price for resistance, in trouble and tragedy.

But today the Malian conspiracy was exposed and in utter wreckage. The Grenadian regime was wiped out. The Singaporeans had had a revolution. Even the European data bankers—*Los Morfinos*—had lost their safe havens and were scattered to the winds. (Applause.)

Even Vienna had been shattered in the world upheaval, but Rizome was stronger than ever. They had proven their right to the future. They—the Lodge personnel—could be proud of their role in global history.

Everyone applauded. They were shiny-eyed. She was getting much better at this sort of thing. She had done it so many times that all the fear was gone.

The formality broke up and people began circulating. Mrs. Delrosario, Mrs. Rodriguez, were both in tears. Laura consoled them. She was introduced to the Lodge's new coordinator and his pregnant wife. They bubbled on about how nice the place was and how much they were sure they'd enjoy it. Laura did her "humble Laura" number, patient, detached.

People always seemed surprised to see her speak reasonably, without hair-tearing or hysteria. They had all formed their first judgment of her from watching Gresham's tape. She had seen the tape (one of the innumerable pirated copies) exactly once, and had turned it off before the end, unable to bear the intensity. She knew what other people thought about it, though—she had read the commentaries. Her mother had sent her a little scrapbook of them, carefully clipped from the world press.

She would think about those comments sometimes when she was introduced to strangers, saw them judging her. Judging her, presumably, by the kind of crap they'd seen and read. "Mrs. Webster was thoroughly convincing, showing all the naive rage of an offended bourgeoise"—*Leningrad Free Press*. "She recited her grievances to the camera like a cavalier's mistress demanding vengeance for an insult"—*Paris-Despatch*. "Ugly, histrionic, gratingly insistent, a testament that was ultimately far too unpleasant to be disbelieved"—*The Guardian*. She had read that last one ten or twelve times, and had even considered calling up the snide little creep who'd written it—but what the hell. The tape had worked, that was enough. And it was nothing compared to what they said about the poor wretched bastards who used to run Vienna.

All that was old news now, anyway. Nowadays everybody talked about the submarine. Everyone was an expert. It was not, of course, an American Trident submarine—FACT had lied to her about that, small surprise there. She had told the whole world that she'd been on a "Trident" submarine, when a Trident was actually a kind of missile.

But Gresham had asked her for a description and the description had made it clear. The boat was a former Soviet Alfa-class missile sub, which had been sold years ago, to the African nation of Djibouti, and reported sunk with all hands. Of course it had not sunk at all—the hapless crew had been gassed by FACT saboteurs onboard as mercenaries, and the whole sub captured intact.

Almost the whole story was out now, new bits and pieces coming in every day. They had the FACT computer files, captured in Bamako. FACT agents overseas were surrendering right and left, naming their associates, ruining their former employers in a septic orgy of confession.

The Countess herself was dead. She had shot herself in her bunker at Bamako and had her remains cremated, leaving a long, rambling, lunatic testament about her vindication by history. So they claimed, anyway. No genuine proof of her death. She'd seen to that.

They still weren't even sure of the woman's true identity. There were at least five solid candidates. wealthy right-wing women who had vanished at one point or another into the underworld of data piracy and global spookdom. That didn't even count the hundreds of goofy folk tales and bullshit conspiracy theories.

The weird, sick thing was that people *liked* it. They *liked* the idea of an evil countess and her minions, even though the testimony and confessions were showing how squalid it was. The woman had been mentally ill. Old and trembling and out of it, and surrounded by people who were part zealot and part profiteer.

But people couldn't see it like that—they couldn't grasp the genuine banality of corruption. On some deep unconscious level people liked the political upheaval, the insecurity, the perverse tang of nuclear terror. The fear was an aphrodisiac, a chance to chuck the longterm view and live for the moment. Once it had *always* been like that. Now that she was living it, hearing people talk it, she knew.

Someone had invited the mayor. Magruder began explaining to her the complex legal niceties of reopening the Lodge.

He was defensive about what he'd done, in his own aggressive way. She fended him off with empty pleasantries. "Oh, wait," she said, "there's someone I simply must meet," and she left him and walked at random toward a stranger. A black woman with a short fringed haircut, standing alone in the corner, sipping a soda-and-ricewater.

It was Emily Donato. She saw Laura coming and looked up with an expression of pure animal terror. Laura stopped short, jolted. "Emily," she said. "Hi."

"Hello, Laura." She was going to be civilized. Laura saw the resolve for it stiffen her face, saw her control the urge to flee.

The hubbub of conversation dropped an octave. People were watching them over their drinks, from the corners of their eyes. "I need a drink," Laura said. A meaningless utterance, she had to say something.

"I'll get you one."

"No, let's get the hell out of here." She pushed open the door and stepped out onto the walkway. A few people out on the landing, leaning on the rail, watching seagulls. Laura walked through them. Emily tagged after her, reluctantly.

They walked around the rampart, under the awning. It was getting cold and Emily, in her simple short-sleeved dress, clutched her bare brown arms. "I forgot my windbreaker. . . . No, it's okay. Really." She put her drink on the wooden railing.

"You cut your hair," Laura said.

"Yeah," Emily said, "I travel pretty light these days." Thudding silence. "Did you see Arthur's trial?"

Laura shook her head. "But I'm glad now you never introduced me to the son-of-a-bitch."

"He made me feel like a whore," Emily said. Simple, abject. "He was F.A.C.T.! I still can't believe that sometimes. That I was sleeping with the enemy, that I spilled the whole fucking thing, that it was all my fault." She burst into tears. "And then this! I don't know why I even showed my face here. I wish we were back in Mexico. I wish we were in hell!"

"For God's sake, Emily, don't talk like that."

"I disgraced my office. I disgraced the company. And God knows what I've done with my personal life." She was sobbing. "Now look what I've done—I've betrayed my best friend. You were in prison and I was sleeping with your goddamned husband! You must wish I was dead."

"No, I don't!" Laura blurted. "I know—I've been there. It's no good at all."

Emily stared at her. The remark had stunned her. "I used to know you really well," she said. "I used to *depend* on you. You were the best pal I ever had. . . . Y'know, when I first came down here, to see David, I thought I was doing you a *favor*. I mean, I *liked* him, but he wasn't exactly doing Rizome morale much good. Complaining, abusing people, drinking too much. I said, my dead pal would want me to look after David. I tried to do something really good, and it was the worst thing I've ever done."

"I'd have done it too," Laura said.

Emily sat in one of the folding lounge chairs and pulled in her legs. "That's not what I want," she said. "I want you to tell me how much you hate me. I can't stand it if you're so much nobler than I am."

"Okay, Emily." The truth burst out of her like an abcess. "When I think of you and David sleeping together, I want to tear your fucking throat out."

Emily sat there and took it. She shuddered and flung it off. "I can't make up for it. But I can run away."

"Don't run, Emily. He doesn't need that. He's a good man. He doesn't love me anymore, but he can't help that. We're just too far apart now."

Emily looked up. Hope dawned. "So it's true? You're not gonna take him away from me?"

"No." She forced the words to come lightly. "We'll get the divorce. It won't be that much trouble. . . . Except for the journalists."

Emily looked at her feet. She accepted it. The gift. "I do love him, you know. I mean, he's simple, and kind of dizzy sometimes, but he does have his good points." She had nothing left to hide. "I don't even need the pills. I just love him. I'm used to him. We're even talking about having a baby."

"Oh, really?" Laura sat down. It was such a strange

thought that it somehow failed to touch her. It seemed pleasant somehow, homey. "Are you trying?"

"Not yet but . . ." She paused. "Laura? We're gonna survive this, aren't we? I mean it won't be like it was, but we won't have to kill ourselves. We'll be okay."

"Yeah." Long silence.

She leaned toward Emily. Now that it was out between them some ghost of the old vibe was coming back. A kind of subterranean tingle as their buried friendship stirred.

Emily brightened. She could feel it too.

It lasted long enough for them to go back in with their arms around each other.

Everyone smiled.

She spent Christmas at her mother's place in Dallas. And there was Loretta. A little girl who ran when she saw the lady in the hat and sunglasses, and hid her face in her grandmother's dress.

She was such a cute little thing. Spiky blond pigtails, greenish eyes. Quite a talker, too, once she got going. She said, "Gramma spill the milk," and laughed. She sang a little song about Christmas in which most of the verses were "na na na na" at top volume. After she got used to her, she sat in Laura's lap and called her "Rarra."

"She's wonderful," Laura told her mother. "You've done really well with her."

"She's such a joy to me," said Margaret Alice Day Garfield Nakamura Simpson. "I lost you—then I had her—now I have both of you. It's like a miracle. Not a day passes that I don't marvel at it. I've never been this happy in my life."

"Really, Mother?"

"I've had good times, and I've had bad times—this is the best time, for me. Since I've retired—shrugged the yoke off—it's me and Loretta. We're a family—it's like we're a little team."

"You must have been happy when you and Dad were together. I remember it. I always thought we were happy."

"Well, we were, yes. It wasn't quite this good, but it was good. Till the Abolition. Till I started doing eighteen-hour days. I could have chucked it—your father wanted me to—

but I thought, no, this is it, the greatest turning point I'll ever see in my lifetime. If I want to live in the world, I have to do this first. So I did it, and I lost him. Both of you.''

"It must have hurt you terribly. I was young and didn't know—I only knew that it hurt me.''

"I'm sorry, Laura. I know it's late, but I apologize to you.''

"Thank you for saying that, Mother. I'm sorry too.'' She laughed. "It's funny that it should come to this. After all these years. Just a few words.''

Her mother took her glasses off, dabbed at her eyes. "Your grandmother understood. . . . We never have much luck, Laura. But you know, I think we're working it out! It's not the old way, but it's something. What are nuclear families, anyway? Preindustrial.''

"Maybe we can work it better this time around,'' Laura said. "I blew it so much worse than you did that maybe it won't hurt her so much.''

"I should have seen more of you when you were growing up,'' her mother said. "But there was work and—oh, dear, I hate to say this—the world's full of men.'' She hesitated. "I know you don't want to think about that right now, but believe me, it does come back.''

"That's nice to know, I guess.'' She watched the Christmas tree, flickering between two Japanese wall hangings. "Right now the only men I see are journalists. Not much fun there. Ever since Vienna took the leash off, they're running hog wild.''

"Nakamura was a journalist,'' her mother said thoughtfully. "You know, I was never very *happy* with him, but it was certainly *intense*.''

They had supper together, in her mother's elegant little dining nook. There was wine, and Christmas ham, and a little spread of newly invented scop from Britain that tasted like paté. They could have eaten pounds of it.

"It's good, but it doesn't taste much like paté,'' her mother complained. "It's a bit more like, oh, salmon mousse.''

"It's too expensive,'' Laura said. "Probably costs about ten cents to make.''

"Well," her mother said tolerantly, "they have to recoup the research fees."

"It'll be cheaper when Loretta grows up."

"By then they'll be making scop that tastes like everything, or anything, or nothing ever seen."

The thought was a little horrifying. I'm getting older, Laura thought. Change itself is beginning to scare me.

She put the thought away. They played with Loretta until it was her bedtime. Then they talked for another couple of hours, sipping wine and eating cheese and being civilized. Laura wasn't happy, but the edges were off, and she was something close to content. No one knew where she was, and that was a blessing. She slept well.

In the morning they exchanged presents.

The Central Committee had gathered in Rizome's Stone Mountain Retreat. There was the new CEO, Cynthia Wu. And the committee itself, enough for a quorum: Garcia-Meza, McIntyre, Kaufmann, and de Valera. Gauss and Salazar were away at a summit, while the elderly Saito was off somewhere taking the waters. And, of course, Suvendra was there, happy to see Laura, unhappily chewing nicotine gum.

Rusticating. They were doing a lot of that lately. Atlanta was a major city. There was always the whispered suggestion that it might become Ground Zero.

It was a typical Central Committee feed. Lentil soup, salad, and whole-grain bread. Voluntary simplicity—they all ate it and attempted to look more high-minded than thou.

The telecom office was a Frank Lloyd Wright revival, gridded concrete block pierced with glass, stacked and undercut in severe geometrical elegance. The building seemed to fit Mrs. Wu, a schoolteacherish Anglo in her sixties who had come up through the marine-engineering section. She called the meeting back to order.

"Thanks to contacts," she told them, "we're getting this tape three days early, and before the network cuts it. I think this documentary serves as a capstone to the political work we pursued under my predecessor. I propose we use this opportunity, tonight, to reassess our policy. In retrospect, our former plans seem naive, and went seriously awry." She noticed de Valera's hand. "Comment?"

"What exactly are you defining as success?"

"As I recall, our original strategy was to encourage the data havens to amalgamate. Thus maneuvering them into a bureaucratic, *gesellschaft* structure that would be more easily controlled—assimilated, if you will. Peacefully. Is there anyone here who thinks that policy worked?"

Kaufmann spoke. "It worked against the EFT Commerzbank—though I admit it wasn't our doing. Still—they're legally entangled now. Harmless."

"Only because they fear being killed," Suvendra said. "The anger of the Net is become an awesome force!"

"Let's face it," de Valera said. "If we'd known the true nature of the F.A.C.T. we'd have never dared become involved! On the other hand, the havens did lose, didn't they? And we did win. Even our naivete worked to our advantage—at least no one can accuse Rizome of having ever supported FACT, no matter how badly the havens pestered us."

"In other words our success was mostly luck," Mrs. Wu said crisply. "I agree—we've been fortunate. With the exception of those Rizome associates who paid the price for our adventuring." She didn't have to glance at Laura to make her point.

"True enough," de Valera said. "But our motives were good and we fought the good fight."

Mrs. Wu smiled. "I'm as proud of that as anyone. But I can hope we'll do better in the present political situation. Now that the truth is out—and we can make what we laughingly call informed decisions." She sat down, touching her watchphone. "Let's roll the tape."

The lights dimmed and the display screen at the head of the table flashed into life. "This is Dianne Arbright of 3N News, reporting from Tangiers. The exclusive interview you are about to see was made under conditions of great personal danger to our 3N news team. In the wilderness of Algeria's Air Mountains, isolated, without backup, we were little short of hostages in the hands of the now notorious Inadin Cultural Revolution. . . ."

"What a glory hog," Garcia-Meza rumbled.

"Yeah," McIntyre said from the comfortable *gemeineschaf* darkness. "I wish I knew her hairdresser."

Footage followed, with Arbright's narrative. White jeeps jouncing cautiously through rugged mountain scenery. The news team in dashing safari outfits, hats, scarves, hiking boots.

A sudden crowd of Tuaregs on dune buggies, emerging from nowhere. The jeep surrounded. Leveled guns. Real alarm on the faces of the news team, jerky cinema verité. Cameras blocked by calloused hands.

Back to Arbright, somewhere in Tangiers. "We were searched for tracking devices, then blindfolded. They ignored our protests, bound us hand and foot, and loaded all four of us into their vehicles, like sheep. We were hauled for hours through some of the roughest and most desolate territory in Africa. The next footage you will see was taken in the depths of an ICR 'liberated zone.' In this heavily guarded, supersecret mountain fortress, we were finally brought face to face with the so-called strategic genius of the ICR—ex-Special Forces Colonel Jonathan Gresham."

More footage. They caught their breath. A cave, crude walls blasted out of living rock, dangling lightbulbs high overhead. Arbright sitting cross-legged on the carpet, her back to the camera.

Before her sat Gresham, turbanned, veiled, and cloaked, his massive head and shoulders framed in a spreading wicker peacock chair. Behind him at left and right stood two Tuareg lieutenants, with slung automatic rifles, black bandoliers, ceremonial Tuareg swords with jeweled hilts and tasseled scabbards, combat knives, grenades, pistols.

"You may proceed," Gresham announced.

Mrs. Wu froze the tape. "Laura, you're our situation expert. Is it him?"

"It's him," Laura said. "He's been to a laundry, but that's Jonathan Gresham, all right."

"Do they *always* look like that?" de Valera asked.

Laura laughed. "They wouldn't last five minutes like that out on operations. Those silly swords, all that hardware—they've got everything but flyswatters. Gresham's trying to put the voodoo on her."

"I've never seen a more terrifying figure," said Mrs. Wu, sincerely. "Why is he hiding his face? His photo must be on file somewhere anyway."

"He's wearing the *tagelmoust*," Laura said. "That veil and turban—it's traditional for male Tuaregs. A kind of male *chador*."

"That's a switch," McIntyre said. Deliberate lightness. She was scared, too.

"Thank you, Colonel Gresham." Arbright was shaken but she was going to tough it out. A professional. "Let me begin by asking, Why did you agree to this interview?"

"You mean why *you*—or why at all?"

"Let's begin with why at all."

"I know what's happened in your world," Gresham said. "We blew Vienna's shell game, and the Net wants to know why. What's in it for us? Who are we, what do we want? When the Net wants to know, it sends its army—journalists. So I'm willing to meet with exactly one—you. I depend on you to warn the rest off."

"I'm not sure I follow you, Colonel. I can't speak for my media colleagues, but I'm certainly not a soldier."

"The Malian regime gave us a war of extermination. We understand that. We also understand the far more insidious threat that you pose, with your armies of cameramen. We don't want your world. We don't respect your values and we don't care to be touched. We are not a tourist attraction—we are a revolution, not a zoo. We will not be tamed or assimilated. By your very nature, by your very presence, you would force assimilation on us. That will not be allowed."

"Colonel, you've been a journalist yourself, as well as a soldier, and, ah, cultural theorist. You must be aware that popular interest in you and your activities is very intense."

"Yes, I am. That's why I fully expect to litter this desert with the bones of your colleagues in years to come. But I'm a soldier—not a terrorist. When our enemies—your colleagues—are killed in our liberated zones, they'll die knowing the reason. Assuming, that is, that I can trust you to do your job."

"I won't censor you, Colonel. I'm not Vienna, either."

"Yes—I know that. I know you pushed the coverage of the

Grenada terror attack well past Vienna's limits, at some risk
to your career. That's why I chose you—you have some
spine.''

The second cameraman had now wandered into range and
got a reaction shot. Arbright smiled at Gresham. Dimples.
Laura knew what she was feeling. She was fairly tight with
Arbright these days. Had done an interview with her, a good
one. She even knew the name of Arbright's hairdresser.

"Colonel, did you know that your book on the Lawrence
Doctrine is now a best-seller?''

"It was pirated," Gresham said. "And expurgated.''

"Could you explain a bit of the doctrine for our viewers?''

"I suppose it's preferable to having them read it," Gresham
said reluctantly. Feigned reluctance, Laura thought. "Over a
century ago, Lawrence . . . he was British, First World War
. . . discovered how a tribal society could defend itself from
industrial imperialism. . . . The Arab Revolt stopped the Turkish
cultural advance, literally in its tracks. They did this with
guerrilla assaults on the railroads and telegraphs, the Turkish
industrial control system. For success, however, the Arabs
were forced to use industrial artifacts—namely, guncotton,
dynamite, and canned food. For us it is solar power, plas-
tique, and single-cell protein.''

He paused. "The Arabs made the mistake of trusting the
British, who were simply the Turks by another name. The
First World War was a proto-Net civil war, and the Arabs
were thrust aside. 'Til oil came—then they were assimilated.
Brave efforts like the Iranian revolt of 1979 were too little too
late . . . they were already fighting for television.''

"Colonel—you speak as if you don't expect anyone to
sympathize.''

"I don't. You live by your system. Vienna, Mali, Azania—
it's all imperial hardware, just different brand names.''

"The British political analyst Irwin Craighead has described
you as 'the first credible right-wing intellectual since T. E.
Lawrence.' ''

Gresham touched his veil. "I'm a postindustrial tribal anarchist. Is that considered 'right-wing' these days? You'll have
to ask Craighead.''

"I'm sure Sir Irwin would be delighted to discuss definitions.''

"I'm not going to Britain—and if he tries to invade our zones, he'll be ambushed like anyone else."

Mrs. Wu froze the tape. "This litany of death threats is very annoying."

"Arbright's got him rattled," de Valera gloated. "Typical right-winger—full of bullshit!"

"Hey!" Garcia-Meza objected. "You should talk, de Valera—you and your socialist internal-money system—"

"Please don't start on that again," Kaufmann said. "Anyway, he's *interesting*, is he not? Here's a fellow who could be a world hero—not to everyone perhaps, but enough of us— and not only is he staying out there in hell, but he's talked these other poor souls into joining him!"

"His ideology sucks," de Valera said. "If he wants to be a desert hermit, he could move to Arizona and stop paying his phone bills. He doesn't need the shoulder-launched rockets and the whole nine yards."

"I'm with de Valera on this one," McIntyre said. "And I still don't see how the Russian space station fits in."

"He's confused," Laura said. "He's not sure what he's doing is right. It's like—he wants to be as different from us as he can, but he can't get us out of himself. He's full of some kind of self-hatred I can't understand."

"Let's give him his say," Garcia-Meza said.

They ran more tape. Arbright asked Gresham about FACT. "The Malian regime is finished," Gresham said, "the submarine is just a detail," and he began talking about Azanian "imperialism." Detailing how roads could be land-mined, convoys ambushed, communication links cut, until Azanian "expansionism" was "no longer economically tenable."

Then without warning he started in on plans to heal the desert. "Agriculture is the oldest and most vicious of humanity's bio-technologies. Rather than deracinated farmers in Azanian sterilization camps, there should be wandering tribes of eco-decentralized activists. . . ."

"He's a screwball," de Valera said.

"I think we're all agreed on that," Mrs. Wu said. She turned down the sound. "The question is, what is our policy? Is Gresham any less threatening to us than Grenada or Singapore? He certainly cultivates a line in aggressive bluster."

"Grenada and Singapore were pirates and parasites," Laura said. "Grant him this much—he only wants to be left alone."

"Come on," de Valera said. "What about all that high-tech hardware? He didn't get that by selling handmade jewelry."

"Aha!" said Garcia-Meza. "Then that is where he's vulnerable."

"Why we should harm someone who fought the F.A.C.T.?" Suvendra said. "And if *they* could not frighten or defeat his people, could we?"

"Good point," said Mrs. Wu. They watched Gresham lean back briefly in his peacock chair and mutter an order to the lieutenant on his left. The Tuareg saluted smartly and swaggered away, off-camera.

"He is in a desert no one wants," Suvendra said. "Why force him to come after us?"

"What the hell could he do to us?" de Valera said. "He's a Luddite."

Laura spoke heavily. "Can you run the tape back? I think that man who just walked off-camera was Sticky Thompson."

They stirred in shock. Mrs. Wu ran it again. "Yeah," Laura said. "That walk, that salute. Under that veil, it's got to be him. Sticky—Nesta Stubbs. Of course—where else would he go? I wondered what had become of him."

"That's horrible," de Valera said.

"No, it's not," Laura told him. "He's over there in the desert with Gresham. He's not over here."

"Oh, my God," McIntyre said. "And to think I stay up at night worrying about atom bombs. We'd better tell Vienna immediately."

They stared at her. "Smart move," de Valera said at last. "Vienna. Wow. That'll really scare him."

Mrs. Wu rubbed her forehead. "What do we do now?"

"I can think of one thing," Laura said. "We can protect his supply lines, so no one else bothers him! And I know one supply that's got to mean more to him than anything. Iron Camels, from GoMotion Unlimited in Santa Clara, California. We should make inquiries."

"Rizome-GoMotion," McIntyre said. "Doesn't sound half bad."

"Good," Garcia-Meza said. "He is vulnerable, as I said. Transport—that would give us influence over him."

"We might be better off forgetting all about him," de Valera said. "It's hot in the Sahara. Maybe they'll all evaporate."

"No one's ever going to forget Gresham," Laura said. "They never forget what they can't have. . . . We'd better get hold of that company." She looked around the table as they sat in the flickering television dimness. "Don't you see it? Iron Camels—the Jonathan Gresham Look. Every would-be tough guy and rugged individualist and biker lunatic on this planet is gonna want one for himself. In six months Arizona will be full of guys in nylon *tagelmousts* breaking their necks." She propped her head in her hands. "And there's not a damn thing he can do about *that*."

"Could be worth millions," de Valera mused. "Hell, I'd bet on it." He looked up. "When does this thing air?"

"Three days."

"Can we do anything in that time?"

"In California? Sure," said Mrs. Wu. "If we get right on it."

So they got right on it.

Laura was cleaning her kitchen when her watchphone buzzed. She touched it and the door opened. Charles Cullen, Rizome's former CEO, stood out in the corridor in denim overalls.

"Mr. Cullen," she said, surprised. "I hadn't heard you were back in Atlanta."

"Just dropping in on old friends. Sorry I didn't call, but your new phone protocols. . . . Hope you don't mind."

"No, I'm glad to see you. C'mon in." He crossed the living room and she came out of the kitchen. They hugged briefly, cheek-kissed. He looked at her and grinned suddenly. "You haven't heard yet, have you?"

"Heard what?"

"You haven't been watching the news?"

"Not in days," Laura said, throwing magazines off the couch. "Can't stand it—too depressing, too weird."

Cullen laughed aloud. "They bombed Hiroshima," he said.

Laura went white and grabbed for the couch.

"Easy," he said. "They fucked up! It didn't work!" He rolled the armchair behind her. "Here, Laura, sit down, sorry. . . . It didn't explode! It's sitting in a tea-garden in downtown Hiroshima right now. Dead, useless. It came flying out of the sky—*tumbling*, the eyewitnesses said—and it hit the bottom of the garden and it's lying there in the dirt. In big pieces."

"When did this happen?"

"Two hours ago. Turn on the television."

She did. It was ten in the morning, Hiroshima time. Nice bright winter morning. They had the area cordoned off. Yellow suits, masks, geiger counters. Good helicopter overhead shot of the location. Tiny little place in wood and ceramic in some area zoned for small restaurants.

The missile was lying there crushed. It looked like something that had fallen off a garbage scow. Most of it was engine, burst copper piping, ruptured corrugated steel.

She turned down the gabbling narrative. "Isn't it full of uranium?"

"Oh, they got the warhead out first thing. Intact. They think the trigger failed. Conventional explosive. They're looking at it now."

"Those *evil bastards*!" Laura screamed suddenly and slapped the coffee table hard. "How could they pick *Hiroshima*?"

Cullen sat down on the couch. He could not seem to stop grinning. Half amusement, half twisted nervous fear. She'd never seen him smile so much. This crisis was bringing out the bizarre in everyone. "Perfect choice," he said. "Big enough to show you mean it—small enough to show *restraint*. They're evacuating Nagasaki right now."

"My God, Cullen."

"Oh," he said, "call me Charlie. Got anything to drink?"

"Huh? Sure. Good idea." She called the liquor cabinet over.

"You've got Drambuie!" Cullen said, looking. He picked out a pair of liqueur glasses. "Have a drink." He poured, spilled a sticky splash on the coffee table. "Whoops."

"God, poor Japan." She sipped it. She couldn't help but blurt her thought aloud. "I guess this means they can't get *us*."

"They're not gonna get anybody," he said, gulping. "The whole world's after 'em. Sound detectors, sonar, anything that can float. Hell, they got the whole Singapore Air Force scrambling for the East China Sea. They picked the bomb up on airport radar coming in, got a trajectory. . . ." His eyes gleamed. "That sub's gonna die. I can feel it."

She refilled their glasses. "Sorry, there's not much left."

"What else have we got?"

"Uh . . ." She winced. "Some plum wine. And quite a bit of sake."

"Sounds great," he said unthinkingly. He was staring at the television. "Can't send out for liquor. It's quiet here in your place . . . but believe me, it's getting very strange out in those corridors."

"I've got some cigarettes," she confessed.

"Cigarettes! Wow, I don't think I've smoked one of those since I was a little kid."

She got the cigarettes from the back of the liquor cabinet and brought out her antique ashtray.

He looked away from the television—it had switched to a public statement by the Japanese premier. Meaningless figurehead. "Sorry," he said. "I didn't mean to barge in on you like this. I was in your building before I heard the news and. . . . Actually, I was just hoping that we could . . . you know . . . have a good talk."

"Well, talk to me anyway. Because otherwise I think I'm going to have a fit." She shivered. "I'm glad you're here, Charlie. I'd hate to be watching this alone."

"Yeah—me too. Thanks for saying that."

"I guess you'd rather be with Doris."

"Doris?"

"That *is* your wife's name, isn't it? Did I forget?"

He raised his brows. "Laura, Doris and I have been separated for two months now. If we were still together I'd have brought her with me." He stared at the television. "Turn it off," he said suddenly. "I can only handle one crisis at a time."

"But—"

"Fuck it, it's *gesellschaft* stuff. Out of our hands."

She turned it off. Suddenly she could feel the Net's absence like a chunk taken out of her brain.

"Calm down," he said. "Do some deep breathing. Cigarettes are bad for us anyway."

"I didn't know about Doris. Sorry."

"It's the demotion," he said. "Things were fine as long as I was CEO, but she couldn't take the Retreat. I mean, she knew it was coming, that it's customary, but . . ."

She looked at his denim overalls. They were worn at the knees. "I think they take this demotion ritual a little too far . . . what do they have you do, mostly?"

"Oh, I'm in the old folks home. Change sheets—reminisce—pitch a little hay sometimes. Not so bad. Kind of gives you the long view."

"That's a very correct attitude, Charlie."

"I mean it," he said. "This Bomb crisis has people totally obsessed right now, but the long-term view's still there, if you can back off enough to look at it. Grenada and Singapore . . . they had wild ideas, reckless, but if we're smart, and very careful, we might use that kind of radical potential sensibly. There's a world of hurt to be put right first . . . maybe a lot more if these bastards bomb us . . . but someday . . ."

"Someday what?" Laura said.

"I don't really know what to call it. . . . Some kind of genuine, basic improvement in the human condition."

"It could do with some," Laura said. She smiled at him. She liked the sound of it. She liked him, for having brought up the long term, in the very middle of hell breaking loose. The very best time for it, really. "I like it," she said. "Sounds like interesting work. We could talk about it together. Network a little."

"I'd like that. When I'm back in the swing of things," he said. He looked embarrassed. "I don't mind being out of it a while. I didn't handle it well. The power. . . . You should know that, Laura. Better than anyone."

"You did very well—everyone says so. You're not responsible for what happened to me. I went into it with my eyes open."

"Jesus, it's really good of you to say that." He looked at the floor. "I dreaded this meeting. . . . I mean, you were nice enough the few times we've met, but I didn't know how you'd take it.''

"Well, it's our work! It's what we do, what we are.''

"You really believe in that, don't you? The community.''

"I have to. It's all I have left.''

"Yeah,'' he said. "Me too.'' He smiled. "Can't be such a bad thing. I mean, we're both in it. Here we are. Solidarity, Laura.''

"Solidarity.'' They clicked glasses and drank the last Drambuie.

"It's good,'' he said. He looked around. "Nice place.''

"Yeah . . . they keep the journos out. . . . Got a nice balcony, too. You like heights?''

"Yeah, what is this, fortieth floor? I can never tell these big Atlanta digs apart.'' He stood up. "I could use some air.''

"Okay.'' She walked toward the balcony; the double doors flung themselves open. They stood on the balcony looking down to the distant street.

"Impressive,'' he said. Across the street they could see another high-rise, floor after floor, curtains open here and there, glow of television news. The balcony was open above them and they could hear it muttering out. The tone rising.

"It's good to be here,'' he said. "I'll remember this moment. Where I was, what I was doing. Hell, everyone will. Years from now. For the rest of our lives.''

"I think you're right. I know you are.''

"It's either gonna be the absolute worst, or the final end of something.''

"Yeah . . . I should have brought the sake bottle.'' She leaned on the railing. "You wouldn't blame me, Charlie, would you? If it was the worst? Because I did have a part in it. I did it.''

"Never even occurred to me.''

"I mean, I'm only one person, but I did what one person can do.''

"Can't ask for more than that.''

There was a bestial scream from upstairs. Joy, rage, pain, hard to tell. "That was it,'' he said.

People were pouring into the streets. They were jumping

out of vans. Running headlong. Running for one another. Distant leaping bits of anonymity: the crowd.

Horns were honking. People were embracing each other. Strangers, kissing. A mob flinging itself into its own arms. Windows began flying open across the street.

"They got 'em," he said.

Laura looked down at the crowd. "Everybody's so happy," she said.

He had the sense not to say anything. He just held out his hand.